WINTER

THE STORM KING'S DAUGHTERS - BOOK ONE

STELLA WHITCOMB LANE

ARROW & RAVEN
BOOKS, LLC

The star of the unconquered will,
He rises in my breast,
Serene, and resolute, and still,
And calm, and self-possessed.

And thou, too, whosoe'er thou art,
That readest this brief psalm,
As one by one thy hopes depart,
Be resolute and calm.

O fear not in a world like this,
And thou shalt know erelong,
Know how sublime a thing it is
To suffer and be strong.

- Henry Wadsworth Longfellow

PROLOGUE

LARS

I STARE BLANKLY through the wide windows of my office at the dense forest and the icy sea just beyond it. The dark morning sky bathes the snow-covered trees in a pale blue light. This home, this prison, is a fortress of steel and concrete wrapped in thick swaths of glass. Ice cold and magnificent, the wild landscape of this hidden island is my only companion.

I fight against it, but the forced isolation is weighing on me. I take a sip of coffee and lean back, putting my feet up on my old wooden desk. My boots are worn, as is the denim of my jeans, but I can't be bothered to care. I haven't seen anyone in too long, but change is coming.

It is almost time.

My phone chimes, and I answer without looking. Only one person calls me.

"Mikkel. Is the book in play?"

"Good morning to you, too, brother. Yes, the volume is on its way."

By necessity, Mikkel runs the more hands-on side of the family business. He is a ruthless and terrifying man with his power barely contained in the best of circumstances. There is constant tension in his speech, but today it is especially pronounced.

"Any concerns with the package?"

"No, the book will do what you require, and all the pieces are in motion." Mikkel is withholding information. I can always sense an omission of truth.

"Excellent. Now tell me what the problem is." The authority in my voice is absolute.

Mikkel grumbles, but gives in. "Our man on the inside tells me the IMA is aware of the package and its destination."

I mutter a curse. If the Agency intervenes, they could ruin years of preparation.

"How bad is it?"

"It's not good, Lars. They've assigned Lundqvist. He's leaving for the States within the hour."

Unlike most people running the Agency, Stellan Lundqvist is intelligent as well as powerful. While I remain one step ahead for now, the magic I use to stay hidden will not go undetected much longer. Lundqvist needs to be removed. This is too important.

"Let me know when you land, brother." I laugh, but it's been so long since something amused me that it's more of a raspy bark.

"No, Lars. That is simply not possible. I already have too much to manage here."

"If this plan fails, we may not have another chance."

"She's your daughter. You go." Mikkel sounds petulant. I hate having to ask when I should be obeyed.

"You know I can't set foot off this property. I need her. We need her. Go and take additional men with you. Unless you have offspring I am not aware of, there is no other option. And besides, you owe me."

Mikkel curses. I can almost see the wheels turning in my brother's mind. He grunts in agreement and disconnects the call without another word. He knows I'm right even if he doesn't like it.

I throw the phone on my desk and run a hand through my hair. It's long enough now that I can tie it back, and it's beginning to gray on the sides. I detest the reminder that time is passing, that I might be losing my edge.

I have to depend on others for the first time in decades, and it's a weakness that sickens me. A poison that slowly eats me away from the inside. I am accustomed to the solitude with only my research to occupy me, but not for much longer. My daughter will soon be home.

PART ONE

VERMONT

CHAPTER 1

THERE'S something in the repetitive motion of scanning a book that settles me. Lift, turn, press, push, repeat. I'm already several pages into this heavy volume of Vermont State Legislation balancing on my hands. The comfortable rhythm of turning pages and the dull hum of library activity lures me away from our basement office and into another deep daydream.

My mind is wandering more frequently lately, and I'm finding it harder to stay present. I'm not sure if it's stress or boredom or some potent combination of the two. I let the errant thoughts come without purpose, like a meditation. They float to the surface, and I decide whether to explore them. Scanning reference material when I'm physically safe in the library is the perfect time to let my mind go.

Random images appear: a childhood playground, a sexy stranger, a white-capped lake. It's the lake where my family has a cottage that catches my attention. I have countless memories associated with this place, but this flashback is a particular moment in time. Standing on the shore, watching rough waves on the water and autumn leaves whipping around. The wind tickles my face, making me shiver. My hands press deep into the pockets of my favorite red sweatshirt as I watch the variegated sky of a storm approaching over the horizon.

The familiar sense of fear and excitement that comes before a thunderstorm settles over me. The emotions are vivid, almost tangible things. I can taste the freshness of the air, feel the water on my face. Awareness of a presence behind me pricks the back of my neck and a rough hand clasps my shoulder.

There's a spark of electricity that shoots through me at the connection and my father's strong pine-scented aftershave fills my nose. In the memory, I tense up and the heavy weight of apprehension settles on my shoulders. In the library, a tight knot twists inside my chest.

Some memories are better left buried.

I place the book down on the mahogany reference desk and shake off the sluggish remnants of the past. I have enough to worry about in the present.

The special collections department in the library at the University of Vermont is usually quiet, but this afternoon it's especially painful. With no distractions, I'll spend the next half hour obsessing over the meeting we've been summoned to.

Dr. Edwards, or "Harvard Dave" as I call him in my head, is the director of the library and the number one thorn in my side. We acquired a collection of new books, and he scheduled a mandatory meeting to show them off.

Admittedly, they are pretty marvelous. Prime examples of late medieval codex from countries all over Europe. They'll be excellent for teaching and research, and I'm dying to get my hands on them.

Unfortunately, my position as the Collections Assistant means my contact with these magical volumes will be limited to whatever Dr. Edwards believes I can handle, and I already know that won't be much.

It doesn't seem to matter that I have degrees from highly reputable institutions, or that I frequently hear praise from colleagues and researchers. Dr. Edwards will only ever see me as support staff and that is where I remain.

"You ready?" Jim Grant's voice calls down the hall. His large frame leaning against his office door. Jim is the head of our department and my immediate boss. His gray hair reflects the fluorescent lights, and he appears to have brushed it into something that resembles smooth. His shirt is wrinkled and the knot in his tie is crooked.

He's about as different from Dr. Edwards as you can get. He's kind, understanding, and smart as a whip. But he's also messy and often lost in his own head.

"As I'll ever be."

Jim's footsteps fall heavy on the wood floor. He leans against the reference desk.

"You could always leave, you know," he says quietly. "I'd miss you, but I would understand it."

Jim has been advocating for my promotion in the months since our cataloger retired. Dr. Edwards won't agree to it, and I'm guessing Jim is starting to give up.

"You know there aren't other jobs here, and I can't leave Vermont."

Jim just dips his head and gives me a sad smile.

It's not like I haven't considered it. I'm bored out of my mind. I scroll through job listings daily, hoping for something that might call to me. Something that might make me feel alive and productive again, even if it's not directly related to libraries.

But with everything I'm responsible for here, I can't leave.

I follow Jim to the library's larger meeting space. It's set up for a lecture with rows of chairs facing a selection of the new books lined up on a table. All of them nestled safely in the book cradles I recommended.

Dr. Edwards spots us the moment we walk in and charges over on his spindly legs.

"There you are, Jim. I expect you will stand up with me as the head of your department."

"Sure, but I was thinking that it would be best if Willa does the honors. She knows far more about these kinds of texts than I do. You know my expertise is more 19th century."

"Of course," Dr. Edwards replies with a curl of his lip. He gestures to a spot on the far side of the table.

"Wilhelmina, you will stand next to the table and out of the way, there."

He glances up and down my outfit with a wrinkle of his nose.

I'm wearing what I consider professional attire for early November in Vermont. A black shift dress over gray tights and black ankle boots. Maybe it is too much black, but it's not like I'm in a flannel and jeans.

My dark brown hair is in a much smoother bun than normal, and I checked my makeup to make sure I don't have raccoon eyes. I know I look fine. Maybe even nice.

I catch the eye of my closest work friend, Justine, at the back of the room. She gives me an encouraging smile and an enthusiastic thumbs up. Justine is the most cheerful person I know, but even she has to realize this is my nightmare.

I read once that it's our animal brain taking over when we're afraid of public speaking. It's all the eyes fixed on us like we're about to be eaten. Jim prepped me for this as best he could, but I'm still nauseous and shaky. I inhale and exhale slowly, but it doesn't do much to lessen my simmering panic.

While Dr. Edwards works the room and greets faculty entering through the wide double doors, my attention diverts to the books on the table. I haven't seen them up close, and I'm a little star-struck. My fingers itch to run over the rough spines and assess the texture of the parchment.

One book in particular draws my eye. The cover is a rich black, and the vellum pages are charred around the edges. It's striking, so much so that it almost glows despite the harsh overhead lights in the library, and there's something about it that forces my eye. I can't look away. There's a sharp tug inside my chest almost like it's calling to me.

I'm so close to reaching it when Dr. Edwards clears his throat, announcing the start of our meeting. I turn away reluctantly. The sharp burn inside my chest remains, and I rub my hand over the spot.

"Thank you all so much for joining us. We are delighted to share our latest acquisition with you all..."

Dr. Edwards pontificates in his seasoned professor voice. Speaking as if this is the kind of donation we receive all the time and not just this once ever. Most of our collection is from the 1800s with some odd colonial bits thrown in here and there. What we're known for is our strong connection to the State of Vermont and its history. For us to take in a collection of texts from medieval Europe is way out of left field.

"Wilhelmina, would you please..."

And I have absolutely no idea what he just said.

Half of his speech so far has been about his own accomplishments, which I've heard at least ten times already. I watch in confusion as Dr. Edwards puts on a pair of white cotton gloves and gestures for me to do the same.

"Oh no, Dr. Edwards. In the field of Special Collections, it's widely understood that gloves aren't necessary when handling most collection material. It might surprise you, but it's more likely for us to cause damage if we put…these on."

My words falter when I catch Dr. Edward's face. His nostrils flare and his eyes narrow on me.

I hear a gasp that sounds distinctly like Justine and the shifting of seats in the uncomfortable silence. Jim hangs his head and rubs a hand across the back of his neck awkwardly.

Oh, fuck.

I was only trying to protect the fragile bindings, but I doubt he'll ever see it that way.

"Never mind," I say quickly and take the gloves, shoving them over my now sweaty fingers. "I'm sure I'm mistaken."

"Yes, I'm quite sure you are. Please hold up a book and explain its significance to our audience, Ms. Martin."

My cheeks heat. I pick up the black book even though I don't know as much about it. I swear it shakes in my hands. The sharp push inside my chest increases, and I have to swallow to keep the nausea at bay.

"Well, Ms. Martin, are you going to tell us what makes you so *experienced* on this topic?"

Dr. Edwards taunts me and someone in the audience laughs.

"Yes, of course." I straighten my spine. I'm not going to let him make more of a fool out of me.

"These volumes, of which there are 23 in total, are a representative selection of texts found throughout the mid to late medieval period."

I swallow hard. The crowd's eyes are on me and there's expectation on their faces. It's the encouragement I need to ignore Dr. Edwards and his homicidal glare.

"The primary purpose for the written word at the time was religion. We have several prayer books here as well as a variety of Bibles, Books of Hours, and psalters."

I glance down at the book in my hands and note the

hurried nature of the text and the change in penmanship. The lines are separated by what appear to be dates.

"This particular text is likely a church ledger, or a record of the comings and goings of a community. I have no doubt that it's of incredible research value and will be a wonderful addition to any classes on medieval history or religion. As soon as we have them cataloged, they will be available as a teaching tool. We hope it opens up opportunities for further collaboration with the library so that students can gain first-hand experience with these remarkable works."

There's some polite clapping while Dr. Edwards turns his angry eyes away from me and pastes on his fake smile for the audience. I embarrassed him, and I am certain I'll hear about it later.

CHAPTER 2

WILLA

MY STUDIO APARTMENT is just off Battery Street and across from the park. The apartments on the other side of my building have lake views, while mine has a beautiful view of my neighbor's bedroom. But it's close to work and down-town, and I can't do much better.

The apartment is tiny, but enough for me and the cats. Reginald and Goldie are fairly recent additions to my life. They were available for adoption at the local humane society, and I put my name in on a whim. I liked the idea of a bonded pair, that way they can keep each other company while I'm at work or out visiting my mom.

Goldie is a ginger cat with a sweet and sunny personality, while Reginald is pure black and cuddly, but only on his terms. He's also a complete lunatic. He digs holes in all my plants, and sleeps right on top of my face every night.

As soon as I walk in, I notice he's barfed on the rug again.

"Reggie," I hiss and shake my head. He licks his paw like

he has no idea what I'm talking about. The vet tells me that he's fine and he just does it when he's upset about something, but that appears to be all the time.

I hang up my coat, drop my bag on the table, and clean up Reg's mess. I finally flop onto the green velvet couch that I love with my whole heart. It's like sitting on a cloud, but it takes up half the room.

For a moment, I just stare at the ceiling. I probably lost my job today. And if I didn't, my promotion definitely died in the water now that I made Dr. Edwards look like an uninformed idiot in front of an audience.

The fact that he is an uninformed idiot doesn't matter. I'm smart enough to know that success in academia is often more about perception than actual knowledge.

Deciding I'd rather do anything than think about my job, I dial my mom's number.

"Hello!" Her voice is high and sounds much younger than a woman in her 40s.

"Hey, Mom. How are you?"

"Oh, fine." She exhales with a sigh.

"Did you get my package?"

"I did! Thank you! I love them. They'll be nice and warm."

I sent her some new work gloves. Mom has a tendency to wear things down to nothing, and I noticed her old pair had giant holes the last time I was visiting. I don't want her burning her hands on the wood stove this winter.

Mom's house is out in the woods in a part of Vermont known as the Northeast Kingdom. The winters are long and harsh, and wood fires are a necessity.

"Great. Have you seen Tim lately?"

"I have! He stopped by this morning with some more meat from the farm. We had a good chat. He's working on a new fence for the horse."

"That's nice. I'll try to come up in the next week or two. I need to check on the cottage. We haven't had any guests since the foliage peaked, and I want to make sure everything's in order."

"Sounds good, but I have to go, sweetheart. I'm working on a new piece and the paint is drying."

"Alright. Love you, Mom."

I hang up and clutch a pillow to my chest. I wish I didn't worry about her so much, but between her and the twins, I'm always worrying. Dad left when Beatrice and Wren were toddlers, and Mom has been on her own ever since. Her mental health has improved, but I'll never shake the fear of calming her through panic attacks in the middle of the night.

On one of my visits a few months ago, I discovered she hadn't been buying food regularly. She's an artist and a writer and sometimes gets lost in other worlds. She said she just forgot, but it's made me extra vigilant.

Tim Hawkins is her oldest friend, and he lives on one of the farms nearby. I asked if he'd check on her periodically. He and mom were close once, and he seemed happy to have a reason to reconnect.

My mother's life has not been easy. She's spent all of it in Vermont with no reprieve for college or much in the way of vacations or travel. Her great-great-great grandfather settled in the Northeast Kingdom, and her family never left. I think she likes being there. At the very least, she expresses no inclination to leave.

My grandparents passed when my mom was young, and she inherited our property on the lake. It's the ultimate escape from reality and my favorite place on earth. Mom gladly let me take over caring for it even though she lives much closer.

I have a feeling she doesn't like the memories of my father that linger there.

From what I remember of our dad, he was temperamental and often away for work. He was tall and gave good hugs when the rare mood struck him, and cold and closed off when it didn't.

I do, however, remember distinctly what it was like when he left.

The night it happened was violently windy with torrential rain and deafening thunder. It was evening, right before dinner, and Tim was visiting mom. I can still smell the pot roast in the oven and hear the rain against the windows. The twins were playing in the living room, and I was alone in the kitchen.

I heard the front door open and knew instinctively that my father was home. Then there were raised voices, my father's loudest of all. I didn't see what happened, but I remember a flash of light and my mother's screams ringing in my ears. The flash was probably just my imagination, but it's always there when I think back on that night.

I don't know what took place, just that it was serious. Mom was hospitalized for a few days, and we stayed with Tim and his sister until she came home. She was different after. Quieter and less vibrant, and I could hear her crying at night. Even though I was young, I would climb into bed and put my arms around her until her breathing settled.

She always hugged me tight but never told me anything. I thought it was better not to ask. After that night, we never saw my father again, and we saw Tim less and less.

After dad left, we also lost mom in a way. I've never doubted her love for us, but her pain needed an outlet, and she found it in her art. My mother's books and paintings tell incredible stories of magic and nature. She's won awards and recognition in fantasy circles for her stories about The Storm King. It meant that we didn't starve as children, but it also meant that she vanished for long periods of time while she shut herself away in her studio.

My sisters inherited her talent and they're both brilliant artists in their own right. I'm the practical child. Though it could be argued that I didn't have a choice in the matter.

Focusing on mundane details like whether we had shoes that fit for the school year or whether the electric bill had been paid were not in my mother's nature to remember. Perhaps it had been before our father left, but certainly not after.

I don't feel burdened by taking care of my family. I love them and making sure they're happy and safe gives me comfort. But, if I'm honest, I do have a little resentment for always having to hold myself together.

Sometimes, it's like there's this wild thing inside me trying to escape and terrible events will unfold if I let it out. I feel it in my chest sometimes, like a caged animal trying to escape. I always have to be controlled, cautious, and diligent. And I have to be nearby in case mom loses herself again.

Because if not me, who else will do it?

Beatrice and Wren live their own lives in Providence. They went to RISD, and I'm unbelievably proud of everything they're accomplishing in their careers. They were too little to remember the change in our mother. To them, she's always been this way, and so the burden of responsibility falls on my shoulders.

Reginald rubs against my leg, purring as he snuggles up to me. I pet his back and fire off a quick message to my sisters.

Willa: Talked to mom. She seems good. I love you.

Beatrice: Love you, too, Willie!

Wren: <3

I heat up some leftovers and pour a glass of wine. I refuse to think anymore about work or my family. I pick up the sweater I've been knitting and put on a British crime show I've seen a bunch of times. At some point, I call it a night and fall asleep with Reg curled around my head, dreaming of lightning and my boss's furious eyes.

CHAPTER 3

THE HUM of the plane drowns out the circular argument happening across the aisle of the private IMA jet. Ronan Banks and Greta Adamu, two of my invaluable colleagues and closest friends, can be counted on to fight like good-natured cats and dogs whenever the opportunity arises.

I flick through another page of the document in my lap. I've read and re-read the dossier Soren Westerholm, the other member of our team, pulled together on our target. Soren is exceptional at what he does, and I know more about Wilhelmina Sophia Martin than she probably knows about herself. It's a welcome distraction from whatever Banks and Greta keep on about.

Willa Martin, as she prefers, is 27 and the eldest daughter of Anne Martin and Lars Stromberg. She was raised in Greensboro, Vermont along with her two younger sisters, Wren Selene and Beatrice Penelope. They all adopted their mother's last name after their father left abruptly when they were children.

Willa lives alone in a small studio apartment in Burlington with her two cats, and works as an entry level librarian at the local university. She earned an undergraduate degree with honors in medieval history from Fordham and a master's in library science from McGill. Both degrees were paid for by her mother, but based on her apartment and general lifestyle, that appears to be the only money she has accepted from her mother's ample net worth.

I flip to the next page of the document. Her closest friend is Samuel Henderson, a geologist for the State of Vermont. Her free time is spent at coffee shops, the yoga studio, or visiting her mother in the country. She frequents local restaurants and spends a staggering amount of money on yarn and books. She was most recently dating Nicholas James Granger, a local musician who, based purely on his photos, is a completely smug little shit. A man who pays next to no rent, freeloading in the house owned by her friend Sam.

Willa Martin's social media is private, but that has never stopped Soren before. She posts regularly, but nothing of consequence or anything that speaks to the inner workings of her mind or her motivations. It's all photos and videos of knitting projects, nature scenes, and her cats.

Beatrice has tagged Willa in several images throughout the years, and the black and white photo that Soren attached to the top of her file stares up at me. Our target faces straight at the camera with a wide smile that takes over her features. A portrait taken by her sister in a moment of levity.

But her eyes are wrong. There's a darkness, a seriousness, in her gaze that surprises me. Willa doesn't appear to be the kind of person who truly lets herself enjoy anything.

Perhaps she can't.

Perhaps there are responsibilities or the weight of guilt or some other heavy burden.

Whatever it is, I intend to uncover it. We've been led to believe none of the Martin women has had contact with Stromberg since he vanished 20 years ago. But if there is any chance he's spoken to them or they're harboring his secrets…

It's a lead we can't ignore.

I flip through more pages of the thick packet.

There's something off about the turn this investigation is taking. Something my colleagues sense, too. Apprehension is thick in the air.

A text alert chimes on my phone. I see it's from Ingrid, and I clear the notification. I should have pushed harder when Olsen foisted her on us. I've never worked with a woman I've been involved with, no matter how brief the encounter or how pretty she is.

My interaction with Ingrid was one dinner and some uninspiring sex at her apartment, but I put these rules in place for a reason. Women and work never mix. But when Director Olsen determined that we needed more resources for the case, it wasn't feasible to say no.

I don't ignore Ingrid, but I don't encourage her either. I cannot afford any distractions. Distractions like the soulful eyes staring up at me from this photograph.

I immediately dismiss the thought. For all we know, Willa Martin is working with her father. There is too much unknown. Too many unanswered questions and pieces that don't fit.

As if reading my mind, Greta pipes up from her seat by Banks.

"I do not like this," she states, her French accent becoming more pronounced while she flips aggressively through her own copy of the report. Greta was born in Nigeria but moved to her mother's home in Paris as a small child. We all attended boarding school together outside London.

"Why not?"

I'm curious if her thoughts are in line with mine.

"Why would Stromberg reach out to his daughter so indirectly? Wouldn't it make more sense for him to come himself? And why now? He's left his wife and children alone for the last 20 years. What changed?"

"Lars can't leave his hiding place. We're too close to finding him," I reply. "He'd be caught within hours and he knows it."

"My contacts underground haven't said anything definite," Banks adds in his rough brogue. "Just that there are whispers of changes in organizational leadership that are making people nervous. Nothing concrete."

Ronan Banks is a gruff Irishman with a dark and complicated past. His contacts are rarely wrong.

Another chime from my phone draws our attention.

"What could she possibly want now?" Greta asks with an exaggerated eye roll.

I read through the text from Ingrid. It's professional. Mostly.

"She's just checking in."

"That woman is a snake," Greta says.

"Ingrid is a member of our team for the duration of this investigation. We might be used to a certain dynamic, but we cannot sow dissent."

Greta sniffs in disapproval but doesn't say anything else. She knows I'm right, even if she doesn't like it.

"Though it is unusual for me to agree with Greta," Banks says with a twinkle in his eyes. Greta shoots him a fiery but mostly affectionate glare. "I sense discord in Ingrid. Though I can't place the cause."

Banks is the most intuitive member of our group. His shrewd observations are invaluable, but unless I have concrete evidence that Ingrid's presence is counterproductive or somehow nefarious, there is little I can do to remove her. So far, she just seems keen to prove herself.

"I appreciate your insights, but I also have to trust Director Olsen. Ingrid is new to our team and the way we operate and that is causing some very normal tension. Nothing more, nothing less."

Greta huffs something in French that sounds an awful lot like, *"les hommes sont les idiotes,"* and Banks crosses his arms over his barrel-sized chest and frowns.

"Getting back to the matter at hand." I turn my attention back to the dossier. "I think it might be best if I make initial contact."

"But that is not what we agreed." Greta furrows her brow in confusion. "I'm posing as a researcher to befriend the target and extract the information. That is why I am here."

"You are here because I need you here," I state plainly. "Your skills and expertise are applicable to a wide range of situations. You know that as well as I do."

Greta nods, but her lips are pressed in a thin line. It is unusual for me to change course so close to the contact point. She's right to question me.

"Will Greta and I handle the library director then?" Banks asks.

"Yes. The two of you will find out what you can about the illegally obtained books while I focus on the target. The only change is that Greta and I are swapping roles. The mission remains the same."

"May I ask why?" Greta is cautious, but firm.

I scrub a hand over the short beard I've grown out before answering her. It's not my usual clean-shaven look, but I admit to enjoying the rough feel of it.

We always make an effort to blend into the environment. It's impossible for us to completely assimilate anywhere, but three agents walking through the doors of a university library would raise alarm bells and attention we do not need.

"I'm not sure, Greta." Her eyes soften at the uncertainty in my voice. "Call it instinct or simple intrigue, but there's something about Willa Martin that I can't place. Something that's calling to me to figure out. I am certain that she is central to the investigation, but why? Why her? Why now?"

I take out the black and white photograph again. Greta and Banks watch on with silent curiosity.

"Despite the extensive research in the pages of this document, I still don't have a clear picture. We know she's important to her father and uncle, but we don't know why. There's something hidden, something we're missing."

My voice trails off and I realize I'm running my finger along the outline of her face.

Banks clears his throat and my hand abruptly stops moving. Greta gives Banks a furtive glance.

"It's settled then," I say, ignoring their inquisitive expressions. "I will be the one to make initial contact with the target and you will handle David Edwards. We should be landing soon."

"Yes, the pilot will be making the announcement shortly." Greta grabs on to my change of subject. "I'll go check with the flight attendant." She unbuckles and rises from the beige leather airplane seat and exits through the curtain that separates us from the flight crew.

The emotionless mask that Banks always wears slips into the slightest smile.

"What are you smiling about, Banks?"

"Me? I don't smile. You know that."

"I do. It's why I'm asking."

Banks rises and claps me on the shoulder.

"Your instincts are sound, Lundqvist. They've not led you wrong yet, but don't allow training to dull your natural senses. I suspect that solving this case will require more agility than we are accustomed to."

"Care to elaborate?"

Banks's eyes dart back down at the photo of Willa in my hand.

"Just that there are unpredictable variables at play. Our perceptions will likely be challenged and what we expect is needed may differ from what is required."

Banks leaves in search of Greta with his head ducked. The jet is ample by aviation standards, but Banks is an uncommonly large man. He has a way of speaking in riddles, but he's rarely wrong.

I flip to another photo of Willa Martin attached to Soren's dossier. It reflects the light above me, her eyes a brilliant shade of electric blue and a dusting of freckles across her nose and cheekbones. There may be some truth in what Banks says, but experience dictates that deviating too far from the set path causes disruption and, on rare occasions, utter devastation.

No matter how intriguing I find her, the eldest Stromberg daughter cannot draw me too far off course. I won't allow it.

CHAPTER 4

WILLA

I ARRIVE at work too early. I couldn't sleep. Thoughts of Dr. Edwards and the unknown but inevitable retribution I'll face today kept me up most of the night.

I practiced over and over everything I'll say to defend myself when the time comes. It wasn't intentional. I was simply trying to protect the books and share my knowledge.

But Dr. Edwards isn't rational when it comes to his ego and won't care that I'm right. And I won't say what he deserves to hear. I'll apologize and placate and fight the urge to run away.

I'm tired of it. Tired of remaining silent in my own discomfort while I let someone else steal more of my pride.

Isn't that why I barely complained when I found Nick in bed with…

Nope, we are not thinking about that now.

If I can manage it, I won't think about that particular brand of humiliation ever again.

I dressed in my typical work uniform of a comfortable

black dress and paired it with tights and my trusty black heeled boots. As I left, I threw on a chunky knit cardigan that I made a few winters back to fight off the late autumn chill.

We're well into the semester, which means we already have a library peppered with anxiety-ridden students. I can always tell what's happening on campus by the mood in the building. Even at this early an hour, the timbre of their conversations changes during high stress periods.

I grab a quick coffee in the library cafe and enjoy the strong clicking of my boots on the tile floor. I might not be the boss, but the sound of my heels making their way to the basement of the library reminds me that I could be. My spine straightens, and I push my shoulders back.

I've got this. I am an intelligent, powerful woman, and I don't have to take any shit from anyone.

Right.

Maybe if I keep telling myself I'll eventually believe it.

I shift my bag and coffee to one arm, and insert my key in the department door. Jim and our other coworkers don't usually come in until 8:30 so I'll be the only one here.

I unlock the door and step into the dark office. I go through the motions of opening the reading room, turning on the lights and arranging our pencils and paper on each table.

It's my day to sit at the reference desk, but I don't need to be out there until 9. I hang up my coat and bag in my office. I take another sip of my coffee and turn on my computer.

An email pops up with Dr. Edwards's name and my stomach sinks. I was checking messages on my phone all night. He must have sent it while I was on the way in. My heart beats with excess speed and a sick sensation settles in my gut.

"Wilhelmina,

The newly acquired books need to be cataloged ASAP. They

were moved to your department's secure storage and require your immediate attention. Please see that they are fully available for patron access by the end of the day.

There is no metadata to accompany the donation, but I trust that with your *vast* expertise, this will not be an issue.

Regards,

Dr. David H. Edwards, PhD"

So, this is how my career ends.

That prick knows there is no conceivable way I can catalog from scratch all 23 volumes in 8 hours. Even just bare bones cataloging on rare material takes more time than that. There's so much research required, and I'm going into it blind with no information on the donor. To do all the books justice would require months, if not years, of work.

Not to mention how far above my pay grade this is. Of course Dr. Edwards would refuse my promotion but expect me to do the work anyway. I can't get through all of them, but maybe I can do part of one and explain rationally that his request is unreasonable.

Jim will back me up. He understands the complex nature of describing unique material. No one, not even the world's most prolific rare books cataloger, could possibly do anything truly useful with all these books in a day.

Part of me knows I should report this to Human Resources. But I also know that Dr. Edwards would only get a slap on the wrist, and then he'd make my life a living hell until I quit. That's usually how these things go.

Instead, I wind my way through the work area to our secure storage space and unlock the door. I find the volumes stacked on a book cart in the middle of the cool, dark room.

I push the cart back to my desk and force the tears welling in my eyes to remain at bay.

I cannot get fired. *What would I do?* I might not love my job as much as I should, but I need it to support myself.

Pushing those worrisome thoughts aside, I pick up the closest volume. It's clearly a Bible.

OK, I know Bibles.

It's in Latin, which I expected. Even though it's much smaller, it reminds me a little of the famous Bury Bible at the University of Cambridge. That would make it probably mid-12th century.

How the hell did we get these books? And with nothing from the donor indicating what they are? It was a ridiculous donation to accept. They could be stolen for all we know.

I'll have to comb through each page to see how its unique from others of its kind, and if there's any indication about the scribe and where it was created.

This will take forever.

I set the book down gently and rub my temples.

My eyes catch on the book from yesterday. The one that intrigued me. Black with unusual runes etched along the gilded cover.

It's gorgeous.

I pick it up and open it to a page in the middle. My assessment was correct, and it's definitely some kind of old church ledger based on the hurried and irregular script. But it's in a language I'm not entirely familiar with. Possibly Old Norse or Old Swedish.

Without warning, something strange like an invisible vine clamps onto my fingers. It snakes up my hands from where they hold the binding.

Holy shit.

I try to drop the book, but it's like my fingers are glued to it. I can't let it go.

My office slowly fades and fuzzes around the edges. My stomach lurches and my head spins as my vision tunnels.

The strange sensation of vines climbing up my arms continues and steadily relaxes me. It reaches my chest, and I can barely hold myself upright. I'm so tired. So warm and sleepy.

I slump to my knees, and I can't stop the sudden, overwhelming desire to lay on the floor.

Just for a moment. Just a little while.

I curl up on the rug by my desk, and between one blink and the next, I'm fast asleep.

I wake up in a field. A dry expanse of tan grass and short ochre-colored leaves. A field in November, before the real snow falls. Browns and grays deepened by an overcast sky. Across the field, a pine forest covers one side and the tall amber grass of a marshland on the other. Golden tamaracks dot the dark evergreens. The only needle tree that sheds in winter.

A shadow steps out of the forest and approaches me at a slow pace. The earth around me rumbles, and the wind picks up as if this figure is drawing it in and pushing it toward me. I can't run or hide. I'm afraid, but the fear is disembodied like I'm watching this happen to someone else.

The figure approaches closer. I can't see clearly through the growing wind. It whips my face and hair, and I should be cold but instead I'm warm like a fire is lit inside me.

The rational part of my brain is screaming at me to run, but I'm riveted to the spot. I have to know who is coming. The shadow man moves closer, and though he's cloaked, I feel a deep sense of familiarity. This person is someone I know, but I can't quite place.

He steps in front of me and removes his gloves. He reaches out and touches my forehead with one finger. A sharp pain sears through me and a surge of power passes between us. It feels ancient and dark, but not malevolent. Just potent and unpredictable like a thunderstorm. I fall to my knees, breathing hard against the wind. The figure vanishes and I collapse into darkness.

I wake again in a deciduous forest in early spring. The tranquility of the trees flows through me, and even though I don't recognize these surroundings, I'm safe and at peace. The leaf buds just sprouting, the mist of fresh rain, the faint scent of violets.

The vision shifts, and I'm in the same forest in summer. Broad leaves, heavy green mosses on gray rocks, birds calling overhead.

It shifts again, and the forest is in full autumn glory. Golden light, deep orange leaves, the sweet smell of decay.

Then it's winter. The sun is shining and lighting up the snow like diamonds. The bare tree branches sparkle with ice. It's cold, but I look down and see I'm wearing a bright blue cloak with white fur lining the hood. It makes the cool air on my face pleasant and welcome. In my hands, I'm carrying a white stone, a black feather, and a green vine. I don't know what they mean, but they feel significant.

Power radiates from my outstretched fingers. I breathe deeply, and I begin to hum and tremble like I'm drawing in power from the earth itself.

The sound of running water and the cold, clean scent of fresh snow are calming and fortifying.

The forest is feeding me its strength and its calm, its power and its serenity.

The man approaches again. The cloak is gone. And he is definitely someone I know.

It's my father.

His eyes crinkle as he smiles at me in greeting. He hasn't changed much over the years with his tall, broad stature, long blonde hair and aqua blue eyes that are just like Bea's. He's as much the Viking as I remember.

"Willa, I'm delighted to see you again," he says. His voice and his accent are long-lost memories resurfacing.

I have so many questions for the man before me, but I land on something simple.

"Where are we?" I ask.

"In a dream," he shrugs like it's obvious.

"That doesn't explain anything."

I shake my head, and he smiles like he finds me endearing, which only makes the jumbled mix of emotions more difficult to untangle.

"I came to speak to you," he says. "There are so many things you need to understand, and I need to ask your help."

"OK…"

"The first is that I never set out to hurt you or your…"

My father's face begins to fade. The forest around me darkens. Panic crosses my father's features.

"Stay with me, Willa. Please. I have to talk to you. It's imperative that you understand…"

He fades further, and I hear a faint call. My name. Someone in the distance is calling to me. I want to hear what my father has to say so desperately, but I can't seem to stay in the dream. I'm being forced out of it.

"Now that you're no longer trapped, I'll find you again," his voice is faint, like it's through a thick wall. "You can find me, too, if you try…"

My father vanishes. His shadow completely dissolves, and his voice floats away like a leaf in the wind. The forest is long gone.

With no ceremony or explanation, I'm back in my office with a pair of the most gorgeous blue eyes I've ever seen staring down at me.

CHAPTER 5

"WHAT THE HELL?" I cry out. I'm incensed. I don't know how to get back to the woods and my father and the thought enrages me. There's also a deep sense of loss. I miss the calm of the forest, and I have to know what my father was trying to tell me.

I'm lying on the floor next to my desk with an exceptionally large man kneeling over me. My eyes drift to the dark gray cotton shirt covering his broad, muscular chest. There's a faint outline of washboard abs and thick biceps coiled beneath his long shirtsleeves.

Sweet Jesus. Am I still dreaming?

I sit up, waving off his attempt to help me, and make the mistake of really looking at his face.

He's so handsome I lose the ability to speak. Real men don't look like this. Especially not men who come into my library. He's maybe in his early thirties. His beard is trimmed close, and I can make out the hard angles of his jaw. Then there's the masculine shape of his nose and the fullness of his lips. His brown hair is on the longish side, soft looking and a little untamed, like he regularly runs his fingers through it.

"Are you alright?" the ridiculously gorgeous man asks.

He has an accent. *Of course, he has an accent.*

It's English, but with a lilt to it that's familiar. As if he learned English somewhere in the UK.

My heart speeds up when I realize I recognize it because it's the same as my father's.

I'm instantly wary and alert. This undeniably hot man is Swedish. I just met my Swedish father in a dream state.

Coincidence? Is that even possible?

I don't know how I know the dream was real, but I do. I know with my whole heart and soul that I just spoke with my father for the first time since I was a child. My insides buzz with energy. The swirling and churning inside my chest that I've felt faintly inside me at various points in my life is suddenly and painfully alert. I rub my chest, trying to calm it down.

"What are you doing here?"

My voice isn't friendly, but I can't bring myself to care at the moment.

The man glances at my hand, which is rubbing my chest in small circles. I stop the movement and clasp my fingers together on my lap.

"I just found you passed out on the floor and woke you up. I believe a thank you is in order. But I'm here to do research on one of your collections. My colleague and I made an appointment with Jim Grant."

He smiles slightly so I don't think he's offended. Perhaps more amused than anything.

The man stands and reaches a hand down for me. He's tall. Over a foot taller than my 5'3" and at least twice as wide with a muscular chest and broad shoulders. Reluctantly, I reach for his hand. The moment our skin connects, the churning in my chest pitches forward. Something uncontrollable runs down my arm to reach him.

The man's eyes widen a fraction, but he recovers quickly. I draw my hand back.

"Oh, that's right. Jim mentioned it earlier in the week."

"My name is Stellan Lundqvist. It's nice to meet you."

"I'm Willa Martin. It's nice to meet you as well."

I shake my head to clear the cobwebs and get a handle on myself. It's not this man's fault he prevented me from speaking to my father for the first time in 20 years.

He dips his head slightly and his lips press together in concern. His eyes are drawn to the books on the floor. He watches as I scramble to pick them up and set them safely on the book cart. Cataloging them will have to wait.

"Are you sure you're alright?" he asks, scanning me up and down as if searching for injuries. "Do you faint regularly? Do you need a doctor?" His deep voice rumbles over me like a caress.

"No," I clear my throat. "I've never done that before, but I'm fine." I awkwardly rub my hands against the soft fabric of my dress along my hips. His eyes follow the movement and I stop.

And it's true. Despite how uncomfortable it is that this god among men found me passed out on the floor, I feel great. Strong, even. As if the power from the forest is still alive inside me.

"Hmm, if you're sure."

He doesn't believe me. I mean, it's a strange thing to stumble upon.

I lead him to the reference desk in the front of the office. Jim still isn't in yet. A quick glance down at the computer tells me it's only 8:29. How did all this happen in less than a half hour?

I want the time to process everything my father was trying to communicate with me, but that doesn't appear in the cards. The gorgeous patron stands expectantly by the desk.

"Jim already pulled the boxes you need. I just have to ask you to fill out our patron registration form. If you expect your visit to extend over multiple days, we'll set your materials aside on a cart in the back."

"Thank you, that's perfect. I'll be here until early next week."

He pulls a notebook and some papers out of his leather shoulder bag and hands me a list.

"I'm hoping to look at these ten or so folders today," he says.

He leans closer, and I catch the scent of his cologne. There's something fresh and natural about it, like a sunny forest in early spring, newly budding leaves and earth covered in fresh rain. Petrichor. Cologne doesn't usually do it for me, but this man's scent draws me in, like there's an invisible cord connecting us.

My eyes flutter closed, and I'm sure I catch him breathing in slowly, as though he's feeling the same magnetic attraction. Just as abruptly as it starts, he takes a step back and severs the connection.

"I'll just, um, go get your boxes," I say with as much composure as I can muster. "Please feel free to take a seat in the reading room."

"Thank you," he says and blinks a few times like he's clearing his vision.

I grab the nearest cart and head to the back room to fetch the boxes. I catch him looking at me as I walk away, my heart pounding like I'm a teenager at a school dance. I'm glad to have some distance between us.

It has to be a coincidence that he's here. He doesn't know

me or my father. He can't know that he woke me from that dream.

Right? I mean, that's crazy. But then, this whole thing is crazy.

I gather up the boxes and try to look unruffled as I push them toward him. He sets his bright blue eyes on me, and I look down at my feet. I've gone from feeling semi-confident to not being able to make eye contact.

At least I manage not to trip over myself with him watching me like that.

I push the cart up to his table.

"Here you are, Mr. Lundqvist. I'll just be at the reference desk, if you need anything."

I give him my politest and most professional smile.

"Thank you for your assistance. And, please, call me Stellan," he says and returns the smile.

I should move or say something, but I can't. I just drink him in. His eyes are kind, and they sparkle in a bright and clear blue like fresh water in the sunshine. His hair is this beautiful, wavy mix of browns and his short beard is sexy and masculine.

I blush again, the heat making my cheeks burn.

"Sure, Stellan. No problem," I reply before I finally convince my legs to walk me back to where I belong.

It's just my luck that he picked the table closest to the reference desk. If just his smile makes me blush, I'm in for an exceptionally long day.

CHAPTER 6

STELLAN

I PRETEND to take notes and flip through folders while keeping an eye on our target. When I found her on the floor, my heart sank to my stomach. Her supine form on the ground, her face pale. It was startling. Thankfully, she woke easily enough.

The incident also very likely means her father reached her before I arrived. Our intel clearly indicated that Stromberg would contact her through one of the rare books he had spelled in his lab.

I won't question Willa directly just yet, but I'll find out soon enough. I have to know if he spoke to her and how she fits into his plans.

If she's aiding and abetting her father in any way, it won't matter how pretty she is; she will need to be under my control.

Unfortunately, that's a thought I like a little too much.

I shift uncomfortably in my seat, disgusted with myself. I

cannot have thoughts like that about Lars Stromberg's eldest daughter.

I was assigned to this case six months ago after it had been left dormant for nearly two decades. This is the most tangible progress we've made, and I can't risk losing this lead.

Willa is trying not to glance in my direction, but her interest in me is obvious. I can't be certain if it's just that she finds me attractive or that she suspects I know what happened with the book. Perhaps it's both. I can't get a read on her, and that is unusual in itself.

It's conceivable that Stromberg warned her about us. He must know I'm hunting him. It's entirely within the realm of possibility, which will make this an uphill battle. But if she is attracted to me, I can use that to my advantage. It wouldn't be the first time.

The thought sours my stomach. I never feel guilt doing my job. The mission is always more important than anyone's wounded pride. But something about deceiving Willa Martin, especially lying to her in that way, makes my chest ache uncomfortably.

Willa's superior checks in on her. They have a hushed and tense conversation that I can only hear in snippets. Something about an email and some books she's meant to catalog. I hear Dr. Edwards's name repeated. It's clear the man has done something to upset Willa. Anger fires the air around her. Her spine is ramrod straight, and a flush of red crosses her cheeks and her eyes sparkle.

She is lovely when she's angry. I can't help but wonder what all that intensity and passion would look like in another, far more enjoyable setting.

I'm saved from my unwelcome thoughts when the man in question rushes into the office. His face a bright purple and his rage blazing.

"You bitch! This is entirely your fault!"

He shouts at Willa and she freezes, startled and shocked. Her eyes wide in surprise.

"Dave! How dare you speak to her like that!" Jim shouts. His own anger rising in a dark cloud.

Banks strides in right after Dr. Edwards, so I remain where I'm sitting. Keeping myself in character as a curious patron for the time being.

"You stuck these people on me! They said they're here to collect the donation. Why would they do that if not for you!?" Edwards shouts right in Willa's face, but she doesn't cower. I force myself to remain where I am.

"I don't know what you're talking about," Willa says, and I find that I'm proud when her voice doesn't falter. "I haven't spoken to anyone but Jim about them."

"You lying..." Dr. Edwards swings his fist back as if he's going to hit her, and I'm off my feet in a second. I'll be too late to stop him, but not too late to pummel him into the ground.

Luckily, Banks is right there and grabs Edwards's arm, spinning him around and slamming his furious face against the glass wall of the office with a loud bang. Edwards yelps in pain. He struggles as Banks twists his arm, but he's no match for my colleague's strength.

"Right, mate. That's quite enough," Banks barks at him. Onlookers from outside their department are drawn to the noise. We need to wrap this up. "Do you think you can parcel up the books for us?" he asks Willa much more gently.

"Oh, yes of course." She pushes to standing but then turns to Banks. "But wait, who are you?"

Banks pulls out his badge with his right hand, holding Edwards still. The piece of metal is mostly meaningless, but it does the job. "I work in the cultural heritage sector, primarily stolen artifacts and rare objects. The books in your possession were obtained illegally, and we tracked them here. We need to return them to their rightful owners. I have paperwork I can show you."

"Oh no." Willa claps a hand to her mouth. "I knew something wasn't right. I'll go get the books by my desk now. Jim, the rest are still in the back."

Jim turns away after another disgusted glare at Edwards. Banks makes a grimace and a slight shake of his head at me, but otherwise we remain silent while Edwards hangs his head in defeat.

"Here you go," Willa says after returning to us. "I put the ones I had in two record boxes. I can wrap them up better and more securely, if you need it."

She's helpful and thorough, and her concern for the books is endearing.

"No, this is perfect. Thank you. After I take this gentleman upstairs to greet the local authorities, I'll be back to collect them. We appreciate your cooperation."

"Of course," Willa responds and wrings her hands. She stares at a fixed spot, lost in thought.

Jim returns moments later with his own stack of boxes and sets them by Willa's. Banks escorts out a quietly seething Dr. Edwards with a cursory nod in my direction.

"My God, Willa. I'm so sorry," Jim says and wraps her in a fatherly hug.

I push down the growl at another man, even one old enough to be her grandfather, touching her. There is something seriously wrong with me today.

"I'm fine," she says, but she's shaking. My protective instincts drive me to comfort her, but I remain rooted to the spot.

"I'll go fetch you some water," Jim says helpfully, giving me my moment alone with her.

"Are you alright?" I ask cautiously, my chair scrapes

against the floor as I step away from the desk. Her face opens in surprise.

"Oh! I'm so sorry you had to see that, sir. How ridiculous and unprofessional. You came here to work and…I'm so sorry."

"Ms. Martin, what are you apologizing for? From my perspective, you did nothing wrong. That man behaved abominably."

She wrinkles her nose. "He did, didn't he?"

She smiles as if she wants to laugh. She even lets out a tiny giggle and her whole face lights up.

I'm struck by how uncommonly pretty she is.

She claps a hand to her mouth when she notices my startled expression and mistakes it for something else.

"You must think I'm crazy, wanting to laugh at a moment like that. I'm just so relieved," she sighs. "Dr. Edwards has been bullying me for months, and I knew something wasn't right with the donation. I'm just so glad it came to light when it did."

I let her see my most charming smile. The one I use only for work. She swallows hard. Her throat bobs, and I want to run my fingers along her neck, feel her pulse rise as I whisper my dirtiest thoughts in her ear.

My pretty catch has taken the bait. Now to reel her in.

"Perfectly understandable." I approach closer, putting myself in her orbit. "I apologize if this is too forward, but would you like to have dinner with me this evening?"

Willa blinks a few times like she's processing the request. Her fingers twist around the hem of her cardigan nervously.

"Oh, um, well, I have plans tonight." She is adorably awkward.

"Could you cancel them?" I press.

"I'm afraid I can't, but I'm free Saturday. You said you're here until next week." I smile again at her boldness.

"I did say that. Saturday it is. Here, give me your number." I create a new blank text and hand her my phone. She types quickly and hands it back. I text her a brief introduction. "Send me your address and I'll pick you up at 7."

"Actually, could I just meet you somewhere? I don't like to let strangers know where I live. Not that you're scary or anything, but, well, you know what I mean..." she explains with a wave of her hand.

I'm taken aback by her caution, but also a little impressed. I refuse to examine what it says about me, but most women just do what I ask in these situations. She'd also be shocked to discover that not only do I know where she lives, I know what she eats for breakfast, her favorite cat food brand, and the middle names of all of her grandparents going back several generations.

"Of course. That's very smart, and I can't fault you for being careful. I'll text you where to meet me. I think I've had enough excitement for the day though. Can you set these aside for me when I return next week?"

"Absolutely. I'm sorry again for the disruption."

"Don't mention it, Willa." I wink at her, and she blushes.

I leave the library with a satisfied smile. Initial contact with the target went better than expected. Much better.

CHAPTER 7

JIM SENT ME HOME EARLY. After I gave a statement to the police, he told me to pack up for the day and take as much time off as I need.

I know myself, and I'll be back on Monday. There's no point wallowing in what ifs. And really, despite being yelled at and nearly punched, nothing terrible happened. If anything, I'm relieved. I'll be replaying for a long time the moment when that giant, dark-haired man grabbed Dr. Edwards and shoved him against the wall.

But I am grateful for the extra time at home. This morning was something out of a fantasy story. Beyond the insanity with my boss, I genuinely don't know how to process the fact that I spoke to my father.

How could I ever explain that to anyone? It's so farfetched, and anyone with a sound mind would argue it was a dream. But I am certain beyond a shadow of a doubt that it was real.

The same peculiar vibrations from the forest still hum beneath my skin. The swirling in my chest is so active it's almost painful. If I close my eyes, I can see it, like a great ball of twirling light next to my heart. It's strange but so familiar, like it's been there all along.

Something about that dream woke it up. It's far more intense than just anxiety or some kind of psychosomatic reaction to seeing my father. It's powerful and undeniable.

But what is it?

The churning grows so strong while I focus on it that I'm afraid I'm going to explode. It's like I'm one trigger away from detonating all over my apartment only to be found days later half-eaten by my cats.

I remember some breathing exercises my mother taught us when we were little. It had to do with focusing on a ball of light inside us. Breathing in and out and imagining that we're protecting our inner power, keeping it secure.

She can be such a ridiculous hippie sometimes, but that's not uncommon where we grew up. Everyone's either new-age and witchy or salt of the earth and practical. There's little in between. But perhaps my mother was onto something because after a few minutes of deep breathing and meditating on control, the swirling has slowed and I'm less volatile.

I made plans to meet Sam a little early so we can catch up before our other friends arrive. Sam moved to town with his mom and brother when we were in first grade, and we've been close ever since.

On his first day at school, he walked into our classroom full of confidence in his worn Batman t-shirt and a dimpled grin. He took the spot right next to me like he belonged there, and we were pretty much inseparable from that point on.

I was small for my age and painfully shy, but Sam always

seemed to know how to draw me out of myself. We both came from single-parent families, and as we got older, he spent most afternoons at our house while his mom worked. Our friendship has an ease to it that I've never found with anyone else. We try not to go more than a couple weeks without catching up.

Still, it was hard to say no to Stellan Lundqvist when he asked me to change my plans for him. I was definitely tempted. Denying someone that out of my league felt wrong on a fundamental level.

If it was anyone other than Sam, I probably would have. But I haven't seen my best friend in a while and I didn't want to cancel.

We're seeing a band later, so I put on something a little spicier. One of my shorter dresses and my sexier boots. I give myself a smokey eye and curl my long hair into waves.

I throw on a thick cardigan and my jacket and head out. The walk is short, but the air is cold. The wind off the lake bites through my clothes like I'm barely dressed instead of wrapped in multiple layers. Typical Vermont in November.

I hurry along Battery Street for a couple blocks and turn up College Street toward downtown. Before rounding the corner, I notice a group of men a few blocks ahead moving in my direction. They aren't close to me, but they stand out enough that I pause.

Three uncommonly large and intimidating men, dressed in black from their boots to their hats walk toward me with a practiced kind of swagger. I've never seen anyone like them in Burlington, or anywhere else for that matter.

One of the men notices me looking. I can feel his eyes on me before I can confirm it. Fear creeps over my skin like spiders. He nudges another man, and all of them stop moving and stare directly at me.

Alarm bells blare in my head. A little voice in the back of

my mind tells me to run. So, without a second thought, I do. I sprint hard and don't look back to see if they're following, but I swear I can hear the pounding of feet on the pavement behind me. My instincts tell me to put as much distance between me and these men as possible. The tension in my muscles and the swirling in my chest rise to a fever pitch as I fly up the hill.

I keep running until I find a familiar alley way and slip through it. I snake my way into town through side streets and more alleys until I'm in the heart of downtown Burlington and can hide myself in the Friday night crowd.

I stop close to the restaurant where I'm meeting Sam and catch my breath. I lean against a brick wall clutching my chest. Blood pounds in my ears, and my lungs burn from the cold air. I have no idea who those men are or if they really were following me, but I've never been so freaked out all the way to my bones at just the sight of someone.

An older couple looks at me curiously as they walk by. I must seem crazy standing outside a restaurant breathing like I ran a marathon.

With distance between me and the men, I realize I probably overreacted. It reminds me of games my sisters and I used to play as children, imagining that we were being chased by monsters. How real it felt in the moment, but also safe in the knowledge that it was just make believe. The panic subsides and it's replaced with embarrassment at my strong reaction.

Justine made a reservation at one of the many farm-to-table places in town. She picked it because her girlfriend works here and we'll get free drinks. But I don't care where we are, I'm just glad to be surrounded by people.

As soon as I catch my breath, I open the door and hang my coat up on the rack. The interior walls are all painted dark gray and offset by local abstract art. Candles light the dining room in a warm glow. The change of scenery eases away the rest of my anxiety.

Sam is seated at the bar already but stands when he sees me approach. He's dressed in black jeans and a red and black buffalo check shirt. Sam's mom was born in Seoul and he looks just like her except for his height, which he got from his dad. He has the kindest brown eyes I've ever seen, and his model-worthy dark hair flows down to his shoulders.

"Willa!" Sam calls and wraps me in an embrace before pulling back to look at me. He must notice my flushed features or something in my eyes. "Are you OK? You look all keyed up."

"Oh yeah. I'm fine!" I lie and sit down in the open stool next to him and pick up the ice water the bartender sets in front of me. "So, when you were leaving the house tonight did you plan on dressing like a logger in a shampoo commercial?"

Sam laughs. "Fair enough. That's a great cardigan, by the way. I didn't know there were auditions for Miss Marple happening tonight."

I roll my eyes. "You are hilarious."

"You started it. Let's get you a drink and then you can tell me why you obviously sprinted here."

I cough on my water as it goes down the wrong pipe.

"I should have known I can't hide anything from you. I ran here because there were these scary men near College Street. It's been a weird few days and some insane stuff happened at work, and I think I just freaked myself out for no reason. I'm fine."

Sam takes a sip of beer and stares like he's reading all my inner thoughts. Sam is protective of me. Sometimes overly so, but I know it's because he feels like there's no one else to do it.

"Odd stuff like what?"

I wish more than anything that I could tell him about my father. But that's impossible. He'd have me committed.

"My boss sort of tried to attack me and accused me of siccing some federal agents on him for stealing rare books. And also, I kind of passed out in my office. It's no big deal though. I don't want to talk about any of that."

"It's no big deal, Willa!? Your boss tried to attack you! And you passed out!? Are you OK?" His voice dips low and dark. "Do you need me to kill him?"

He would, too.

"No, Dr. Edwards got what he deserves, and I actually feel pretty great."

"Yeah, alright. I'm not sure I believe that you're fine, but I'll let it slide since Justine and her housemates will be here soon. I imagine you don't want them to know about any of this."

"You got that right, my friend. Justine's probably going to grill me for details about Dr. Edwards that I definitely can't share. Open investigation and all that."

"Fuck, Wil. That is wild." Sam takes a long drink of beer and my cocktail arrives.

We sit in companionable silence for a moment.

"Oh! I didn't tell you the best part though. I'm pretty sure I got asked out on a date!"

"Really?" Sam's face lights up. "That's great!" He smiles so genuinely that his eyes crinkle. People like Justine don't understand our friendship. They think we're secretly in love with each other, but that's really not it at all. When Sam says it's great that I got asked out on a date, he means it.

"Well, tell me about the guy…" he hedges.

I puff out a breath that makes him laugh. "He's hot, Sam. Volcano hot. He came into the office this morning to do research and asked me out for dinner tomorrow night.

He's…I don't even know how to describe him. He's Swedish, I'm pretty sure. He has an accent anyway, and he's crazy tall and just all sexy muscles."

I laugh at myself for rambling.

"Look at you!" Sam teases. "You're all flustered."

I laugh again. "It's just dinner, but I'm excited about it."

Sam's expression turns earnest. "I haven't seen you this way in a while. It's like the old you." His voice drops and his brow furrows. "You won't admit it, but I know that Nick really hurt you. I'm just glad to see you smile like that again."

"Thanks, Sammy. I appreciate it." I take a sip of my drink to ease my suddenly tight throat.

Nick is Sam's housemate and our friend of several years. We were in what I thought was a serious relationship until I caught him in bed with one of the yoga instructors from the studio I go to. She couldn't be any less like me, in appearance and in personality, which really makes it sting when I see how happy they are together. Nick is sexy and charismatic and the lead singer in a local band. I felt lucky to be his girlfriend.

It's stupid now that I think about it because he's also pretentious and judgmental and not very much fun to be around. I've spent a lot of time over the last few months undoing all the hits he took to my confidence.

"Sorry, I didn't mean to bring the mood down," Sam offers apologetically.

"No worries. I'm cool. Nick's old news. Is he still with the Quinoa Queen?"

Sam laughs. "Yup, he's still with Jessa. She was over last night, and I swear she's the most boring person I have ever met. I've met rocks with more personality."

I can't help but laugh. Sam's a geologist, so he's probably not lying.

"I do feel better, and I'm sure that spending time in the company of a Scandinavian sex god had a little to do with it."

And as if on cue, the door to the restaurant opens and cold air wafts in, drawing my attention along with the scent of fresh rain despite the recent dry spell. I look up at the exact moment Stellan Lundqvist walks in.

CHAPTER 8

STELLAN STRIDES into the restaurant in dark trousers and a white button-down shirt. The top two buttons are undone showing off the taut muscles around his neck and chest. Despite the cool evening, his sleeves are rolled up, and my mouth goes dry at just a glimpse of his strong forearms. He is arrestingly handsome. It wasn't just my imagination.

"Sam!" I hiss. "The hot guy from the library just walked in!"

"No way! Let me know when it's safe to look so I can check him out."

His easy excitement is one of the many reasons I love my best friend.

"Do. Not. Turn. Around." I growl, which just makes him smirk at me. I take another glance back up and notice that he's not alone. His hand rests lightly on the shoulder of the most beautiful woman I have ever seen while he says something to her.

"Shit. He's here with someone."

My face falls for a second before I can control my reaction.

"Oh no, are you alright?" Sam reaches over and touches my hand.

"Of course," I shrug in feigned nonchalance. On the inside, I feel foolish for crumbling a bit. "He asked me to dinner, but it's not like we had any promises to each other. Maybe she's a colleague, or maybe she's his wife and he just wanted to go to dinner with me to talk about his research. It's entirely possible I misread the whole thing."

In fact, now that I think about it, I probably did misread things. There is no planet on which a man that gorgeous is interested in me. I know my strengths and I'm comfortable with myself, but I also know my limits. Men like Stellan go for women like the one he's with tonight.

She's tall with the most flawless skin, and her dark, wavy hair shines in the dim light. She's dressed professionally in a navy pencil skirt and an off-white silk blouse that accentuates her hourglass figure. Her heels click across the floor. It looks like she just finished up her day as a C-suite executive. There's no way I can compete with that.

"You're killing me, Wil. I have to check this out."

"OK," I reply. "They're walking to their table, so you should be able to get a safe peek." Sam turns, pretending to check for our friends. He pauses for a moment and then whips back around to me with the most astonished look on his face.

"What the fuck, Willa! That amount of sexy isn't legally allowed in Vermont!"

His eyes are so wide with shock that I burst into laughter. It just explodes out of me. I start laughing so hard I have to hide my face in a napkin, which just makes Sam laugh, too, and we fall onto each other.

As I try to pull myself together, I feel Stellan's eyes on me.

I know he's looking at me before I can confirm it. I glance over Sam's shoulder and we make eye contact. I force my lips together and give him a polite wave. He simply nods in return then his eyes grow harsh and cold. I realize he's not looking at me, but instead at Sam who has his hand on my shoulder.

Justine arrives in the next moment with her wild housemates, and I lose track of Stellan as we're hurried off to our table for dinner.

"Are you seriously not going to tell me what the hell happened at work today?" Justine asks after we've had our fill of food and drink. She's wearing a cute red dress, and her pixie hair is styled to perfection.

"I wish I could," I say in earnest. "But I was told not to talk about it."

"I'll tell you what I heard, and you blink twice if I'm right, OK?"

"Listen, Teenie, I'm not sure that's a good idea. I really could get in a lot of trouble for talking about it."

She just brushes me off. "Well, I heard that Dr. Edwards was arrested in your office. I also heard from Rachel who heard it from Carlos in Public Relations that the rare books we just got were stolen!"

Well, she heard correctly.

I grimace. "I really can't tell you anything. I'm sorry."

"I know, I know. But the fact that you aren't denying it means it's definitely true!"

"You heard nothing from me," I say adamantly.

"Not a word! Alright, let's go dance!!"

Sam gives me a commiserate smile, and we follow Justine to the exit. I'm immensely proud of myself for not glancing over at Stellan's table on my way out.

* * *

THE BAR where we end up always has a line at the door even in winter. I don't know who we're seeing tonight, but I figure it will be a welcome distraction.

Another perk of going out with Justine is that we can skip the wait. She always knows someone. People groan as we cross ahead of them.

Justine is in rare form as she leads us through the crowd to stake out a decent table close to the music. Waving at everyone she knows and blowing kisses at the bartenders.

All the surfaces inside are painted black, and the lights from the stage dance around in hypnotic patterns. We round the corner of the bar and on the stage in front of us is Nick setting up his equipment.

My heart drops to my stomach. I definitely should have asked who was playing tonight.

He's fiddling with the knobs on his guitar while his band-mates chat with each other. A vaguely nauseous sensation settles over me.

Justine turns with a look of horror on her face.

"Willa, I am so sorry. If I had known they were playing tonight, I wouldn't have suggested it. I thought for sure it was someone else."

I bite my lower lip and nod slowly, taking in what she's saying while watching Nick work. Looking at him usually sparks a deep longing that's hard to shake, but it's not there this time.

"It's fine," I say and surprise myself by meaning it.

Justine smiles in relief and we settle in at a table close to the stage but further off to the side.

"Are you sure, Wil?" Sam asks in my ear as we approach the table. "I'm sorry I didn't realize they'd be here either. I told Nick days ago that we were thinking of coming here this weekend. I think he must have assumed we were coming to see him."

Oh, great. That's good for his ego, I'm sure.

"It's really no big deal. I see him at your house all the time." I shrug. I don't actively avoid Nick, I just make sure we're never in the same space for very long and never, ever alone.

"Yeah, but it's the first time you've seen him like this," Sam says, gesturing to the stage. He watched me fall hard for Nick, especially Nick with a guitar.

God, I was so stupid.

"I know," I say. "It will be weird, but I'm fine. Catching your boyfriend balls deep in someone else changes your perspective pretty quickly."

Sam laughs like he's relieved and wraps me in a bear hug. I breathe in his woodspice and whisky scent and relax. I have plenty of love in my life. I don't need Nick and his dumb, sexy voice and his stupid hair and fuckboy attitude.

It's my turn to get drinks, so I leave the safety of our table to locate an open section of the bar.

I'm just finished ordering when a familiar voice calls my name.

"Hey there, Willo," Nick says, smooth as silk. He always called me that, even before we were dating.

I spin slowly on my heels to face him. He leans with his arms against the bar.

"Hey, how's it going?" So casual. Not bothered at all.

"Good, good. Thanks for coming tonight. Means a lot."

Right.

"To be honest, I didn't know you were playing." I offer a smile and gather up my drinks.

Nick laughs. "Uh huh, I'll buy that. Listen, I just wanted to thank you."

I'm taken by surprise at the sudden shift and Nick's strangely earnest tone.

"Thank me?"

"Yeah, I know it's still a little awkward between us or whatever, but I think we can get past it. Go back to the way things were before. I miss our friendship. And honestly, dating you was a turning point for me. It made me realize what I really want."

He does that infuriating hair flip that used to drive me wild. Now I just want to punch him in the throat.

"What you really want?" I ask slowly repeating his words, not sure I'm hearing this correctly.

"Yeah, what I need in a partner. It wasn't until you that I figured it out."

"Right," I say, not sure how to process that. "You're welcome?"

"Yeah, now I know that I need someone a little less practical. Someone a little more chill and fun who knows how to be open to what the universe is providing. Someone who isn't afraid to let go with me. So, uh, thanks."

I blow out a breath through pursed lips.

What the actual fuck?

"Glad to be of service," I manage to say through my shock as the acid in his words washes over me.

I grab my drinks and march off holding my head up high. I'll never let him know how much that stung.

"Bye, Willo!" Nick calls after my retreating back like he didn't just rip my insides to shreds.

Sam knows something's up with me, but I'm not getting into it right now. If we leave, Nick will win. It's a foolish thought, but one I can't seem to stop.

Sam's hovering nearby, shooting worried glances at me. With the loud music coming from the stage, it's not like we can have a conversation anyway. I sit at our table nursing my final cocktail of the night. I don't know if I'll even bother telling Sam what Nick said. They're longtime friends and roommates, and I don't want to make it awkward between them.

And it's not like I don't know that I'm not "fun," and I'm definitely the opposite of "chill." I had to become an adult in elementary school. When other kids were learning to tie their shoes, I was balancing bank accounts and packing lunches for my sisters. I'm not going to apologize for it or let some asshole make me feel bad about what I had to do to survive.

I guess it's a good lesson. Sometimes the person you love wants something you can't provide. And isn't it better to know that and cut ties than constantly feel the weight of not being enough?

"The next song we're going to play is a little different from our usual stuff." Nick picks up his acoustic and sits on a stool, adjusting the mic. "It's for someone who means a lot to me and all the trials and tribulations that brought us to our time together."

My bruised heart sinks even further. I just try to focus on breathing in and out. I really am over this breakup, and I have been for a while, but I'm not sure I have it in me to listen to him sing a love song to his new girlfriend.

In all the years we were friends and even when we dated, Nick never once played a song for me onstage. That probably should have been a red flag.

I scan the crowd and find Jessa standing on the other side of the stage. She's tall and willowy, wearing a slate gray jumpsuit that wraps around her yoga-toned body. She does this swishy thing with her hair like she's trying to play it cool, but it's obvious she's deeply thrilled.

I should leave, but something holds me to my spot. Curiosity, maybe? Self-mortification?

Sam pushes out of the crowd and sits next to me. His hand rests on my shoulder and the warmth of it is comforting. When the first chords play on Nick's guitar, the hair on the back of my neck stands up. Sam squeezes my shoulder and our eyes meet.

Oh, shit.

Nick plays a soulful version of a song that I helped him write. We spent many summer evenings on the porch sitting next to each other trading lyrics. And judging by the sound of it, Nick took all my suggestions.

It's a song about friendship and falling in love. Honestly, I thought it was a song about us since that's what I was thinking when I gave him the lyrics.

When it ends, the crowd loses it. Nick pulls Jessa onto the stage and kisses her like his life depends on it.

Sam tries to stop me, but I need air. Desperately. So, for the second time tonight, I run.

CHAPTER 9

THE MOMENT THE COLD, Vermont air hits my face, I feel better. Behind me, Sam calls my name.

He's carrying my coat as he jogs up to me. The trees along the pedestrian street are already wrapped in twinkling Christmas lights. They bathe us in a cheerful glow against the midnight sky. A welcome warmth in a dreary time of year and an unpleasant evening.

Stick season. That's what my mother calls the gloomy period between the beauty of the fall foliage and the bright snow of winter. She hates this time of year. It's cold, and we steadily lose the daylight. It's also the time of year when dad left.

I've always liked this season though. It's a good reminder that transitions are necessary. Even when they're dark and gray.

Sam holds out my coat and watches me with wary eyes as I slip into it. He's not sure whether I'm going to explode in anger or burst into tears.

"You good, bro?" he asks, keeping it casual.

I nod. "Yeah, I'm fine. That was just hard to witness, you know?"

Sam lets out a slow breath. "Yup, I get it."

He puts his arm over my shoulder and I lean into it.

"You hungry?" I ask, looking up at my friend.

Sam makes a face of humorous disbelief. "What the hell kind of question is that? Of course I'm hungry. Pizza at your place?"

"Yeah, yours would not be an ideal spot tonight."

I stare up at the dark sky and breathe the cold night air deep into my lungs. This was one of the most emotionally draining days of my life.

We walk up Church Street in silence, and I'm grateful that Sam isn't pressing for more information. I'll talk about it once I sort it all out in my mind. Tonight, I just need to feel it.

We approach Pearl Street when I hear footsteps behind us. Soft at first but definitely gaining. There has to be more than one person, maybe three or four based on the cadence. Sam notices it, too, and squeezes his arm tighter around me.

I don't dare turn around. If it's just another group of late-night bar hoppers, it won't matter. But if it's the same group from earlier in the night, I don't want to know. I just want to get further down the street to the pizza place where there's more light.

Burlington is more populated than most places in Vermont, but it's nowhere close to a big city where there are people around all the time. At night, there are dark corners everywhere, and walking home late never feels safe.

Sam and I pick up our pace. The footsteps only get louder. My heart pounds in my ears, and the swirling sensation in my chest rises to a dangerous new level. It pushes against my bones like it wants to rip out of me. I try to breathe slowly, calmly, but I'm losing control. Every footfall echoes inside my brain, and chills run up my spine.

My instincts tell me to run again. To flee. Would Sam know to follow me? I look up into his face.

He nods.

Together, we take off down the street. Sam is faster and his legs are longer, so he half-runs, half-drags me along with him.

The footfalls behind us pick up speed, and I hear someone shout. Eventually we make it to the small park by the bus station and sneak around the side of a building.

"What the fuck?" Sam asks through deep breaths.

"I don't know!" I cry. "I told you some people were following me before. I thought I was just being paranoid, but…Sam?"

Sam's usually happy face is awash with horror. Before either of us can speak another word, a leather glove clamps around my mouth and an arm like a tree trunk grabs me painfully around the waist. I release a muffled scream into the man's hand.

Sam makes a rush for me, but another man comes out of the shadows. Tall and terrifying, he's dressed all in black with his face hidden by darkness. I'm struggling to breathe, and my heart hammers beneath my ribs. Sam takes a hesitant step but then loses himself to rage.

He swings wildly at our attackers, but my easy-going friend doesn't stand a chance. The man from the shadows effortlessly grabs Sam's fist and slams down on his arm, breaking the bone with a horrifying snap.

"No!" I scream into the glove as tears flood down my cheeks. Sam makes a choked sound in his throat and cradles his broken arm, his face white as a sheet. He doesn't seem able to speak through the pain. The man cocks back his arm and hammers his fist against Sam's temple. Sam grunts and falls to the ground unconscious.

The man behind me is a solid wall of muscle. He loosens his grip just enough to spin me to face him. I've never seen a person this large before. Not even the man who arrested Dr. Edwards in the library.

In just a black sweater and black pants, this man's body is boxy like he spends his life in the gym, and his face and neck are meaty and gross. His head is covered in a black beanie, his features cruel and thick.

"Why…why are you doing this?" My voice sounds faint and far away even to my own ears.

"We have orders to bring ya to yer uncle, and that's what we're doin'," the man says in a thick South London accent. "But don't worry, so long as you don't cause a fuss there'll be no reason to hurt ya."

"That's right, darlin'," the man who broke Sam's arm agrees.

"You must have the wrong person. I'm just a librarian."

"Ah, Mikkel said you'd be confused, but it's his job to explain this to ya. We're just the muscle. Right, Gav?"

"Right, Hank."

A third man dressed in a similarly intimidating black ensemble steps out of the shadows. They are without doubt the men I saw earlier.

"There has to be some kind of mistake," I say, desperation clawing at me. "I don't even have an uncle."

My mom is an only child and my dad's family lives in Sweden and we've never heard from them. But guess I don't even know if he has brothers. *Does this have to do with him?*

"I wouldn't be so sure of that," Hank says and squeezes my middle with one arm while his other hand clutches my nape so I can't move my head. I gasp and struggle, but he just grips me harder.

The swirling in my chest rises up again in a frenzy and my arms start to tingle in anticipation.

For what, I'm not certain. Something about it is comforting though. It will take care of me, if I let it. I just don't know how.

Hank's hold on me is suffocating, and I feel bruises forming all along my ribs and neck. The reality that he can break me with a flick of his wrist hits me hard. I'm small in the best of circumstances, but I'm merely a toy to these beastly men. I have no way to fight back.

His breath is stale and disgusting as it washes over my face. A sick dread churns in my gut as he tightens his grip even harder on me. I want to scream, but I can't get enough air.

My hands push against his chest, but he holds my neck and waist in his vise-like fingers so tight I can't budge. I'm trapped, and I lose myself to panic.

The swirling pushes harder against my chest and my ribs. Fighting me to escape its confines, I scream in pain and surprise as it slips out of my control. My sternum feels like it's splitting in two as a storm rumbles in my ears.

I have no idea what's happening, but in the next moment, a powerful current flies down my arms and explodes out of my hands. A bright light blinds us, and the scent of ozone fills the air. My arms vibrate with a crackling electricity that shouldn't be possible.

Hank howls and shoots backwards several feet, landing on his back with a thud. This must be a dream. It has to be my brain creating a scenario to protect me from my bone-deep fear. I can't have created lightning. That's not a real thing that people do.

With Hank's hands no longer on me I want to run, but the thought of leaving Sam is impossible. He needs medical attention. Instead, I stand frozen to the spot with my heart pounding.

The cold wind whips through the trees blowing around my loose hair and stinging my tear-stained cheeks.

Gav steps forward with pure fury in his eyes and back-hands me across the face. Pain splinters over my cheek, splitting my lip and making blood run down my chin.

I cry out in alarm and hold a cold hand to my face. I've never been hit in my life. More than the pain, it's the shock of it that's overwhelming. Tears fall down my face in a steady stream.

The third man steps forward. "You're coming with us. Now."

Gav squeezes a hand around my neck and lifts me off the ground like I weigh nothing. I am officially out of options. I don't want to go anywhere with these men, but what am I supposed to do?

The churning power in my chest rises up again, but it's weaker. I can't access it like before.

I start to lose oxygen, and black dots form in my eyes. I kick out with my legs, but it does nothing against the brick shithouse of a man with his hand around my throat.

As I succumb to the oblivion, the overwhelming scent of a rainstorm permeates the air. As terrifying and violent as a flash flood and destructive like a hurricane. Whatever it is, I'm not alone in sensing it. The men around me go still, and their eyes shift nervously. Fear lines Gav's face. The men start yelling at each other, but I can no longer understand them.

Gav drops me like I'm on fire. My legs won't support me, and I collapse on the ground. They run, assisting a limping Hank as they flee.

The ground is cold and hard against my back. My eyes blink slowly. In and out of awareness.

I'm worried about Sam, but as much as I want to, I can't move to reach him.

The freezing air blows over me and smells the same as the cologne Stellan was wearing this morning. After everything that happened tonight, it's almost funny that my oxygen-starved brain conjures up that particular scent to comfort me. I picture his face. So beautiful, with his calming blue eyes and that soft beard I wanted to touch.

Sadly for me, Stellan's probably tucked up in bed with that sexy woman while I'm about to pass out in the park, staring up at the sky.

The stars are lovely tonight at least. I sink deeper into the earth. Let it swallow me. The darkness beckons, and I can only hope that someone finds us soon.

CHAPTER 10

THE MORNING LIGHT shines through the sheer curtains in Willa's bedroom and casts an ethereal glow over her sleeping form.

Her ridiculous black cat with the crazy eyes makes another attempt to suffocate her while she's sleeping. I pick him up and set him on the floor.

He simply climbs back up and puts his back right next to her face instead and gives me a look as if to say, "Is this acceptable, your highness?" I shake my head at him, and he huffs while setting his chin on his paw.

Willa's other cat leaps into my lap and languidly stretches across my thighs. I pet its orange fur as it settles on my legs.

"Thanks for not sleeping on my face this time, Reggie," a sad, hoarse voice calls from the bed and Willa gives her black cat a slow pat.

"It's only because I move him every time he tries to climb up," I state from my seat next to her bed.

She shoots up in the direction of my voice and winces as

her battered body protests against the movement. I'm going to find those men, and I'm going to kill them for doing this to her.

We just stare at each other for a moment. Her eyes cast over my navy sweater that's draped on the back of her chair and then down to my lap where her cat is sleeping peacefully on my lap.

"Shit, I'm dead," she says. Her mouth parts. "Apparently, the afterlife includes that hot library patron in my bedroom, but fuck. I'm dead. Who's going to look after mom now?"

She rambles in a panic. It's cruel of me, but I let out a chuckle. She's endearing and funny without trying. I set her cat down and let it saunter off to find another spot to sleep. I lean forward with my elbows on my knees and my fingers interlaced. She stares at my hands and presses her lips together.

"I'm pleased to inform you that you are not dead. You were, however, attacked and quite badly injured. I imagine if you were dead, you'd probably feel less sore right now."

"Ohhhhh, God," she says slowly as realization dawns. "Do you know who those men were? Why did they come after me? Is Sam OK? Where is he? Wait…"

She pauses and tilts her head.

Here it comes.

"Mr. Lundqvist? Why are you in my apartment?"

She shoves the covers off her and swings her legs over the side of the bed. Her face turns pale, and she grabs her head before falling back onto her pillow. "I guess I'm not ready for that."

I stand and approach her cautiously. This is going to be a delicate matter. Explaining everything is impossible, but too little will only entice her inquisitive nature. If she becomes frustrated, she will ask questions I'm unprepared to answer.

"I am sorry," I say and offer an arm to help her return to

sitting. I ignore the heat of her fingers against my forearm. "I should have found you sooner, but I lost track of you."

The confusion on her face brings a smile to mine. She is achingly sweet.

"So, first, I asked you to call me Stellan. And second, your friend is perfectly fine. My colleagues, Banks and Greta, brought him home. They've healed him. He will remember that you left the bar together and after that it will all be a rather vivid and unpleasant dream."

"I'm glad to know that he's OK, but what do you mean by 'healed'? I watched a man break his arm and knock him out. That's not something you slap a Band-Aid on."

I exhale a long breath and grab her hand from where it rests on her blanket. I trace my finger along her palm. The unexpected connection makes her breath catch beautifully.

"With everything that occurred last night, did it escape your notice that you used lightning to fight off those men?" I ask with a slight raise in my eyebrows.

Her mouth opens in surprise, no doubt remembering the power in her hands. I was still at too much of a distance to see with certainty, but the crack of electricity had to be Willa.

She smiles, but it trembles. "I thought I must have made that up."

I draw a pattern over her fingers. I'm playing with fire, but the urge to touch and comfort her is too strong.

"Have you ever observed the sensation that something was alive in your chest? As if there's an entity or a power pushing for freedom?"

The recognition in her eyes tells me everything. She presses her other hand against her heart.

"We believe that something has been suppressing your natural abilities and that it was recently released."

If she were to mention the book and her father, now

would be the time. Instead, her eyes cast down for a moment as she mulls over what I've told her.

"So, am I a witch or something?"

Her sudden question startles me, and I can't help but laugh. The way her nose wrinkles when she asks and the excitement in her eyes is unexpected and charming.

"If that is what you want to call yourself, but I warn you that the people who like the mystique of witches and wizards often end up on the wrong side of my Agency's radar."

Confusion crosses her face, but I continue on.

"People with our unique skill sets are most frequently called Mages. In some parts of the world Wielder is used, but you'll also hear Ancients, *Fortis Magicae*, and Humans with Advanced Capabilities, though that is not heard in everyday conversation."

"Right," she says.

She furrows her brow. What I'm telling her is slowly sinking in.

"This is very overwhelming. But why were those men after me? What did they want and why did they keep talking about my uncle? I didn't even know I had an uncle…"

She rambles in nervous confusion. I will tell her as much as I am at liberty to share, but now is not the time. She needs rest, and I need to check in with my team.

"We are only scratching the surface of all there is to discuss. I have dinner reservations for us tonight at 7, when we will continue our conversation. But I must caution you not to leave your house until then."

My intensity surprises her. I am right to continue this conversation in a public place. It will help temper her reactions and allow me to better control how much we discuss.

"Uh, sure. That sounds great. Though I'm not sure I'm really fit for dinner in this state." She points to her throat, which is badly bruised. She has the beginnings of a black eye forming. I choke down my rage at what they did to her.

"You are not the only one here with unique abilities, Willa. I have every intention of healing you before I leave."

"Healing me?"

"Yes. Like you, I have a certain set of skills outside the normal range for most humans. One of these is the ability to heal wounds and internal injuries. I do need to touch you, and I want to make sure I have your permission before we begin."

Her cheeks turn pink. "Um, yes. That's fine. Thank you for considering that. Very thoughtful."

I suppress a smile.

"I'm just going to touch the areas where you're injured, and an energy will flow from me and into you. It won't hurt, but it will probably tingle and you'll feel some heat."

"OK. Should I just stay here?"

"Yes, I'm going to put my hands here and here." I place one on her bruised cheek and one over her throat. Her pulse beats fast. "Just try to relax. Close your eyes, sometimes that helps. Then I want you to take a deep breath with me."

She breathes in and out with me, and her skin heats beneath my touch as my magic trails over her bruised skin. At this close proximity, her spice and evergreen scent lingers in the air around me. The tightness in her cheeks and the stinging around her throat should be easing. My magic takes very little time for this type of injury.

"There," I say when I'm finished. "How do you feel now?"

"Fine. I'm fine now. Perfect even. Thank you." She deflects my attention but struggles to get comfortable.

I'm aware of her other injuries. I can sense them, though she doesn't know that.

"I know you are lying." I cross my arms over my chest and

raise an eyebrow. I do not appreciate being lied to, even about something like this.

"I'm sorry, but I am fine. They'll heal on their own soon enough." She tries to wave me off.

"Willa, I have the ability to take your pain away. I'm not leaving until you let me."

"I don't need anyone to take care of me." She shakes her head. She states this as plain fact, like she has said it and thought it a thousand times.

"Listen to me closely, Willa." I lower my voice an octave and she stops fidgeting. "You might not be used to accepting help, but while you are under my watch, you are my responsibility. I will give you some privacy to lower your dress, and then you will let me help you."

She swallows and pinches her lips together, but she nods.

Very good.

I rise and turn away from her, watching the neighbors rake leaves out her window while she unzips her dress.

"Mr. Lundqvist. Sorry, Stellan. Um, I can't quite reach." Her voice is soft, but she sounds frustrated with herself. "It's too hard with the...with the injuries."

"Of course." I turn and she's kneeling on the bed with her back to me. Her long dark hair flows down her back and her tight black dress from the night before riding up her thighs. A perfect picture of innocent seduction.

Gud rädda mig. God save me.

I gather up her soft hair, which feels like silk between my fingers and place it over one shoulder. My fingers whisper ever so slightly over her skin as I lower the zipper to her waist.

The slope of her back and shoulders is elegant but strong, and the spotted lace of her black bra is surprising. I crave to see the rest of it. To rip it from her body and let her ample breasts fall into my waiting hands. To feel her nipples pebble against my palms.

Enough, Stellan.

I came to get a job done, not play out fantasies. The sooner she's healed, the sooner I can get out of this bedroom.

Her heart beats erratically, fear or arousal. Both perhaps.

"I won't hurt you," I say.

"I know," she whispers. I lift my eyes to the ceiling and say a prayer for strength.

I prod along her ribs. She winces, and I regret causing her more pain.

"Just relax. It won't be long. You're very bruised, but it will heal quickly."

I help ease her arms out of the sleeves. I cup her sides, and my fingers splay around her ribs.

The pressure is firm, but careful.

"Take another breath with me," I tell her, and we breathe together like before. Her wounds do heal rapidly, but I allow myself the liberty of a last lingering caress against her waist. She trembles just slightly beneath my hands, goosebumps rising across her soft skin.

I pull away, and she sighs in contentment before twisting her body and rolling her neck, testing the efficacy of my efforts.

"Good as new."

She begins righting her clothes.

I stand, giving us both the space we need.

"So, what am I meant to tell Sam?" she asks.

Her question catches me off-guard. And I don't relish the thought of her best friend with the wandering hands.

"What do you mean?" My voice is more clipped than before and it makes Willa hesitate.

"Well, he is going to call me today and want to swap

stories. We were meant to get a pizza and come back here. Obviously, that didn't happen."

"You can confirm for him that you left together. Play up how drunk you both were. I am pleased you seem aware of the required level of confidentiality, but I am obligated to state that no one can know what really happened last night, and it is imperative that our abilities remain strictly classified. The penalty for revealing our secrets even to close friends and relatives is severe."

"Of course. I'll just say that we drank more here, and then he decided to head home at some point. If he says anything about his dream, I won't give anything away."

"Thank you."

I nod in approval and gather up my belongings. I need some space from Willa Martin and her tantalizing innocence.

"Your apartment will be monitored today, but I expect you to remain inside at all times. If you notice anything unusual, you have my number. A car will come for you later. You and I have much to discuss."

CHAPTER 11

WILLA

"Wɪʟ, how much did we drink last night?"

On the phone, Sam sounds sleepy and confused. I pace back and forth across my tiny apartment, my bare feet are cold against the wood floors. I really don't like lying to Sam, but the reality of what happened last night and what is happening to me is too unbelievable. I'm not even sure I believe it.

"Well, Sammy, I can't say for sure. We got pretty drunk here, and you decided you'd rather go home than sleep on my couch. You left around three."

"I've never forgotten stuff this badly before. It's like a whole chunk of the night is missing. I hope I didn't do anything embarrassing. Like that time I passed out in Wren's closet."

I laugh at the memory. "Not that I can remember anyway. I crashed pretty hard after you left. Anyway, have you seen Nick at all?"

I don't actually care if he's seen Nick. I just want to steer the conversation away from topics we can't discuss.

"I wandered down for coffee not too long ago. He was in the kitchen. I barely acknowledged him, so I think he knows I'm pissed. I can't believe he did that to you. He took the song we all know you wrote together and played it for someone else while you were in the same room. I mean, that's just… Honestly, I'd kill him if I wasn't so hungover."

I laugh, but it's mostly humorless. "It's fine, Sam. I don't love Nick anymore, and I don't want Nick anymore. It definitely hurt, but more because I'm angry with myself for being so stupid. I let myself care for someone who clearly didn't reciprocate. It was foolish, but I'm just going to take it as a lesson learned and move on."

"You're a better person than me. I want to string him up by the balls and break both…his…arms."

Sam's voice slows like he's remembering something from last night.

Shit.

"You OK, Sam?"

"Yeah, dude. I'm cool. I just remembered the most vivid dream I had last night. These super scary guys jumped us, and one of them broke my arm. It was so vivid. I can almost feel it still, like a phantom pain or something."

"Wow, that's crazy. Well, I should go get ready for the day."

I grimace. I shouldn't have cut him off so abruptly, but I'm not a natural liar and I panicked.

Thankfully, Sam doesn't seem to notice.

"Alright, my friend. I'm going back to bed."

"Good idea. Bye, Sammy."

* * *

AROUND QUARTER TO 7, the large shadow of a man darkens my doorstep, and there's a loud knock.

"Ms. Martin, I work with Stellan Lundqvist, I'm here to take you to dinner." A rich, deep voice with an Irish brogue calls from behind the closed door.

It sounds familiar. In fact, it sounds exactly like the man who arrested Dr. Edwards.

I push back the curtain on the window next to my door and peer out onto the porch. It's definitely the same man. I can just make out the tattoos on his hands that I noticed in the library.

"It's you!" I say as I open the door.

The man doesn't smile, but his eyes twinkle. He dips his head in acknowledgment.

"Ronan Banks, at your service, but everyone calls me Banks. Are you ready?"

"But…what? I mean, yes. Let me just grab my coat."

He follows me inside. He has to duck to fit through the door. Stellan has a broad, muscular physique and an obvious masculine strength, but there's a gentleness to him. The man who barely fits in my apartment is all rough edges and hard lines.

Handsome in his own way, but rugged and so intimidating it's difficult to make eye contact.

When I do meet his dark green eyes as he helps me into my coat, it's like being stripped bare. As if he can read into my soul with just one glance.

My hands shake slightly as I lock the door and put my keys back in my bag. Banks takes my small arm in his massive one and leads me to the waiting car. I notice he has some kind of communication device in his ear, and he's wearing a Secret Service-style black suit with a black tie.

"Wow, this is way weirder than I thought it was going to be," I say mostly to myself.

He doesn't respond, but I think I catch another ghost of a smile.

We only need to travel about four blocks to Stellan's hotel, but after being followed and attacked, I'm glad for any added security. Not to mention, it's freezing outside.

If this man works with Stellan and he was in the library interrogating Dr. Edwards, does that mean Stellan is also connected to the books somehow? Does he know what happened when I touched it? Is he somehow connected to my father? How? Why?

I'm completely in the dark. It's a sad realization that I know absolutely nothing about the man who provided half my DNA.

I twist my fingers together nervously in my lap. I'm wearing one of my nicer dresses, but simply for the confidence boost. It was only when I was in the shower washing my hair that I really put it together. Stellan was definitely not asking me on a date in the library. And now that I know he's working with the Irish giant sitting next to me, that's even more obvious.

The only silver lining is that I'm too anxious about everything to be overly disappointed about it.

Banks drives the way I'd expect him to. Smooth and confident. He pulls up in front of the Hotel Vermont.

"Agent Lundqvist will meet you inside. I'm going to let you out of the car and walk you to the entrance. I will be ready to take you home when your dinner is finished."

He does exactly what he says, softly guiding me with a hand on my lower back. His touch is not possessive or unwelcome. I don't understand it, but I feel supremely safe around this man. I smile at him as he says goodbye, and though he doesn't return it, his green eyes twinkle again.

The restaurant at the Hotel Vermont is one of the nicer ones in town. The cocktails are excellent, and it's conveniently dark and cozy with a mix of modernity and old Vermont charm. There's a burnished metal bar lined with stools that are all occupied, and a large fireplace crackles with a roaring fire, warming the space and sending a golden light throughout the room.

Despite having seen him only a few hours before, when Stellan comes into view my heartrate picks up. His strong upper body is fitted in a tailored white Oxford shirt, and his caramel-colored hair is perfectly tousled.

He's simply the most gorgeous man I've ever seen. No big deal.

Our table is far in the back and secluded from most of the other patrons. Stellan looks up from the menu he was perusing as I approach. Clear blue eyes meet mine. I'm sure I'm mistaken, but I think I catch him glancing down my body briefly before offering me a very business-like smile.

"You look lovely, Ms. Martin. Thank you for joining me. Please, sit." Stellan points to the seat across from him.

We order some drinks and food, and I stifle all the burning questions lingering on the tip of my tongue while the waitstaff are hovering.

"So, what do you want to know?" Stellan asks as soon as the waitress leaves our drinks. He takes a sip of his scotch and holds it in his right hand. "You are physically assaulting me with your anticipation, and it's starting to hurt."

It takes me a moment to register what he's really saying. That my thoughts are somehow causing him pain.

"Hold on, can you read my mind?"

I hope not because that would be seriously embarrassing.

His lips curl into a smile at the sudden shock on my face. "No, not your mind exactly, but enhanced empathy is one of my abilities. I can sense the emotions and mood shifts in every person in this room. Though it is interesting that with you it only works when you're projecting it."

I shrug and give a half-smile. "That actually doesn't surprise me. Maybe all those years of practicing control were not for nothing."

Stellan examines me thoughtfully for a moment as if I've given him something new to consider. "Can you explain what you mean by that?"

I focus my attention on the flickering candle in the middle of the table. I spent the day wondering and worrying about these so-called "skills" I've come to acquire. Stellan talked about them like it was something hidden inside me. It's made me wonder what was keeping it locked up, and it's changing the way I viewed certain elements of my childhood.

"Well, my mother is kind of witchy. She's always been big on breathwork and crystals and stuff like that. We used to do these breathing exercises when we were little where she would guide us through various meditations. One of the most frequent involved building a fortress in our minds and imagining that our brains and hearts were glowing lights that we needed to protect deep inside it. It was something I always found kind of silly, and I just assumed it was my mother being her odd self. Now I'm not so sure. She was so serious about it."

Stellan frowns. "That suggests to me that your mother knew about your abilities. Has she ever mentioned anything to you?"

"No." I shake my head. "Never." My stomach sinks. *Would she hide something this important from us?*

"Curious." Stellan takes another sip of his drink and places it firmly on the table. "I need to ask you some questions, Willa. I must impress upon you the vital importance of your honesty and cooperation."

His stern, law enforcement voice and the change in his demeanor is abrupt and startling.

"Of course. I'll tell you anything you want to know."

Before he can start, we're interrupted by the arrival of our food and the wine we ordered to accompany it. We settle into eating quietly for a few moments though my appetite has completely vanished.

Stellan clears his throat and sets his utensils on his plate and picks up his wine glass.

"You mentioned earlier that you thought there was something unusual about the donation of rare books your library took in. Can you expand on that?"

I gently place my own utensils down and wipe my mouth with the corner of my napkin.

"Sure. So, we do occasionally receive old books from donors. Most typically, it's an alum looking to give us some volumes that belonged to their great-grandparents or whomever. Often, they're not really that useful or even that rare, despite what the donor might think. It is extremely unlikely that a UVM graduate or some random friend of the university had twenty-odd medieval texts just hiding out in their attic that they would then graciously give to us."

"What else?" Stellan asks and leans back in his seat.

"Well, for books that valuable and rare to change hands, metadata typically accompanies them to describe at least basic information on what they are and who owned them over time. We received nothing of that nature."

"So, you have this stack of rare books that you feel strongly didn't belong in your care. Did it occur to you to contact the authorities?"

"Good question. To be honest, probably eventually? But I was mostly worried about keeping my job when you showed up."

"Your job was in jeopardy?"

"It felt likely. I embarrassed Dr. Edwards in a meeting the day before. He's never particularly liked me, and he was setting me up to fail."

"Interesting," Stellan says and motions for the waitress to return. She comes to the table with a little swish in her hips that makes me smile to myself. He orders another scotch and she refills my water glass.

"Was there a book in the collection that particularly grabbed your attention?" There's something eager and determined in his eyes.

I clear my throat and shift uncomfortably in my chair.

"Yes, there was."

"Can you tell me about it? Why did it appeal to you?"

"I mean, it's just me being a nerd, it looked really cool." I laugh, but Stellan doesn't even smile.

OK...

"But it also sort of called to me."

"Explain." He uses his investigator voice again. It makes me anxious and unsure of myself.

"So, the feeling in my chest that we talked about, well, it perked up when the book was nearby. And then as soon as I touched it, I fell asleep."

Stellan leans forward, resting his elbows on the table.

"What did you dream about, Willa?"

His stare is so intense, so all-consuming that I have to look away.

"A field."

"A field?" He has an incredulous, almost disappointed expression on his face.

"And a man."

"Tell me about the man," he urges.

"He was wearing a cloak. He touched my forehead, and it hurt. Then I was in a forest and I was full of all this power. The power stayed after I woke up."

"Anything else?"

I pause. I don't really want to talk about this with him or anyone. He might be attractive, but he's essentially a complete stranger. He already knows more about me than he should.

"It's personal," I answer and lower my eyes. Denying anyone what they want is hard for me, but why would he need to know about the private conversation I had with my father?

"Personal?" he asks, affronted.

"Yes, and I don't really want to talk about it."

"Hmm, alright." Stellan takes a slow sip of scotch. "Let's try something else then. What can you tell me about your father?"

He gives me a pointed look, as if daring me to deny him again. I puff out a sharp breath.

"Nothing, really," I answer honestly. "He left us when we were kids. He wasn't around a lot before that. I don't really remember much, and my mother never speaks of him."

Stellan considers my statement as he watches the scotch swirl around the ice in his glass, as if weighing the validity of my statement.

He lifts his head and his expression is deathly serious. "I'm only going to ask you this once and I expect a real answer."

He speaks with so much authority that my spine snaps to attention.

"Did your father speak to you in your dream? If so, what did he say?"

I'm getting really pissed off now. I don't appreciate the accusation in his tone. A day ago, I thought this man was interested in me, now I'm being interrogated by him like a criminal. I'm angry, but I'm also embarrassed that I can't seem to tell reality from pretense when it comes to men.

"Listen, Stellan. I don't know who you are or why you think you get to speak to me like this, but I haven't done anything wrong."

My voice shakes. I have the desperate urge to flee, but I stay rooted to the spot.

"You might not have done anything wrong," he counters. "But your father definitely has."

"What are you talking about?"

Stellan takes a breath and in a single sentence cuts me wide open.

"Willa, your father is currently the most dangerous and wanted criminal in all of Europe."

I swear my heart stops beating, but Stellan continues without giving me a moment to catch my breath.

"Lars Stromberg has been on my Agency's radar and has engaged in questionable and illegal activity his entire life. About twenty years ago, he blew up one of our labs in Stockholm. The explosion and ensuing fight killed several Agency personnel. Since then, he's been in hiding.

"Recently, we heard rumors about a rise in the circulation of black-market objects, like the book that found its way to your library. There have also been reports of missing persons and a handful of unsolved murders that all fit a familiar profile.

"My team was asked to investigate. We believe that your father and his brother, Mikkel, are planning something and likely have been for some time. That something now involves you and I would like to know why."

Stellan pauses in his story and eyes me. Gauging my reaction. Checking for deceit? Corroboration? I don't know.

All I can do is swallow down the nausea that's creeping up my throat and attempt to blink away the tears forming in my eyes.

The silence between us stretches on. Stellan sits back in his seat and runs his thumb over his bottom lip thoughtfully.

When I finally speak, my voice is thick.

"I...have always wondered about my dad." I swallow hard

and clear my throat. "I never knew why he left or if he ever thought about us at all. I certainly never expected it was something like this."

I cast my eyes down at my hands, and a stray tear falls onto my fingers. I quickly wipe it away. Stellan curses under his breath and runs a hand through his hair.

"I appreciate that this is difficult, but if your father made contact with you, if he said anything, I have to know about it."

I nod.

"I understand. He was only in the dream for a moment before you woke me up."

Stellan looks frustrated. *Yeah, no kidding, buddy.*

"Did he say anything at all?"

"He said that he needed my help and that there were several things he wanted me to understand, but then I woke up and that was it. Honestly."

Stellan mutters something in Swedish under his breath and scrubs a hand over his beard.

He downs the rest of his scotch.

"Well, we might not know why," he says in an exasperated tone. "But at least we know for sure. The Storm King has indeed returned."

My eyes widen in panicked dismay, and my mouth opens in surprise.

Oh, my God.

The room feels like it's closing in on me.

"Willa?" Stellan asks, his eyes full of concern.

"I'm alright." I manage to speak. "But we need to have a very difficult conversation with my mother."

CHAPTER 12

STELLAN

"Why can't we come with you again?" Greta is not naturally a complainer, but she is pushing close to the boundary.

"I already explained it." I don't bother hiding my frustration.

I finish lacing up my boots and sit back in the patterned chair facing the window. Our hotel rooms have beautiful views of Lake Champlain and the Adirondack mountains, but I haven't had a spare moment of quiet since we arrived to admire it or anything else about this small city. It's not why we are here.

"I know, but I want to go through it another time."

Greta's manicured hand is on her hip, and her blazer hangs over her shoulders. Her matching navy skirt is perfectly smooth, and her 4-inch heels give her an added height she doesn't need. To anyone unfamiliar with her easy smiles and soft heart, she is intimidating and it is entirely intentional.

Greta wasn't always so polished. I'll always remember her

as a scrappy tomboy with ripped jeans and smudges of dirt on her nose. Now she's a model IMA employee. We all are.

But not today.

Today, I'm dressed how I would if I was alone. Just me. Stellan Andreas Lundqvist. Not Senior Special Agent. Not IMA employee #58376. Just a man.

Because I fucked up.

"You can't come with me because I need you and Banks here to track down the men that attacked Willa," I explain for the third time. "They haven't left. They're just waiting until the heat dies down. Soren reports that a few partial hits on facial recognition show Mikkel outside London meeting with a handful of high-profile Mages. We don't know if he'll come himself, so we need personnel here, scouring the area. Mikkel has yet to slip up and do anything that warrants his arrest, but I am not taking any chances with a man of his ability."

"Right, you said that. I understand it. But I don't under-stand this." She points to my outfit.

I glance down at my jeans and sweater.

"What about it?"

All she does is raise an eyebrow.

"Alright, fine," I concede. "Yesterday, I crossed a line with Willa." I finish folding clothes and gathering my toiletries into a travel bag. "I was too aggressive with her. Too accusatory. I let my assumptions and my drive to find her father cloud my judgment. She doesn't know anything. Not one thing about her father or her parents' relationship or her abilities. She was devastated when she learned her father is a criminal, Greta. I made her cry."

The memory of the tears on her face gives me a sharp pang in my chest.

Greta frowns. "You have made countless people cry, Stellan. Your job is to upset people. What is different here? Help me understand."

"It is different because she is going to need help and guidance. Willa is powerful. Likely, as strong as her father. If that is the case, her entire life is about to change. But more importantly, her father reached out to her in a dream that I interrupted. He will try again and I intend to be there when it happens."

"And in order for her to trust you with the truth, you need to be you?" She asks, pointing to my clothes again. But it's not just about what I'm wearing, and Greta is smart enough to know it.

It's everything.

"Yes. I need her to trust me. I need her to know that we are safe for her. If she doesn't, she might run in the wrong direction."

Greta hums. "It could work."

She picks a piece of nonexistent lint off her shoulder.

"What aren't you saying?"

"Oh, nothing," she sing-songs. "Just that I suspect it also has to do with the fact that Willa Martin is your kryptonite. She is exactly your type."

"Willa is nothing like the women I date," I scoff. She's truly not. When I bother to date at all, I date women like Ingrid. Tall, sexy women who are interested in a good time and no long-term commitments. My work is too important, and my free time is too precious.

"Exactly," she says, like it's obvious. "You don't date women like Willa because then it might actually mean something."

"You know I love and respect you, G. But you are incorrect. I don't date women like Willa because our lives are too vastly different and it would be a waste of time and only result in hurt feelings and disappointment. And besides, I'm not attracted to her."

Lies. Lies. Lies.

"The lady doth protest." Greta mocks me, and I scowl at her for reading my mind. But I suppose even with my advanced shields, her magic would pick up on my attraction anyway. Sometimes it's infuriating to be surrounded by such high caliber Mages all the time.

"Are you done psychoanalyzing my nonexistent love life, or should we invite Banks in so we can do him next?"

"Oh, *mon ami,* that would take far too long," Greta laughs. "I'll leave you to your packing."

Greta's heels click along the floor. She stops with her hand on the doorknob.

"I agree with you, by the way," she says.

"Pardon? Can you repeat that? Did you just say you agree with me?"

She smiles over her shoulder.

"Yes, I think your approach to be honest and earn Willa's trust is the right one. She will need friends."

"That she will."

"Good luck and keep us informed. We'll do the same."

"Of course."

The door closes softly behind her.

The world Willa Martin just stumbled into is cruel and harsh. There are monsters lurking in the shadows that not even we can see. Willa will need more than just friends before all this is over. She will also need our protection.

CHAPTER 13

IT'S ABOUT 70 miles from my apartment in Burlington to my mother's house in the countryside.

That's simultaneously too much time alone in a car with Stellan and not nearly enough time until this dreaded conversation with my mother.

Before Banks brought me home, Stellan instructed me to pack a bag for a few days. We're going to visit my mom and then stay at my family's cottage so he can evaluate my new abilities and I can stay out of sight.

I packed up a bag and went to bed, though I slept poorly and couldn't shut off my mind. Even Reg refused to sleep next to me because I was moving too much.

I let Jim know I was taking him up on the offer of a few days off. I also called Sam and told him I was going to the lake for a while and that I'd need him to check in on the cats.

I didn't give Sam any details. He'd want to know more about Stellan and why we were together. He'd be mistakenly excited about it. But sadly, the only time a handsome man whisks me away to a lakeside cottage is when it's part of an international criminal investigation.

The man in question showed up at my house this morning in a handknit sweater and jeans, looking more casual than I've come to expect. I realized too late that I'm also wearing a handknit sweater in a similar pattern.

We're going to arrive at my mother's house to ruin her day in matching tops.

She'll love that.

It's one of those early winter days that's perfect for driving. The snow has yet to fall, and it's bitterly cold with a bright, clear sky. The sun's rays warm the car, and the sky is a perfect blue set against the browns and grays of the November trees.

We drive about 15 minutes in silence before I'm crawling out of my skin. I have so many questions and so many things I'm worried about. The scent of him, earthy and masculine like rain and fresh air, is all around me. It's hard to breathe.

Stellan's deep voice breaks through my inner tumult. "You're rather quiet this morning. I expect you have questions for me. I'm a captive audience."

He's coaxing, but cautious. Softer than before when he was demanding answers and all but accusing me of collusion. The curious and beautiful scent of him grows stronger, too. Like when he was using his abilities to heal my wounds.

It hits me that the scent and his enhanced abilities are one and the same. The scent isn't cologne; it's his magic.

"Are you using your powers on me right now?"

"No?" He draws out the word in a question. "Why do you ask?"

"Because I've noticed that when you do, your scent gets stronger. Is that accurate?"

Stellan exhales a slow breath but doesn't take his eyes off the road.

"You're very observant."

"I guess I am, yeah."

"To answer your question, I was not using my magic on you, but some parts of it are always switched on. It's nearly impossible to shut it off completely."

"Right," I say and turn back out the window.

"You smell like Christmas," he blurts out of nowhere. His deep voice almost echoes.

"What? I smell like Christmas?"

"Yes, I've only caught hints of your magic here and there, but it reminds me of Christmas in Sweden. Of evergreens and winter spices and fresh snow. Like the winter solstice and Lucia Day. It's lovely."

"Thanks." I don't really know how to respond to something like that.

We're quiet again for a few miles. The turns of the highway and the hum of the car quiet my racing thoughts for a moment.

Stellan breaks through the silence.

"Willa, I need to apologize."

"Oh?"

"Yes. I was wrong to lie to you about who I am. And it was wrong to interrogate you over dinner last night. I should never have told you about your father's crimes in a public setting, and I shouldn't have forced you to tell me what he said to you that way."

"No, you shouldn't have," I agree. "But I haven't cried in public in a while, so I guess I was due."

Stellan's laugh is mostly humorless. "I've worked for the Agency for over a decade, and I've had many cases in my career, but tracking your father is the one case I've yet to close," he says. "He's kept himself hidden from us for so long most people in the Agency don't think we'll ever find him again."

I play with the hem of my sweater. Twisting the soft wool between my fingers.

"You must have been pretty excited to have such a solid lead then. Sorry I'm not an accomplice. That would have made things easier." I'm not trying to be funny. His intensity makes more sense now.

Stellan's laughter is real this time. "Why is it you never say what I expect?"

I shrug. "Someone's gotta keep you on your toes."

"I actually have someone for that already. His name is Soren."

I tuck my foot under my leg so I can face Stellan while he drives.

"He sounds fun. Where does he live?"

"In Stockholm. Very far from here. And you'd hate him, he's hideous. Covered in scars."

"Sounds very Beauty and the Beast. I like it."

"I'm joking. Soren is the most disgustingly handsome person on the planet and my closest friend. But he's off-limits. I can't have the two of you ganging up on me."

"Wouldn't dream of it."

He takes his eyes off the road for just a moment to smile at me. It's breathtaking.

Stellan clears his throat and turns back to face the road.

"We still have time until we reach your mother's house. Are there any questions you have for me about your abilities? Things I could clarify for you?"

"Only around a thousand or so. I stopped myself from making lists, but it was close."

He laughs again. "Let's just start and we'll see what we have time for."

"OK, first question: what kind of enhanced capabilities do I have, and how do you classify them?"

"Wow. You are definitely a librarian."

"Yes, I am. If you're going to tease me, I'll go find this Soren fellow and see if he can answer my questions."

"You wouldn't dare."

"Just answer the question."

He suppresses another laugh. "We predict that less than one tenth of a percent of the world's population have enhanced abilities," he begins. "It's a very rare, but usually a dominant gene that passes from parents to their children. We believe it has always been present as long as humans have existed, but most people manifest it subtly. It might make someone a highly skilled doctor or a brilliant artist, but it's not something that raises alarm bells.

"However, there is an even smaller subset of people like you and me, the *fortis magicae*, who have capabilities that fall under the umbrella of 'magic.' We tend to think of it as the natural progression of human evolution, but you can imagine how the public at large would react if they knew you could shoot lightning out your fingers."

"Uh, yeah, I imagine that wouldn't go well for me."

"No, it wouldn't. Secrecy is vital to our survival and our relative freedom in society. But to answer your question, our powers don't fall into perfect categories, but that hasn't stopped the human need to label and classify everything. Much like the terms we use to describe whether someone is male or female, gay or straight, we know that everyone falls on a spectrum. The same is true for our magic. Since our powers often mimic natural phenomena, they have been classified over time using the language of nature. In the shorthand, we refer to our magic as seasons, which are simplistic and Anglo-European descriptors, but they work on a very basic level."

"That makes sense," I say. "I've spent a lot of time with library classification systems. They tend to favor a colonialist perspective as well. So, what kind of magic do you have?"

"I am a Category 4 *Vere Magi* because I have high level abilities in healing, empathy, and water manipulation. Spring Magic tends to be lauded in our community, but there is a dangerous element to any powerful magic. In my line of work, the same magic that can be used to heal can also be used to pinpoint weaknesses and exploit them.

"That's really intense, Stellan."

"Does it scare you?" he asks with genuine interest.

"Maybe it should, but I think I'm still processing all of this. Are there a lot of people like you?"

Despite our rocky start, I trust Stellan not to hurt me. But someone else with that power? Not a chance.

"We are aware of around a dozen or so strong *Vere Magis* in the world. Banks is one as well, though he and I are considered some of the most powerful currently on record. Those like us either work for the Agency or other governmental organizations, or they have agreed to heavy monitoring and to never use their magic except in predetermined settings.

"There are varying levels of power associated with each category. We rank them on a 1–5 scale. Any Mage within Categories 3–5 is required to submit to periodic evaluation and regular monitoring. It's unfortunate, but it keeps us safe."

"I see. So, what kind of magic do I have?"

He hesitates a moment before answering. "You are very likely a Winter Mage or a *Heims Magi*. It is the rarest and often the most powerful of all the categories. And because of that, also the most feared.

Oh. That's...something.

"All magic has a mental or emotional element to some degree or a physical manifestation. People with our level of power generally have both. Spring Mages can manipulate water. Summer Mages can wield fire, and Autumn Mages can control metal and earth matter. Winter Magic is associated with air and weather manipulation or *atmokinesis*. Though since the nature of weather requires it, the most powerful Winter Mages can control water and fire as well. That's something your father can do, and it is highly probable that you can as well.

I shake my head in wonder.

"What about a mental ability? Will I have one of those, too?"

"Your powers are just waking up, but it is possible that you will have some form of *somnokinesis*, or the ability to manipulate sleep and dreams. Most of the powerful Winter Mages in the Agency's records have that listed in their dossiers, and obviously you experienced it firsthand."

I let out a slow breath.

"If I hadn't experienced it and watched lightning fly out of my own hands, I'm not sure I'd believe you right now."

"I know, Willa. I'm surprised by how well you're adjusting. You're remarkably calm for someone who just found out a different world exists around them."

We pull onto the tree-lined dirt road that leads to my mother's house. Quiet and secluded, with not much to see besides plants and wildlife. Dense woods surround the unkempt and bumpy road. Even without the canopy of leaves, the woodlands shut out the light, drawing us farther away from civilization and deeper into the wild darkness of my mom's property. The closer we get to home, the more it's like stepping back in time or into some kind of fantasy world.

I consider the last thing Stellan said about how I'm handling all this. What he's shared with me is surreal and should have been unbelievable, but it wasn't. It was more like the shifting of train tracks, connecting me to the right destination when I hadn't realized I was on the wrong path. It was all the off-kilter pieces of my life clicking into place.

I smile at Stellan.

"I suppose that's because you haven't seen where I grew up yet."

CHAPTER 14

THE HOME where I spent my childhood is an old white farmhouse with green shutters surrounded by a few acres of dense forest. A different owner might have cleared out more land, but my mother likes the privacy and has a fondness for the trees.

Hydrangea bushes full of long-dead flowers line the property on one side and a grove of old cedar trees marks the entrance to our forest. My mother's flower and vegetable gardens on the southern side of the yard are still beautiful even when put to bed for the winter.

Stellan and I exit the car and the scent of woodsmoke comes from the house while the clean, cold northern Vermont air fills my lungs. This is not going to be an easy visit, and my heart is heavy as we approach the front door. It's painted green to match the shutters and fairy runes are carved around the edges. Anne Martin is no casual artist and fantasy writer. She fully immerses herself into the worlds she creates, and her home is an extension of her work.

My mother opens the door to let us in and gives me a wide-eyed look with a funny nod of approval after Stellan is inside. I shake my head and can't help but smile a little. Like most mothers, she wants me to be happy, and I know what she's thinking. Unfortunately, this is not a "meet the parents" situation. We're about as far from that as you can get.

An odd sensation grips me as I step across the threshold of our house. Being home always sets me on edge, and I anticipated the familiar veil of apprehension that settled over me in the driveway.

But this is sharp, pronounced. Tight and constricted, my magic doesn't like it, and it pushes against my chest painfully. I wince, and both Stellan and my mother turn to look at me. Stellan's eyes narrow in suspicion as I rub my chest.

"I'm fine. Just a weird feeling." I shrug. "You look nice today, Mom," I tell her as I give her a hug.

"Thank you." She pulls back to look at me. My mother always looks nice. She had us very young so she's only in her 40s with the same bright blue eyes and dark hair I inherited from her. My mother's hair is flecked with a few grays, but it's pulled back in a messy bun. We are often mistaken for sisters.

She is wearing her usual paint-stained overalls and a linen blouse. Her face is bright and youthful. Despite the pain in her past, there's an innocence about my mother that never seems to fade, and I expect it will always be there as long as she lives.

"So, who's this fellow?" she asks with a gesture toward Stellan.

"Mom, this is Stellan Lundqvist. Stellan, this is my mother, Anne Martin."

"It's a pleasure to meet you." Stellan offers a hand to my mother. She takes it, but her smile falters. Stellan's accent is mostly English, but she can't have missed the Swedish name or the Scandinavian lilt.

"Of course. Please call me Anne. Come in and have some coffee." Her wariness is unmistakable, and Stellan's tight smile tells me he picked up on it as well.

Mom leads us through the house to the kitchen. We renovated over time to lighten up as much of the space as possible. Our furniture is a mix of antiques and family heirlooms and a few funky pieces that Beatrice fixed up when she went through an upholstery phase. My family's art and photographs are all over the walls.

My mother has a fire going in the woodstove, and it's warm and homey with the familiar scent of coffee and woodsmoke. We take seats around the worn wooden table and mom's old mutt, Boomer, puts his head on Stellan's knee. He gets suckered into scratching Boomer behind the ears while he takes in his surroundings. The kitchen has a very lived-in feeling, but it's clean and full of light.

While most of the other rooms are painted white, this one is a light yellow that accentuates the midday sun coming through the large French windows that look out over the garden. A bouquet of dried flowers sits in a milky white vase on the table.

"So, tell me, how did you two meet?" Mom asks carefully, breaking the silence as she pours us some coffee.

"At the library," I say without thinking, but it quickly dawns on me what she still thinks is the reason for our visit. "Oh, Mom. No. I mean, he's not...we're not...well, it's not like that." I panic and turn pink.

Stellan comes to the rescue. "I think what your beautiful daughter is trying to say is that we are not in a relationship. We came here to talk with you."

"OK..." She looks really worried now. I ignore the stupid flutter in my stomach from Stellan calling me beautiful. He meant it as a compliment to my mom and now is definitely not the time for butterflies.

I clear my throat and focus. "Mom, there's really no easy way to say this, but we need to talk to you about Dad."

Her jaw clenches. The ice coming from my mother is arctic, but her eyes always give her away. All this time and even just the mention of my father devastates her. The pain she still carries is plain to see. Her hand shakes slightly as she sets down her coffee.

"I gave a statement to the Agency years ago. I don't have anything new to add." She directs her anger at Stellan.

Her irritation doesn't faze him, and I figure he expected it. "And we thank you for your cooperation then and now. I understand that this is difficult, Ms. Martin. But recent developments make it very likely you have information that will help us in our investigation."

"I can't imagine how. I told you what I know, and I haven't heard from Lars in two decades. I don't appreciate you coming into my home and bringing up memories that don't deserve the light of day."

It's the coldest and most closed-off I've ever seen my mother. She's being obstinate, and while I understand it, I can't accept it. Not after everything that has happened to me.

But unlike the riot happening in my head, Stellan remains calm and unaffected. "Do you realize that it's illegal to have those ward runes along your entryway?" He's even-tempered and clearly used to this kind of meeting, but I'm seconds away from losing it.

The magic in my chest pushes against whatever is containing it. I can hardly breathe from the pressure. It sends a sharp tingling pain down my arms. I massage my temples and try to breathe through my rising anger so I don't say something I'll regret.

"Mom, I'm not even going to touch what Stellan just said

about the runes because I'm too close to exploding as it is. I understand that this is hard for you. I really do, but you need to tell me what the hell is going on. I've discovered that I can shoot lightning out my hands, and I need you to tell me why. Why am I only learning about my father's fucked-up super-powers from a man I just met and not you?"

My mother pales and bolts from the room. She chokes out a sob before the door to her studio slams shut.

"Shit. Mom, wait!" I call after her. This is exactly what I wanted to avoid, but I couldn't control my anger.

Stellan puts his hand on mine. "Give her a minute, Willa. This can't be easy for her."

I swallow down the lump forming in my throat and sit back down. Every muscle in my body is stiff and tense.

"The runes on your door were put there by a powerful Mage. I'm sure you felt it trap your powers as you stepped into the house. I'm speculating, but I assume those runes are part of the reason you and your sisters never developed your abilities. Your mother hasn't wanted anyone using magic in her home. I would wager there are other protective measures throughout the house."

I release a long exhale. This new development isn't surprising, but it's now painfully clear that my mom knew about all of this and never shared it.

"I don't blame her for doing what she needed to feel safe in her own home. I just wish she'd told us."

Stellan squeezes my shoulder with one of his strong hands. His magic tingles against my skin beneath my sweater in a cool, calming vibration, but it's faint. The runes are working on him, too.

"I can only imagine what you're feeling right now, Willa. Unfortunately, we don't have a lot of time, and we need information that only your mother has."

"I'll try to speak with her. She has a history of closing

herself off from everyone when her anxiety is triggered, but I'll do what I can. I need answers, too."

I pass through the dining room. The spot where Bea's piano used to sit is now home to a collection of Wren's impressive handmade swords. On the opposite side is the white door with black metal latches that leads to my mother's studio.

Her workspace has its own set of stairs from her bedroom so in certain moods she rarely has to leave this side of the house. As children, we knew better than to disrupt her, and even now it goes against my nature to open this door without invitation.

"Mom?" I call out gently. The door isn't locked, and I creep into the brightly lit studio. It smells like paint and the papery scent of canvas and wood. The warm, sunny space is a stark contrast to my mother's dark mood. She's sitting in the window seat, staring outside with blank eyes. Tears streak her face.

She doesn't look away from the window while she speaks. "I'm so sorry, darling." Her voice is thick and rough.

My feet creak against the wood floor, and I take the spot next to her. "I know, Mom."

Hugging her tight, she leans into me. She feels especially small and fragile, like she's made of nothing but glass.

"All the decisions I made and the secrets I kept were to protect you and your sisters. I just need you to know that."

"I know how much you love us, and I trust you did what you thought was best. But now that I'm aware and this power inside me is awake, I need you to be honest with me. I'm… I'm scared." My voice breaks. My mother's eyes soften and more tears spill down her face.

We hold each other for a long moment, but Stellan is waiting and we can't put this off any longer. I clear the emotion from my throat.

"I need you to talk to Stellan. I know it's hard, but Dad sent me something and it woke up my magic. I've had people following me. I've been attacked. I'm only safe and here with you because of him. He can help us."

I didn't think it was possible, but Mom's face turns even more white. Her whole body stiffens and the air heats around her, fiery and molten hot. There's a sudden and strong scent of summer flowers. It burns and my magic perks up in alarm inside my chest.

"Mom, are you OK?"

Her voice is tight, strained and her hands shake. "No, Wil. I'm not OK. I haven't been OK since I was 18 years old. I'm angry. Just so angry that this is now your problem and that your father still has the ability to reduce me to rubble with just the mention of his name."

She wipes the tears from her face in defiance, as if she's done being sad and afraid.

"I'll tell you and that man what you want to know, but you're not going to like what you hear."

CHAPTER 15

STELLAN

THE PAINTING IS REMARKABLE. It's mostly black and white with varying shades of gray and tiny wisps of dark blue, sap green, and golden yellow. A woman dressed in dark armor carries a long, glinting sword with her hair wild around her like the inside of a storm.

She's powerful. Daunting. Her face is partially shadowed, but it's clearly a portrait of Willa. Perhaps as her mother sees her. Perhaps what she dreams or fears for her.

"This is a beautiful painting," I say when I sense them enter the room. My eyes shift from Willa to her mother. My magic is dulled by the wards and runes in this house, but anger, sadness, and worry roll off them in waves. Subtler emotions like curiosity and anticipation are there, too. Today will be hard for both of them, but unfortunately necessary.

"Thank you," Anne replies curtly. Her ire with me hasn't receded and I doubt it will. "I'd like to get this over with, please."

"Of course, Ms. Martin. Thank you for agreeing to talk

with us. Are you comfortable with me recording this conversation?"

Her eyes narrow momentarily, but she just shrugs as if she's past the point of caring. I gesture for them to sit down on the couch, and I take the chair opposite.

International laws prohibit me from contacting a witness who has already given a statement unless new information surfaces. The Agent who interviewed Anne Martin twenty years ago was a product of a different time. The questions he asked were pointless and routine, and the information he gathered has proved to be of very little value.

I have read Anne's books. Though they are written in a high fantasy style, it is obvious to me that the character of The Storm King is based on Lars. But that connection alone was not legal recourse to contact her.

I have desperately sought an opportunity to speak with Lars Stromberg's wife, and I am certain this will be a pivotal moment.

I set a recording device on the coffee table between us and state the date and subject for our records. "Ms. Martin, can you please tell me how you met Lars Stromberg?"

Anne inhales slowly and releases a steadying breath. Willa holds out her hand and her mother takes it.

"I met Lars at the bookshop in town where I worked," she begins and her voice grows steadier as she speaks. "He was in Vermont to teach a few classes on climatology at a college nearby. At least, that is what he told me."

"Can you describe the nature of your relationship?" I keep my voice impassive and professional despite my mounting anticipation.

"We were in love. Well, I was at least." She speaks slowly, trying to keep herself in check. "He was older than me and sophisticated. Just so unlike anyone I'd ever met. Meeting him was the most thrilling thing that had ever happened to me. We were inseparable almost from that first day.

"He was very possessive of me and insisted on providing for us. I quit my job, and we moved in together shortly after we met. We got married in a private ceremony after just a few months. He always told me that I was special and powerful, I just needed his help to blossom."

She glances down at her lap and her chin quivers. She's using all her strength not to break down. Willa squeezes her hand, offering encouragement.

"When you are able, can you elaborate on that?"

This is the crux of everything. I'm certain of it.

The atmosphere in the room shifts and tension simmers as we wait for Anne to speak. Willa's eyes shine with unshed tears. Whatever story she has told herself, whatever theories she has constructed about her mother's life and her father's departure are all about to be blown out of the water.

Anne swallows hard and gains control over her voice though it comes out thick and hoarse.

"One day, almost a year into our relationship, Lars told me he had finally found a way to unlock my potential. A way that would ensure we could be together forever. Silly me, because I thought we already were. We were married, committed to each other, or so I thought. But Lars said he had family obligations that would prevent us from ever truly staying together unless I did something for him. I loved him so desperately, I would have done anything to keep him. But what I let him do was…"

She trails off, but I have to know.

"What did he do, Anne? This is very important. Please be as specific as possible."

Anne nods and stares at a fixed point on the floor. Lost in her memories.

"Lars asked me to lay down on our bed while he sat on

the edge. There was this odd sensation like a thick blanket on top of me. It was suffocating, and it smelled so strongly like Lars that I knew it was him, or part of him anyway. He always smelled like spruce trees and icy fields, but this was so strong I could taste it.

"My limbs were weighed down and my eyes grew heavy, and then I was locked in a dream. A horrible dream of fire and violence. I tried to wake up, to move, to do anything to escape, but I couldn't. I couldn't wake up. I saw myself in the middle of a raging fire. I wasn't sure how, but I knew I had caused it. Everything around me was engulfed in flames, and this sharp hot pain in my chest began to swell and burn me from the inside. I woke up screaming with our bed on fire. I nearly burned the house down."

Willa gasps, horrified, and wraps an arm around her mother.

"Can you tell me what happened after that?" I am grateful for my years of experience staying calm under pressure because, fucking hell, this is bad, bad news.

"Once he put the fire out, Lars was elated. He told me I was his first success. I spent the next few weeks in a daze as he performed tests on me and my new powers. He made me do *horrible* things."

Anne finally breaks down, and Willa hugs her mother tight to her chest as she cries. Willa meets my eyes over her mother's sobbing head, and the fierce determination and rage on her face are magnificent. She wants to kill her father.

"I don't like that this is making you so upset. We should stop," Willa urges.

"I need to do this. I've held it in for so long." Anne sits up and wipes at her eyes with her hands.

I see a box of tissues by the mantle and offer it to Anne. She clears the tears as if she's removing the pain itself.

"I think your dad assumed I would be thrilled, but I was

terrified of what I could do," she goes on. "I could burn an object to the ground in seconds with just a thought. I could manipulate people's desires and make them feel and do whatever I wanted. He forced me to practice on people I'd known my whole life.

"They never seemed to remember it, but I have never forgotten the control I had over them. I had always thought of myself as a good person, but it wasn't until I had all this power that I realized my true nature. I wanted more than anything to prove to myself that I was strong. I wanted to hurt the people who had hurt me. And as soon as I realized I could, I wanted to burn the whole world to the ground. All the rage and frustration I felt growing up bubbled to the surface, and it absolutely terrified me. What I could do. What I would become if I let it.

"So, I taught myself how to control my magic. It was hard to go against your father's wishes, but I refused to use my powers on anyone again. And I've never used them since."

My jaw is clenched so tight I'm afraid I'll break a tooth. I can't imagine a world where I don't use my powers. They are part of me, but I grew into them naturally. I was born knowing they would develop with puberty, and I had the help of parents and teachers to master them. It is not surprising that Anne would want nothing to do with her magic when it was forced on her so cruelly and with so little support.

"When you refused, how did Lars react?" I ask.

"He was very angry with me, but I think disappointment is how I would describe it best. He was severely disappointed in me, which in some ways was harder to take than his anger. But then after a month or so, we just carried on like it never happened.

"That was also when I found out I was pregnant with you, Willa, and it was like that strange, painful time didn't exist. I had this image in my head of the happy family we could be if I just ignored what had happened. I was willing to do almost anything if it meant I wouldn't lose Lars. But then, he was gone so much for work that it was just me and you a lot anyway.

"Over time, a great divide formed between me and Lars. He was always secretive, but it became clear something wasn't right. He was gone even more than usual, and he'd snap at the littlest things. When I found out I was pregnant with the twins, I thought it might bring us closer together, but it only seemed to drive him further away.

"He was distrustful of my relationship with Tim, but he was away so often and I relied on Tim to help me around the house. A few days before it happened, he accused me of having an affair with Tim. Lars said he could sense his magic in Willa, but he couldn't feel it in the girls. He was sure it was because they didn't belong to him.

"He left again for what he said was work, and I invited Tim over to tell him we had to stop seeing each other for a while."

Willa snorts in disgust, and Anne gives her a sad smile.

"You have to understand that I was entirely dependent on your father, Willa. I was afraid to be without him. He had awoken something dangerous in me, and I was scared I couldn't control it on my own."

Willa rubs the back of her mother's hand with her thumb, encouraging her to continue.

"That night is very fuzzy for me. But I do remember that Tim was here when your dad came home. His face in the doorway was the most terrifying thing I've ever seen. I'll never forget it. There was fighting. Tim and Lars were shouting. I remember this massive flash of electricity and excruciating pain. When I woke up several days later, your dad was gone, and Tim said that your father lost control and attacked me. Tim didn't say exactly what he saw, but I'm certain your father struck me with lightning and then fled."

A tear slides down her cheek, but her voice stays strong. Willa's eyes are red-rimmed, and her cheeks are wet with tears.

I make a mental note to follow up on Tim Hawkins. It's been twenty years, but I can't allow any loose ends.

I click off the recording device, and both Willa and Anne startle as if they forgot I was here.

"Thank you for sharing your story with us. The information you provided is more helpful than you realize. Would it be acceptable to ask you a few more questions off the record?"

Anne agrees with a subtle nod.

"When did the Agency get in touch with you?"

"About six months after Lars left. Some Agency people came to ask me some questions. They didn't tell me what they were investigating, just that I was a person of interest because of my connection to Lars."

"What did you tell them?"

"I was afraid of what would happen to me or the girls, especially the girls, if I told them about my powers and how they came to exist. I feigned ignorance about Lars's magic, and I truthfully never knew much of anything about his work or what he did when he wasn't here.

"I just told them he attacked me and left, and that I hadn't heard from him since. I promised that I would call if he made contact, and they were satisfied. This is the first time I've heard from the Agency since then, and Lars is a ghost as far as I'm concerned."

Sadness blooms around her like funeral flowers. Even after all this time, it still hurts her that she never found closure.

"Thank you for telling us your story, Ms. Martin. Please

know that we would not have come here if we were not concerned about the extreme danger Lars Stromberg poses to innocent people and your daughter."

"Is Willa really in danger?" She grabs her daughter's hand.

"Yes, she is. Though to what extent, we don't know for certain. All we know so far is that Stromberg's known associates, including his brother, are on the move and that Lars attempted to contact Willa. I will help your daughter through this," I add when I catch the horror on her face.

"We recently discovered that Stromberg has been hiding on a small island off the coast of northern Sweden for years. My team is closer to tracking him down than any of our predecessors. I assure you, arresting him is our highest priority."

Anne rises from the couch. Her slippered feet glide along the floor to the mantle over their fireplace, and I'm struck by how timid and small she looks. She lifts open the base of an old black clock and pulls out an envelope.

"This letter arrived earlier in the year. It's not from Lars, but from his older stepbrother, Albert. I haven't opened it. I have nothing to say to Lars or anyone else in his family. But take it in case it's useful."

"Thank you," I tell her earnestly. "Between this and the information you shared, we have a lot more to work with than before. We are well aware of Lars's brother Mikkel, but much less is known about his mother's first marriage."

She turns to Willa. "I met Albert once when you were small. He came to visit Lars. I believe they were close when they were younger, but that was the first time they'd seen each other in years. It was before the twins were born. I wasn't permitted to ask certain questions about his past or his family, and I didn't press for information. I never met the younger brother. Lars said Mikkel was busy with the family business, and I had learned when to pick my battles by that point."

The thunderclouds gathering in Willa's eyes are violent. She's ready to explode. I'm impressed by her strength, but I'm worried for her. It's been an excruciating few days.

"I'll give you both a few minutes. Thank you again, Ms. Martin."

I squeeze Willa's shoulder in a reassuring gesture and let just a hint of my magic brush against her. She glances up at me in surprise, and I smile warmly. I'm here to help her, and I want to make sure she knows that.

Anne doesn't miss the exchange. I catch the knowing expression she gives Willa as I leave the house, and I wonder what kind of warning she's giving her daughter about me.

CHAPTER 16

OUR FAMILY'S cottage isn't far from my mother's house. It's just beyond the village and a few miles down more dirt roads toward the lake. In the summer, the town is busy with tourists and families returning to their vacation homes. But once the foliage fades, it's desolate and quiet.

It's my favorite time to be here, when the emptiness and absence of others is a sweet kind of sadness.

The building itself is painted red with white trim and surrounded by cedar trees. It has a rustic charm, but it's a large house with five bedrooms. There's a gazebo porch where my sisters and I string up fairy lights and hang a swing in the summer. It faces a picturesque view of the lake and the hills and farmland across it.

I'm still dazed after the meeting with my mother, but I had enough wherewithal to take Stellan to the village general store. It has everything anyone could need, so we stocked up on enough food, beer and wine to last a few days. I have no idea how long Stellan expects to stay, but I figure it's better to be prepared.

It's special showing this place to someone new, but the significance weighs more today. Stellan now knows more about me and my family history than anyone else. More than Sam. More than even my sisters.

I hate keeping Bea and Wren in the dark, but Mom insisted we wait until we could tell them in person and I reluctantly agreed.

Inviting Stellan into a space I hold sacred peels back another layer. It opens me further to his scrutiny and draws him deeper into my life. I feel raw and exposed, but I can't do any of this without him. I have no choice but to trust him and accept his help.

Standing on the porch overlooking the lake, I watch dark clouds roll in as the cold wind bites my face. I wrap my arms tightly around myself.

In summer, the view before me is a jewel-toned mix of greens and yellows, crisp blue skies and sparkling waters. In stark contrast, early November is a mottled mix of browns, dark orange hues, and a lot of gray. The first snow is around the corner, but for now, the frigid white-capped lake is nestled beneath bare hills studded with dark evergreens and dormant fields.

I hear Stellan approach with the rest of our bags. He sets them in front of the door before coming closer to take in the view. His solid body projects a warmth behind me that is so reassuring it's nearly an embrace. I shiver, though it has nothing to do with the cold.

"Willa, you're exhausted," he says gently. "You should rest."

I spin around to face him. He's close, too close, and his heat and rainwater scent is dizzying. He raises his arms slightly as if he's going to touch me, but closes his fists instead, letting them fall back to his sides. His eyes are dark and his jaw set.

"Thank you. I think more than anything I'd like to take a bath. Do you mind?"

Stellan clears his throat. "Not at all. Of course, that's fine." His nostrils flare, and he abruptly diverts his gaze, taking a step back.

I'm suddenly and acutely aware that we are staying here together without another soul around. A tension I don't want to examine too closely charges the air around us.

I unlock the door and lead Stellan inside. The walls are mostly white and bare wood with wide windows that over-look the lake. There are two bedrooms on the main floor and three upstairs.

A few years ago, Bea decided each bedroom needed to be painted its own color. The gray room and the blue room are downstairs, and upstairs are the gold, burgundy, and green rooms. Over time we've matched the furniture, accent wall-paper, and linens to each color.

The kitchen is stocked with staples and has all the uten-sils and cooking supplies anyone might need, and the bath-room has a clawfoot soaking tub. There's a stone fireplace in the living room that's flanked by a deep blue couch and big, squishy armchairs in an antique floral pattern.

We kept some things in their original state, like the giant tub and the fireplace, but modernized everything else to appeal to visitors looking to experience country life, but with almost all of the familiar comforts.

"The, um, kitchen's just through there, and you can pick whichever bedroom you'd like. There are more upstairs, but the two down here are generally warmer this time of year."

"Thank you," he replies a little woodenly, and sets his bag down in front of the blue room off to the right of the stairs.

"Tomorrow we can begin an assessment of your abilities, but you should take the afternoon to rest."

I acknowledge him with a nod and bring my own bag to the gray room. This one is my favorite with a king sized four poster bed and a toile linen duvet that matches the slate-colored walls. The sheer gossamer curtains let in just enough light so no matter the season it's always bright and airy. I put away a few things in the antique dresser and grab a change of clothes to take to the bathroom.

Turning on the taps, I pour some lavender-scented bath soap into the tub. I undress and pile all my hair on top of my head. The tub is deep and large enough for two, though I make a conscious effort not to think along those lines with my companion in the next room.

Who am I kidding though? I'd love nothing more than to feel the steely strength of his body behind me or soap up those lickable abs and watch the water drip off his shoulders and down his thick biceps. I puff out a resigned breath. It is incredibly inconvenient how attractive that man is.

The water is so hot my skin turns pink. My muscles relax, but my mind still reels from everything my mother shared. The more I mull over her story, the angrier I become. I have little love for my father, but sitting with the full extent of his crimes is suffocating. It's no wonder my mother never fully recovered.

And now Lars is trying to contact me, though I can't fathom why. From the moment he stormed out of our lives, he never made an effort to contact us. It wasn't like he sent us birthday cards or checked in during the holidays. We just didn't exist to him anymore. It doesn't make any sense that he's interested in me now. And if he wants to talk to me so badly, why not come himself?

I shudder at the thought of seeing him now that I know

what really took place. What he did to my mom. I wonder if he'll try to manipulate me or use me like he did with her.

I toy with the bubbles in the bath and promise myself that no matter what happens next, I'll keep the people I love safe. Whatever this new power is inside me, I'll embrace it and not fear it. I squeeze my fists together and the magic simmering in my chest rises, pushing its confines, demanding to break free.

I breathe deeply, tipping my head back against the bath, and settle the roaring beast inside my chest. If I have anything to say about it, Lars Stromberg will never hurt anyone I love ever again.

I drain the bath and put on a pair of black leggings and an old band t-shirt that used to belong to one of the girls and set off to find my phone. I send Sam a quick text to let him know I made it and to thank him for watching the cats.

I take my phone with me and wander out to see what Stellan is doing. I find him at the island in the kitchen chopping vegetables. There is a large pot on the stove, and the smell of something delicious greets me. My eyes drift to his hands as they skillfully handle the knife.

"Oh, dear. He knows how to cook, too?"

Stellan looks up from his work and smiles as I approach.

"I know the basics. You'll have to see for yourself if it's any good."

"Would you like some help?"

He shakes his head. "No, I have it managed. You could open a bottle of wine though." He gestures toward a bottle with his knife.

I open some white wine and pour us both a glass.

"So, what are you making?" I ask as I sit back down.

"It's called *gryta*, and it's essentially a beef stew. I occasionally make it with my sister and her family. Our mother used to make it for us when we were small. It's what you might call comfort food. I thought we could use a little of that this evening." He lifts the cutting board and deposits the vegetables into the pot.

The thoughtfulness of the gesture makes my heart swell inside my chest.

When has anyone ever made food for me because they thought it might make me feel better?

Not even my mother. Not that I blame her. Bea did a lot of the cooking when we were younger, but that was simply because she was good at it and we needed to eat. I've looked after everyone else for so long that I never bothered to think what it might feel like to have someone look after me.

"That sounds really nice, thank you." It comes out a little wobbly. I clear my throat. "Do you see your sister often?"

"When I'm not traveling," he says. Stellan's eyes dart over to me briefly before focusing back on his task. He observed the emotion in my response but wisely ignored it. "We have dinner once a month. She lives in Stockholm with her husband and their children."

"Do you travel a lot?"

"I do, though this is a little farther afield than I usually need to go. Most of the work I do is based in Europe," he explains as he fills the pot with stock and adds a bundle of herbs he tied with butcher's twine.

He told me earlier that the woman with him in Burlington is a colleague like Banks, but what if he has a significant other back home? My gut twists uncomfortably at the thought.

"Does your wife or partner mind you being away?" I ask and I know I'm not half as casual as I intend, but I take a sip of wine to cover it.

Stellan lets out a small laugh. "She might, if she existed. My job is demanding and doesn't really offer a lot of time for relationships." He looks up to assess me as I take in his answer.

"I was just curious," I reply with a shrug. "I'd hate to think I was keeping you from your wife and three lovely children or something."

His blinding smile hits me right in the heart. "That's enough interrogation, Ms. Martin. I'm here to find out about you, not the other way around."

We settle into an easy conversation. He's engaging and open but always shifts the focus back to me. We discuss light topics like the books we like to read and how we both enjoy cross-country skiing. We have weird little things in common, like the fact that we both have a cottage on the water. Stellan's holiday home is on the island of Sandhamn in the Stockholm archipelago. I'd love to see that part of the world, but I don't know if that will ever be a reality for me.

The dinner Stellan prepared was simple and delicious, and I light a fire when we're finished washing up. We sit on the floor in front of the fireplace with our backs against the couch so we can tend to the logs and be closer to the warmth.

In an alternate universe, everything about this would be romantic, but I make sure to put plenty of space between us. There's nothing amorous or intimate in what we're doing here, despite how much I wish everything was different.

"You did really well today," Stellan says, breaking the easy silence we settled into as we watch the fire.

"What do you mean?"

The fire deepens the shadows on his face, accentuating the hard lines of his cheekbones and jaw. He shifts, putting his elbow on his knee to face me. Even sitting on the floor, he's impressive and overpowering.

It's more than physical strength and the graceful, confident way he holds himself. It's also how his intelligent eyes catalog everything around him, ensuring he's constantly alert and aware of his surroundings. I doubt Stellan will ever fully relax here. I wonder if he can relax anywhere.

"You faced something that was exceptionally difficult. The things you had to hear were horrific, but your presence was invaluable in gathering information from your mother. Understanding your father's past actions can help us figure out what he's planning. And I don't want to overstep, but I think it was beneficial for both of you to have the truth out."

"Thanks," I say, quietly. "It was difficult, but my mother needed to do that. To release what she was holding inside. But now I'm struggling a little with the weight of it all. The enormity of my father's crimes and all the secrets that were hidden from me and my sisters. I just want to fix it. To take away all this uncertainty and put everything right again."

"Willa, you are not responsible for your father or any of the damage he has caused," he says almost sternly.

"I know that. I might not be responsible for his actions, but I also can't sit around and let other people solve this problem for me."

"You have fixed problems for everyone else your entire life, but you are only just waking up to your abilities. Please, just promise me that you won't do anything rash." He sounds genuinely worried.

"I promise I won't put myself in a dangerous situation unnecessarily, but it's pretty clear danger is coming for me already. I want to be prepared."

But as I say it, the exhaustion of the day hits me hard. I yawn and lean my head back against the couch. I can prepare after eight hours of uninterrupted sleep.

"Get some rest, Willa. We'll begin assessing your abilities tomorrow. I should warn you that I am very strict and I plan to be very hard on you." He smirks playfully.

"Promises, promises," I quip back and rise from the floor.

I stretch and my shirt rises up. He tries to be discreet, but I catch Stellan's eyes as they trace over the small strip of skin that appears and the curve of my hips.

I brave a hand on his shoulder. It's hot beneath my palm, and his muscles are so much firmer than I expected.

"Thank you for today. I don't think I could have handled that conversation alone."

"You're very welcome, Willa." Stellan sets his hand on top of mine. His fingers are warm and slightly calloused, though from what I can't imagine. Picturing what they'd feel like gripping my waist or trailing up my thighs is a terrible idea, but I've already maxed out my willpower for the day.

"I'm truly sorry to have met you in these circumstances," he says. "But I'm glad to be the one here with you."

I don't know what to say in response to that. The man makes me yearn for things I can't have, but I'm glad he's here, too.

"Goodnight, Mr. Lundqvist," I call over my shoulder as I walk into my bedroom.

A low chuckle responds. "Goodnight, Ms. Martin."

CHAPTER 17

WILLA

I WAKE EARLY and throw a sweater over my nightgown, braiding my hair loosely over one shoulder. When I leave my room, Stellan's door is still closed. Not knowing his morning routine, I make a pot of coffee and a little breakfast for myself. After I eat, I move to the couch and take out my latest knitting project and add a few rows.

Making something with my hands is exactly what I need. I'm nervous about today and what I might discover. Now that I know about my potential and the looming dangers, I desperately want to prove myself. I want to be strong and not run scared like I so often do.

I'm adding another row to the sweater when Stellan opens the front door. I jump and clutch a hand to my chest. He's dressed in cold-weather running gear, and it looks like he's been out for a while.

"What the hell!?" I start to chastise him for scaring me half to death, but then I catch the expression on his face. It's soft, almost wistful.

He doesn't speak for a long moment, but his eyes stay locked on me. I can't imagine what's causing him to stare at me in my pajamas like that.

I place the unfinished sweater in my lap and tilt my head. "Stellan? Are you alright?" He shakes his head as if clearing his vision.

"Yes, of course. My apologies." He starts toward the blue bedroom door, but then stops and adds, "You are creative even if you don't think so."

"What do you mean?"

"Your knitting," he says and points to the sweater I'm making. It's one of my own patterns. "I know you don't think you're like the rest of your family, but it's not that you aren't creative. It's that you need a practical application for it to feel worthwhile."

"You're probably right." I smile. "Thanks."

Is it that obvious I don't feel like the rest of my family, or is he just ridiculously observant?

"I'm going to shower and change. You should put on something close-fitting but comfortable. When I was out, I found a decent spot where we can work and remain unseen."

Stellan is back to using his business voice. The moment of soft expressions and candor is over.

I change into black leggings and a black wrap shirt that I use for yoga. I redo my braid so it's tight and decide it's as ready as I can get. My face is pale next to all the black, but my cheeks are rosy and my blue eyes sparkle. The anticipation looks good on me.

I laugh when Stellan comes out of the other bedroom. He's wearing a black long-sleeve t-shirt that shows off the ridges of his muscles and black jogging pants.

"We have to stop dressing the same. We look like we're auditioning for a play."

Stellan's deep booming laugh answers, and my stomach

somersaults. He's so serious, and I love that I can make him loosen up a little. I smile to myself as we grab our coats. Stellan picks up a bucket and some kindling wood to take with us.

It's a cold but brilliantly sunny morning. The sun will eventually warm things up a little, but I expect snow will make an appearance this week. This is the kind of autumn weather that I love, cold and bright with the promise of winter just around the corner.

Stellan takes us about a mile from the cottage to a small clearing around a stream that connects mountain runoff to an inlet feeding the lake. The stream weaves through a tiny meadow and back into the forest. Lichen-covered rocks line where the water bites through the earth. It's lovely even when the leaves have fallen. The darkness of dying plant life and bare trees against a cornflower blue sky.

Stellan finds two logs and moves them to the middle of the clearing. We sit across from each other with our knees almost touching. He takes my hands in his and turns my palms face up on my legs. Despite being out in the open, the intimacy of our bodies so close together is heady and intense. Nerves make my pulse pound in my ears, and my breath can be heard over the wind through the trees.

"Try to relax, Willa," Stellan says patiently.

I take some deep calming breaths.

"To start, we would normally work on shielding your magic, but your mother already taught you those skills."

"Yes, I've come to realize that."

"Please close your eyes and tell me what you see when you focus on your magic?"

I draw my thoughts inward. "It's like a ball of bright light inside my chest."

"Very good. What color is the light? Is it blue or gray?"

"Neither. It's gold," I answer without a second thought.

Stellan freezes across from me and falters before responding. "Tell…tell me what you do when you shield your magic."

I'm a little troubled by his strong reaction, but I keep going. "I imagine my light and my mind are safely hidden deep within a fortress. I've probably read too many fantasy novels, but I always picture it like a medieval keep. It's made of stone and iron, and no orcs or evil wizards are getting in."

He makes a noise like a stifled laugh, and some of the heaviness around us lifts. "I can believe it. I'm just going to gently test your strength and make sure they're as sturdy as you say."

I close my eyes tight together and imagine my power inside the protective boundaries of the keep. A foreign power gently brushes against my mind. The scent of rainwater and earth. The steady warmth and calm I associate with his presence tries to break through my defenses. I almost want to let him in, but I keep my shields up no matter how hard he pushes against them.

"That's impressive, Willa," he says with a rough edge to his voice. The compliment does wonders for my confidence, but the truth is that control and protection were drilled into me from birth by my mother. It wasn't only the Vermont stiff upper lip like I thought.

"I'm certain you have the basics down, but now I'd like to see what you can do. Are you ready?"

"As I'll ever be," I shrug.

"We know that you can create lightning. Can you demonstrate that for me? Pick something to focus on and light it up."

An old rotten stump stands out of the ground not too far from us and I set my attention on it. When I used my magic before it was in self-defense. This time I'm using it with intention, but I'm not entirely sure what I'm meant to do. I visualize a raging storm inside me and close my eyes, holding out my hands in front of me. I don't really know what to do with my body, but it feels right so I go with it.

The storm intensifies in my mind, and electricity builds up around me, making me tingle and shake. I think I can hear Stellan calling my name, but he sounds faint and far away. I push my hands out instinctively, and a massive bolt of lightning pours out of me and out of the sky at the same time.

Stellan yells my name and rushes toward me just as the stump explodes.

We're thrown backwards onto the ground. I land on my back in the grass with Stellan on top of me. I hit a rock and cry out in surprise as bits of old stump rain down on us. I look up to find Stellan's face inches from mine with his eyes wide in shock.

"Are you OK?" I ask.

"Yes, I'm fine. Are you?"

"I think so. I hit my back on something sharp. Also, you weigh a ton." I give him a shove. Stellan's deep laugh answers, and he rolls off me.

Still on the ground, Stellan props himself on his elbow and considers me seriously. "I have never seen anyone so new to their magic do something so powerful." He shakes his head like he can't believe it. "How do you feel?"

"A little out of breath and maybe a little tired, but otherwise fine." I don't know how to verbalize what I really feel, but it's almost like I'm tired because I was trying so hard to rein myself in and not incinerate half the forest.

Lying next to me on the dry grass, it would be so easy to reach out and touch Stellan's face or his unruly hair. His eyes darken as they wander down to my lips. For one brief moment, the heat in his gaze is an inferno.

But it's gone in the next second, his professional mask

firmly back in place. Stellan stands and offers me his hand. Pulling me up, our bodies are close for a moment too long as though we can't quite break the spell. I take a step back before I embarrass myself.

"So, what's next?"

"Are you certain you are ready for more?"

"Yes, of course. Like I said, I feel fine."

He considers me with determination, and I feel his magic whisper over me, checking for injuries. When he seems satisfied, his power retreats.

"So long as you are sure," he continues. "As I explained yesterday, magic manifests uniquely in each individual, but some traits always appear among the broader categories. As a Winter Mage, your ability to conjure lightning is consistent with others on record. However, there are some, like your father, who have access to a broader range of abilities. I'd like to assess if that has passed on to you."

"What would you like me to do?"

He grabs a piece of kindling wood he brought with us.

"I'd like you to light this on fire." He presses the thin piece of wood into my hands.

"Um, sure. Any ideas how?"

"Trust your instincts. If this is part of your magic, it will be clear to you."

I turn the wood over in my hand and stare at it with my brow furrowed.

"I'm not sure scowling at it is going to work," Stellan says dryly.

"Thank you, Mr. Lundqvist. Your tutelage is truly inspiring." He clears his throat like he's suppressing another laugh.

I close my eyes and picture a fire inside me. It starts in my chest and slowly creeps down my arms. I take a deep breath and release it slowly. As I breathe, I envision the fire flowing down my arms and igniting in my palm where the wood rests. It doesn't burn me, but I can sense it growing hotter and it tickles beneath my skin.

When I smell smoke, I open my eyes. The wood in my hand is in flames. I'm holding fire in my palm. It doesn't hurt, but I scream because there's actually fire in my hand and I drop the fully engulfed kindling.

"Excellent!" Stellan exclaims and pulls me into a bear hug. I cry out in surprise again, but he just laughs and draws me in tighter against his chest. It's just as nice in his arms as I imagined. I lean into it, hugging him back. He breathes into my neck. It's intoxicating. So potent it's dangerous. I tap his back, and he releases his hold with an apologetic smile.

I can't meet his eyes.

"Let's try something different and perhaps more difficult," he suggests.

"Sure," I agree with another shrug of my shoulders. I am growing tired now, but his confidence in me and his enthusiasm are inspiring.

Stellan grabs the bucket and fills it with water from the stream.

"I would like to know if you can freeze this water. It's already very cold so if you can do it, it shouldn't take much effort."

It sounds simple enough. I place my hand over the water, and in the same way I pictured the fire, I imagine my chest is full of a glowing blue ice. It spreads down my arms.

Though, unlike the fire, this time it hurts. A chill moves through my blood. The blue ice expands, and I can no longer control it. It's so cold that I shake uncontrollably.

I try to open my eyes, but I can't. Stellan shouts my name. He sounds too far away. I can't make anything out through my frozen lips when I try to call back to him. I'm encased in ice and I can barely breathe. And then there's nothing.

CHAPTER 18

STELLAN

MY MAGIC WRAPS us both in a blanket thicker than the fleece I've tucked over Willa's bare shoulders. With one arm, I hold her around the middle, pressing her back close against my chest as I continue my assault on her overactive magic, keeping her body warm while her magic tries to freeze her from the inside.

I should never have pushed her so hard in one day. *What was I thinking?*

I wasn't, that is the problem. I've never seen anyone so effortlessly switch on their magic. It was thrilling to witness, but also extremely worrisome. What it means for her, if it's discovered...

No. Of course, it will be discovered. I have to share whatever I find with my team and with Director Olsen. Willa's life is about to change dramatically, but that is beyond anything I can control.

I'll help her through the transition as best I can, but the trajectory of her life is ultimately not my business.

It doesn't sit well with me, but none of that matters if she dies from hypothermia. I give my magic another push. Willa's magic is wild, and it wants freedom after so long existing in a cage inside her. Our magic is not meant to be locked up. As Willa's body warms against my chest, her magic also calms. Lulled to rest by mine.

Willa's eyes stay closed, but she finally stirs and twists in my arms so her face is now against my chest. This is the first time she's moved since I brought her inside.

Tack Gud.

Her eyelashes flutter.

"Willa?" I call to her. I need to see her pretty eyes open so I can fucking breathe again.

"Hmmm," she says sleepily. "Shhh, I don't want the dream to go away. It's so nice."

"Willa, you're awake." I'm so relieved. I tuck her into me and squeeze her tight.

"Stellan, I can't breathe," she squeaks.

I just laugh. She tries to sit up, but I'm not letting her go anywhere. My arms form a tight band around her waist.

"Stop squirming, Willa. I've just spent the last two hours keeping you from turning into an icicle. Please don't move until I know you're no longer in danger." I pull back so I can examine her face.

Her cheeks are beautifully flushed, and her heartbeat is steady and strong.

"I'm glad to see the color back in your cheeks. It was close for a while."

"What happened? And…where are our clothes?" She looks down at the tops of her breasts, which are spilling out of her bra and pressed against my chest. Her eyes linger on the small dusting of hair on my pecs. Her arms are trapped against my abs, and she startles the moment she realizes that

I'm only wearing boxer briefs and that my calves are wrapped tightly around her legs.

I've done everything in my power to remain a gentleman. It was easy when I was concerned about her well-being. Now that I know she's fine, it's becoming harder to stay unaffected.

"What do you remember?" I ask, willing myself to remain professional despite our near-nakedness.

"I remember freezing the water. The fire felt like a tickle, but the ice was excruciating. I couldn't breathe. Then everything went black. I'm so sorry." She lowers her eyes.

"You have nothing to be sorry for." I pull her closer and run my fingers across her back reassuringly. She's especially petite and fragile in my arms, and I can't deny how right it feels to hold her this way.

"It's entirely my fault. I pushed you too hard. I was so focused on discovering what you could do that I didn't think about how it was affecting you."

I'm furious with myself, but it doesn't stop the need for her rising inside me. Holding her this close is torture. I lean in slowly. My tongue wets my bottom lip. Her heart thumps in anticipation.

But I can't do this to her. I can't abuse her attraction to me.

"You've been through too much today. I apologize for our state of undress, but it was the surest way for me to regulate your body temperature."

She clears her throat and swallows her disappointment. Her shields are lowered in her weakened state. I don't want to invade her privacy, but it's impossible for me to ignore when her moods are on the surface and so strong.

"Yes, that does sound logical. Very smart."

She shifts in discomfort. She wants to escape, but I can't let her go. Not yet. I just need her in my arms a little longer.

To know she's safe and unharmed. Her body trembles, and I feel her nipples harden through the thin fabric of her bra.

"You're shivering. How are you feeling?"

"Fine," she says breathlessly. "Better than fine. Thank you for taking care of me." She speaks in just above a whisper, sultry without trying, and so sweet. Using her free arm, she brushes her fingers lightly against my chest, right near my heart. My body tenses. I sense her inner conflict.

She knows she shouldn't, but she can't help herself.

Willa draws a slow circle in the center of my chest. My eyes close, and my breath grows shallow, controlled. Her touch is a blaze across my skin. She trails down and flattens her hand over the peaks and valleys of my abs. She's slow, cautious, like she just wants to feel me beneath her palm. Not wanting to push a boundary she's unsure she should cross.

Willa travels lower, and I grab her hand. No matter how much I might want that, there are firm lines here. Our eyes are open and locked. Our breath mingling, her heart pounding in time with mine.

Bells ring in my head like a five-alarm fire.

She's your responsibility. She's vulnerable. Back off.

Now.

Too abruptly, I push away from her and sit up. "I'm sorry, Willa, but we can't."

She blinks a few times and her face falls, but she gathers herself. Drawing the blanket around her shoulders and holding her head high. Her strength and grace impress me more every day.

"Of course, I'm sorry. It was just so warm…" Her cheeks flush in embarrassment.

"Willa, I know," I acknowledge. "It's fine, but we can't."

She lowers her eyes to her hands. Her discomfort and embarrassment physically wound me, but I was right to stop her.

"I'm going to draw you a hot bath, and I want you to relax for the rest of the day. Can you do that for me?"

"I can try."

Her eyes roam over my body while I put on sweats and a t-shirt. My magic reads her reactions: desire, lust, and something else. Something soft and affectionate before she shores up her shields and I'm cut off from her emotions.

Stopping her was nearly impossible, but it was the only appropriate course of action. I refuse to take more from her than she should give me. Willa is here for my protection and guidance, and I don't want to confuse her or lead her on. Even though she has done nothing wrong, we are still on very different sides of this investigation. The sooner we both remember that the better.

CHAPTER 19

WILLA

I WANDER into the kitchen the next morning to find Stellan sitting at the table staring at the lake through the wide French windows. It's a calm day, and I love when water is like glass and you can see all the way to the bottom. Stellan is lost in thought and doesn't move or acknowledge me when I enter the room.

I quietly pour myself a cup of coffee from the pot on the counter, not wanting to interrupt whatever he's mulling over. But the milk is on the table next to him, and I reach over to grab it.

As I do, my arm brushes his chest, and I realize too late how far into his personal space I've stepped. His back straightens, and he slides as far away from me as possible while still seated. We've been awake together for all of two minutes, and I'm already making it awkward.

Nice work, Willa.

Thinking of yesterday's supreme lapse in judgment, I take a hurried step back.

"Sorry."

Stellan clears his throat. "It's fine."

It sounds like a lie, but he gives me a reassuring smile. He stands and refills his own coffee mug. His t-shirt stretches across the muscles of his back and I'm suddenly much too hot. I place my coffee mug down and push it away from me.

He was so kind after I practically threw myself at him yesterday. Thankfully, he seems to have chalked it up to the heat of the moment and not something we need to discuss further. I'd rather not relive the rejection, if I can help it.

Last night, he drew me a bath and fixed us with plates of leftovers, and then he worked and I knit in comfortable silence until it was time to go to bed. Any hint of the intimacy or flirtation from earlier in the day was gone, but I enjoyed spending time in his company without it.

"So, what's on the schedule today, Boss?" I ask.

"Boss?" He raises an eyebrow.

"Yeah, I don't know. It just felt right." I shake my head at myself.

"I thought we'd stay inside today and work on testing some of your mental and emotional abilities."

"That sounds fine. I'll just change, and we can begin whenever you're ready for me."

At the mention of changing, Stellan's eyes travel down my body. I have on a black nightgown with a scalloped edge around the collar. I've never been one for pajamas.

"Is that what you sleep in? I thought only the elderly wore night dresses."

I pause. "Wait, are you teasing me?" I try to be indignant, but Mr. Serious can be funny when he wants to be and I like it.

"Maybe?" He sips his coffee to hide his smile.

"I'll have you know that many young people wear nightgowns, and even if they didn't, I wouldn't care. It's what I find comfortable. I don't like anything touching my legs while I sleep."

Stellan rises from his seat at the kitchen table. "Oh, Willa. There are so many things I could say in response to that. Go get dressed, little old lady. I'll meet you in the sitting room."

* * *

STELLAN and I sit across from each other on the couch. I'm small enough that I can sit fully sideways with my legs crossed. Stellan doesn't look quite as comfortable, but he's still more relaxed than how I'm used to seeing him.

"Take a deep breath and reach out for me again with your magic." We've been trying for the last half hour to see if I can sense his moods or his thoughts. So far, it is clear those are not my strengths.

I inhale and focus on my magic inside my chest. It surfaces, twisting and pushing against my sternum. I breathe out and let a little of it loose. I'm growing more familiar with it, and with my eyes closed I can "see" it as it travels toward Stellan. It's a shimmering gold vine that gently curls and twists around Stellan's face and chest. Through the vine, I seek feedback from him or his magic. I can feel his warmth and the sensations of calm and protection that I associate with him, but I can't read anything more specific.

"Yeah, I got nothing. I don't think this is one of my gifts."

"You're doing a wonderful job tickling me, though, if it's any consolation."

"I mean, that does make me feel better." The overachiever in me struggles with any perceived failure.

"I didn't think you would be able to do this. There's no record of a Winter Mage who can sense or manipulate emotions or thoughts. It's just not part of your ability profile,

138

and that's probably a good thing. Learning to control the magic you already have will be enough."

"I suppose that's true," I concede. "What's next?"

"The Agency would frown on this, but I'd like you to attempt putting me to sleep."

"You cannot be serious. What if I hurt you?" He can't want me to put him in such a vulnerable position.

"I trust that you won't," he says with confidence. "You'll just need to be careful because you could put me to sleep permanently." He smiles as if he thinks it's reassuring.

It's not.

"Stellan, that's really not funny. I can't do this." There's no way I can trust myself enough to keep him safe. "What if I go too far?"

"You'll know when to pull back."

"This is a terrible idea." I twist my fingers together nervously.

"Probably, but let's try it. It's something I'm sure you can do, and we need to explore it. If it makes you feel better, I'll write down Banks's phone number. If something goes wrong, you can call him."

He writes down two numbers on some paper on the coffee table.

"I added Greta's number as well, so you have both."

"Thanks. Would you like to try it here?"

"Hmm, no. I think we'll try it in the bedroom." Stellan must see the look of concern on my face because he adds, "If only because I'm afraid I'll fall off the couch."

"Uh, sure," I say and follow him to his room.

"I'm going to lay here in the middle of the bed, and you're going to use your natural abilities to put me into a gentle sleep and then you're going to wake me up. Does that sound acceptable?"

"Right. I just wish we could practice on an animal first or something." Though even that makes me feel ill.

"Well, we don't have any animals available, and it's not going to take long."

"You sound so confident when I've never done this before."

"You are powerful, Willa. You simply need to trust your magic. It will guide you."

Stellan lays down with his arms behind his head. His long legs stretch out, and he looks at me with cocky assurance. He has way more faith in me than I do in myself. I'm terrified I'm going to put him in a coma.

"There is a possibility that you will put yourself to sleep the first time. Try to avoid that," he says without opening his eyes.

"Oh, really? I could use a nap, actually."

"Alright, funny lady. Focus."

Stellan isn't going to let this go until I try. I breathe in and out a few times to steady myself. Turning inward, I search for what might help me do this. A new vine appears in my mind. It's gold like the others, but there's something calm about it that makes me think of sleep and dreams.

I let it rise up and travel down my arm. Instinct tells me to touch Stellan in order to make this work. I reach out and put my hand on top of his. He surprises me by taking my hand and entwining our fingers.

I sink some more energy into the vine and focus on beautiful sleep and pleasant dreams as it travels down my arm and into where our hands are connected. I attempt to pass on to Stellan the kind of sleep that cleanses your soul and refreshes your mood. A gentle sleep of peace and clarity.

I continue to breathe slowly. Matching my breath with Stellan's as I lull him into this easy sleep. I know the moment it works. But I also know that Stellan is safe and that he'll wake up. I haven't gone too far.

I'm about to pull the magic back inside myself when I feel it curl up my arm. So soft and pretty and peaceful. I try to fight it, but the lure of a beautiful rest is too strong. The warmth in the room. The muted morning light. I can't stop it. I don't want to stop it. I fall onto the bed next to Stellan and pass out.

Some time later, I wake up enough to realize where I am. I try to sit, but Stellan grabs my waist and pulls me into his chest. He holds me to him like I'm something precious. His heavy arm around my waist and the other underneath me as he tucks me into him with my back fully pressed against his front. I fall back to sleep almost immediately.

We wake up at the same time two hours later. Sleep clings to us like a heavy veil, but Stellan's low rumbling laugh brings me back to reality.

Stellan is fully wrapped around me, caging me inside a protective embrace. In turn, I cling to him like a koala on a tree trunk. My leg is hitched up around his thighs and my arm around his chest.

There are definitely worse ways to wake up.

I clear my throat and extract myself from Stellan. "I'm sor…"

"Don't," Stellan interrupts in a husky voice. "Don't apologize." He draws me in closer to him for a moment longer. "That was the best sleep I can ever remember having."

I lift my head off his chest and our eyes meet. He's almost reverent in the way he gazes back at me. I offer a shy smile before pulling away. I can't trust myself not to melt back into him.

"You were right about putting myself to sleep. I'll have to remember that." I brush my hair away from my face, avoiding eye contact. After the incident by the fire, I don't trust myself. I don't have the constitution for risking my heart to rejection over and over again.

"Willa," he says my name earnestly. He sits and cups my face in his hands, forcing me to meet his eyes. "Thank you."

One hand stays on my cheek, and the other moves to my waist. His touch is intimate and familiar, but I know he won't cross the line he's drawn.

"You're welcome?" I say, breaking the spell. "Why are you thanking me?"

"Sleep has always been hard for me. Harder since..." He pauses and shakes his head. "Well, it's difficult for me to fully relax, and I always sleep lightly or not really at all. That was the first time since probably my childhood that I've slept so soundly and peacefully. So, thank you. It was an unexpected gift."

"Well, you're welcome, then. Thanks for believing in me enough to try it. Sorry about the cuddle, though. I didn't mean to pass out right next to you. I'll work on that for next time."

"Willa, you can cuddle with me anytime you want."

I know he doesn't really mean it, but part of me — a really big part of me — wishes I could believe him.

CHAPTER 20

WILLA

AN ODD ORANGE glow lights this unfamiliar bedroom. It's almost as if there's some kind of barrier between me and the room. I can't make out much except the shadowy shapes of hotel furniture. A man with a thin frame sits at a mahogany desk smoking a cigarette. The scent of tobacco, new and stale, is thick in the air, like he's been waiting here for a long time. He plays with a hunting knife, twirling it around his fingers.

A phone rings. The man shifts the cigarette to his other hand to answer it, and a one-sided conversation takes place. It's in Swedish, and the man speaking sounds harsh and angry, his voice rough like sandpaper. I can't hear the person on the other end of the call, just a sense of urgency and an air of frustration.

I catch my name a few times, and a word that sounds like daughter. The smoker has to be my uncle, Mikkel Stromberg. I can't see him well, but enough to know he has similar features to my father.

I listen for more, hoping to piece together anything I can gather. It's not much, but my blood runs cold when I hear Mikkel say "Lundqvist" a couple of times before he stabs the table with his knife. The blade shines, catching what little light there is in the room. I do not need a translator to know what he's talking about.

My heart beats fast. I press my fingers against the barrier between me and my uncle. It begins to fade, like frosted glass turning clear beneath my hands. Mikkel comes more into focus. His head turns in confusion. *Can he see me?*

He stares directly at the spot where I'm standing. My pulse thunders in my ears. He speaks into the phone, but this time it's in English. He wants me to understand him.

"Lars," he says in a teasing voice. "We don't need to worry. Your daughter is very much a Winter Mage. Practicing her powers, too, by the look of it. We'll bring her home soon."

* * *

"No!!!" I shout, and bolt upright in my bed.

The light is gaining on what promises to be another cold but sunny day. The bedding all around me is rumpled, and my hair is wild from tossing and turning. I feel nauseous and weak. I shuffle off the covers and swing my legs over the bed, too shaken to stand just yet.

Stellan bursts into the room. "Willa! Are you alright?"

I'm jumpy from the dream. He's lucky I didn't try to electrocute him.

"My apologies. I heard you shouting, and I thought you might be in danger."

"I'm fine..." I say, but then I take in what he's wearing. The man is in my bedroom entirely naked except the tightest boxer briefs that leave very little to the imagination. I'm completely motionless as I look him up and down. I swear my brain fritzes out.

He catches me staring at his rippling abs, and the bastard smirks at me. He knows exactly what I'm thinking about, which is nothing short of wondering what they'd feel like against my tongue. My face heats in embarrassment, and I collapse back onto the bed so I don't have to look at him anymore.

"I'm fine," I repeat, speaking to the ceiling. "But it was a dream. About my uncle."

"Right." The amusement fades from his voice. "I'll just go get dressed."

He leaves, and I change into some comfortable clothes and tie my hair back. Despite the nap yesterday, I'm tired from a restless night's sleep and anxious about the dream and what it means.

I meet Stellan at the kitchen table. He's already sipping coffee and reading something on his laptop.

I pour myself some coffee and sit across from him. He's wearing jeans, but he's put on a stiff white dress shirt. He looks more like his investigator self.

"Tell me about your dream." He is all business this morning.

"I am pretty sure that it wasn't a dream, but something that really happened. Like I traveled in my sleep."

Stellan puts his mug down firmly on the table with a loud thud. He sits taller in his seat. "To where?"

"To my uncle's hotel room."

"Elaborate."

"Bossy..." I tease, but he doesn't smile. He just narrows his eyes. It seems the time for playfulness is over. I swallow down my disappointment and fill him in on what I saw and heard in my dream, fidgeting with a piece of old laminate stuck to the kitchen table.

"Thank you for telling me," he says, still in his professional mode.

"Of course. I promised I would tell you if I ever had another dream."

"Continue to practice shielding your mind. It will help." He states the words with so little warmth that I nearly shiver. "This morning, I need about an hour alone to make some calls and check in with my team. I can use one of the bedrooms upstairs."

A sharp and unexpected pang lights up my chest. "Sure, I'll take a walk so you have some privacy." My voice is too tight, and I clear my throat. "I should make some calls, too."

I feel foolish for caring, but it bothers me more than I want to admit. I guess I don't relish the reminder that this man is not here to laugh and cuddle with me. A massive and unquestionable divide exists between us, and I would do well to remember it.

I leave the house a half hour later, bundled up for a cold walk. There's a stretch of lake that ought to be secluded this time of year. The air is perfectly still this morning, and steam rises from the quiet water in an ethereal mist.

I wonder idly when it will snow. It's usually come by now. I walk for a few minutes before I make my first call, giving the brisk air a chance to perk me up a little. I sit down on a rock overlooking the lake with a wall of cedar trees behind me, blanketing me in their woody scent.

Even though I know she won't answer, I dial Wren's number first. Wren and I were close as children, but something I don't understand happened around the time she turned 18 and she's grown steadily distant as the years pass. She'll text back one- or two-word answers, but we never talk anymore. I hate to think that I did something to upset her, but since I can't figure out what took place and she brushes me off whenever I ask, I can't fix it.

Wren looks just like me and mom, with the same dark hair and deep blue eyes. She's covered in gorgeous tattoos and is never seen without several complex and beautiful pieces of jewelry that she made herself. Wren studied metal-smithing and all her work is extraordinary.

It always stings when her voicemail picks up. I don't bother leaving a message.

I try Beatrice next. She looks nothing like me or her twin sister. She's fair and blonde just like our dad with his bright aqua blue eyes. She's endlessly kind and funny and nothing ever gets her down. She's a phenomenal painter like our mother, and so sweet and sincere. I often worry about her trusting nature. She nearly always answers on the first ring.

"Hi, Willa!" she shouts down the phone. "Mom told Wren you had a hunky guy with you on your visit. Who is he, Willa? Tell me!"

I can't help but laugh at her enthusiasm. It's also pretty standard that Stellan's appearance is what made it into conversation and nothing of actual substance.

"I see Mom is telling tales again."

"Nope! No way. I know you're at the cottage with a man. You are required by the Laws of Sisterhood to give me details."

"Fine. Yes, I am at the cottage with a man." Bea has a way of sniffing out the truth anyway, so I might as well tell her.

"And…"

"And he is very attractive." I puff out a breath. "Like, 'holy shit the world is on fire' hot, Bea."

She giggles. "Yes! I love it. So, why are you there with this guy? Wren said Mom didn't think you were dating."

"That…is complicated." I can't tell them everything yet, but I won't continue in my mother's footsteps of keeping secrets. At the very least, my sisters need the basics to keep themselves safe. Who knows what could happen if their own magic starts waking up.

"I actually called so that you and Wren can keep an eye out for anything odd. The man with me is from an organization kind of like Interpol, and he's based in Stockholm. He's here as part of his investigation into our father's criminal activities. Basically, our dad is up to something, and I'm being targeted."

The line is silent for a moment too long.

"Bea, you there?"

"Yeah, sorry. I'm just processing. What the actual fuck?"

I stifle a laugh. "I know, Bea. It's a lot. I can't tell you much more because there's so much I don't know myself. Just be careful, OK?"

"Yeah, we'll be careful. You, too, though. This is really awful. But ugh, I gotta go. I'm late for work again."

"Aren't you always?"

"Yes, but I'm especially late today. The last time I was this late, I had a mutiny on my hands. The nursing home staff were ready to kill me."

"I can imagine." Among other things, Bea teaches highly popular art classes to senior citizens in Providence. "Tell Wren I said hello and let her know what I told you."

"I will. Stay safe! Love you!"

I make a few other quick calls to my mother, Jim, and Sam. I don't plan to do it, but I give Sam a bare bones story about the situation with my dad because I don't think it's fair to keep him totally in the dark. He's confused and worried, but I assure him I'm fine. I think he sort of believes me.

Unfortunately, there's nothing he can do to help me anyway.

Mostly, it's nice to hear his voice and remind myself that the person I was before is still somewhere inside me.

I feel like I'm unraveling the more time I spend with Stellan and the more I learn about myself and my family. The sturdy and comfortable structure of my identity is coming undone, and I'm not sure what I'll find underneath when all this is over.

CHAPTER 21

"We tracked them to a hotel near the airport. The men who attacked Willa were definitely staying there. We found traces of magic and a few empty bottles of vodka in their room, but the mercs have vanished."

I curse in Swedish. "Keep looking. They need to be found."

"They haven't left the area, but the trail only grows colder as more time passes," Greta adds. She looks especially grim. Her usually bright face is downturned. "Soren says Mikkel is still in London, but he's helping them somehow. They have to be working with someone powerful, or we'd have found them by now."

She's frustrated. We all are.

"How is Willa?" Banks asks.

"Handling this better than expected. I keep waiting for her to break down, but she continues to surprise me."

"Is she as powerful as we imagined?" Banks asks.

"We'll discuss that when I see you later in the week. There are several more tests I'd like to run."

"Are we still on target?" Greta asks.

"That depends on if you find the mercenaries or if we have evidence of them leaving the area. I won't risk Willa's safety."

"But what if she comes with…"

"No, we already discussed it. Fuck, Olsen's calling me," I cut Greta off. My computer flashes with an incoming call. "Keep me updated." I exit the meeting.

"Good afternoon, Director," I answer, sitting up taller.

"Lundqvist. I need an update."

Henrik Olsen is the Director of the Northern European Office of the IMA's Investigations Branch. He's in his early 50s with salt and pepper hair and a body that has gone slightly to seed. He and my father worked together years ago, and while I don't always like his tactics or his politics, he is my boss and I give him the respect he is due.

"The investigation is progressing well. We have trails to follow here and some leads for when we return."

"Excellent. Ingrid said you haven't responded to her questions. You know, she's a very bright girl, not just a pretty face. Don't discredit her, Lundqvist."

My jaw clenches. I can already feel a tension headache blooming at the base of my skull. "Yes, I am aware of her skills and intelligence. But as Ingrid technically reports to Soren, I have not needed to update her directly. You don't normally take such an interest in my staff, sir."

I try to keep the accusation out of my voice, but I'm certain I fail.

"I have my reasons, but she's good for your team. You'll see. Just keep her informed."

"I'll do my best, sir."

"And what of the Stromberg girl? Is she one of your leads?"

"Yes, Willa Martin has proven to be an invaluable asset."

"An asset?" His interest is piqued, and I instantly regret my choice of words.

"Yes, she is an asset to the case, and I am working with her directly."

I can practically see the cogs turning in Olsen's mind, and I'm certain I won't like the direction he'll want to take.

"Is she a Mage?"

"Yes, she is."

"What kind? Surely, you know this is important, Lundqvist."

Fuck. I had wanted to keep this information to myself as long as possible.

"I suspect she is a Winter Mage."

Olsen perks up. "Like her father? Is she powerful?"

His keen interest unsettles me, and I pause for the briefest moment before answering. "It seems only moderately so." The lie slips out much too easily.

I have never once denied information to a superior. My career is the most important part of my life, and our hierarchy serves a purpose. But protecting Willa Martin is more important than my professional scruples. Olsen's interest in her tugs on my instincts and unsettles me.

"She'll need to come in, Lundqvist."

"I don't think that will be necessary. Once we are sure the threat is neutralized, she will report to New York or the Montreal office for periodic check-ins. There's no reason for her to relocate."

"No reason to relocate?" Olsen repeats, his voice rising in frustration. "Lundqvist, she is Lars Stromberg's daughter. She's ours to deal with. I won't have some New York hack taking our assets from us. For all we know, she's working for her father. She needs to be evaluated by our medics and assessed for psychological anomalies. Bring her in, Lundqvist. Any means necessary. Just get it done."

"Yes, sir," I concede, and the video call ends.

I scrub a frustrated hand over my face.

I was primed my entire life to work for the IMA. My father was a Senior Agent. His father was before him. When you're born into power like ours, you don't have many options outside of Agency work. It is expected that you will use your abilities in the service of others. That's how I was raised and the philosophy that guides me.

This is not the first time in my career that my orders don't align with my preferences. But it is the first time my orders have conflicted with my personal convictions. It's the first time that following a command leaves me sick with guilt.

And I have no idea how to reconcile it.

CHAPTER 22

I TAKE the long way back to give Stellan more time alone. Approaching from the road, I hear the steady thud of someone chopping wood. I round the corner to see Stellan furiously swinging an ax.

Despite the cold air, he's wearing just a thin white t-shirt and jeans as he cuts through piece after piece of wood. His arms and shoulders contract and stretch while little flashes of his abs tapering into his jeans appear with every swing. Sweat dusts his brow, and his cheeks burn red.

I shouldn't stare. I should let him know that I'm standing here, but I can't move. The sight is all my erotic lumberjack fantasies come true. And I didn't even know I had erotic lumberjack fantasies.

He's swinging the ax so hard I think he might break it. There's fury in his movements. He is absolutely incandescent about something, and he's taking it out on my wood pile.

He swings the ax hard into the stump, lodging it in place with a grunt. He wipes the sweat off his forehead with the bottom of his shirt, showing off his abs in full and the fine trail of dark hair from his belly button leading into his jeans. I swallow hard and bite my lip. I know I need to rein in the heat blossoming between my thighs, but I crave all that fierce intensity directed at me. I want him to grip me in those Herculean arms while he…

Stellan unexpectedly roars with anger and throws his hands in front of him like he's pushing away an invisible foe. The power he releases is so strong I feel it in my bones. My own magic springs to life inside me, responding to a threat. I clutch my chest just as a tree on the other side of the yard explodes into a thousand splinters. They rain down while Stellan breathes hard and runs a hand through his hair.

I squeak in surprise and he whips around.

"Willa, how long have you been standing there?"

"Not long. You looked occupied. I didn't want to interrupt."

My face must show my shock because his eyes soften for just a moment before he turns back to stone.

"Are you OK? You seem…upset," I ask, carefully.

"I'm fine," he all but growls.

"Sure. Do you want to talk about it?" I know he doesn't, but I figure I should offer.

"No." The hard line of his jaw is set. His teeth clenched. He doesn't owe me an explanation, but his behavior isn't something I can ignore.

"You just blew up a tree. I didn't know you could do that," I add, trying to stay casual, but I feel like a gazelle standing in front of a lion.

"I can control water, Willa. That means anything with water inside it as well."

"Cool. That's pretty intense. Well, if you need me, I'll just be inside." I think about the fact that human bodies are 60% water. That's a terrifying amount of power.

"We have to continue the assessment of your abilities," he says with a curl of his lip. He's pissed, but I'm most of the way certain it isn't because of anything I did.

"Uh, sure. Right now?"

"Right now." Stellan holds himself rigid, fists clenching and unclenching at his sides.

Whatever happened while I was gone was definitely not good.

"You sure? You look like you're about to Hulk out."

"Don't, Willa." The look he gives me brooks no argument. OK, then. No jokes. Got it.

It's getting hot in my coat, so I take it off and place it on the ground. The air is brisk but pleasant, and the maple trees high above us are still against the deep blue sky like fine cracks on pottery. Apart from my grumpy companion, it's a beautiful day, and I'm ready to see what else I can do.

The memory of passing out and almost freezing to death is fresh in my mind, but I have faith that no matter his mood Stellan won't push me too hard again.

"Today, I need to see if you can impact other natural phenomena. We won't try freezing water again, though I feel strongly that is something you can do. I'd rather not risk it today."

"You and me both," I mutter under my breath.

If he hears me, he ignores it. "As you know, your father's primary power is *atmokinesis*, or the ability to manipulate the weather. We know you can create lightning, but I'd like to see if you share the ability to control more. Can you start by manipulating the wind?"

I step away from him and take in my surroundings. It's a perfectly calm day. Birds are calling and the stream feeding into the lake is bubbling, but the trees are silent.

"Just like yesterday, picture what you want to happen and if it's something you can do, the path will become clear. For me, I can sense all the water in everything around us. I focus on connecting with it and then providing the instructions."

Directing his attention to the task of assessing me is calming him down. The anger is still there, but it's dissipating.

I close my eyes and breathe in and out slowly. I imagine a breeze. With each inhale, I draw more power inside myself, and with each exhale, I push it away from me. The power in my chest churns and expands as it flows through me. I continue breathing, drawing in more power as I exhale pure force. My hair tickles my face as the air around me stirs. I hear the trees bending and quaking as I draw in and press out more and more energy with each breath.

I open my eyes. Stellan is staring with rapt attention. We make eye contact, and I can't help but smile. "That's me, isn't it?" I ask, indicating all the wind now blowing around us.

"Yes, Willa. It is you," he says with admiration. My hair has fallen loose. My cheeks are flushed from exertion. Creating lightning took power, but this takes control. It's the strongest and most badass I've ever felt in my entire life. I breathe in one more time and imagine the twisting vines of my power drawing back inside me. The wind calms almost immediately.

"Excellent, Willa. That really was impressive." He still doesn't smile, but I believe he means it.

"For the next test, do you think you can create cloud cover over us?"

"I'll try." I was fine creating a breeze, but changing the day's weather makes me uncomfortable in a way I don't quite understand. But I suppose it's just for the assessment, and I'll put things back to normal after.

I close my eyes again and let my magic guide me. As Stellan suggested, I connect to the water in the air and instruct my magic to pull it together into clouds above us. In no time at all, the sky darkens over our heads as the power inside me flows in and out with my breath.

"Brilliant!" Stellan says with more enthusiasm. "That's excellent. Do you think you could make it snow?"

"Yes," I answer quickly. I'm sure I can do it. I envision a snowstorm. The white flakes falling, coating the ground. The first snow of the year. But the thought gives me pause, and the uncomfortable feeling returns. I know that I can do it, but I desperately don't want to.

"Stellan, I can't do it," I say quietly.

"What do you mean? He asks, confused.

My shoulders slump, and I draw all my magic back inside myself. The storm clouds above disappear, and the brilliant sun shines down on us again.

"I mean, I can do it. I know I can make it snow a blizzard right now if I want to. I can feel it right here." I touch a hand to my chest. "It's in there, but I can't be responsible for the first snowfall. I mean, it's the weather! It determines every-thing in our lives, from the food we eat to the activities we enjoy. I guess I don't feel right making snow fall before its time. It feels like playing God. I know it's silly, but I just..."

Before I can continue, Stellan is on me.

Breathing hard, he clutches me to him roughly in an embrace that is both ravenous and somehow tender.

His control hangs by a thread. He lifts me effortlessly into his arms, and I throw my hands around his neck to steady myself. I don't know what's happening or why he's holding me, but I'm going with it. I wrap my legs around his waist while he stares hungrily into my eyes. His mouth is mere centimeters from mine.

"Fuck it," he growls. Then he takes my lips in a blinding kiss.

CHAPTER 23

WILLA

RAW, animal power radiates out of Stellan as he crashes into the living room with me in his arms, his lips locked on mine. He's a man possessed, and it's all I can do to hang on for dear life.

Stellan holds me up with a strong arm around my waist while the other grips the nape of my neck. Dizzy and panting, rational thought evaporates as pure, unfiltered desire takes over. He tastes like magic. His lips are warm and soft and perfect.

Stellan shoves me against the nearest wall with a grunt and unbuttons my sweater with eager fingers. He thrusts his thick arousal against the junction of my thighs in a rhythm that matches the determined pace of his kisses. I groan while leaning harder against him, seeking more pressure. He rips off my cardigan and breaks our kiss just long enough to lift my shirt over my head.

I reach back to unhook my bra. I need his skin and all his

masculine heat against me. The movement causes Stellan to pause and he stops my hand, pulling back to look into my eyes. Searching for answers to unasked questions while he breathes heavily, his chest rising and falling in passionate exertion.

"Willa," he says in a dangerously low voice that makes me tremble.

"Stellan?"

"Are you sure you want to do this?" He backs away just slightly. His arms hold me up, but his hips draw away. Even just the temporary loss of connection is torture.

He is giving me a way out. If I say no, he will stop. We'll go back to being distant and professional. Then he'll eventually leave and that will be the end of it. But that isn't at all what I want.

As I look into his gorgeous face, there's only one answer. His lips swollen and red from our kisses, his eyes hooded and cheeks flushed. I know that no matter what happens after this, all the pain I will inevitably feel when he leaves, I can't say no. I want this. I want him. I won't regret it.

"Yes." I kiss a trail up his neck, pulling him back to me. My tongue and lips playfully tease his soft skin. His short beard rubs deliciously against my cheek, and his grip on me grows tighter as he loses more of his tightly wound control.

I reach his ear and whisper, "Fuck me, Stellan. Please."

He emits a wild growl as he marches us to the bedroom and flings me down onto the bed. Towering over me, Stellan reaches behind him and pulls his shirt off over his head in one smooth motion.

My breath catches as I take in his broad shoulders and strong chest tapering down into abs that seem to go on forever. His skin is mouthwatering and smooth with the perfect dusting of hair on his chest and leading down into his jeans. Stellan is a Greek statue come to life, and I'm going to savor every single second that he's mine to touch.

He doesn't stop me this time when I reach back to unhook my bra. I fling it off and sit up on the edge of the bed. Stellan's eyes are wide and fixed firmly on my chest. He mutters something to himself in his native language and licks his bottom lip. Leaning over me, he palms my breasts with both hands while he devours my mouth in another scorching kiss.

Reaching for the button on his jeans, my knuckles brush against the hot skin of his stomach. I break away from his lips and kiss a trail down his chest, licking and tasting as I go.

Stellan grips my shoulders. My eyes flick up to meet his, and I slowly unbutton his jeans. A primal part of me wants to make him lose control. I want him crazy with lust and to know that I'm the one driving him over the edge.

"Is this OK?" I ask, needing to be sure.

Stellan swallows hard and nods. "More than OK." His voice is strained and his eyes darken.

I kneel down on the floor in front of him. He gazes down at me with an awed expression and runs a hand over my hair and down my cheek. His thumb plays with my bottom lip, and my tongue flicks out to taste him. He releases a shuddered breath.

I pull his jeans down over his hips and take out his rigid cock. I run my hand along the thick shaft and watch his eyes glaze over as I lick the underside, swirling my tongue over the tip.

Stellan hisses through his teeth. Emboldened by the sound, I take him fully into my mouth, pulling him all the way to the back of my throat until I gag. I repeat the motion, laving the tip with my tongue as I go.

"Fuck, Willa. You are so fucking pretty on your knees for me."

His control slipping further, he fists my hair and thrusts. Gently at first and then steadily deepening the movement as he loses himself to my hot, wet mouth. I take him even deeper into my throat, his growls and praise ignite a new fire in me. A fire I've never experienced before that burns inside my veins as my magic pulses in a hypnotic rhythm inside my chest.

I gyrate and squirm, seeking friction and a release from the budding ache between my thighs. Stellan catches the movement and with blazing eyes lifts me off my knees and pushes me onto the bed. He makes swift work of his jeans and pulls my leggings and panties off in one sharp tug.

Stellan stands above me, his eyes trailing over every inch of me as I lay fully exposed before him.

"So beautiful," he rasps in a harsh whisper. His fingers trail up my thighs as he leans over me. So close to where I need him and yet not close enough.

"Are you wet for me, darling?"

"Why don't you find out?" I ask in a sultry voice I don't recognize. I am never this bold.

My back arches when he finally touches me with his warm, rough hands exactly where I ache the most. He teases my soaking wet pussy making my legs tremble and my heart race.

"I can't wait. I need to feel you, Willa." There's desperation in his voice that mirrors my own. He grabs a condom from his travel bag and slides it on his long, hard cock.

Settling between my open thighs, he aligns himself with my wet heat. I whimper unintelligibly, lost in the storm we're brewing together and the sweet anticipation of what's to come. As he slowly sinks into me, his blue eyes meet mine, and the depth I find there steals the breath from my lungs.

A low moan is wrenched from my throat when he's fully

seated inside me. The intensity and the relief. The burning fullness and the beautiful connection.

"You feel so good. So fucking perfect." He whispers encouraging words while I adjust to his size.

I suck in a ragged breath as he begins to move. Nothing has ever come close to this. With every powerful thrust, he ruins me for anyone else. The onslaught of sensation is more than I can contain, and a few errant tears leak down my face from the sheer, overwhelming pleasure.

I hook my ankles around him and claw at his muscular back, desperate to find something to ground me. But caged in his massive arms, all I can do is take what he gives me, thrusting into me with powerful strokes that shake the cottage walls.

My blood is liquid fire, and the heat coils tighter and tighter. I lose sense of time and space as he hits places inside me I didn't know were there. Stellan grips my hips with feral hands, his breath growing harsh and erratic.

"That's it, Willa. Come for me."

His thrusts match the tempo of my cries as I follow his command and explode. The orgasm tears through me in waves of intense pleasure that flow out like an electrical current. I struggle to breathe, my mind blanks. My body trembles and shakes as Stellan draws up tighter and with two more powerful thrusts stills inside me, groaning out my name along with his own release.

Mindless, liquid, and dazed. Breathing heavily, I trail my hands softly along Stellan's back. He sighs in contentment, his breath tickling my neck.

Stellan frames my face between his forearms and kisses my cheeks and my eyes and my forehead, doting and reverent. Eventually, he gets up and disposes of the condom and comes back with a glass of water and hands it to me to drink.

We don't speak, but he bundles me up in his arms and

holds me against him, his hands playing a delicate pattern over my bare skin. More of his sweet kisses dot my hair and face. A million thoughts and conflicting emotions run through my head as we hold each other in the afternoon light.

But one thing is abundantly clear, there is no way I'm getting out of this with my heart in one piece.

CHAPTER 24

WILLA

"So, where did you go to school?"

It's our third morning waking up and sharing breakfast nestled into armchairs in the living room by the fire. Stellan and I are falling into a steady rhythm of pretending we are two normal people getting to know each other.

I read and work on a new sweater, and he types for hours at a time on his laptop and occasionally takes private phone calls. I have no idea what he's doing, and I'm not in a position to ask.

In between, we cook together and take walks around the lake. Stellan shows me more methods for controlling my magic, and we have mind-blowing sex on every available surface inside the cottage and occasionally outside of it.

In the back of my mind, the awareness that we're on borrowed time is never far away. I don't know how long this will last, but I know it's not a forever situation.

We both seem afraid to bring up certain topics. Topics

that might lead us to the inevitable conversation about what happens next and when he plans to leave.

Whatever the conclusion, it won't be with us riding off into the sunset together. He'll go back to hunting criminals, and I'll have to figure out what my life looks like now that I'm a Mage. My unfulfilling library job is not a long-term option anymore, but I'm not ready to think about any of that right now.

"Well, as you can probably tell, I went to school in England," he says, answering my question.

"Yes, I assumed that with the accent."

He smiles. "When I was 12, it was confirmed that I'm one of the *fortis magicae,* and I was sent to a school called Darlings Academy. Before you bother, you'll never discover anything about it. It's a Mage-run school outside London, and only children with exceptional power are welcome to study there."

He must see the look of amused curiosity on my face because he adds, "It's nothing like fucking Hogwarts so don't even ask."

"Fair enough." I can't hide my smile. "Do you think my father went to Darlings Academy or a place like it?"

"I know for a fact that he did. Just about all the *fortis magicae* children in Europe have attended Darlings. Since magic is generally hereditary, it's relatively easy to keep track of which children will grow into greater power.

"It is becoming more common for magic to remain dormant in a family line and suddenly appear. A subsection of my organization is dedicated to tracking down these individuals and helping them adjust to their new life.

"It is highly unusual that someone like you, a descendant of an incredibly powerful bloodline, is unfamiliar with their power or the potential for it. You are a bit of an anomaly."

What would life have been like if my father had stayed?

Would I have attended a school like Darlings? Would I have been primed for a position in this Agency or something more sinister? I can't say, and it doesn't really matter. I can't change the past or control the choices that were not mine to make.

"Do other people in your family have enhanced abilities?" I ask instead.

"Yes, my father. He went to Darlings. My older sister has some as well, but they are subtle. They've made her an incredible doctor, but she's lucky enough to live a normal life."

I don't miss the wistful expression on his face when he says it. I wonder if he secretly desires a normal life. "Do you have any other siblings?" I ask. He referred to his sister as "older" so maybe he has others.

"I did," he replies with hesitation. "It's not something I talk about." It's impossible to miss the dismissal and the frost that now blankets the room.

"Stellan, I didn't…"

"I'm just going to wash these up." He stands and takes his dishes to the kitchen.

I sit for a moment not sure how to proceed. Something terrible must have occurred in his past and my question expectedly brought it to the surface.

I follow Stellan into the kitchen and find him at the sink washing our breakfast dishes. I wrap my arms around his waist from behind. He leans into my embrace enough for me to know he welcomes it.

"I'm sorry. I didn't mean to pry. I'm just curious about your life and how it's different from mine."

He shuts off the water in the sink and turns to face me. I take a step back, but he puts his arms around me, keeping me close.

"No, I'm sorry, Willa. I should have anticipated your very

innocent question, but it took me by surprise." His eyes are full of remorse.

"It's alright. You can't always control what triggers you. In the same way you can't always know what might hurt some-one. You don't have to tell me anything, but I'm sorry. For asking. For your pain."

"Thank you. You are a remarkable woman, Willa Martin. I hope you know that."

Stellan leans down, gently smoothing his thumbs across my face. My breath slows as I take in the scent of his magic and the warmth of his hands on me. He lays gentle kisses on my nose and forehead. My eyelids and cheeks. As if he's memorizing my features with his lips.

He kisses down my throat and over my chest, pushing the top of my nightdress to the side for access to more skin. He lets the fabric spring back and kisses over my breasts on top of my clothes before kneeling down in front of me. He kisses my stomach and slowly trails his hands up my legs, gathering up my dress. My knees threaten to buckle.

Stellan inhales, breathing in my magic, and sighs before pulling down my panties, exposing me to him fully.

He dips his head between the juncture of my thighs and kisses up my legs and across the curve of my stomach before laying a gentle kiss on my already soaked pussy.

"I'm becoming addicted to the taste of you," he purrs against my skin. "It's like sin and salvation, and I can't get enough."

Stellan swirls his tongue expertly over my clit, and I moan as my knees finally give out. Stellan catches me and laughs in a deep rumble against my heated flesh, sending vibrations all over me.

He scoops me up like I weigh nothing and carries me to the living room, laying me down on the couch. Kneeling in front of me, he parts my thighs and feasts on me.

I arch against him, my chest heaving and my body shaking. He dips two fingers deep inside me and curls them up, pressing against the spot that makes my eyes roll back in my head. He teases in and out in a gentle rhythm that builds and swells my desire. My legs tremble against his shoulders as he worships me with his mouth and his hands, bringing me closer to the point of no return.

The glorious and electric frenzy of his touch continues until I break open. My body tenses and shivers as ecstasy ripples through me. My back lifts off the couch, and I grip Stellan's hair and press him into me as he slows his movements and wrings out every last drop of pleasure.

"Fuck, that was amazing." I'm breathless and shaking.

Stellan laughs, "Oh, *älskling*, we are far from finished."

I have no idea what he just called me and no time to question it as he lifts me to standing on unsteady legs and drags me by the hand to the bedroom.

* * *

"WE SHOULD GET DRESSED. I have some calls to make, and then perhaps we can go for a walk?" Stellan gets out of bed and starts putting on his clothes.

I'm naked with my hair spilling out of my braid and my cheeks flushed from exertion. "Sure, that sounds nice."

"You are so gorgeous just like this." He leans down to kiss me sweetly. The wistful expression on his face is back, but he doesn't say more.

I dress in leggings with thick wooly socks and another oversized sweater. It's especially cold today, and it finally snowed overnight so there are a few inches of powder coating the ground.

Stellan is already outside on the phone when I come out of the bedroom. I think about checking my work email or maybe calling Sam or my mom again when I notice we're out of wood.

I lace up my boots and don't bother with a coat since I'm not going far. The woodshed is out behind the cottage, and I crunch my way through the newly fallen snow. It's a dark gray morning, and I hope it means more snow is on the way to ease us out of late autumn and fully embrace all the beauty a Vermont winter has to offer.

Grabbing a handful of logs out of the woodshed, I trudge across the frozen earth back toward the cottage. Stellan is in a conversation around the corner near the car. I'm not trying to listen, but I hear my name and I pause.

I peek around the building, and Stellan comes into view. He's on a video call with his back to me, talking to a distinguished looking older man with a Scandinavian accent I can't quite place. Norwegian maybe. I hear the man ask, "How are things progressing?"

"Very well," Stellan replies cooly. "The asset is only moderately powerful, like I said, and I still don't believe we would benefit from her relocation."

The man cuts him off. "We have been over this, Lundqvist. She is a Winter Mage, and with her bloodline, this is the only option. The other Directors are growing impatient."

"Yes, sir." Stellan's voice is so flat and emotionless, I almost don't recognize him. I should back away, but I can't. Not when they're talking about me like this. Like I'm just some resource to be managed.

The man continues in a clipped tone, "I don't care how you do it. Have you charmed her? When we last spoke, I said you could fuck her if you had to. She needs to be brought in for testing and evaluation, and we can't risk her father getting to her first."

Oh, my God.

I'm dizzy, the world tilting on its axis. I couldn't have heard that. It's not possible. I've always known this time with Stellan wasn't destined for long, but I was foolish enough to believe it was something real. Something precious.

"No need to worry. I have her well in hand. I'll make the arrangements for relocation this afternoon." He clicks off the phone and hangs his head, sighing in frustration.

My heart hammers wildly.

How could he do this? *How could I have been so stupid?*

"You bastard!" I shout and throw all the wood I'm holding on the ground in a great, loud tumble. Stellan whips around and registers me standing there. He knows I just heard all of it. His face is a mask of horror.

"Fuck, Willa! What the hell are you doing out here?" His voice is angry and accusatory, like it's my fault for over-hearing him.

"What am I doing here? I was getting firewood. What the fuck does it look like I'm doing?!" I shout back at him.

"Willa, what you just heard..."

"Save it, Stellan." I cut him off. "I should have known." My voice starts to break. I swallow down the lump in my throat. "I should have known a man like you would never..." I can't even finish it. I don't want to give him the satisfaction of watching me cry over this.

He steps closer to me. "Willa, I..."

"Stay away from me." I take a step back. "I mean it. Don't touch me." He keeps stepping closer like he wants to reach for me and pull me into his arms. As though he still has the right.

"Don't do this," he says. His voice is hard and cold. "You know as well as I do that what was happening between us was never something I could..." He stops himself and rakes frustrated hands through his hair before coming even closer. I swear he sounds sad and desperate, but I can no longer trust my instincts around this man. He reaches out to grab my shoulders, and I lose it.

"I said don't fucking touch me!" I push out with my hands, and a blast of benign energy shoots out and knocks Stellan onto his back. He calls after me, but I'm already running. I run as fast as my legs can carry me. I don't care that I'm not dressed for the weather. It doesn't matter that it's cold, that the air stings my cheeks and burns my lungs. I need as much distance between us as possible.

I need to be where no one can see me when I break apart.

CHAPTER 25

WILLA

I sprint along the road and away from the cottage. My breath rises as steam in the cold air. I stop when I reach the clearing in the forest. The brook winding through it peppered with ice-covered rocks. The air is bitter, but I welcome how the cold numbs me. I throw myself onto a fallen log with tears paving a frozen trail down my face.

How did I let this happen? How could I have allowed myself to get so caught up in the fantasy that I didn't see what was so obvious? I didn't bother to stop and think that maybe it was too good to be true. Too perfect to be real.

He lied so expertly that I thought maybe he was falling for me just as I was for him. But no, his boss had told him to seduce me. They need me agreeable so I'll do whatever they ask.

I am so monumentally stupid.

If I hadn't overheard them talking, how long would it have taken to find out the truth? Would I have ever known? When we got on the plane would he have said he was sorry and it wasn't me it was him? That it was just a bit of fun while it lasted, and now he had to focus on the job? Even with all my pride, I would have followed Stellan anywhere. I would have bought any lie.

Now it seems I have no choice but to go anyway. I have to be brought before this Agency and answer for the sin of being born to the wrong father.

I'm lost in bitter thoughts when I register the sound of footsteps approaching. I turn, expecting to find Stellan, but instead three burly men in black coats step out of the woods.

I wipe away my tears and stand up slowly, keeping my eyes on them. They're the same men that attacked me and Sam in Burlington and a shiver runs over my freezing skin. The largest man, the one I recognize as Hank, steps toward me.

He motions for the other two men to flank me. They're giving me fewer options to flee. My pulse races, and my magic surges up angrily in my chest.

"Ah, Ms. Martin," Hank says in his heavy South London accent. "So nice to see ya again."

"Wish I could say the same. What do you want?"

"Like we said before, the boys and me are here to take ya to a little family reunion. I thought we'd have our work cut out for us with yer big boyfriend, but ya made it so easy out here on yer own. Haven't ya, luv?"

Hank has an impressive scar running down the side of his face. His giant arms strain against the black leather of his coat, a little woolen hat sits askew on his bald head.

"This is my only warning: you need to stay away from me. You do not want to mess with me right now."

My magic is in tune with my emotions, and it's already agitated. It's becoming harder to control it as it rises up to protect me against a clear threat.

It's almost funny that my anxiety is sky-high when people

watch me talk about books, but when real predators have their eyes on me, everything comes into sharp focus. I'm not anxious. I'm pissed. They picked the wrong moment to find me alone.

"We have our orders, sweetheart. Take ya to Uncle Mikkel alive. But nobody said anything about the state ya have to be in when ya get there."

He pulls a knife out of an inner coat pocket and brandishes it at me. "Let's not make this difficult, lovely."

The man on Hank's right grabs his dick with a suggestive tug and winks at me. The other men laugh, as I shudder in fear and disgust.

"Stay back," I shout and hold up my hands.

The scent of ozone and electricity builds in the air around us and thunder rumbles in the distance overhead. They refuse to listen and draw closer. I'm breathing hard against the force of my magic trying to free itself.

Hank lunges for me, and my freezing-cold body isn't fast enough. He grabs hold and spins me around so my back is against his chest. I struggle in his grasp, but he's too big, too strong. His beefy fingers grip my neck. His breath is a disgusting warmth against my cheek.

"I told ya not to make this difficult." With no other warning, he slices across the top of my arm with his knife. I look down in horror at the tear in my sweater and the blood pooling on my skin as it runs out of a long, deep gash in my arm.

"LET ME GO, YOU BIG ASSHOLE!" I scream and fight for freedom. He just squeezes me tighter. I'm numb from the cold, but the physical pain sharpens my other senses.

I take a deep breath, gathering the thunderstorm, letting it build up inside me and all around me. I inhale another deep breath, expanding my lungs, filling me with power.

The men in front of me pause. "Oy, Boss. There's something weird happening."

I breathe vast amounts of air and energy in and out. I've never given my magic full freedom or allowed it to push boundaries the way I do now. My body shakes with terrible intensity, and Hank releases me. The men all back away like skittish animals.

I lift my arms open, concentrating the brewing storm into one location. I exhale sharply at the same time I bring my hands together and push them out, unleashing all my magic in one massive explosion.

Lightning flashes and strikes the ground with a deafening crack. All three men are thrown backwards.

I stagger, breathing hard. The sizzle of electricity coming off their bodies is sickening, and I fight back the nausea at what I know I have done.

My knees buckle, and I sink to the ground. I'm so tired. So cold.

The deep cut on my arm throbs in sharp bursts. I fall onto my back, and the last thing I see before my eyes go dark is my blood painting the snow crimson.

* * *

"I NEED backup at the cottage immediately. Three bodies. Two code blue. One alive, but barely. I have the target in my custody. Just get here now."

I float in and out of consciousness. Numb to my surroundings. I think I hear orders being issued and new voices heavy with concern and white-hot anger. I'm lifted off the ground and carried against a warm chest. I wake briefly, surrounded by an incredible heat, shaking uncontrollably.

I hear someone whisper soothing things to me as I shake

and my teeth chatter. My eyes won't open, and there is no way to be certain what is real and what is a dream.

"You're safe, Willa. You're safe now." I hear Stellan's voice clear as day, and the scent of his magic surrounds me. How easy it would be to give in to the comfort. To allow him to care for me and pretend the phone call and what happened after was just some horrible dream.

But I can't do that.

"Please...please go, Stellan. I can't..." I manage to whisper before I fall under completely.

PART II

STOCKHOLM

CHAPTER 26

THE FOREST IS UNFAMILIAR. Dense coniferous trees tower overhead, and shrub brush covered in deep snow litter the ground. I'm wearing a familiar long cloak in a blue like the morning sky with a fur-lined hood. It keeps out the cold, but the harsh, salty wind bites my nose and stings my eyes. I'm trapped in an endless expanse of darkness lit only by starlight.

The sound of footsteps in the undergrowth draws my attention. Crunching snow. Snapping twigs. The silhouettes of three men all in black come into view. Their eyes glowing red in the darkness. The men are eerily silent except their footfalls, which grow closer through the dense brush. The largest of the men steps closer and I catch the outline of a thin scar along his face. His eyes drip with something viscous and dark against his deathly pale face.

I'm struck dumb with panic. They found me. I want to scream but nothing comes out. I turn hard and run.

My feet are covered in heavy boots lined with fur and I

stomp clumsily through the thick snow. I trip over bushes and mossy rocks coated in ice.

I run and run until my lungs burn and my legs ache. I can't let them catch me. A faint light in the distance appears and grows steadily as I approach.

The trees open to reveal a towering building. Built like an industrial fortress with walls made of steel and glass, the building lights up the darkness around me. There must be magic keeping it hidden as it was nothing but a faint light one minute and then looming in front of me the next.

A door opens revealing a tall man with long blonde hair and familiar blue eyes.

I slow my running to a cautious walk, breathing hard.

The man pushes the door wider and greets me with open arms.

"Welcome home, my dearest daughter."

* * *

WHEN I WAKE in the darkness, the first thing I notice is that the birds are all wrong. The group of ravens that reside in the trees by my apartment don't sound anything like this. It's too loud, and the call is almost like laughter. I've never heard a bird make that sound before.

The air is wrong, too. It smells faintly like cinnamon with the musky scent of old stones and salty water.

A gap in the curtain lets in a sliver of moonlight. I'm in a bedroom. But where?

"You're awake! Excellent!" A woman with a French accent calls from the doorway to my right.

A crystal chandelier switches on over my head. My eyes sting in the sudden light. The bed has a brilliant white duvet, and I'm wearing what looks like very expensive satin pajamas. The room is mostly white with an accent wall of floral wallpaper behind the bed and art hung up everywhere like a gallery.

"What the hell?!"

The beautiful woman I saw with Stellan what feels like a decade ago stalks closer to the bed. Greta, he had said.

She's uncommonly pretty with deep brown eyes and striking features.

"My apologies, Ms. Martin," she says with a smile. "I wanted to wake you sooner, but my orders were to let you sleep."

She puts her hand on my shoulder, and I catch the scent of tropical flowers and a sunny beach.

"Welcome to Stockholm."

What...

"Stockholm? What time is it? What day is it? How...how did I get here?" I admit that perhaps my tone isn't friendly, but honestly...

Stockholm. That's like 4,000 miles away from home.

The woman laughs. "You have been unconscious for about 12 hours, and in that time, you were transported to Sweden. You have a meeting with the Directors at 0900 hours, and I am to take you to Headquarters along with Banks, whose snores you may just hear in the next room."

A faint snoring sound reaches my ears. I shake my head and rub my temples. This is hard to wrap my mind around.

"I'm Greta Adamu. It is delightful to finally meet you," she says cheerfully.

I try to return her smile, though I'm certain it doesn't reach my eyes.

"I'm going to leave you with something to eat, and then you can get yourself ready for the day. I have a set of clothes for you in the bathroom. I'm positive they will fit. We will leave for Headquarters in an hour."

Greta starts toward the door, but reality hits me like a sledgehammer, making my head spin and my heart race.

"Greta, wait," I call after her. "My mother? Does she know I'm here? I'll need to tell her or she'll worry. And my job? I can't just leave the country without letting them know."

"All of that has been taken care of," she explains like it's obvious. "Your mother is very well and understands the situation. She said she will check in with Sam Henderson and Tim Hawkins periodically and asked me to tell you that you need to worry about her less. Your boss gave you a leave of absence. Everything is in order."

"Uh, thank you. I think? I would still feel better if I could speak with her myself."

Greta smiles warmly again. "I understand. My colleague is setting up a phone for your use. It will be ready later in the day." I nod woodenly, and she returns to what must be the living space of this very well decorated apartment.

This is so messed up.

I flop back onto the bed and stare at the chandelier, the light refracting through the crystal in pretty patterns on the ceiling. I have a lot of questions, and I'm pretty sure I killed at least two people yesterday.

That alone is enough to devastate me, but I also lost consciousness and was somehow taken to a foreign country. I heard Stellan say they needed to "relocate" me, but I didn't expect it to happen so abruptly and without my consent.

I sit up and undo the knot on my bun and let my heavy hair fall down with a sigh. I run my fingers through it before throwing the covers off the bed.

The biggest question is how much therapy I'm going to need when I finally get home. Because what the actual fuck is happening to my life?

I find the food Greta left. I drink what feels like a gallon of water and eat a little of a cinnamon bun and some fruit.

My stomach is in knots, but I'll regret it if I don't at least try to eat something. The last thing I want to do is pass out again. Who knows where I'd end up next, Finland?

I feel surprisingly well rested and not too weak or shaky the way I might expect after such an ordeal. I run a finger over the cut on my arm only to find it's nothing but a thin scar. Stellan probably healed it after he picked me up out of the snow.

The thought makes my heart ache, and I squeeze my eyes closed to stop the tears from falling.

I hate how I came to have this scar and everything that happened leading up to it. But all the same, I welcome the little white line across my bicep. A permanent reminder to always be more careful.

I pad along the trendy area rugs leading into the world's fanciest bathroom. It's all white tiles with black accents, a giant clawfoot bathtub and one of those showers that makes you feel like you're in a hot rainstorm.

There's a brief moment after I shower when I think that maybe not everything is terrible, but then I find the clothes Greta left out for me.

She's correct; they fit to perfection. However, it's like playing dress up as a CEO. Everything is tailored and stiff. I have on a tight, charcoal gray pencil skirt in a thin wool and a white blouse.

Even the nude undergarments feel executive. Greta also provided a pair of black heels in exactly my size with a wool blazer that matches my skirt.

I've never worn anything so professional in my life, and it feels fraudulent. The woman looking back at me in the mirror is a version of myself I barely recognize.

The only consolation is that I look like a stone-cold fox.

I'm not sure if it's just a trick of the light, but my cheeks and lips are rosy and my dark blue eyes sparkle like sapphires against my dewy skin. I twist my hair up in a clip I find in the vanity and set out to meet my fate.

My fate turns out to be a comically large man in a black suit. Banks is waiting for me in a high-backed chair in the living room, but it's dwarfed by his impressive stature and massive shoulders.

Banks has a way about him that exudes confidence. Maybe it's the tattoos that peek out of his sleeves and onto his fingers, or the hard lines of his face and the dark set of his green eyes. He leaves no doubt that he chews up smaller men for breakfast and knows exactly how to make a woman scream his name in ecstasy. And yet for some reason, I don't find him intimidating.

I mean, I do. I'd be a fool not to, but there's also something about Banks that makes me feel safe.

"Morning, Banks. Where's Greta?"

"Agent Adamu was called into Headquarters early," Banks says gruffly. "I will be accompanying you to the office." His face is hard, and his eyes narrow on me. He's the same man I met in Vermont, but he's different in this environment. Somehow more serious and more official.

"Alright," I say. "I guess I'm ready to go then."

I swallow down my nerves, but Banks zeroes in on my shaking fingers.

His expression shifts completely, turning softer and kind. He reaches for me with one of his large, tattooed hands and holds both of mine gently. It spreads warmth up my arms, and I breath in a deep deciduous forest scent. It's like mosses and leaves covered in mist. His magic is serene and beautiful. It's unexpected for a man who exudes such natural dominance.

"I'm here to watch out for you," he promises. "While you are with me, you will be protected. Do you understand?"

I nod and choke back the tears that threaten to spill. I

refuse to cry. Because if I start, I'm not sure I'll ever be able to stop.

* * *

BANKS ESCORTS me out of the old building and onto a quiet, cobblestoned street. He tells me this is where distinguished visitors stay when they're in town. We approach a black SUV where a driver and an armed guard are waiting for us. Banks sits in the back next to me, and the man with the gun sits next to the driver.

I've never been this close to such a powerful weapon, and I'm frightened into silence as we move through the city in the dark. I take in the lights of the city as it wakes to a new day, not registering much of what I see.

The car stops in front of a series of ornate neoclassical stone buildings. The sound of water lapping against stones comes from the Stockholm harbor behind us where the lights from boats going about their business twinkle in the distance.

Banks takes my arm as I exit the car, and we enter a drab and unimpressive lobby where an attendant sits behind a small desk. The woman smiles at Banks as he scans his badge against a keypad on the back wall. After a series of beeps, a doorway opens into a long hallway.

We walk for several minutes until we reach another panel where Banks holds his palm against a biometric access scanner. The wall slides to the right and a second, far more elegant reception area comes into view. A large crest hangs on the wall over a tall desk where several attendants sit working.

Greta exits an elevator at the back and comes over to greet us as we move through the security checkpoint. I'm patted down and thoroughly prodded with a metal detector and several other unknown sensors by three different security personnel. I adjust my skirt back in place and try to remain calm. *Keep breathing*, I tell myself. *Just keep fucking breathing.*

"Welcome to Headquarters," she says with a kind smile as she approaches us. "I'll take you upstairs and introduce you to everyone. Your meeting with Director Hawley and Director Olsen is in 45 minutes."

"OK, sounds good," I say with a forced smile.

Actually, it doesn't sound good at all. In fact, it sounds horrible, and I want to run away and never look back, lighting the whole place on fire as I flee. But I know there's no hope for escape. The man at my back silently carrying a military-grade weapon isn't just here for my protection. He's here to make certain I know I'm at their mercy. That the only reason I'm alive and walking around is because they're allowing it.

We enter a glass elevator with Banks and Greta on either side of me and slowly make our ascent to the 25th floor. I catch our reflection in the glass. I'm surrounded by two of the most awe-inspiring people I've ever met and a man with an automatic rifle.

All my life I've run or shied away when faced with confrontation and conflict. I ran when I found Nick in bed with Jessa. I ran when I caught Stellan in his lie. I never once stood up to Dr. Edwards when he belittled me, and I have to admit I've used my mother as a convenient excuse to avoid taking risks or making changes.

Being in this elevator is the most trapped I've ever felt and yet it's also the most liberated.

With all the control taken from me, my choices are limited to crumbling in panic or facing it head on.

I watch my reflection as it hardens in resolve. Whether I'm ready or not, the time for running is over.

CHAPTER 27

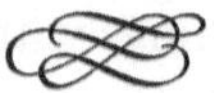

WILLA

WE EXIT THE ELEVATOR, and Greta leads us to an open-plan office area with high-tech workstations and several glassed-in conference rooms. Private offices with ultramodern furniture line the opposite end of the space.

Agency personnel crane around their computers and stand up from their chairs as we walk through. Some try to be subtle about it, but mostly they just openly gawk. I wonder what they've heard about me. Based on their faces, it doesn't seem overly positive.

We stop in the back by the private offices. A tall man in a dark gray suit is talking to a thin woman in a black pencil skirt and a dark green silk blouse. She's at least 5'10" with perfect blonde barrel curls that fall down around her shoulders. I can't see her face, but I'd bet anything she's drop-dead gorgeous.

The tall man peers around her when he spots us. He is so handsome that I actually gasp out loud, and Greta makes a groaning noise as if she expected it. The man has an angular face with a chiseled jawline and high cheekbones. His full lips are made for sin, and his honey-colored eyes match his wavy, dark blonde hair. It's cut short at the sides and longer on top, so it flops around rakishly. He exudes a sensuality I have never witnessed in another human being. I blush just looking at him.

Seriously, does this Agency only hire models?

The handsome man smiles so genuinely that my nerves melt away for a brief moment. At least until the woman whips around and pierces me with a glare so sharp it stings. She has a cold, cruel face like an evil stepsister. She's undeniably beautiful with hazel eyes and red painted lips, but she's completely devoid of warmth.

She crosses her arms and scowls as if daring me to step closer. Unfortunately for her, I left all my patience back in Vermont, so I scowl right back.

The tall man notices our stare-down, and with a slight roll of his eyes steps forward to greet me.

"*Hej*! You must be Willa Martin. I am thrilled to finally meet you." He has another hybrid British-Swedish accent, though there is a haughtier edge to it than Stellan's. "I'm Soren Westerholm."

I pick up the scent of rich spices and sandalwood as he moves closer.

"Hi. Yes, I'm Willa. It's really nice to meet you, too." He smiles at me, showing off his perfect teeth, and I can't help but smile back. So, this is the good friend Stellan was talking about.

My smile falters at the memory of us laughing in the car that day.

Nope, I am not going there.

"Oh, you are quite the little beauty," he goes on. "I can see why Lundqvist..."

"Ms. Martin, allow me to introduce you to our team,"

Greta interrupts with a disapproving glare at Soren. "Soren is the technical, if not tactful, brains of our operation. He leads our research department. You've obviously met Banks. He's our security specialist. I work in human intelligence and conflict resolution. And this is Ingrid Davis. She is a senior intelligence analyst."

"It's a pleasure to meet you," I tell Ingrid with no inflection.

It is definitely not a pleasure.

"Likewise," Ingrid says in an American accent that surprises me. She doesn't come any closer, and she doesn't make eye contact. She just turns on her heels and goes back to her office.

OK, then.

"Banks will take you to your meeting with the Directors momentarily. Perhaps you have questions for us?" Greta asks, drawing my attention away from Ingrid.

I laugh humorlessly. "I have more questions than you can possibly imagine. But who exactly am I meeting and why seems like a decent place to start."

I cross my arms over my chest.

Greta purses her lips a little in annoyance, but it's Soren's indignant scoff that surprises me.

"You cannot be serious?" he asks. "She's about to meet with the Director of the Northern European Office and the Director of the entire European Division, and she hasn't been briefed?"

Greta glowers at Soren. "You know none of this has gone to plan. You'll have to take it up with Agent Lundqvist. I'm just following orders."

"Oh, I intend to. This is ludicrous," he says and rakes a hand through his hair. "Ms. Martin, please accept my apology on behalf of our team." His jaw is set in frustration, but his eyes are kind.

"You are about to meet with two very high-level Agency Directors. I have not been privy to the agenda of your meeting, but I expect it will establish the baseline of your involvement going forward. I wish I could provide you with something more concrete to ease your mind."

"Honestly, I appreciate you telling me anything."

The sadness that comes through my voice is more than apparent. There is one person who could have told me these things and should be here with me, but he's conspicuously missing.

As if sensing my inner turmoil, Banks steps closer and gently takes me by the arm. "Alright, Ms. Martin. It's time to go."

* * *

THE ARMED GUARD follows me and Banks up the elevator to the 27th floor where I'm escorted into a conference room with black leather chairs surrounding an ornate wooden table. From the portraits of powerful figures on the walls to the harsh lines and dark wood accents, everything about this room is meant to impress and intimidate. Meetings in Dr. Edwards's office were a spa day in comparison.

"Willa, you are going to be just fine," Banks attempts to reassure me. But it's pretty clear from his expression that "just fine" is a bit of a stretch. He motions for me to sit at the table facing the door.

The armed guard moves with me to stand behind my chair, which does nothing to ease my rising panic.

"I'll take you back to the hotel when the meeting is over."

Banks spares me one last glance and then leaves me on my own.

I inhale and exhale on a count of eight to slow my heart

rate. My hands still shake, but I think I might not vomit all over the table.

I silently curse Stellan for not preparing me for any of this. I wonder what would have happened if I hadn't overheard that phone call. How long would he have continued the charade? Would I find this new situation any easier if I didn't know all that came before it was a lie?

I have no idea. But I do know one thing for certain: I am an idiot, and it's going to take a long time to forgive myself.

The door opens and stops my thoughts from spiraling. I stand respectfully, smoothing my skirt and trying to smile. The first person through the door is a dignified older woman in a tweed blazer. She's short and a little round with long dark hair flecked with gray that she's twisted up in a bun. Her thick rimmed black glasses make her watery blue eyes seem impossibly large. She gives me a brief smile in return and sits at the head of the table.

The next person through the door is a man in an ill-fitting brown suit with cropped sandy brown hair that's graying on the sides. I recognize him as the man Stellan was speaking to the day everything went straight to hell. His face is stern, and I get the impression he's used to giving orders and not taking shit from anyone.

The last man comes through the door a moment later and sucks all the air out of the room. My heart stops and my face heats with all the emotion I'm struggling to control. A familiar and devastating rainwater scent assaults me as Stellan Lundqvist stands directly across the table refusing to meet my eyes.

CHAPTER 28

WILLA STARES at me with unblinking eyes. Her gaze like a brand against my skin. She's cataloging all the ways I've changed my appearance since she last saw me. My hair is cut short and my face clean-shaven. I'm in a tailored suit, and my shirt is pressed to perfection.

I'm back to the man I was before I met her.

But no, that's not quite right. That man is long gone.

I am the man she believes me to be. The one capable of hurting her to achieve my own goals.

She would be correct.

"Ms. Martin, it's very nice to meet you," Director Hawley says. She motions for Willa to sit. "Please be seated." Willa offers a polite smile, but hasn't found her voice yet.

"My name is Alice Hawley, and I am the Director of the European Division of the International Monitoring Agency, henceforth to be referred to as the IMA, or 'The Agency' when in conversation. The man to your left is Henrik Olsen, the Director of the Northern European Office. His focus is criminal investigations. I believe you are acquainted with Senior Special Agent Lundqvist. Do you have any questions for us before we begin?"

"Not at this time. Thank you," Willa says. Her eyes tell a different story as she flicks her gaze back to me. She has a lot of questions, but none of them can be answered at this meeting. Questions I can't and won't answer despite her desire for clarity.

"Excellent," Hawley continues and opens the folder in front of her. Willa's photograph is stapled to one side, and I catch Willa flinch as realization dawns on her.

Yes, all that time we spent together in your cottage, I was writing a report about you.

She swallows hard and clasps her hands together to mask the shaking. She's shielding herself from our magic, but I know her face. She's hurt, and she's furious.

Good. *Use that fury, darling. You'll need it.*

"To begin, we need to confirm that you have not had contact from your relations," Director Hawley goes on.

Willa clears her throat and answers after a furtive glance in my direction. "Apart from the initial contact with the book and then the two failed kidnap attempts by men working for my uncle, I have not seen or heard from my relatives."

I note she doesn't mention the most recent dream. I intentionally left it out of my report, and I wonder if she suspects the severe repercussions of sharing that information in this room.

"You will alert us if you have any contact. Is that understood?" Director Hawley's tone leaves no room for argument. Willa agrees.

"Ms. Martin," Director Olsen interrupts as if he can't wait a second longer to berate her. "Are you aware that you killed three men in what you call a 'failed kidnap attempt'?" His voice is accusatory and full of disdain.

I have had my work cut out for me the last 24 hours. Olsen wants her locked up, but I've held him off for now.

"I suspected," she says. Her sadness over what she had to do is clear to me, but her chin remains raised and her face impassive. She's refusing to show Olsen any weakness.

"Is that all you have to say for yourself? You used extremely powerful and unauthorized magic resulting in the death of three individuals. Do you have any idea..."

"Director Olsen," I interrupt. "We have gone over my report of the incident in question. You are aware that it was determined to have occurred in self-defense. Ms. Martin was protecting herself, and as you know that falls under Section 1.3.5 as a legal use of power."

I speak with authority and composure though I'm raging inside. Director Olsen huffs but doesn't say more.

"Thank you, Agent Lundqvist," Director Hawley speaks serenely. "I am in agreement that Ms. Martin acted in accordance with our laws and that she does not deserve punishment for protecting herself from mercenaries intent on causing her harm."

Willa's face remains stony, but her eyes are alert and surprised. She is unaware of how close she's come to a prison cell.

Olsen's magic whispers across the table toward Willa. He assumes I can't sense him, but he's not nearly as subtle as he thinks he is. Willa tenses as the scent of cold air and damp autumn leaves greets her. I watch as her jaw sets and her eyes narrow. If he's trying to break into her mind, he has his work cut out for him. His scowl deepens as he realizes she's not the easy target he assumed.

"That being said, I do have reasonable cause for concern," Director Hawley continues. I shift higher in my seat, and Willa stops breathing as she waits for the other shoe to drop. "You are gifted, Ms. Martin, and while that is to be celebrated, with your bloodline and recent history, we are recommending that you be detained for testing and evaluation until we are certain you are not a harm to yourself and others."

This is not what we agreed to. "With all due respect, ma'am," I interrupt. "If you read pages 15-23 of my report you will find that my evaluation was thorough and I concluded that…"

"Enough of this, Lundqvist!" Director Olsen snaps. "She will report for testing, and that is the last I will hear on the matter. I have agreed to your terms on her accommodation, but I will not bend on anything else. She is dangerous, and as she is Lars Stromberg's eldest daughter, I am not convinced she shouldn't be in the secure facility. We will not discuss this further."

My fists clench, and my jaw snaps shut so tight my teeth ache. A lesser person would flinch at the look I give Olsen, but he just ignores me.

"Very well," I concede. "I will see to the arrangements."

"Excellent," Director Hawley says, her voice cold.

"We have a few ground rules that you must abide by, Ms. Martin," Director Olsen directs his attention back to Willa. "The first is that your abilities must not be used except in the evaluation rooms at Headquarters. You are not allowed to leave your rooms without authorization. You must be attended by Agency personnel at all times. Any failure to follow these rules will result in the harnessing of your magic and your immediate relocation to the secure facility. Do you understand?"

Willa's eyebrows lift in surprise before she regains her composure.

"Sure, that sounds great." She smiles in false sweetness. Olsen scowls. He doesn't trust her, and it seems the feeling is mutual.

There's a hint of a smile on Director Hawley's face as she watches the exchange. "I have several meetings to attend while I am in town. It was a pleasure, Ms. Martin. Agent Lundqvist, please keep us informed on your progress."

Olsen follows Hawley out the door without a spare glance at Willa and a curt nod to me.

Willa clasps her hands to her face and rubs her temples. Attempting to calm the raging storm inside her. The storm I had a major hand in causing.

"Willa, will you please say something?" I ask after too much time has lapsed in silence. The stern mask I wear around my superiors slips slightly.

She sits back in her chair and breathes in one deep breath. The disgust on her face is a dagger in the heart, but it's a look I deserve.

"How long am I stuck with GI Joe?" she asks and points to Eriksson behind her. He shifts uncomfortably at being addressed, but I catch the twitch of his jaw. He wants to smile, but he's too much of a professional to allow it.

I let out a humorless laugh of my own and shake my head. Of course she'd make a joke now.

"As of this moment, you are under my watch. We will keep you guarded when you travel between here and your hotel. However, while you are with me or another member of my team, armed reinforcements will not be necessary.

"I have to warn you, Willa. This is serious. As you've just seen, there are people here who want you locked up until we find your father. I have prevented that for now, but any unauthorized use of your magic will change things."

"I understand," she says with a frown. "They think I'm dangerous because I am dangerous."

"You are no more dangerous than me or anyone else here, Willa. They just fear the unknown, and you are very unknown."

"I'll be on my best behavior."

There is more I want to say, but I glance up at Eriksson. I trust him, but not with everything.

"I'll take you back to the office. Arrangements will be made for your evaluations tomorrow morning."

We travel in uncomfortable silence down the elevator and through the hallways. Soren is the first person to greet us when we return.

"So glad to see you on the other side," he says and squeezes Willa's shoulder. My eyes narrow.

"Thank you." She visibly relaxes as Soren's warm disposition soothes her.

I've never had the urge to kill my best friend, but with his hands on her, I'm close to the edge.

"Westerholm, why are you here? Don't you have CCTV footage to process?" I ask, short and irritated.

He shrugs. "I do, but I wanted to make sure our new arrival survived the meeting she was so ill prepared for." I can't miss the censure in his voice. "I also wanted to ask if she has plans for dinner." He says with a wink in Willa's direction.

"I'm not sure I'm allowed dinner plans on house arrest, but thank you for asking." She tries to make light, but apprehension tightens her face and shoulders.

"We could all go over to the hotel. What do you think, Lundqvist?"

"I am busy this evening," I reply curtly.

"Suit yourself," Soren says with another saucy wink at Willa. I breathe in and out through my nose like a bull. Soren shoots me a teasing grin.

Bastard. He's punishing me on purpose.

Banks approaches, and I latch onto the opportunity to refocus.

"Please take Willa back to the hotel and see that she's

settled. Tomorrow morning, one of us will bring her back here for evaluations."

As I'm finishing my instructions, Ingrid saunters up to us and places a hand possessively on my shoulder. I glance at Willa, her eyes locked on Ingrid's hand.

"May I help you, Agent Davis?"

"The security footage you requested is available," she says in a far more flirtatious voice than necessary for the kind of information she's relaying.

"Excellent, thank you," I respond stiffly. Ingrid flips her hair over her shoulder and licks her red lips seductively.

"If you don't have time now, we can always talk about it later over dinner," she says and looks me up and down like I'm her favorite dessert.

Willa inhales sharply. It's subtle, but I notice it. So does Ingrid, who smiles triumphantly. The two women face off in a silent battle. Willa refuses to lower her eyes or cower despite all the assumptions that must be running through her head. Assumptions I don't bother to correct. It's better if Willa hates me. It's no more than I deserve.

"Let's get you out of here, love," Banks speaks gently to Willa, picking up on the tension with a lingering glance at me.

"Yes, thank you," Willa says. "Enjoy your evening," she adds with only the barest hint of sarcasm.

Her head high, she lets Banks lead her to the elevator. If Ingrid notices the tension, she ignores it and stands in front of me, straightening my tie. The intimate and familiar gesture is the last thing Willa sees before the elevator door closes and she's lost from my sight.

CHAPTER 29

WILLA

THE SECOND BANKS closes the door to my suite, I collapse onto the floor in a flood of tears. I kick off my stupid black pumps and my horrible wool skirt with tears streaming down my face. I shed my shirt and crawl into bed in nothing but my ridiculous executive underwear.

I'm proud that I held it together for as long as I did. But with my restraint no longer necessary, I let go. I cry until my eyes are swollen. I slip under the covers and just let myself feel all of it.

At some point, I fall sleep.

When I wake up, I'm in a strange room. I appear to be in a distillery. It's mostly concrete and steel with four towering copper stills on one side and a work area on the other. It smells sharp like alcohol and herbs.

My uncle works quietly measuring quantities of liquids in glass vials. Holding them against the light, he pauses and writes down notes in a black book.

A door on the far side of the facility opens, and someone

with their back to me walks in. I can't make them out fully in the darkness, but their body language is that of deference and anxiety.

"Sir, you asked for me?"

"Yes, I did," Mikkel spins his chair away from his work to face the quivering man. "You've failed. You know how I feel about failure."

"I…I am sorry. It is true that our first attempt at infiltration has not gone as planned, but I have it on good authority that someone else in the Agency is willing to talk. Someone much higher up. I meet with him this week. I won't fail again."

"See that you don't." Mikkel flicks a finger, and the poor man screams. Blood curdling and sharp. I have no idea what Mikkel did to him, but it clearly hurts. The man doubles over, his breathing ragged.

"Get out of my sight," my uncle commands.

The man struggles back to his feet and limps out of the room. Blood dots the floor in his wake.

Mikkel tears his eyes away from the man and fixes on the spot where I'm standing, with a merciless glare full of malice and rage. I clasp a hand to my mouth. Mikkel's face isn't that of a man who wants to capture me and take me to my father; it's that of a man who wants to flay me alive and revel in every second of my screams.

"Enjoy the show, little niece?"

* * *

"WAKE UP." A concerned male voice cuts through the fog. "Willa, wake up."

I launch myself upright, my eyes springing open. I'm back at the hotel. I have no idea what time it is or how long I've been asleep, but I'm panting like I've been sprinting and my heart is pounding.

"Shh, it's alright. You were having a nightmare," Soren says from beside me. A lamp on the bedside table is switched on, casting deep shadows over his handsome face.

I make another decision not to share what I dreamed about. My instincts were correct in that meeting with the Directors. I won't risk a prison sentence because of these dreams. Soren seems nice enough, but I don't really know who I can trust.

I smooth a hand through my hair, getting it out of my face and notice my bra-covered breasts are fully on display. I make a mental note not to sleep naked since privacy clearly isn't a thing here.

"Is there a robe or something somewhere?" I ask. My face turning red.

Soren just laughs and hands me the robe hanging on the back of the door. "You don't need to be embarrassed, Willa. I can assure you I have seen plenty of people in their underwear."

I smile. "I have no doubt about that."

Wrapping the robe around myself, I follow Soren into the sitting room.

This part of the hotel suite has two velvety couches in bright blue and a burgundy red. They are situated around an oval coffee table with pointed legs. There's also a glass and wrought iron desk with a leather office chair. On the desk is a mobile phone and a computer.

"I set these up for you myself," Soren says. "They're Agency-issued, so I will be able to see and hear whatever you do, but I thought you might appreciate having contact with the outside world."

More tears well in my eyes. Whether from appreciation

that I can check on my mother or general misery from the situation, I can't even tell anymore.

"Thank you."

"You're welcome." He leans against the desk with his legs crossed at the ankles. His shiny leather shoes look like they cost more than a month's rent, and he's wearing argyle socks, which I find endearing.

He's in the same clothes from earlier, but he's lost the jacket and tie. His white shirt is unbuttoned enough to show off the top of his chest, and he has his sleeves rolled up. I catch the hint of a tattoo on the inside of one of his forearms, but I can't make it out. Tonight, he has on thick black rimmed glasses that make him look like a hot professor.

Soren holds up the phone. "I programmed your contacts into this, as well as all of ours. I want to make it clear that I will be able to read your messages and listen to any phone calls you make. It's the only way I could get authorization. So, if you want to tell Sam about the handsome man you just met, you might want to hold back."

He winks, but I know his warning is serious.

"I suppose it shouldn't surprise me that you know who my friends are, but I can't deny it's a little unsettling." I absently rub my hands against the silky robe.

"You'll learn soon enough that privacy is an illusion, especially for people like us. My team compiled the beginnings of your dossier long before we set foot in Vermont."

I stare into space while I absorb what he's saying. How long had they been watching me?

"Why don't you find something to put on, and I'll see what's taking the others so long," he says, sensing my shifting focus.

"Uh, yes. Of course."

I find a dress in the bedroom closet that's slightly less

professional and drag a brush through my hair before twisting it up and out of my face. After crying all afternoon, I'm not winning any beauty contests, but I look presentable enough.

Greta and Banks arrive with bags of take out. They're also wearing the same clothes from earlier, but they're less polished like the day has taken its toll on them.

Greta unpacks the food while I accept a glass of wine from Soren. "This is from a place nearby that specializes in quintessentially Nordic cuisine," she says. "Since you can't leave, we thought we'd bring the city to you."

Greta is a very serious and professional woman. It's the way she carries herself and the brief conversations I overheard in the office. But she also glows with her own inner light. There is something warm and comforting in her presence.

"I really appreciate you doing this for me," I tell her earnestly. They could all go about their business and leave me here alone, but they're not and I'm grateful.

"We're happy to support you in any way we can," she says. "The way Olsen..." She trails off and glances at Banks who shakes his head. "Well, please consider us your friends, Willa."

I thank her, but still I wonder what it is they aren't able to tell me.

I haven't eaten since breakfast, and I'm ravenous. The food they brought is delicious. Comforting even though it's unfamiliar. Mostly fish and vegetable dishes seasoned with dill and other herbs I don't recognize.

The conversation flows easily along with the wine. Though they're watching how much I drink since I have medical exams in the morning. Even Banks is more relaxed off-hours, though he never loses the steely edge he wears like armor. Greta is more playful, and Soren is funny and charm-

ing. They all seem to know each other well, and their cama-
raderie is infectious.

"How long have you all worked together?" I ask.

"Oh, forever," Greta says with an exaggerated sigh. "I have
known these fools since we were climbing trees and
throwing rocks at passing trains."

I must have a quizzical look on my face because Soren clar-
ifies further. "We attended Darlings at the same time. Stellan
was always our unofficial leader, so when he was putting a
team together, we were his natural choices. We have the kind
of trust built up over years that you can't easily replicate. The
Agency supports it because we're the best at what we do."

"It's really wonderful that you have such a strong bond."

"We do," Banks says and puts a hand on Greta's shoulder.
They seem to have a special connection, and it makes me
wonder if it ever goes beyond friendship.

It also makes me think of Stellan with Ingrid today and
how she clung to him like a leech while marking her terri-
tory. Peeing on him would have been more subtle.

"Did, um, Ingrid go to Darlings with you, too?" I ask with
as much nonchalance as I can muster. Soren never seems to
miss much and raises an eyebrow at me. I just shake my head
and he smirks.

"*Mais non.* That woman is a snake," Greta snaps, her
French accent coming out.

Banks makes a disapproving sound in his throat.

"What? She is," she says with an unapologetic shrug.
"She's one of Olsen's. She was appointed to us when Olsen
realized he had no one on our team who would report to him
willingly. We do not trust her, but she does her job well
enough so Stellan has to keep her."

"Greta, remember what Stellan said," Banks says to her.
She purses her lips in annoyance.

"Yes, yes, I remember." She waves her hands dramatically before frowning as if an unwelcome thought occurred to her. "Does anyone else think something is the matter with Stellan lately?"

I tuck my legs up on the couch, making myself smaller.

"He's their perfect soldier, but at what cost?" she goes on. "Olsen demands more and more from him, and I think one of these days he's going to break. He should be in charge of the region. He deserves it after everything he's accomplished."

Greta seems to forget that I'm here, or maybe she knows more than she's letting on and saw this as an opportunity to provide me with context. I can't be sure. I just know that it's difficult to hear.

I care for the man I thought I was getting to know in Vermont. I could have loved him, if given the chance. I know that in my bones. I know it now as I consider the sadness that settles over me thinking about him being unhappy and overworked. How I want to be the one to make him smile and help him relax.

God, I'm pathetic. Vermont Stellan was a character. I'd do well to remember that he's spending his evening with another woman.

Banks whispers something in Greta's ear, and she smiles up at him. They rise to leave. Greta gives me a quick hug and apologizes for being emotive before leaning a little too hard on Banks. I thank them for spending time with me and for dinner.

Soren gives me a long and unexpected hug. He smells like warm spices, and when he pulls me close to him all the tension leaves my body. It isn't a sensual feeling. I don't get the same tingles up my spine like when Stellan touched me. It's like being hugged by Sam, and honestly I need that more right now.

When they leave me alone, the aching emptiness from earlier has dulled. I'm still sad and angry, but it's not so acute and desperate.

My father's cruelty and my mother's justifiable lies have left me anchorless and in need of a place to land. The world I built for myself in Vermont was founded on falsehoods and the fantasy of a banal existence. Even my heartbreak over Nick is mundane in comparison. I won't be able to navigate this new world alone. I need friends here.

I send off a few messages with the computer Soren left for me. I keep things light and full of half-truths. I'm in Sweden. I'm OK. I'll be home as soon as I can.

I get ready for bed and take the phone with me to call my mom before I fall asleep. I notice I have two unexpected texts.

Soren Westerholm: "It was nice getting to know you better. Sleep well."

The other name that pops up makes my stomach flip.

Stellan Lundqvist: "Someone will be there early tomorrow morning to take you to headquarters. Be sure to get some rest."

I ignore them both with intention and fall into a blissfully dreamless sleep.

CHAPTER 30

WILLA

IT'S OFFICIAL. Greta is secretly a sadist. She fully stocked my closet with rows of pantsuits and pencil skirts and not a single piece of loungewear. With all this pent-up anxiety, I need to move my body, but I have nothing to wear.

I found a silk nightgown in one of the drawers last night and wear that while I do some yoga poses and bodyweight exercises. It's nothing fancy, but it's the best I can do in this small space.

Afterwards, my face is flushed, and I have a nice, sweaty glow. I strip off the nightgown just as the doorbell rings.

"What on earth?" I say out loud. I thought Stellan said early, not the crack of dawn. Though dawn is a bit of a misnomer here since the sun hardly rises.

I throw on a robe so I'm no longer totally nude and answer the door. I'm about to reach it when the door swings open on its own. I jump back in surprise as Stellan steps inside the suite looking powerful and confident in a navy suit. He freezes when he sees me. His lips

208

thin and his jaw twitches as he takes stock of my appearance.

The robe barely covers my chest and legs, my face is flushed and glowing from exercise, and my hair is tied over my shoulder in a messy braid. A sight he's seen before in a very different context, and we both know it. My face grows even redder as I blush.

"Are you…is there someone here with you?" he asks. His tone is accusatory, and his eyes dart around furiously like he's looking for whoever I'm hiding.

I laugh. A joyless and enraged laugh before I turn away without a greeting. This day is already shaping up to be something extraordinary.

"I'm serious, Willa. Is there someone here?" His voice is too close behind me. I turn around, and he's right there. His rainwater magic soaks the air around us like a downpour. Electricity crackles as my magic answers his. I don't cave or capitulate. I just cross my arms and scowl.

"Yeah, I got lonely and fucked one of the guards." I roll my eyes like a teenager. "Is that what you wanted to know?"

"Don't be childish, Willa," he says, his words clipped. "This is not a laughing matter."

"Believe me, Stellan. I'm very aware how not funny all of this is." My magic flares and tingles my skin as it moves down the length of my arms. I want to punch something.

Stellan blinks, sensing the shift in energy and my red-hot anger, but he doesn't back down or apologize. He just sighs and runs a hand through his much shorter hair.

"You should get dressed. We don't want to be late," he speaks evenly, his voice detached. Then he sits down on the couch without another word. He pulls out his phone and starts typing. He could say something now that we're alone together. Anything. Instead, he ignores me.

Lovely.

I take the angriest shower. I wash my hair and body furiously. Could he not have sent Banks or someone else? He didn't need to come here himself if he's only going to accuse me of sleeping with someone and then not speak to me.

It doesn't help that I can't stop thinking about him spending the night with that awful woman.

My blood is boiling. Even my magic is in a bad mood. I keep having to take deep breaths to calm it down. Rationally, I know it's just an extension of myself, but it's almost easier to think of it as its own ragingly mad entity. A companion of sorts.

I dress as quickly as possible in the first thing I touch, put my hair up in a bun, and consider myself ready. I glance at the mirror and want to laugh. I put on a navy pantsuit.

Of course, I did.

I exit the bedroom, and Stellan's eyebrows raise a fraction as he assesses me from the couch. He stands and continues his silent appraisal. I can't tell if he approves of what he sees or if he's being critical.

"The matching isn't intentional," I deadpan and point at my suit. "It was just the first thing I grabbed."

I swear I catch him trying to hide a smile. "We don't have time for you to change," he says in his business voice. I shrug.

"You look nice," he says flatly, and I get the impression he's trying to ease the tension from earlier.

"I look like I'm trying to sell you a condo." He doesn't look amused in the slightest. "Let's get this over with."

Before we can make it to the door, Stellan shoves me to the side and pushes me against the coat closet like he's going to kiss me.

"What the hell?" I try to shove him off me.

"Quiet!" Stellan interrupts with urgency and I stop fighting.

He speaks in a whisper close to my ear. "I am fairly

certain we removed all the bugs from your rooms, but I don't want to risk it. Nod if you understand me."

I nod.

"I lied on your report," Stellan says and his hands tighten around my hips. "There is no doubt in my mind that you are a Category 5 Winter Mage, but I listed you as a suspected Category 3. If Olsen finds out how powerful you really are, he'll lock you up and I won't be able to stop him."

I swallow hard. "What do you want me to do?"

"Hold back. Make it look harder than it is to use your magic. They will believe you used an extraordinary amount to defend your life, but they need to think it was an anomaly."

Having Stellan so close is a painful reminder of everything I thought was real. He lets go of me abruptly and opens the door to the suite. He walks out without sparing me another glance. It takes me a second to recover enough to follow him.

We embark on another dark morning drive through Stockholm, though I catch a little more of the city this time. It's a beautiful mix of old and modern. The city is surrounded by water and bright, twinkling lights. I wonder what it would be like to visit for a normal reason. To be a tourist and not a prisoner.

"Did you have a pleasant evening?" Stellan asks. He's in the backseat of the car next to me while the driver and a guard sit in front. We spent the first 10 minutes of the journey in silence.

"It was nice," I reply, a little confused by his question. I wonder if he's only asking for the benefit of the two men in the front seats who are quiet and definitely listening. "Greta, Banks, and Soren brought me some dinner and stayed for a while."

He makes a noncommittal noise in response, but I swear I hear him say "better than mine" under his breath.

"So, what were you doing when I arrived?" he asks, abruptly switching gears.

"If you must know," I say with my eyes out the window. "I was exercising. Though it was a challenge considering the only clothes in the suite are for my corporate alter ego."

Stellan laughs a little, but it isn't the carefree chuckle I remember. If anything, it simply sounds sad.

* * *

STELLAN LEADS me to a metal door that's flanked by two more guards with automatic weapons.

It's strange becoming accustomed to this. I don't want to feel numb around such powerful tools of destruction, but it's happening whether I like it or not.

A weaselly man and a pinch-faced woman greet us at the entrance to the medical ward, though it's unlike any doctor's office I've ever seen before. The two wear white lab coats and expressionless faces. Everything is cold and sterile. White walls, steel tables, cold metal chairs.

Fear and unease chase up my spine. I experienced nerves before my meeting with the Directors, but this is different. A sick sense of dread settles over my body. I don't know what's going to happen in this ward, but I suspect it's going to be unpleasant.

Stellan warned me to hold back, but what if I can't? What if I need to do something to protect myself? My magic will want to help me, and I know I'll want to let it.

"I expect to be alerted the moment you have finished your evaluations," Stellan says to the doctors. There is an air of superiority in the way he speaks to them. "I am certain you will handle the asset with the utmost care."

The look I give Stellan could melt glass. He merely ignores it and carries on. "Ms. Martin, this is Dr. Svenson and Dr. Gage. A member of my team will escort you back to the hotel when your sessions are completed." He uses the same authority and cold detachment when he speaks to me.

"Ms. Martin, if you please," the man called Dr. Gage says in a German accent and holds out his hand for me to move ahead of them. Stellan never takes his eyes off me as I'm led away from him and the warm light of the hallway.

The harsh, white fluorescents of the ward sting my eyes and set everything in sharp relief. I can't help but think that it's intentional to make the people they bring here uneasy. People like me who are questionable and therefore problematic.

I'm brought into a small, windowless room and asked to undress and put on a pale blue hospital gown. I sit for what could be 20 minutes or two hours without anyone bothering to check on me. Anxiety weighs me down, and my magic pushes against my chest, seeking freedom.

I know better than to give in to it. Stellan's warning came at personal risk, and his instructions to hold back were for my own safety. It seems my classification as a Winter Mage is considered dangerous, and it's significantly worse as the daughter of a known criminal.

Finally, Dr. Svenson knocks on the door and enters with a phlebotomy kit. Without a word, she takes vials upon vials of my blood for testing. She's careful but not gentle, and she doesn't look me in the eyes or offer me any indication what she's doing with all my blood. My arm aches and stings from the tourniquet and the needle.

Eventually, she finishes and brings me to another room where I'm given a very thorough exam and asked to do a DNA swab and pee in three different cups. By this point, they probably have enough of my genetic material to make a clone army. It isn't the most comforting thought.

I'm then led to yet another room. It's a dark space with a high ceiling, lit only by a few spotlights. They have me stand in the middle of the room where the lights shine the brightest. I feel like I'm about to give a monologue in a black box theater.

Instead, I'm asked to demonstrate my abilities while they watch me from a glass booth on the other side of the room. They speak through a microphone that pipes in their voices with an echo and a weird tinny quality.

"Please show us how you create lightning," Dr. Gage says in his harsh accent.

My face scrunches up in struggle, and I conjure a few lackluster sparks in my hands. The struggle is legitimate since my magic wants to light shit up and I'm holding it back.

"Ms. Martin, please don't be afraid to show your power. We are safe in the booth, and the room is secure. It's made for this kind of procedure."

I guess I have to try a little harder so show them what I can do while still holding back. I make another face like I'm straining to use my magic, when it's really right on the edge of my fingers. The scent of ozone fills my nose, and my hair stands on end. I catch the expectant faces of the doctors in the other room.

Two new figures join them, but I can't make them out. With a deep, dramatic breath, I push out with my hands and a small bolt of lightning cracks with a bang and illuminates the room.

I breathe in and out with effort, keeping up the charade that it was very difficult for me to conjure up that little lightning bolt.

"Very nice, Ms. Martin," the man says. "Just a few more tests."

He then asks me to make fire, manipulate weather, and all the other physical tests that Stellan already went through with me. I comply, but I never show the full extent of my power.

When it comes time to freeze water, I hesitate. I don't want to nearly freeze myself to death in the process again.

"Is there a problem?" Dr. Gage asks from the booth.

"Uh, no. Not at all." I shake my head. I still can't see who else is with him, but it looks like the figures of a tall man and woman in the shadows behind him.

I focus my magic and my mental energy on a deep blue ice and what it will take to freeze the water. I have more control now, and when the chill creeps through my veins, I don't give in to it. I shield my body and mind from the cold while focusing on the water. I create a layer of ice, but I hold back enough so I don't freeze it completely.

I expect some praise or acknowledgement, but there is silence in the booth. At some point, they switch on the mirror so I can no longer see them.

After what feels like an hour, Director Olsen steps into the room with Ingrid right behind him.

Olsen scowls in annoyance, but maybe that's just his usual expression. It's hard to tell since that's all I've ever seen. Ingrid looks gorgeous as expected in another black pencil skirt and silk blouse combo. Her resting bitch face is unrivaled. I almost want to clap.

The two of them in their version of armor and me in a fucking hospital johnny with my panties half out is a power imbalance I do not appreciate. My magic is gunning for a fight, but I hold it together by a thread.

"Brilliant show, Ms. Martin. Now the real fun begins," Olsen says. The darkness in his voice makes my skin crawl.

Then the lights go out.

CHAPTER 31

WILLA

I'M PLUNGED into complete darkness, all sense of direction lost. I can hear their footsteps approaching, and the combined scent of their magic blooms around me, but where they are, I'm not sure.

"It's interesting that someone with such limited powers has such strong shields," Olsen's voice is coming from multiple angles, keeping me off balance. He sounds like he's both behind me and in front of me. My heart races. All of my senses on high alert.

"Is it?" I ask with a slight tremor in my voice, hoping to sound weaker than I am.

"It is. I've only met a handful of people I couldn't break. We're going to find out if you're one of them. Aren't we, Ingrid?"

"Yes, we are." Her obnoxious, simpering voice grates against my already frayed nerves. She is so goddamn smackable.

In the next moment, their magic unleashes and attacks

me from two sides. The scent of dark evenings and wet leaves mingles with magnolia and honey. Ingrid's power could be beautiful, but instead it's sickly and cloying. I struggle to breathe against the assault, their powers suffocating me as they try to crack open my mind.

I can't let them know about my magic, and there are parts of my life and my past that these two do not need to know about. I think about my mother and my sisters, and how desperately I want to keep them away from all this.

Their combined power is strong, but I've been unknowingly building my shields since before I could read. And since I discovered them, I've strengthened them even more. I am a fortress, and it will take more than these two idiots to break me.

"Hey Winter," Ingrid draws my attention while they continue to apply pressure against my body and mind. "Do you want to know something?"

"Not particularly," I say through gritted teeth.

"Well, I'm going to tell you anyway," she says in saccharine sweetness. "It's just too delicious not to share. Would you like to guess how many times Stellan made me come last night?"

Nausea creeps up my throat at the triumph in her voice, and my magic fights with me for supremacy. It wants to take Ingrid out, and I can't blame it. I'm not stupid though. They're trying to provoke me. They want a reason to lock me up, and I'm not giving it to them.

But for all I know she's telling the truth. And it hurts. It hurts more than I ever want to admit, but I won't give her the satisfaction.

"He said you were so pathetic. Coming on to him the way you did," she continues. "As if he'd ever be interested in someone like you when he already has everything he wants right here."

Olsen pushes harder with his magic while Ingrid makes her attempt at distracting me. I want to scream, but I hold it in. It's like an ice pick stabbing at my skull over and over.

I wince, but I'm not going to cave. I can't. I call on some of my magic. Just a fraction and give it permission to slowly, carefully push back against theirs. Not enough for them to notice, but enough to weaken their assault and force them to work harder. I breathe more easily, and I can think a little more clearly.

"It's funny you say that." I hate that my voice sounds so strained. "But he told me the same thing about you. There's this woman in Stockholm, and she's so clingy. He said you throw yourself at him and that he's forced to play along."

I can't see her, but I know the moment Ingrid loses concentration. I use the opportunity to push back just a little more with my magic. Olsen hisses when he realizes he isn't making a dent in my shields. He's growing tired.

"This is ridiculous," Ingrid snaps. "Henrik, it isn't working."

"Tie her to a chair," he says, his voice rough from exertion.

The room turns from impenetrable black to a dim yellow glow. Olsen grabs my arms while Ingrid drags a chair into the middle of the room. They shove me into it and secure my hands behind my back with handcuffs that block my magic.

My wrenched shoulders ache, and my magic screams inside me at being contained. It pushes with an agonizing pressure against my sternum, but the handcuffs won't allow me to release it. I have only limited experience with my magic, but now it's like a missing limb without it.

Where have my medical friends gone? Why aren't Weasel and Pinch Face here when I need them? I'm alone with these two monsters and completely at their mercy. Helpless without the use of my magic or even my hands. I'm terrified, but it's almost like an out-of-body experience. As though this is happening to someone else while I look on.

But then Ingrid's fist slams into my face, and a sharp pain splinters across my nose where she breaks it. Blood runs hot and fast down my face.

"Fuck! That hurts!" I shout.

Then I start laughing and I can't stop. It's the deranged laugh of someone pushed beyond her limits.

"Ingrid! Stop!" Olsen calls out. Ingrid looks like she's about to unleash her fury on me.

I think Olsen might be the good cop in this situation, but then he steps forward and swings at me. His fist connects with my jaw.

The pain is otherworldly. It erupts through my skull. I check that my teeth are all still present and accounted for. My mouth fills with blood. I spit it at Olsen's feet. He sneers but doesn't hit me again.

"You are going to do exactly as I say, or I'll have to hurt you."

"Have to hurt me? What the hell have you been doing?" I say, my words sluggish.

"Warming up." Pure malice steeps every word. He squeezes my throat and tips my face up to look into his fiendish eyes as his magic pummels my shields with such force that I see stars.

"Wow! That's intense." I let out another hysterical laugh. I'm starting to lose it.

"That's nothing," he says. Two quick swipes of his magic against my chest produce deep cuts in my skin right below my collar bone. The sight of my blood running down my chest and the sharp pain fills me with a nauseating sense of dread.

I might actually die here.

"What is it you want from me?" I manage to ask. Surely,

there's a purpose to this. They wouldn't just do this for fun? *Would they?*

"You're going to tell me everything I want to know about your father's work," he explains slowly and with exasperation. As if all this is obvious and I'm taking up too much of his time. "Why does he want you? Where is he hiding? Tell. Me. What. You. Know!"

He punctuates his words with more strikes to my face and chest. I scream in pain as a rib cracks and blood pours out of new wounds where he's sliced me open with his magic.

I spit out more blood and watch it run down the hospital gown from my broken nose.

"What if I don't know anything?" I ask. My words are slurring. I'm losing a lot of blood, and the pain is pulling me under.

"You must know something!" He roars. "You're his daughter, for fuck's sake!"

I laugh again. "Yeah, the daughter he hasn't seen in 20 years, you idiot. It's not like the fucker sent me his notes."

"Henrik, this is pointless," Ingrid whines. "She's too stupid and weak to know anything important."

I start laughing again, and Ingrid grabs my hair and pulls my head back so I can look her right in the eyes.

"You're garbage. Stellan would never want anyone like you."

I just smile at her. A weak, definitely lopsided smile, but it's enough to piss her off even more.

She grips my hair tighter. I wince as pain shoots across my scalp.

"Since Ingrid is likely right and you don't know anything useful, you're going to prove your worth in another way," Olsen says.

He steps forward, so close his nose nearly touches mine.

He smiles like he's never enjoyed anything so much as this.

"You," he says, "will be my bait."

Ingrid laughs cruelly as though the thought delights her. Rage blackens my vision.

I hate her.

I hate them both.

God, I hate them so fucking much.

I'm slipping away. My magic wants me to fight. It wants me to show them they're messing with the wrong girl. It's pushing me to release it, and it takes all I have left not to scream from the pressure.

"First, though," Olsen says, "we're going to heal you so no one knows about our little meeting."

Meeting. That's a word for it.

"Ingrid, do the honors."

"With pleasure. We wouldn't want our Stellan to see you this way now would we?" I want to claw that cruel smile off her face. Her magic trails over me, sickly sweet and disgusting.

Stellan's healing magic is gentle, but this is like drowning in honey. I want to push her away, but my body needs this as much as I hate it. I swallow down the waves of over-whelming nausea.

It takes much longer than with Stellan, but eventually, my wounds knit together and my nose clicks back into place. The tight bruises vanish. I breathe and my damaged lungs fill with much needed air.

"Now get up, you worthless piece of shit," Ingrid spits at me. I stand on shaky legs and picture all the horrific things I want to do to her. She chucks my clothes at me and shoves me in the direction of another room with a shower.

"Clean yourself up," Olsen says with a haughty tilt of his

head. "A word of this to anyone and your usefulness will be reevaluated."

"In other words, you'll be dead," Ingrid says with a flip of her hair.

"Yeah, I kinda got that," I say. Her smug face turns sour again.

My body is healed, but I'm exhausted. My legs wobble, but I won't let them see that.

"Well, this was real fun, friends," I say. "Let's do it again sometime."

Ingrid rolls her eyes, and Olsen leads her out of the testing room.

We'll definitely do this again, I vow. And the next time, I won't be the one left bleeding.

* * *

SOREN AND BANKS arrive at the medical ward to escort me back. One glance at my hollow expression and they pounce. I washed all the blood off and put my clothes back on, but I'm pale and there's a dead look in my eyes that I can't hide.

"What happened, Willa?" Soren asks. He puts his arm around me, and I lean into the comfort. I need it so badly.

"Nothing," I tell him. "I'm fine."

"I'm not sure I believe you," Soren says and his concern borders on frustration.

I should tell them. I know I should, but I can't. I can't take the risk. I won't survive the pain of not being believed.

They share a silent look, but don't say anything else.

Stellan is in conversation with two people I don't recognize when we arrive back at the office.

He continues talking even though he sees us approach. Soren leads me to a small seating area by the windows and helps me into a chair. Banks hands me a glass of water. They both hover like nervous mothers.

"Guys, I'm OK."

"I'm not buying that, Willa. You look like death," Banks says.

Soren sits next to me and rubs my hand. "Tell us what happened, sweetheart."

I fight against the tears I refuse to shed over this. "I…I can't. Please just trust me that I'm fine."

Physically, I'm not torn apart anymore, but I'm still weak and shaky. I will probably never be truly fine again after all this. Soren draws an arm around me. Banks cups my face in his massive hands and looks into my eyes. His deep forest scent infuses the air.

"Have you lost blood? Your pulse is weak, and your blood pressure is very low." His eyes carve into me as he uses his magic to scan for injuries.

Stellan's footsteps echo along the tile floor. The man whose comfort I long for more than any other. But after everything that just happened to me, I can't even look at him.

"Is she hurt?" Stellan asks Banks.

"She's not telling us, but I'm going to say yes. Her vitals are all over the place."

"What on earth would have caused…" Stellan starts to ask, but Ingrid appears before he can finish.

"Oh, no. Is she OK?" she asks with fake concern. I flinch. I hate myself for it, but I can't help the physical response. The memory of her fist in my face is far too fresh.

Soren tugs me closer while glaring openly at Ingrid. "Where have you been for the last hour, Ingrid? We were looking for you."

She shrugs in exaggerated innocence and picks a piece of lint off Stellan's shoulder. As if he's hers to touch whenever she wants.

How can he stand her?

"I was working with Olsen on a special project," she says with a furtive glance in my direction. If Stellan notices, he doesn't acknowledge it. In fact, he barely registers that she's there at all. He's staring at me like I'm a puzzle he can't solve.

"It's too bad she's not feeling well. I guess the evaluations were too much for someone with her limitations," she says and then walks away with a seductive swish in her hips.

Stellan ignores her and kneels in front of me. He moves to put his hand on my cheek, but I flinch again. His face falls for a moment at my reaction, but he recovers. "Willa, I need you to tell me if something happened while you were in the medical ward."

"I'm fine. I just need a long rest and some food." I try to smile but fail. My eyes are dark pools, and I can't conceal how fully hollowed out I am.

"If you change your mind, please come find me," he says.

"Yeah, sure thing," I retort, too tired to bother masking the sarcasm.

"We'll take her home," Banks tells him. Stellan wants to talk more, but I turn my attention out the window. He gets the hint and leaves with his back stiff and his fists clenched.

"Alright, love," Banks says. "It's clear you're not going to tell us what happened, but at least let us know if there's anything we can do for you."

"Yes," Soren agrees. "Anything."

I close my eyes for a moment. Remembering the powerlessness I felt tied to that chair without the use of my magic.

"There is something you can do. I need you to teach me how to fight without magic." Both men start in surprise at the murderous tenor of my voice. "I want you to teach me how to tear someone apart with my bare hands."

* * *

I FALL asleep on Soren as we travel back to the hotel. He's so warm and comforting. He tries to carry me inside, but I refuse. I can walk. I'm not that broken.

Banks forces me to eat something. I'm not hungry, but eating improves my mental clarity and I can feel my body recovering. Eventually, they're satisfied that I'm not a danger to myself and leave me alone to rest.

My steps falter as I enter the bedroom. I'm not sure my heart can take another surprise today, but on the bed are several skeins of yarn, knitting needles, and two piles of clothes.

I run my hand over the fabric. There's athletic wear, black leggings, wooly socks, and the kind of soft dresses and night-gowns I always wear.

There's only one person here who knows me well enough to get it this right. I slide to the floor and hold my head in my hands, too numb and wrung out to cry.

CHAPTER 32

STELLAN

LYING awake on my couch at 3 a.m. has become a regular occurrence. I rest Anne Martin's latest novel on my stomach and stare at the ceiling. I haven't been able to sleep, so I've stopped trying.

My days are full of meetings, interviews, and so much paperwork my eyes are red and sore. Work keeps me busy and my mind focused.

But the night is when I struggle with my resolve. It's when I leave the office and come home to my empty flat and eat dinner alone that I am forced to face the consequences of my decisions. It's moments like this one when the idea of knocking on her door doesn't feel so impossible. So dangerous.

But I cannot and will not do that. I made the right choice.

And yet, it's in the darkness that my control slips and I just want to see her one more time. It's when I want to make her eyes sparkle as she smiles and bask in her hearth-like warmth. When I want and want and want so much that my stomach hurts and my bones ache.

But then I remember what I'm accomplishing by staying away.

I rise up from the couch and turn off the rest of the lights, forcing my feet to carry me to bed.

I lay down on top of the covers and think back to when she flinched away from my touch. It wasn't so long ago that my hands brought her pleasure. When I made her melt like snowflakes on my tongue.

I don't know what happened in the medical ward, but Willa's response is worrying. Dr. Gage assured me that the evaluations followed protocol, but I can't shake my unease.

The sooner we catch Lars Stromberg, the sooner Willa can return to her life and leave mine completely. Then she'll be free from danger and my fucked-up world. I just have to work harder.

I can only sleep by recalling the exquisite sensation of her magic wrapping around me like a warm bath, gently tugging under.

I fall into a fitful slumber remembering the tiny buds of soft emotions just starting to unfurl at the edges. Emotions I can't begin to uncover or I'll never be strong enough to stay away.

* * *

DAYS LATER, our progress isn't sufficient. We should be closer to locating Stromberg, but instead we're falling further behind. Mikkel has gone dark, and every lead we once had on him has run cold.

Director Olsen's interference is an added aggravation. He piles on tasks that distract me from our true priorities. He's preoccupied with Willa and any contact she may have had with her father over the years.

She's had none, but he won't let it go. When he's not obsessively spinning theories about Willa in my office, he's burying me in red tape and forcing us to chase leads that go nowhere.

I'm frustrated. I have a terrible headache, and everyone is grating on my nerves. Greta, rightly, called me out for being a bear this morning. But I don't understand how my team can be this delayed.

Even Greta's prowess can't get a meeting on the books with Albert Wagner. Lars Stromberg's stepbrother wrote to Anne Martin requesting a phone conversation. But we can't know what he wanted to discuss unless we convince him to talk to us instead.

We could subpoena him, but that's only a last resort. The more Agency personnel involved in this investigation, the more it spreads out of my control. I can't risk a leak that I won't be able to plug. It happens all too often with powerful Mage families, and the Stromberg name carries significant weight.

My footsteps echo down the corridor of offices. I'm on my way to see Ingrid, who has requested an "urgent meeting." If it's anything like her last request for a meeting, it isn't urgent and will only intensify the sharp pain in my skull.

I pass by Soren's office. The lights are dim and he's standing at his desk with headphones on, scanning line upon line of code. I catch the faint scent of winter spices and evergreen trees, and a pang of agony lights up my chest.

I slow my steps and look deeper into the room, finding the woman I spend every waking minute trying to avoid. The woman who visits me in my sleep every night and around whom all this work revolves.

She's sitting in an armchair in Soren's office with a mug of tea and a book on her lap.

Her eyes are downcast, and her thick lashes fan across her cheeks.

"What's Willa doing here?" I ask Soren in a gruff voice I barely recognize as my own.

Willa's eyes shoot up from her book as soon as she hears me. I don't miss the hurt on her face, nor do I miss the concern. She tilts her head just slightly, observing the bags under my eyes and the heavy lines all the days of little sleep and high stress have given me.

"Reading?" Soren offers unhelpfully, barely glancing up from his computer. My friend is angry with me. Hell, I'm angry with me.

But it's not as if that changes anything.

"Can I speak to you for a moment in private?" I ask Soren.

He gives Willa an apologetic smile, and she shakes her head as if to say she doesn't mind. A possessive jealousy darkens my mood further. How wonderful that they've become so close they can communicate nonverbally.

We stop just outside the door of Soren's office.

"Take Willa back to the hotel. She shouldn't be here." I never give commands to Soren, but I'm past caring.

"Are you serious?" Soren comes close to yelling. "I'm not sending her back to the hotel. What is wrong with you? You're an empath, Stellan. Tell me you can't feel how fucking sad she is?!"

Soren's words are a punch to the gut. It's one thing to suspect, but it's another to have it shouted at me. I've done everything I can to avoid Willa and what she might be feeling. I don't need to know. It won't help.

"It doesn't matter what I feel or what I think. What matters is keeping her safe and this investigation moving forward." I hardly register the words as they leave my mouth. It's the same thing I repeat to myself multiple times a day.

"Would you fucking listen to yourself?" Soren yells again. Then he pauses and in a lower, more desperate voice asks, "Did you not learn your lesson the last time?"

My heart leaps to my throat. *Why would he mention her now?* "This has nothing to do with Liliana, Soren. How could you bring that up?"

"Do you think I like talking about it?" Soren is so exasperated that he's on the verge of breaking down or punching me. "I'm only going to say this once, Stellan. Pull your head out of your arse before you ruin this completely. Willa is not stupid. She can't stay in the shadows forever, and we cannot keep her locked up feeling useless and alone or she's going to take matters into her own hands. And then where will we be?"

He pauses and in a lower voice adds. "And where will you be?"

Soren storms off, and I'm left standing alone in the hallway. I realize too late that Willa is just beyond the door and that was a conversation we should not have had in English.

CHAPTER 33

WILLA

THE INTERIOR of the steel and glass building is strangely beautiful. It's cold, but there's something in the arrangement of the furniture that speaks to the care of its owner.

It seems so much more than a house, but it's clearly lived in. There are a few empty mugs scattered here and there, and the brown leather furniture is worn in places. Whoever lives here has a set routine. They only sit on the left side of the couch. They've worn a path along the wood floor by the windows.

"Come to visit?" A voice behind me asks.

"I guess so." I turn and face my father. He's wearing a white t-shirt and jeans over worn leather boots with the laces undone. He appears younger than a man in his 50s, and more physically fit than some men half his age, but his eyes are tired.

"Is there something you came to ask?" He poses the question with a thoughtful expression on his face. Though I can't be certain how I ended up here, I suspect it's because there is something I want to know and my magic took charge.

"Why do you need me?"

My father sighs and sits in his spot on the couch. He stares out the window to the forest and the sea beyond it.

"It's rather complicated, Willa."

"I have time."

"Not enough," he states. "There is much to share with you and much to ask of you."

"Why?" I ask again with more insistence.

"Set yourself free and I'll tell you."

* * *

BANKS AND SOREN have made good on their promise and are teaching me a combination of self-defense, mixed-martial arts, and defensive magic. They sneak me into the training facility at odd hours to avoid unnecessary questions.

It hasn't been long, but I'm growing stronger and more capable. Soren showed me how to break free from a captor, and Banks taught me how to tap into my magic to enhance my physical strength. I feel safer knowing I can defend myself.

The tight knot of anxiety that has lived in my chest since that awful day in the medical ward is starting to loosen. My muscles ache at the end of each day, but I like going to bed physically exhausted instead of emotionally wiped out.

Since I arrived in Stockholm over a week ago, I've seen Stellan less and less. If I thought he cared, I'd assume he was avoiding me.

I have seen Ingrid more than I would like, which is basically anything more than never. She often devises ways to seek me out and make snide comments about my weak magic or how tired she is from being up all night with Stellan.

Even days later, the sharp pain doesn't fade. As much as I don't want to care about Stellan and who he might be in bed with, I really fucking care, and it sucks.

Ingrid is probably lying or at least exaggerating, but I can't trust my instincts in that regard, so I don't know what to believe.

Greta has gone away for some work "in the field." I'm not sure what that means exactly, but I miss our conversations and her company.

"Damn, Willa! That tickles!" Soren laughs. He is on his back, and I've trapped him with my legs while my hands shoot gentle sparks against the underside of his arms. It isn't exactly fair play, but I finally pinned him after an hour of trying and failing to get him on the mat.

"You never said I couldn't play dirty." I wiggle my eyebrows.

"Oh, I'll show you dirty," he counters with a mischievous glint in his eyes.

"No!" I shout and laugh. Soren is much stronger by a long shot and flips us so I'm beneath his hard body with my arms over my head. My legs are twisted up in his, and there's no way to move out of his hold.

His earth magic rumbles through me like a tremor, igniting my senses with the scent of spice and a warmth that sends tingles everywhere. *Holy shit.*

"Ah! That's not fair!" The rumbling travels across my chest and further down my stomach. "Stop that, Soren!" I laugh. "I give up! I give up!"

He smirks and pulls back his magic, but he stays on top of me. The hand holding my arm is the one with his tattoo. The name "Liliana" runs down his forearm in a delicate script. I've noticed it before, but it wasn't until the name was fresh in my mind that it clicked into place. I dart my eyes away before he catches me looking.

Soren is smiling down at me, his expression soft and affectionate. I get the impression he cares for me and enjoys teasing me, but that's it. The man is crazy hot, and I'd have to be dead inside not to notice. But sadly, there is only one man who makes my heart flutter, and we aren't exactly on speaking terms.

"Next time I won't be so easy on you," he jokes. A thoughtful expression plays about his face before he burrows into my neck and inhales deeply.

"Has anyone ever told you that you smell like Christmas?"

My chest tightens at the memory. I swallow down the unexpected emotion and avert my gaze.

"Ah," he says. "I think you just answered my question." Soren sits up and pulls me with him so we're sitting across from each other. His hand on my arm. "I'm sorry, Willa. I know Stellan…"

"What the hell are you doing?" A deep, furious voice asks from the doorway.

Stellan storms over, looking as angry as I've ever seen him. He must have come to work out, wearing gray sweat-pants and a tight white t-shirt, not the suit it seems he hasn't changed out of since we arrived in Stockholm. The five o'clock shadow he's sporting makes him look rougher and more casual. This is the most I've seen of his muscular arms since we were alone together in Vermont.

The memories of how he held me pressed against him bring an unwelcome flush to my cheeks. No matter how angry he makes me, no matter how badly he broke my trust, I still crave him. It's a weakness I can't seem to overcome.

Stellan's jaw is set in anger, but his eyes are red and tired as they move between Soren and me. I wonder again if he's been sleeping.

The two men exchange heated words in Swedish. Soren gets right in Stellan's face. Their magic pulses violently around the room. I'm afraid someone is going to get hurt if I don't intervene.

"Enough!" I yell, infusing magic into my voice like thunder. The loud sound breaks the percolating tension and shifts their attention to me. "Soren, would you mind giving me and Stellan a few minutes alone?"

Soren squeezes my shoulder. "Of course," he says. He pushes past Stellan with an angry shove.

"Willa, you can't train here." Stellan doesn't acknowledge Soren or give me a chance to speak first. He takes a step forward, now dangerously close to my personal space.

"You can't be serious." I cross my arms. This is the one thing that brings me any joy here, and he's going to take it away?

"I'm sorry, but it's just not something I can allow."

"Are you sorry, though? *Really?*"

Stellan stares at me for a moment too long, like he's trying to find the right words.

"I haven't heard so much as a single word from you in days," I go on. "I am not allowed to know anything about an investigation that impacts me more than anyone else on Earth. I'm in a foreign city that I haven't actually set foot in. I'm essentially your prisoner and an 'asset' you manage. So, no, I don't believe you're sorry at all."

"Willa, you have to understand," his voice rising in desperation. "I'm not doing any of this to be cruel. If the Agency knows you can fight, they'll never let you go."

He pauses and my resolve falters. I hadn't thought of it that way. That he might be trying to protect me.

"I never wanted any of this for you," he continues with his hands so close to touching me. "I never wanted you to come here at all. I am sorry..." His voice wavers with emotion, and he runs his hands through his hair in frustration. "Fuck, I'm sorry for so much, but I am trying to keep you safe. Can't you see that I'm trying to make it possible for you to go back to your old life when this is over?"

I close my eyes and breath slowly, keeping my emotions in check. I want to cry, to scream.

"Stellan," I say with all the patience I can find. "Have you ever thought to ask me what I want?"

His throat bobs as he swallows. His eyes are wild. He looks genuinely unwell. I shouldn't have the capacity to worry about him, but I do.

"You know as well as I do that there is no returning from this. Do you really think The Storm King's daughter is going back to cataloging books? Do you honestly believe I can take all this power raging inside me and just do…nothing with it?" I'm utterly exasperated.

"This." I hold up my hands. I push a tiny sliver of magic down my arms and light a small fire in my palms. The task takes no effort, and Stellan's eyebrows raise slightly at how much more easily it comes to me. "This is my world now, Stellan. I have to learn how to find my place in it with or without your help."

We're so close I feel the heat from his body. There is so much I want and need him to say, and I don't know if he will. He reaches for me, and I realize that no matter how badly he hurt me, I want him to touch me. I want him to hold me and tell me he's sorry and show me how much he cares.

He gently touches my arms and the simple heat from his hands on my skin makes my breath stutter. Our eyes are locked in silent communication, igniting a flame inside me that I haven't dared to hope for.

"I have to know," I speak quietly and with all the vulnerability I usually hide behind thick walls. "Was anything real between us or was it all lies? Please tell me so I don't spend the rest of my life wondering."

Stellan releases my arms like I'm on fire when he feels the intensity of my emotions with his magic. The loss of connection is almost violent in its finality.

"Willa, I…" He rubs the back of his neck, his eyes on the floor. Then he exhales heavily, straightening his spine. His professional mask slips fully back in place, and I know that I've truly lost him. My heart sinks, and he hasn't even spoken yet. That small flame of hope is snuffed out.

"What happened in Vermont was real in the sense that we were attracted to each other and we allowed that to run its course. It was a mistake on my part, and I regret causing you pain. What you overheard that day was unfortunate, but this was always the end result. You are here as part of an ongoing investigation, and I can't allow for your emotional response to cause distraction. You are my professional responsibility, and you need to remain in your hotel room until further notice."

Bullshit.

"My 'emotional response'?" I shake my head in disbelief. I think back to all those moments when he kissed my face and held me close. The softness in his gaze. The tenderness. They weren't lies. I'm certain of it now. But does it matter what he felt then if he refuses to follow his heart and not his orders? There is a man beneath that cold exterior who cares for me, but it won't ever be enough to matter.

"Stellan, you can tell yourself whatever you want, but it won't change the truth. I hope someday when you find something you want again, you're brave enough to reach for it."

He closes his eyes, refusing to let me in. I turn away from him.

"Willa, wait," he calls after me. But I don't look back. I just let my magic flow around me like a pissed-off tornado and walk out.

CHAPTER 34

It's another day of not much to do and even less enthusiasm with which to do it. I sit on my burgundy couch hugging a pillow to my chest and survey my fake apartment/prison cell.

From the white and bare-wood kitchen area to my little teak style dining room table, it's all too perfect. The floors are painted a cheerful light blue, and the furniture is trendy and modern in rich colors and fabrics that are simultaneously luxurious and sensible.

I'm grateful that I'm not in an actual prison, but there's something so false and impersonal about everything.

I feel like I'm suffocating inside a Scandinavian minimalist's wet dream.

Stellan icing me out has put me in an even worse mood. It would be easier to believe he doesn't care, but I'm certain he's lying to me and to himself.

But what choice do I have? I have to take what he's saying at face value. He wanted me when it was a charade and a game of playing house, but he doesn't want me in his real life.

It's time to get over it.

Since Stellan insists that I no longer visit the office, Banks told me he'd stop by this morning with coffee and some more books so I reluctantly get dressed and busy myself as best I can with another knitting project.

Much earlier than expected, there's a knock at the door. I open it to find Ingrid standing on the other side, looking perfectly coiffed in blonde curls and a red peacoat.

"What are you doing here?" I don't bother hiding my irritation.

"Hello to you, too," she says with an exaggerated eye roll, as if I'm the one being difficult.

"Stellan asked me to take you to the office this morning."

Right.

"Yeah, I'm not falling for that, Ingrid." Her phony smile slips before she plasters it back on.

"Look, I know we got off on the wrong foot, but I'm just here to take you to the office. Stellan told me this morning when we woke up that you were needed and I offered to give him a break and come get you myself. He's been working so hard lately, and I've been keeping him up at night." She winks and flicks her hair over her shoulder.

I rub my temples and close my eyes. I know she's lying, and I know she's goading me.

"Ingrid, how stupid do you think I am? You handcuffed me to a chair so I could be tortured. I'd say that's pretty much the wrongest foot two people could ever get off on. If Olsen or Stellan want me to come to the office, they can come get me themselves. I don't trust you, and I have no reason to trust you. I'm not going anywhere."

"You're making a big mistake," she says viciously. Her eyes like daggers, she flicks her hair over her shoulder again before crossing her arms. Is there some kind of training course for bullies? Ingrid is a fucking pro at it.

"What mistake is that?" Stellan peeks around Ingrid from the doorway. She turns red and simpers. "Oh! Stell! I wasn't expecting you!" She leans into him and kisses his cheek. "I was just telling Willa that she was making a big mistake not trying the herring for breakfast. It's traditional after all. You didn't tell me you were stopping here this morning?"

Stellan's eyes narrow. He doesn't believe a word she just said. "No, I came to speak to Ms. Martin, and I assumed she would be alone." There's a bite in his voice. He's not happy to find Ingrid at my door.

Whatever the real reason for either of them being here, I'm too tired and angry to examine it. Calling Ingrid out on her obvious lies holds no appeal.

"I guess it's just the day for unexpected guests," I say coldly and leave them both in the doorway. I sit back down on the couch and pick up my knitting. I have no reason to pretend with these people anymore.

"Well, anyway, why don't you and I go grab some breakfast before we head into the office?" Ingrid suggests to Stellan with a flirty smile.

Stellan doesn't appear to know what to do or say. I glance at him, and our eyes meet briefly. I can't trust it, but I think he's trying to wordlessly convey something to me. Unfortunately, he made it clear that there is no reason to spend the energy figuring him out, so I'm not going to bother.

"That's a wonderful idea," I speak for him. "Have a fabulous time."

I keep my focus on my knitting needles until I hear Stellan sigh and the door shutting behind them.

I keep myself occupied as best I can for as long as I can, but eventually even knitting starts to annoy me.

I grab the phone Soren left for me and crawl into bed. I wouldn't normally do this, but times are desperate. I type in Sam's number and let it ring.

"Uh, hello?"

I'll apologize later for waking him up, but right now, I'm so grateful he answered the phone I could cry.

"Hi, Sam. It's Wil."

"Are you alright?"

"Sam, I'm…" I'm about to say I'm fine, but my chin quivers. I hold it in. I refuse to cry over any of this ever again. I sniff. Sam will know I'm warring with my emotions.

"Oh, Willa, it's alright."

"I'm fine, Sam." I stifle the tears. "I just miss you so much. I'm OK, but it's…hard."

How do you explain nothing and everything at the same time? I told him what I could about being here. He knows it's not a social visit, but that barely scratches the surface.

"If you need me, I'm on the next flight to Stockholm."

I wish so much that it was that simple.

"Even if that were possible, you wouldn't be able to help me. This is something I have to do on my own."

"What happened to that guy you were with? Is he still there?"

"Yes, Stellan is here. He's not exactly helping things."

"Uh oh, I know that tone. What did he do?"

"Nothing. Apart from presenting me with an opportunity to break my own heart, and I took it. Dove headfirst and everything. But it's honestly not that, Sam. I just feel so useless and trapped. I haven't been outside for longer than 10 minutes in days. I'm barely seeing the sun. I'm lonely, and I'm frustrated. I don't know. Maybe I'm just sad, Sam."

Saying it out loud makes me feel better in a small way, even if it's not the whole story.

"I'm so sorry, Wil." I can hear him moving around now, turning the light on, sitting up in bed. I can picture him tying his hair back. I miss all the little familiar things about my friend. "I wish I could help you or that there was something more I could do for you."

"I know. Just hearing your voice is enough. I'm sorry for unloading on you so early in the morning. How are you? Are you OK?"

"Apart from being out of my mind worrying about you, I'm alright. I just want you to come home."

I wipe away tears as they fall. I have no idea when or even if I can go back to Vermont. I've had no indication that I'll be allowed to return. That's a frightening thought. But what scares me even more is that the idea of going home doesn't hold the same appeal it once did. I don't want to stay here in this half-life, but I'm certain that my old life doesn't fit me anymore. And I have no idea what to do about that.

"I know, Sam. Hopefully, I'll be able to leave soon." I do my best to sound convincing.

"Good. I hope it's OK that I took the cats home. Going there every day was too much."

"Of course, that's fine."

"Reg keeps puking on Nick's carpet, so I think it's safe to say he misses you, too."

The thought makes me laugh despite everything. "Give them both a big pet for me. I love you, Sam."

"I love you, too, Willa. Please stay safe."

"I'll do my best. Bye, Sammy."

I hang up and stare at the white ceiling and the chandelier over my bed for a moment and then roll over to get up. Banks is standing in the doorway to my bedroom. A dark figure in a black coat against the all-white room. I jolt in surprise and scream.

"Goddamnit! You scared me!" I sit, clutching my chest and swing my legs out of bed.

Banks usually has an expressionless face, likely practiced

over many years in his job, but he seems to be debating with himself.

"My apologies," he says.

"It's alright. You're just remarkably good at sneaking up on people. How much of that conversation did you hear?"

"Enough." Banks moves away from the door to give me space to walk through. "Put your shoes and coat on, Ms. Martin."

"Um, why?"

"As the Chief Security Officer, I am breaking you out of jail."

* * *

BANKS TURNS off the alarm on the fire escape. He waits a few seconds until a call comes through.

"This is Banks. Yes, Lundqvist. I'm testing the unit. Everything is in order. Yes, I have eyes on her. All good. Bye, now."

Banks doesn't say anything for a moment after the call ends, but there's a small smile on his lips.

"Alright," he says at last, "we have a few hours of sunlight. Let's make the most of it."

I follow Banks down the fire escape. The moment the cold touches my face and I breathe in the fresh air, the tension eases in my shoulders. The fire escape is rickety and old, but I'm too in awe of my surroundings to notice. The scant daylight illuminates a view of the city with its bright and colorful buildings and old-world architecture that is absolutely breathtaking.

Banks takes my hand and helps me down the last big step to the ground. I have no idea where he's taking me, but I don't care. Just to be out of the apartment and free for a few minutes is the greatest gift.

We walk along old, cobblestone streets. The route avoids

main roads, but I can see the traffic lights and speeding cars running parallel to our path. It's late morning so the streets are mostly empty while the city is at work.

Twinkling Christmas lights are strung on street lamps and between buildings. Red ribbons and evergreen wreaths dot the doorways. Electric candles light up the windows. The holiday ornaments open up a hollow pit in my stomach. A reminder that time is passing while I'm trapped in stasis.

The few people we pass don't pay us any attention as they go about their business. Everyone is bundled up to keep out the cold. The gray peacoat and white wool hat I found in the closet take the sting off the wind, but the cold still finds its way in and my skin prickles.

We cross bridges and walk through parks and up more side streets until we reach a small restaurant inside a red painted building. The interior is warm and welcoming with rustic tables and white candles burning inside thick glass cups.

A fire is going in an ancient stone fireplace. There's a man at the bar wearing a blue apron wiping glasses with a cloth. We're shown to a small table away from the windows. Banks puts my back to the door so he can watch the entrance. He hangs up my coat and orders us some drinks that he brings back to the table.

"This is a beer from a brewery nearby. It's popular. Would you like to choose some sandwiches, and I'll pick out the aquavit?"

"Sure, that sounds nice." I'm too excited to be out and about to care what we eat.

I'm not much of a day drinker, but nothing is normal these days. Banks sits across from me and eyes the door every so often like he expects someone to storm in.

"So, you're from Ireland?" I ask a little awkwardly.

"I am."

"Cool. What part?" I ask, no less awkwardly.

"Dublin."

"What was that like?"

"Awful," he answers with a flat expression.

I wince. "I'm sorry, I think I forgot how to do small talk. You don't have to answer my questions."

"It's fine, Willa. But I don't talk about my life before Darlings. Going to school and meeting Stellan, Greta, and Soren was the best thing that ever happened to me."

"Your friendship is very special. I can see it when you work together."

"We've seen each other at our worst. There's a lot of trust between us."

We drink our beer in silence for a few minutes and then the food arrives along with the aquavit. I couldn't read the menu, but apparently I chose well. Plates of salmon, shrimp, and herring open-faced sandwiches on rye bread with pickled vegetables and a variety of sauces and fish roe fill the small table.

"You'll want to take a bite and then a sip of the liquor. They make it in house. It's essentially vodka mixed with herbs and other ingredients, and it helps round out the flavor of the food."

I do as Banks instructs and flinch a little at the intensity of the alcohol as it hits my throat. He laughs at the face I make.

"That's good, but I'm not used to drinking vodka at noon."

"They say it keeps you healthy." Banks tips back his glass. Of course, he doesn't grimace like I do.

We eat in friendly silence for a while, and I drink more of my beer. I feel a little floaty from the alcohol. I set my fork down and study Banks. He's a man of great contrasts. Big and burly, but also soft and kind.

"Why are you looking at me like that?" He asks with a quizzical lift of his eyebrow.

"Sorry, I'm just curious why you brought me here."

He leans back in his chair and looks out the window for a moment before answering. "I know what it feels like to be trapped in a situation that wasn't your making. I guess I just wanted to give you a minute of normalcy."

I smile at him. "I really appreciate it. I'm sorry if it gets you into any trouble."

He laughs, gruff but friendly.

"Nothing I can't handle, love."

We finish lunch with coffee and some light conversation. Banks asks me questions about my childhood and my work in libraries. He doesn't talk about himself, and I don't pry.

When we're ready to leave, he hands me my coat, and we step out into the afternoon light. I'm dizzy from the drinks and the cold air hitting my face doesn't do much to help.

"Thank you for today, but I have to tell you a secret," I whisper loudly as I lean against him a little too hard.

"Oh, yes?" Banks asks in amusement.

"I think you might have gotten me drunk."

CHAPTER 35

"Why do you call yourself 'The Storm King'?"

My father and I sit across from each other on an animal skin rug with a roaring fire next to us. Snow falls gently outside the wide windows of his fortress house.

"It's a name that was given to me. When I was younger, I was even more arrogant than I am now," he says as if that explains everything.

He leans back against the front of the couch and stretches his long legs out in front of him. "What else do you want to know?"

I could ask him why he wants to find me so badly. I could ask him any number of the burning questions I have for him.

But there's only one that matters.

"Why did you do it?" My voice shakes, but I keep myself together.

Lars exhales heavily but keeps unflinching eye contact with me. I don't need to explain what "it" means.

"I never set out to hurt your mother. In fact, it was my

love for her that had me searching for a way to unlock her latent magic. It might be hard to understand, but I had insurmountable obligations as the eldest son in my family. Anne's magic was the only way that we could be together. And then when she refused to use it, I was forced to…well, I was forced to do things I later came to regret."

He stares into the fire next to us. Lost in memories. I don't speak. I'm not sure I can. I'm so angry. Part of me wants to kill him for hurting my mother, for causing all the upheaval in our lives.

But something in the sad way that he lives so utterly alone and the worn and weathered expression on his face makes it hard to feel only hate for him.

"Is she happy?" he asks after a while.

I wish so much that I could give him a better answer. That my mother had moved on with her life. That she had met someone and was in love or at least that she was fulfilled in other ways and not so haunted by him.

"She's not your concern," I tell him instead.

"No, I suppose she isn't anymore," he agrees sadly before shifting focus. "Our time tonight is almost up. Someone inside the Agency has given us access to you. Mikkel's men will be there soon. Will you come, Willa?"

His question takes me by surprise. I thought I might have more time to decide how to proceed. I'm not sure I want to go. I know I have to find out more about the man in front of me. It's hard to picture this man as the same one who hurt my mother, who intentionally used his magic to nearly kill her.

And I need to know what he wants from me, but exploring it in dreams is so much safer. If I leave, Stellan and my new friends will be furious with me. I'll become their enemy.

But this problem is mine, despite what others may think.

This might be the only chance I have to fix it. There is really no choice in the matter.

"I suppose it depends on how nicely they ask."

* * *

STELLAN

It's late, and I'm still in the office. The only consolation is that Soren is here as well. The blue light from his computer shines into the dark hallway. I can hear the clacking of his keyboard.

I've read the same sentence in this report six times. I should just call it a day and go home.

My mobile phone rings, startling me out of my thoughts. The name across the caller ID is unexpected.

"What can I do for you, Dr. Svenson?"

"Good evening, Agent Lundqvist. I'm so sorry to bother you this late, but once I had confirmation I couldn't wait." The doctor's voice shakes like she's struggling to breathe.

"Couldn't wait for what?"

She sniffs as if she's holding back tears and when she speaks her voice is hoarse. "The day Wilhelmina Martin came in for evaluations, I knew something wasn't right, but I was too afraid to say something before now. I'm so sorry."

Dr. Svenson begins to weep openly. Anticipation claws at me. My heart rages inside my chest.

"What about Wilhelmina Martin?" I ask with urgency in my voice. Soren appears in the doorway, having heard my end of the conversation from down the hall. I motion for him to join me and he sits. I put my phone on speaker.

"Dr. Svenson, please continue when you are able."

"Of course. I'm sorry." She collects herself with a loud sniff. "We performed the customary evaluations on Ms.

Martin, and she was in good health when we ended our session.

"As we were finishing, Director Olsen and Agent Davis arrived in the booth. They asked us to stop filming and leave them so they could meet with Ms. Martin on their own. Olsen said they had classified evaluations to conduct based on her lineage."

Soren and I exchange worried looks from across my desk. My stomach sinks.

"I thought it was strange and very obviously against protocol, but Dr. Gage insisted that we listen to Director Olsen."

"So, you left?"

"Yes, but I felt so uncomfortable and wrong about it that I switched on the secondary camera without them noticing."

"You left a camera running while Olsen and Davis met with Ms. Martin?" I ask her to repeat herself.

"Yes. I was afraid someone would find out so I buried the file. I was terrified to access it again until tonight when my guilt got the better of me. Wondering what might have been done to that poor woman."

"What did you see?" It takes incredible effort to keep my voice even. But I need her to cooperate and not get scared off. The uncertainty around what took place that day has eaten at me. I have to know.

"It's...awful." She sounds as if she's about to cry again.

"Dr. Svenson, if I send you a secure link to upload the file, would you do that?" I ask. Soren pulls out his phone, and it takes only a second for him to send off the link.

"Or course," she says. "I see it. I'm uploading the file now."

"Please forgive me," she says after a moment and hangs up.

Soren comes around my desk and doesn't bother to ask before he's at my computer pulling up the link to a video file.

The still image shows Willa tied to a chair with blood running down her face and chest.

Soren's hand trembles as he clicks play on a video that I'm certain will change everything.

At first, it's too dark to see. It's just the sound of Willa breathing as if she's fighting invisible forces. Then Ingrid speaks.

"Hey Winter, do you want to know something?"

"Not particularly," Willa answers through clenched teeth.

"I'm going to tell you anyway. It's too delicious not to share. Would you like to guess how many times Stellan made me come last night?"

Soren abruptly directs his furious gaze over to me, but I just shake my head in denial. I haven't touched Ingrid, despite her many obvious attempts at seduction. Her beauty is surface level and unappealing. As soon as Willa entered my life, there was no comparison, no temptation for anything less.

The two women spar back and forth, until Ingrid gives up.

"Tie her to the chair," Olsen speaks and the lights in the evaluation room go up. Willa comes into view. She looks so small and vulnerable in nothing but a hospital gown. Olsen grabs Willa's arms, and Ingrid ties them back with magic containment cuffs. The fear on Willa's face guts me.

But then Ingrid slams her fist into Willa's nose, and Soren and I both gasp.

"I'm going to fucking kill her," Soren growls.

Willa laughs in hysteria as blood drips from her broken nose. Olsen punches her in the jaw. It's all I can do to stay sitting, to keep watching. But Willa suffered through this, and I can suffer through watching it.

Olsen raises his arms, and his magic makes two deep cuts

appear right beneath Willa's collarbones. Blood runs down her chest, her eyes are wide open in fear, pain, and shock.

My hands are clammy, and my head swims. I swallow back the nausea.

Olsen shouts at Willa. He wants her to tell him things she can't possibly know. He hits her again and again, and Willa's screams echo through the quiet of my office. I hear a snap as her ribs break. Soren moves a chair over to sit down. His face is as pale as mine.

Willa takes their cruelty with such bravery and control. I'm shocked by how much she endures from them and how little she cracks under the pressure. The insults, the physical torture. She's weakened by it, but she's not broken. By the time Ingrid heals Willa's wounds and the video ends, I'm ready to commit a double homicide.

The silence in my office is suffocating. I inhale deeply through my nose. Soren's leg bounces.

The storm builds inside me until I release an unholy roar and shove all the papers and bullshit reports off my desk. My hands shake, and the blood in my ears rushes so loudly I'm certain I'm on the verge of a heart attack. What they did to her...how they hurt her...

My magic surges, and Soren's eyes go wide. He feels how close I am to the edge.

"Stellan, calm down." Soren is detached and emotionless though I know he's raging inside just as fiercely as I am.

"We have more than enough information to warrant a search into Olsen and Ingrid's digital footprints," he continues.

I inhale and settle my magic. Forcing myself to think logically. "Let's get this and whatever else you find over to Director Hawley's office tonight," I tell him through the gravel in my throat.

"I'll work on it now. But please don't do anything stupid. You're no use to Willa in prison."

"I'm hardly of use to her now. If it wasn't for me…"

"Don't do that, Stellan. What happened to her was truly horrific, but we won't be able to fix our mistakes if we lose our heads now." Soren points to the computer screen with a look of steely determination. We might have disagreed lately, but our friendship is too deep to let anything come between us for long. Soren will always be a voice of reason when I need him.

"They hurt her because I failed to protect her. Because I trusted them, they broke her bones, Soren. They nearly killed her…" My voice cracks.

I hang my head. The shame of it. The rage and the anguish. I could murder them for what they did. But what destroys me is knowing I just handed her over to them. I trusted them both even though I had doubts. I'll never forgive myself for it.

"We'll make them pay for this. I promise you, Stellan," Soren says. "I bear responsibility, too. Banks and I should have pushed harder to find out what happened when she was so unwell that day. We made incorrect assumptions that she was just overwrought from everything else. Once I'm done with them, death will feel like the preferable option. But what are *you* going to do now?"

He's not asking about Olsen and Ingrid. Of all the problems, they're the easiest to fix.

"I am not sure there is anything I can do. I've messed it all up so badly."

"You have," he agrees. I'm grateful for his honesty. "From what I saw, Willa was upset for a day or two after this happened. She experienced it, she felt it, and she put it away. But you? She's not over that by a long shot. They hurt her physically, Stellan. But you broke her heart."

My chest caves in knowing that he's right. The pain I caused her is partially why I stayed away, but it's only made things worse.

"I thought I was doing the right thing. I thought I was protecting her. I thought that she'd be better off. That she'd stay safe. I…"

"You were wrong, Stellan. She's not better off without you. You're not better off without her either. I know Liliana's death is a burden you carry, but I promise it's not yours to bear."

If only it were as simple as that. But seeing Willa so battered…I'll never be the same. Staying away is no longer an option.

There's only one thought that keeps repeating through my head as I stare at the brutal image of Willa's face covered in blood.

She's mine.

Willa Martin is mine. To protect. To treasure. My heart is hers whether she wants it or not, and no one will hurt her ever again.

My phone interrupts my thoughts, the vibrations radiating across my metal desk.

"Banks, is there a problem?"

"Unusual activity at the hotel. I'm pulling up now. Some additional heat signatures on the top floor. Four men, by the looks of things."

"On the way."

I grab my coat and race out the door with Soren following close behind.

CHAPTER 36

WILLA

I WAKE in midnight darkness and shriek at the sound of bullets firing just outside.

My heart leaps to my throat and my stomach roils.

After what feels like forever, the cacophony ceases, and a disturbing silence remains. I have two options: leave willingly or fight them off. As much as I want answers from my father, I don't have a lot of hope this is going to end well.

The door bursts open and four men in Kevlar vests with automatic weapons storm in. I stand in front of them in just my nightgown with my hair a mass of messy waves around me.

"Ms. Martin, we are here to take you to Mikkel Stromberg." The man in front speaks in another burly English accent.

"Yeah, OK. Can I get dressed?"

"Uh, yes?" He wasn't expecting my cooperation, but he motions for two of his men to follow me.

They come up close behind me as we walk into my

bedroom. They don't seem to know what to do with them-selves, shifting uncomfortably on their feet and glancing around like they're expecting an attack.

I'm probably making a very strategic mistake, but I honestly don't know what else to do anymore. I can't let other people dictate the trajectory of my life while I sit around twiddling my thumbs.

I change as quickly as possible. We return to the living room, and the men nod to their leader that I'm ready to leave. We're moving toward the door when it swings open and Banks bursts in with rage billowing out of him like a hurricane.

Oh, no.

"Willa, stay where you are!"

Banks is unlike anything I've ever seen. He takes out the two men closest to the door almost instantly.

For someone so large, he moves like liquid. He uses his magic to incapacitate his assailants and then his brute strength to disarm them. There's the sick sound of limbs snapping and the crunch of orbital bones breaking. It's terri-fying and astonishing as his raw power takes control of the room in a matter of seconds.

I back away, seriously questioning my decision to walk out of here without a fight. Banks is angry and focused, but there was worry in his eyes when he saw me surrounded by four gunmen.

I'm certain he views me as more than just a job. I care for all of them, too. Even though Stellan stomped on my heart, I don't want him or anyone else hurt because of me.

If anything happens to Banks tonight, I'll never forgive myself.

I'm so focused on Banks that I don't realize until too late that the lead gunman is right behind me again. He grabs me by the hair and shoves the gun in my back.

I guess we're past asking nicely.

But the man's error is that he thinks I'm helpless.

"Let her go right now," Banks demands.

"It's OK." I try to convey with my expression that I can handle it. My magic is thrilled with the idea of a fight. It's pushing hard against me.

Soon.

"No, Willa. It's too dangerous." Banks eyes the other man still standing. The gun in his hands is pointed right at him.

"You're correct about that, mate," the man behind me says and yanks my hair so I'm forced to look up. He digs his weapon deeper into my back, bruising me. I'm sure these guys are just like the other men Mikkel hired and will have no qualms about causing me bodily harm. My magic swells, and I let it swirl out of me without a second thought.

My sleep magic trickles down my hand. I try to be subtle, but it's hard to miss the moment I connect with his arm. He instantly sags and his grip on me loosens.

Banks doesn't realize what I've done and takes the man's distraction as an opportunity to rush toward me. He does something with his magic that freezes the two men in place, but not quickly enough. The gunman already opened fire, and I watch in what feels like slow motion as Banks gets hit in the shoulder and the leg. I scream as a bullet hits his chest, and he collapses onto the ground.

"NO!"

My heart drops to my stomach. This is all my fault. My magic is so much stronger than these men. I could have stopped this before it started. It explodes out of me as my anguish takes over.

I lift my arms up by my sides as I breathe in and out, giving my magic permission to take over. I'm past the point of providing instructions. I just let my power carry us.

Beyond rational thought, I swear I float above the

ground. The room grows cold like a February night. My breath vaporizes before me as the temperature plummets to well below freezing. The men are no longer bound by Banks's magic and are about to run when I turn on them. My magic fills the room as I breathe out a powerful gust of arctic air. It knocks them to the ground and doesn't let up until they freeze. Their mouths gape in silent screams.

I tumble to the ground and run for Banks as my magic draws back inside me, warming the room to a normal temperature. I find my phone and with shaky hands call Soren. As I wait for him to answer, I hold tight to Banks. He's still warm. He's still alive. If they get here fast enough, he might be alright.

"Willa, what is it?" Soren asks, alert and urgent.

"You have to come now. It's Banks. He's…" My voice breaks as I choke on a sob. "Men came to the hotel. We took them out. But Banks. He's…it's not good. Please just come."

"We're already on the way, but there's a fucking traffic blockade. I have no idea who authorized it, but we're driving around. Just stay on the line with me. Are you alright?"

"I'm fine," I say, but tears fall on Banks as I cry over him.

"Tell me what you see happening to Banks. He's a hard man to kill."

I survey his body. His chest rises and falls, but barely.

"He's alive. He's breathing."

"Is there much blood?" Soren asks.

"There is some blood." I glance around Banks. Considering how many times he was shot there should be a lot more. "There's not as much as I'd expect. Should I be doing something to help him? I don't know how to fix this."

"No, sweetheart. His magic is taking care of him, as I hoped."

"It's my fault, Soren."

"Don't say that."

"No, it is. I decided to let them take me instead of fighting. I was going willingly and then Banks turned up and it all just happened."

"Wait, wait. You were going to leave with them? On purpose!?" Soren shouts.

"I'm so sorry," I start to cry. It's all too much. I hear angry shouting in the background and what sounds like Stellan's raised voice. I hold the phone against my chest as I cry. I don't want them to hear me.

But then the door to the hotel room opens, and the last person I ever wanted to see again walks in.

CHAPTER 37

OLSEN STRIDES into the apartment like he owns the place. He has a confidence that doesn't match his thinning hair and the gut protruding from his unflattering khaki trousers.

Silver fox he is not.

But I can't forget what happened the last time we were alone together. There are nights when I lie awake and my mind runs over that day when his magic cut me open with just a flick of his hand. He might be disgusting, but he's powerful. My pulse picks up as he moves closer.

"Oh, dear," he says with mock concern as he takes in the state of the room. His eyes fall on Banks, the mercenaries on the floor, and all the furniture that upended during the fight.

"You know, Ms. Martin, when I said you were going to be bait, that meant you had to actually leave the building."

"Sorry?" I shrug.

"Did you do all this?" He gestures around the room in what I'm sure he thinks is an intimidating swagger.

"Some of it," I answer honestly.

"He wasn't meant to show up." Olsen points to Banks. "Ingrid said she had the distraction covered, but obviously she was mistaken."

"I'd say that's on you for trusting someone as dumb as Ingrid."

"Ah, tut tut. Ingrid is twice the woman you are. Your jealousy is unattractive, though it's certainly warranted. Ingrid fucks like a goddess, but I bet you're a real cold fish in the bedroom."

I suppose that bit of unsolicited information shouldn't surprise me, but I shudder at the thought of them together.

"So, what exactly was your plan here?" I ask, ignoring his poor attempt at taunting me. "Were you going to let them take me and then what? Follow them? I don't see how this was going to work out for you."

Soren said something about a traffic blockade. It must have been part of Olsen's grand plan.

"You wouldn't." His feet thud across the wood floor. I take a step back. I don't want him near me.

"Do you have a bone to pick with my dad, and that's why you're so hell-bent on this? Or is it that you just don't like disobedient women?" The urge to provoke him is too strong.

"I'd be delighted to teach you some obedience, young lady." He encroaches further on my personal space. I have to breathe through my mouth to avoid the sickening stench of his magic as it creeps over me.

"No, thanks. I'm all set."

He pushes himself against me, and I bump into the side of the couch. I'm out of room to move back. He runs a finger over my chest, and his magic splits open my shirt, revealing the black lace of my bra. A cold sweat breaks out across my skin.

"I meant what I said before," he sneers. "Lars Stromberg

cannot be allowed to run free any longer, but it's not just that. While Lundqvist was in diapers, I was out hunting your father and countless criminals just like him. Lundqvist thinks he's untouchable. That he's going to take my job out from under me, but I'm going to prove he's not the hero everyone thinks he is."

Olsen leans in even closer. I turn my face and he runs his nose along my cheek. I squeeze my eyes closed and fight to keep the nausea under control. His thick stomach presses into me, and I feel what is unmistakably an erection against my side. I want to vomit, but more than anything else, I want him to suffer.

I give my magic permission to begin twisting and weaving around Olsen. He's too preoccupied to notice as I knit a special nightmare just for him.

"Now who sounds jealous?" I goad him, even though I know I shouldn't.

My magic coils around him, tightening like a snare. I wasn't fast enough with the gunman, but I won't fail now.

Olsen grits his teeth in anger. He rears back and slaps me hard across the face. A trickle of blood runs down my cheek from a ring on his pinky finger.

While I'm still stunned from the shock, he shoots up a hand and squeezes it around my throat while the other grips my breast hard enough to leave marks. I wince in pain, but don't make a sound as his meaty fingers dig roughly into my skin. I refuse to give him the satisfaction.

"I'm going to enjoy making you scream." He releases my throat and unbuckles his belt, opening the button on his pants and lowering the zipper.

Not happening, asshole.

I grab Olsen's arms with both hands, pushing him away from me. I close my eyes and the sick bastard laughs.

But then I open my eyes wide and lift my chin. "You're

going to regret your decision to come here tonight." My magic deepens my voice, turning it lethal and cold.

His arrogant smile fades.

Before he can react, I force my magic into his mind, plunging him into darkness.

Olsen's shields are strong, but I caught him off-guard. I envelop him in a night terror so hideous and gruesome that I have to shield my own mind against it.

Olsen's eyes close, and he loses his grip on me. He falls to the ground in what I hope is a painful landing. He whimpers, curling into the fetal position as his body shakes. I stand over him, watching my nightmare swallow him whole.

I kick him and he grunts in his sleep. He deserves far worse.

I stagger back over to Banks. His forest magic shrouds his body with the scent of trees and moss. He's warm. Probably too warm, but I hope it's his magic healing him, like Soren said. I lean my head against his uninjured side. I rub my thumb along his hand.

I must doze off for a moment because I'm startled to find Greta kneeling over me.

"*Oh, dieu.*" She pulls me into a hug that I desperately need. I've missed her.

"Can you stand? We need to look at him."

"Of course."

I step aside, and Soren leans over Banks, listening to his lungs and checking his pulse. He dials a number on his phone and starts issuing orders in Swedish. He then strides over to the mercenaries and checks them, too. They're alive, but incapacitated.

On the other side of the room, Stellan is crouched over Olsen's body.

"What did you do to him?" he asks without taking his eyes off Olsen, who is still whimpering and twitching in his sleep.

"I gave him a nightmare," I respond flatly. I'm shaking now. The adrenaline is waning. Greta holds my hand.

"From the look of her, he deserves it." Greta points to my face and then my opened shirt where my lace bra and bare stomach are on display.

Stellan's eyes travel from my exposed chest, which have marks from Olsen's fingers, and then to Olsen where his belt and pants are clearly undone.

He pauses for a moment like a record skipping before his face darkens with rage. His crystal blue eyes practically glow.

I've seen Stellan angry, but I've never experienced the full force of it. His magic charges the air, washing us in the sensation of a rainstorm so powerful it makes me want to take cover.

"Stell, you might want to rein that in," Greta says forcefully. "We've got company."

Stellan growls and pulls his magic back as a group of Agency personnel walk in. A man and a woman in matching uniforms move toward Banks with a stretcher while others do the same with the mercenaries.

I caused so much trouble.

"I'm so sorry. If you need to send me to the secure facility, I understand."

"What are you talking about?" Greta asks. "Of course we're not sending you away. You were attacked, Willa. This wasn't your fault."

I shake my head. It is definitely my fault.

She opens her mouth to continue when there's a piercing wail over by the door.

"Henrik!" Ingrid runs over and kneels by Olsen, trying to shake him awake.

"What did you do to him?!" she shouts at me venomously.

It's the middle of the night, and Ingrid is dressed for a

nightclub. She's in the tiniest dress I've ever seen in a bright red color and sky-high heels.

Olsen was wrong earlier. I'm not jealous of Ingrid because she's pretty. I hate her because she's conniving and manipulative and because she hit me when I couldn't fight back.

Greta's magic fires the air around us, and Soren steps up to stand next to me. I am buoyed by their presence.

"What did you do to him?! You bitch!" she repeats on an even louder howl.

I cross my arms, which only makes me more aware of the fact that my shirt is split wide open.

"Name calling? Really, Ingrid? Director Olsen is fine. He is experiencing a very well-earned nightmare."

"Why are you all just standing there? She used her evil magic on a Regional Director!" she screams in outrage.

"I sure did. But at least I've never fucked the man, which is not something I can say about you."

Ingrid turns red and rushes to attack me with her arms flailing wildly. I catch her fist just like Banks taught me and use her own momentum to flip her onto her back. It's significantly easier to do with a thin woman in heels than a big man like Banks.

She's dazed for a moment, but then she ungracefully gets back on her feet. She makes a clumsy attempt at running for me again, but in the next second, Greta is right behind her.

She grabs Ingrid around the neck, throws her to the ground, and pins her in a series of smooth and well-practiced moves. Greta motions to one of the other Agency personnel and they lock Ingrid in the same magic-binding handcuffs they used on me.

The room is silent except for Ingrid's labored groans.

Soren lets out an incredulous laugh.

"What? I told you she was a snake," Greta says with a satisfied smile.

Stellan shakes his head at the scene before him, but then he turns his attention to me.

I hang my head. Whatever punishment they need to dole out for this, I'll accept it. I tried to escape tonight. Banks is hurt because of me.

But all I hear is a sigh before Stellan steps forward and pulls me close to his chest. He holds me tenderly in a protective embrace.

"Willa," he says, low enough that only I can hear him. I brave a glance up and our eyes connect.

My magic can't read emotions, but there is so much that passes unspoken in his eyes. Regret. Relief. There's also a warmth that I wish so much I could trust.

"Stellan! What are you doing?!" Ingrid wails from where she's now being held by two people in uniforms. "Help me, damn you! I haven't done anything wrong!"

Stellan reluctantly shifts his focus back to Ingrid. He holds on to me like he's afraid I'll vanish, but he addresses Ingrid with a cold and measured anger.

"I've made a lot of mistakes with you, Agent Davis. I let my respect for authority cloud my better judgment. Your manipulation went on far too long, and I will always regret allowing it.

"I am aware that you staged an unauthorized interrogation of an innocent witness. I am also aware that you and Olsen were working together to sabotage my investigation for his personal gain. But what I don't know is why? What did he promise you?"

Ingrid's face twists in outrage. "It's not my fault!"

"That's pathetic even for you," Soren says with a laugh.

"It's not! Olsen wanted me to spy on you. I admit that's why he asked me to work with you, but I was ready to switch sides. I would have told you everything, Stellan. All you had to do was pay attention to me!"

It's Greta's turn to laugh, while Stellan remains stoic next to me. "Ingrid, you can't possibly think we believe that," she says.

"It's true! If Stellan had just…"

"Enough!" Stellan interrupts her whining. "Greta, will you escort our prisoner to Headquarters? There's a cell already waiting for her."

The expression of shock and horror on Ingrid's face will carry me through dark moments for a long time.

"It would be my distinct pleasure," Greta says. Ingrid's cries follow them out the door, and then finally there's silence.

Stellan faces me. "Would you be able to wake Olsen? I understand if it's difficult for you, but Soren and I will be here."

"I can do it."

Soren puts his hand on my shoulder. With the two of them beside me, it's the safest I've felt in ages.

My magic purrs against me, and I give it instructions to draw back from Olsen where he lies, sweaty and pale, on the floor in front of us.

His eyes open. He stares blankly at the ceiling for a moment before sagging in relief and sitting up. His respite is temporary with the three of us standing in front of him.

"She…she did something to me!" Olsen yells, spraying spit everywhere. His eyes are bloodshot and dart frantically around. He lifts his hands like he's going to use his magic on me. I brace knowing how easily he could slice me open. Soren clutches me close to his side, ready to shield me.

But before Olsen can unleash his fury, Stellan is on him. He lifts Olsen off the ground by his shirt collar, his magic rising like a flash flood inside the room.

"Your first mistake was assuming you had loyalty here other than Ingrid. Video footage of Ms. Martin's unnecessary, unsanctioned, and horrifically violent interrogation, along with phone records and emails, were sent to Director Hawley's office tonight. And that's just what Soren found tonight. Imagine what we'll find when there's more time to dig."

Olsen's face grows ashen. "You're lying! She's manipulating you!" He raises his hands to attack me again. The air around us is thick with the stench of his magic, but between one breath and the next, it stops. His body goes rigid, and his face turns purple. Olsen twitches and falls again to the ground in a broken heap.

I glance at Stellan in confusion.

"Blood is mostly water. I stopped the flow for a second. It won't kill him, but it's a distinctly unpleasant experience."

An impish grin spreads across my face. Soren laughs and wraps his arm around my shoulder.

"Stellan, I don't think you need to worry quite so much. Willa is definitely Agency material."

CHAPTER 38

WILLA

I FALL asleep against the car window as Soren drives us to Stellan's apartment. Despite my reservations, they've convinced me it's the safest place to stay.

I wake when we arrive and find Stellan's hand on top of mine. He moves it when I begin to stir, but the warmth of his touch lingers.

Stellan's apartment is immaculate. It's also surprisingly personal. I'm used to the white walls and contemporary furniture, but my eyes are drawn to the record player and the shelves upon shelves of books.

"So, this is my flat." Stellan rubs the back of his neck awkwardly. "There's a guest room upstairs. I expect you'd like to sleep."

I follow him to the second floor. He places the travel bag with my things in it next to the bed, and then stands in the doorway watching me with an unreadable expression.

"Willa, you don't have to talk to me, but I want to make sure you have all the support you might need after Olsen..."

He trails off, unable to speak the words out loud. He's angry, furious even. But he's also concerned for my well-being and letting that take priority. I appreciate it.

"Thanks, Stellan. I'm alright." I run my hands over my arms. I don't want to think about what might have happened tonight if I wasn't a Mage. If I didn't have the ability to defend myself.

"Are you sure?"

"Yeah," I say. "I might want to talk to Greta about it later, but I'm OK."

"If you're sure."

"I am, thanks."

He stands there, unsure whether to go or say what's on his mind. "Well, goodnight, then."

"Goodnight, Stellan."

His feet are quiet on the stairs as he returns to the first floor, and I look more closely at the bedroom. It doesn't have the same homey feel as the rest of his apartment and I suspect it doesn't see as much use.

It's close to 3 in the morning, and I'm that weird combination of exhausted and amped.

I take a shower, which helps me feel more human despite my injuries, and change into a black nightgown.

I think about going to bed, but I hear Stellan moving around downstairs. I pile my hair up in a messy bun and make my way back to the first floor.

Stellan is in his kitchen boiling water in an electric kettle. He changed into gray sweats and a t-shirt that fits him perfectly. I half wonder if Stellan in casual clothing is what will finally finish me off. My chest aches.

"What are you still doing up?" His eyes trail over me from top to bottom and his lips form a sad smile.

"I can't sleep. There's just too much on my mind. What about you?"

"I've seen this hour of the day rather often lately. Can I make you some tea?"

"Sure."

I sit on a wooden stool at the narrow table in his kitchen. A large window offers a view of the harbor. Even in the early hours of the morning, the city lights on the water are beautiful and serene.

Stellan pours me a cup of herbal tea in a clay mug. The scent is calming, and the warmth makes me feel fuzzy at the edges. Maybe I am more tired than I thought. Stellan sits on the stool next to mine.

"I have to ask," he says, interrupting the silence. His blue eyes are tired, but they tunnel into me with all his criminal investigator intensity. "Were you really going to leave with them tonight?"

"Yes, I was."

Even if he's disappointed in me, I'm not going to lie.

Stellan closes his eyes and pinches the bridge of his nose. "Why would you do something so reckless?"

"You can't seriously ask me that, Stellan," I respond with exasperation. "What other choice was I given? Have there been any reasons to stay?"

He flinches but doesn't acknowledge my question. "Did you know they were coming?"

"I did. I've been dreaming. My father was opening up to me, and I thought that if I just did what he wanted and went with them, I could find out more. I thought that I could fix it."

Stellan blanches. "How often? That shouldn't even be possible. There are shield wards all throughout that building."

"It didn't happen for a while after that time in Vermont, but it's been more frequent here. Mostly when my own shields are down, either from injury or when…" I trail off and look down at my hands. I refuse to let him know how badly he hurt me. I've already shared too much, and I'm sick to death of being vulnerable when he gives me nothing in return.

"Or when what, Willa? I need to know."

"Please don't make me say it," I plead. Tears sting my eyes. Stellan stands and the heat of him caresses my skin as he shifts closer. He puts his hands on either side of me against the table. His rainwater scent envelops me in what feels like both a trap and an embrace.

"I need to hear you say it, Willa. Tell me what made you dream of your father."

I close my eyes, shutting out the intensity of his gaze. Why won't he let this go?

"It was when I was injured or when I cried myself to sleep, OK?" I stand in anger, forcing him to back up. "I said it, Stellan. Are you happy now? Is that what you wanted to hear? That I cried myself to sleep too many nights to count because of you and all the fucked up people you left me with?"

He pushes back. Away from the table, away from me. I take the opportunity to move around him, to go back to my room, when he gently grabs my arm.

"Wait."

"Stellan, I can't do this…"

He stares at me for a long moment before falling to his knees. He hangs his head in contrition. The strong, stoic man kneels before me like I hold the key to his salvation.

Stellan tips his head up with red-rimmed eyes and anguish on his face.

"I know there is nothing I can say that will make up for the way I have treated you. I can't do anything to take away the pain you have suffered because of my mistakes, but I need you to know that I have never been more sorry in my life."

He takes my hand cautiously and brings it to his face. He breathes in the scent of my magic like it's some divine and cleansing perfume. He presses my hand gently on his cheek. He leans into it and closes his eyes.

I can barely breathe.

"Stellan," I speak thickly through my tears. "Why? Just tell me why."

He meets my eyes. His pain is so sharp and visceral I want to wrap him in my arms and soothe it away. But there's no space for that now. I need answers and time to think. He might be hurting, but his decisions put us here and that won't just disappear.

"I've been so afraid, Willa. Afraid of what I feel for you and what that means for me, for this investigation, for everything. Afraid of ruining your beautiful life with the cold violence of mine.

"I wanted so desperately for you to have what I can't that I was willing to push you away. If it meant you could be safe and go back to your family and your cats and your library, I would break my own heart a thousand times over. I just didn't realize breaking yours would be so much harder to bear."

Stellan is close to collapse with the weight of his guilt and a bone-deep exhaustion. I can't believe what I'm hearing.

"You are the biggest idiot."

I wrap my arms around him. Placing his head against my stomach, he slowly wraps his arms around my waist as if he can't understand what's happening. I hold him to me for a long moment, breathing him in.

"Come on." I pull him to stand.

"What are we doing?"

"I'm taking you to bed."

I almost laugh at the look of shock on his face. "No, no. You haven't earned that, my friend. But you're exhausted, and it's making me tired and sad to look at you. I'm taking you to bed and making you sleep."

Stellan holds my hand all the way to his bedroom. "You don't have to do this, Willa. I hardly deserve your kindness."

"I know," I agree. "But I'm doing it anyway. I'm going to go brush my teeth and get ready for bed, and when I come back, I want you all tucked in and ready to sleep."

"I can do that," he says slowly, as if he's still struggling to believe what he's hearing.

I'm not at all ready to forgive Stellan. It's too much too soon for the pain he's caused me.

I am, however, ready to move forward.

I need to keep my focus on what's in front of me. Dreaming of my father is only confusing things. I don't believe I can trust anything he says. He might truly be a sad and lonely man, but he's still the same person who nearly killed my mother and destroyed her chance at happiness. I don't know what he needs from me, but after tonight I'm certain that I want no part of the violence he and his brother deal in.

I pad over to Stellan's room. There's a bedside light on, casting long shadows across his bedroom. It's a man's room, well-decorated with midnight blue walls and dark, wooden furniture.

I lay down on top of the duvet. I don't want to push things. As soon as he falls asleep, I'll go back to the other room.

"Please get inside the covers," he says sleepily. "If that is acceptable to you, of course," he adds.

I turn off the light and nestle inside the duvet next to Stellan's warm body. He breathes in my magic and sighs in contentment while wrapping both his arms and legs around me. I feel him slipping into sleep almost imme-diately.

"I haven't used my magic yet." A small laugh bubbles out of me.

"I never thought I'd hold you again, Willa. Knowing you're here and you're safe. That's all I need."

In his next breath, Stellan is asleep.

I spend a few minutes shielding my mind against unwanted dreams. The part of me responsible for self-preservation is certain that this is unwise and that I'm bound to get even more hurt by letting this man anywhere near me again.

But I'm starved for comfort and that wins out. I let the security and warmth of Stellan's embrace and the steady rhythm of his breathing carry me to sleep.

CHAPTER 39

I WAKE CURLED AROUND WILLA. My hand spans her stomach, tucking her into the front of my body as close as possible.

She's still asleep, small and perfect. It can't be real that she's in my arms again, but the events from last night are too vivid to be a dream. And yet, holding her as she sleeps is the last place I imagined I'd find myself again.

I breathe in the scent of winter spices at her neck, and move her dark, silky hair off her shoulder and kiss her exposed skin. My lips press just lightly against her. I long to taste her fully, to have her moaning and gasping beneath me again, but she won't welcome that and I fully accept why.

"You're here." She stirs, her voice husky from sleep. She spins in my arms and rests her head against my shoulder while I take her arm and place it over my chest, exactly where I want her.

"Did you expect me not to be?"

"Honestly? I don't know what to expect. I'm doing my best not to think too hard."

My eyes land on the bruises around her chest. I run my finger along one and examine the cut on her cheek.

"I could kill Olsen for doing this to you." I can barely speak through my clenched teeth. "I would heal them, but I'd like Director Hawley to see the full extent of Olsen's crimes."

"I understand. They don't really bother me. It's the memory of their hands on me when I couldn't defend myself that hurts the most."

I draw her closer, letting her warmth sink into my skin. "I saw the video footage of your interrogation. Dr. Svenson knew something wasn't right and left a camera running. She was too afraid of Olsen and didn't tell me until last night. Soren and I watched it together. I can understand why you didn't tell me, but why not tell him?"

"I couldn't," she says with a sigh. "I know Soren and Banks were concerned, but I was too afraid no one would believe me. It also felt like a battle of wills between Ingrid and me. I wasn't going to tattle on her."

Ingrid. I have to confess the past and clarify the lies. I just hope Willa believes me. I don't dare to hope for her forgiveness, but I need her to know the truth.

"Willa, I need you to know something about Ingrid."

"OK…" She's wary, and presses against my chest to sit up. I let her go. As much as I don't want to lose the connection, I'll give her whatever space she needs to feel safe with me.

Willa tucks her knees up inside her nightgown and holds them against her chest. She looks so tiny and fragile with her bruises and her sleep-mussed hair. But Willa is anything but weak. Her strength rivals that of anyone I've ever met.

"Ingrid and I did have a very brief…encounter. We were introduced at an Agency event, and we went on one date that lasted into the night. This was months ago."

"Why are you telling me this?" Willa asks, her face falling

at my confession. The truth hurts her, and an ache blooms inside my chest at causing her more pain.

"Because I need you to understand that the things she said to you were lies. Yes, I went on one date with her, and we had one unsatisfactory night together, and that was the extent of it. I didn't see her again because it was obvious she wanted more than I would ever give her.

"When Olsen appointed her to my team, my instincts told me it was a bad idea, but I ignored them. I am sorry. For giving her access to you, for allowing you to believe she meant anything to me."

"I don't want to think about Ingrid ever again," she says and her eyes flash with anger and resolve. "She isn't worth the pain she caused me. Not even close."

I don't deserve Willa's forgiveness, and she doesn't offer it. But at least now she knows the truth.

"I have seen incredibly powerful people fall apart under a fraction of that pressure," I tell her. I need her to understand how special she is. "They could have broken you, but they didn't. You have handled everything with so much determination and grace, and I am…"

I stop. I don't quite know how to say everything in a way that will convey how much has changed for me. "You intrigued me from the moment I opened Soren's file on you, but I have come to realize that you're so much more than I could ever have imagined."

"I just did what was necessary," she says quietly.

"Unfortunately necessary. Director Hawley is arriving this afternoon, and your presence has been requested. The confirmation came through very early this morning. Unless you don't want me there, I will accompany you. Though I do warn you that I'm going to find it hard to let you out of my sight for a while."

She stretches her legs and glances out the bedroom

window. "I'm sorry that I was planning to leave. I realize now it wasn't the best decision. I knew it then, too. I've just been so desperate for a resolution. I wanted to talk to my father in person, to confront him myself. I'm so sorry Banks was hurt because of me."

"Banks was doing his job. If anyone can handle a few gunshot wounds, it's him. His magic is unique. I can heal other people's injuries, but Banks can do that and heal himself. I've seen him recover from much worse. I'm not at all worried."

Relief shines on her face. "I'm glad to hear that, but I'm still sorry. I didn't anticipate someone showing up on my behalf. I feel responsible for not stopping them sooner."

I sit up and the duvet slips down around my waist. She averts her eyes after a quick glance at my chest and stomach. Her physical attraction to me has never been an issue, but I want her to desire more than just my body. I want to give her my heart and soul, too.

"If anyone is responsible, it's me. When you told Soren you were planning to leave willingly, I nearly lost my mind. I didn't care about the investigation or my responsibilities. I just needed to make sure you were safe." I brave a touch of her hair as it spills out of her bun. My hand wanders down her shoulder, over her soft skin. She shivers.

"It cut me open, Willa. It wasn't just the possibility of losing a key witness or someone under my protection. It was that you were willingly walking into danger because I'd given you every reason to leave."

"I do feel badly, but..." She makes a funny grimace and shrugs.

I laugh, but it's not lighthearted. "I know. I don't blame you. I would have left, too."

She smiles sadly and looks away from me again.

Willa is beautiful with her dainty nose and rosy lips. But

she's also intelligent, resilient, and strong. I never once bothered to imagine an ideal partner. A perfect match. It wasn't something I thought I wanted or needed.

It wasn't until that first day in Willa's cottage that the thought even occurred to me. When I came back from a run and found her looking just like this with her knitting in her lap.

What would it be like to come home to that every day? To make a life with someone who understood me. Someone to take care of and protect and cherish. I can't stop myself from reaching for her and pulling her onto my lap.

I hold her close to my chest, and she tucks her face against my neck. She embraces me with her arms around my back. I breathe her in, feeling my heart rate settle and the tension in my shoulders melt away.

"I missed you." I bury my face in her hair.

She hesitates as if allowing my words to sink in. Her arms lock and her discomfort washes over me, my magic picking up on the change like a dark cloud raining down on us.

She draws back, her eyes brimming with tears. "I'm sorry," she says and disentangles herself from me and climbs off the bed.

"I'm sorry, but you don't know how badly I've wanted to hear those words from you. How many nights when I would lie awake and imagine you walking into my bedroom. You would say that you missed me and that it was all just some terrible mistake.

"But you never did, Stellan. You never came. You made me feel like I was nothing. That I was just a means to an end. That it was all an obligation."

Willa sniffs but maintains her composure. My throat burns and I swallow back the lump in my throat. I treated her so cruelly and I deserve to feel this.

Her bare feet softly carry her to the door. "I think I'm having a hard time trusting what's real right now."

"You have nothing to apologize for, Willa. I can't erase the pain I caused you with a few simple words. I know that. But I'm not leaving you alone. You will never have to fight battles by yourself ever again. I'm going to prove it to you."

"I hope so," she says with another sad smile and leaves my bedroom with my heart in her hands.

CHAPTER 40

BANKS'S HOSPITAL room smells like antiseptic and his forest magic. I fight with more tears when I see him connected to all the beeping machines.

His giant body in a hospital gown, with his face too pale is excruciating. He's awake and sitting up at least, but it's a blow to my heart and my conscience. He wouldn't be here if not for me and my foolish choices.

"Don't even think about it, Willa," Banks says gruffly.

"Think about what," I sniff. He motions for me to step closer and takes my hand. Stellan follows close behind me, his presence a sturdy comfort.

"You are thinking that all this nonsense," he points to the hospital gown and the wires, "is your fault."

"But it is. I'm so sorry. I'm so much stronger than those men. If I had known you were coming, I wouldn't have decided to leave with them. I would have fought them and then you wouldn't..."

"No. None of that," he shakes his head. "I am disappointed

you felt you had no other option than to leave us, but I won't hear you take the blame for their actions and my own reluctance to accept help. I should have realized sooner what you were trying to do."

Banks opens his arms for me to step in. Careful of the wires, I fall into his hug.

"Thank you for coming to my rescue. You're the only one who has ever done that for me," I whisper.

He pats me gently on the back. "You're worth it, Willa. I'll rescue you anytime you need it." He pats me gently on my back.

The scent of a violent rainstorm suddenly permeates the room, but I don't turn to look at Stellan. I keep my attention on Banks.

"Take care of yourself," I tell him. "I'll come visit again soon."

"Not necessary. I'll be out of here in a day. This is just a precaution."

When Stellan finally speaks, his voice is rough an this jaw is set. "Willa, will you wait outside with Eriksson for just a moment? I have to check in with Banks briefly."

Is he angry about something?

"Sure? I'll be right outside."

The door clicks shut behind me and GI Joe, who apparently has a real name, nods at me before resuming his watch at the end of the narrow hallway.

Some uncomfortable chairs line the wall next to Banks's room. I sit in the one closest to the door to wait for Stellan. I can't help but listen as their conversation floats through the closed door, animated by their raised voices.

"What are you on about?" Banks asks in exasperation.

"What are your intentions toward Willa?"

"My intentions? Did I wake up in the 19th century?"

"I'm serious, Banks." Stellan's voice is suddenly lethal.

"I know you are, Lundqvist," Banks bites back. "My intentions toward Willa are to be there for her however, and whenever, she needs me. As her friend. If you were thinking clearly, you'd remember that it's not possible for me to give anyone more than that."

I don't know much of substance about Ronan Banks, but now I'm very curious.

"Fuck, I'm sorry. I know that. I just…"

"You lost your fucking mind. I can understand that. Really, I can. But don't you ever question my loyalty, Stellan."

"You're right. I apologize for the accusation." Stellan sounds genuinely contrite. "I can't keep a lid on my emotions lately. I haven't felt this volatile since I was a teenager. I don't know what's wrong with me."

Banks laughs. "Seems obvious to me. Now get the hell out of here so I can heal in peace." His words are sharp, but there's a lightness in his voice that was missing moments before.

"Rest up, old friend. We need you."

"Yes, you do." Banks states it as fact. "I warned you that this case would require more agility than we're accustomed to. There's a woman out there who needs you to be the man I know you really are. Sort yourself out, mate."

* * *

I'M FURIOUS. Stellan knows because I barely acknowledged him when he left Banks's hospital room. I stood next to Ericksson and answered his questions in clipped replies. His brow furrowed in confusion, but then realization dawned and he frowned. His little chat with Banks was not as private as he thought.

Now we're in his office. His desk is clear of paperwork, which seems instead to be all over the floor. The high-backed chairs that face his desk look sleek in a dark tan leather. There's a bookshelf with leather bound books and two photographs along the only non-glass wall. The first photo is of him with two little boys, who I assume are his nephews. Then there's an older photograph of what appears to be Stellan at about the age of 12 and a girl who looks just like him.

I take up residence in one of his chairs with my arms crossed and my eyes fixed on the window behind his desk. It's the time of day when there's enough light to see the city below us. Stockholm harbor stretches in the distance and colorful city buildings rise above busy streets. It's beautiful, but I'm not in any mood to enjoy it.

How dare he accuse Banks of…trying to do what, exactly? Seduce me? Care for me? Banks has done a better job protecting me than Stellan. That's for damn sure.

Stellan sits in the chair opposite me. "Willa, I know you're angry with me." He folds forward and rests his elbows on his knees and links his fingers. He has no business looking this hot while I'm so mad.

"Yes. I am," I reply curtly and turn away from him. I can't even look at his face.

"Would it help at all if I told you that I'm sorry?"

"Oh, you're sorry?" I shout. "Sorry for what, Stellan?"

I don't even realize I've stood up until I start pacing and waving my arms.

"Are you sorry for lying to me from the moment we met? Sorry for weaponizing my attraction to you? Or maybe for flaunting Ingrid in my face? Or are you sorry for abandoning me and then venting your anger on the people who actually looked out for me? Because that's what I'm mad about, Stellan. You don't get to treat me like I'm disposable and then turn into a caveman when someone else plays the role you refused."

I'm too loud. I don't notice it until I stop. My hands shake, and my magic is all riled up inside me. Stellan remains seated, but swallows hard.

"God," he says thickly and his eyes darken as he watches me standing there, breathing hard trying to rein in my out-of-control emotions. "You are glorious when you're angry."

"Don't compliment me! We are in a fight!" I cross my arms dramatically. I swear Stellan suppresses a smile, which only makes me want to punch him even more.

"I'm not fighting with you, Willa. You are entirely right, and I am entirely wrong. A fight implies we disagree, but you are completely correct." He stands up, and his shoes echo in the quiet room.

He stops in front of me.

"If I touch you, will you incinerate me?" he asks, half teasing, half serious.

"It's very tempting," I reply, but my anger has evaporated.

Stellan places his hands on my shoulders and bends his head toward mine.

"I'm sorry, Willa. For all of it. I have never felt this way about anyone, and I'm fucking it all up. I just ask that you give me a chance to make it right."

Can I do that? Can I risk trusting Stellan not to hurt me again? It's impossible to think straight with his hands on me, but I know that I desperately want to believe him.

"I can try." It comes out quiet and uncertain.

Stellan cups my cheeks in his hands.

"You won't regret it. I promise."

He leans forward as if he wants to kiss me, but then abruptly stops and looks around the room as if suddenly remembering where he is. We're in his office, and anyone could walk by and see us.

Stellan clears his throat and drops his hands. "Director

Hawley will be expecting us in the conference room soon. Do you have any questions before we meet with her?"

"Yes, I do." I step back, needing more space between us. "Should I be worried? I was caught off-guard for the first meeting, and I'm not sure I handled it as well as I could have. I want to make sure I know what's expected of me."

"Director Hawley is aware that I falsified your records to keep you safe. After what happened with Olsen, she understands my rationale for protecting you. Today's meeting is about you. Not about what you need to hide or what you should be ashamed of, but your strength and your intelligence and your skill. Just be yourself, and everything else will fall into place."

I wish there was a way I could capture the expression on Stellan's face. The soft sweetness and the pride. I'm terrified of the damage he'll cause if he shuts me out again. But seeing him now, looking down at me with so much affection, guarding my heart feels like a battle I've already lost.

CHAPTER 41

WILLA

STELLAN SITS NEXT to me in the same conference room where we first met Director Hawley. I tap my fingers on the table, and my legs dance. I know this is nothing like the last time, but my body is having an anxiety response that I can't control. Underneath the table, Stellan puts his hand on my thigh, stopping the motion.

"It's going to be fine, Willa. This isn't like last time."

"Rationally, I know that. It's just hard to convince the animal part of my brain that we're safe."

Stellan shifts toward me in his seat with remorse on his face. He places a hand on my cheek, and the scent of his magic fills my lungs. It travels over my skin, and I sense it curling up inside my chest, calming me and my magic, enticing us to relax. I'm still nervous, but it's no longer as strong.

"I love that you can do that," I sigh and smile softly.

"Do what?" he asks, confused.

"Your magic. The thing you do sometimes to calm me down. It's nice."

Stellan tilts his head. "Willa, my magic doesn't work that way. I can't control emotions — I just read them. *Pathokinesis* or advanced emotion manipulation, is something very few can do and usually only in certain areas. A powerful Autumn Mage might be able to make someone feel depressed or terrified. A strong Summer Mage can influence wants and desires. Spring Mages don't usually have the ability to change emotional states. It's not one of my abilities."

"But you do," I shake my head. "A few different times now, your magic has alleviated all my anxiety."

Stellan smiles wide and tucks a loose strand of hair behind my ear. "If that's the case, and I do believe you, then my magic only does it for you, darling."

God, I want to kiss this man. As if reading my mind, Stellan bends closer, but a knock at the door has us abruptly pulling apart.

We rise as Director Hawley enters the room. Her commanding presence takes up all the air. She's wearing another tweed skirt and suit jacket, and her graying hair is up in a flawless bun.

"Please, sit," she says tersely. Hawley sits at the head of the table and clasps her hands together. She looks down at them for a brief moment and breathes as if collecting herself. Her burgundy painted lips thin in frustration. I glance at Stellan nervously. He looks back with equal concern.

"Thank you both for meeting with me," she says finally and pierces me with her hazel eyes. "I first need to express that I am horrified by the actions of my colleague. I have known Henrik Olsen for many years, and I assure you that while I have always found him to be a pompous prick, I never anticipated he would do something so heinous."

Hawley glances at my chest and my face, which are still

bruised from Olsen's hands. "Ms. Martin, please accept my apology on behalf of the IMA."

"Thank you, Director."

"I am personally overseeing Olsen's punishment, and I can assure you that it will be thorough."

There's a merciless glint in her eyes that is nothing short of terrifying.

"As a citizen of the United States, Ingrid will be relocated to the Chicago Office for handling," she continues. "I have it on good authority that she has already lost her position and will likely spend the rest of her life restricted and monitored."

Director Hawley turns her attention to Stellan.

"Agent Lundqvist, I am disappointed that this was allowed to happen on your watch. I would expect more vigilance from someone of your caliber. While you are not to blame for their actions, I trust that you will not be so easily distracted in future."

The warning is abundantly clear.

"Of course, ma'am," Stellan says and lowers his head respectfully.

"Very well. I would like a few minutes to speak with Ms. Martin alone. Would you be so kind as to wait for us outside? I will call for you after."

Stellan's eyes shift to me. "I would prefer to stay, ma'am." Director Hawley's eyebrows raise in surprise. It must be rare for anyone to deny her.

"Stellan, it's fine." I don't want him in any more trouble because of me. "I trust Director Hawley." I lean in closer to speak more quietly. "There are some things I need to do on my own."

Director Hawley can still hear me, but I want Stellan to know this is a personal request.

Stellan exhales on a slow breath and rises from the table.

"I will be nearby, if you need me."

When the door closes behind him, Director Hawley turns to me and smiles. "I knew you'd be trouble." She sees the concern I can't hide on my face. "The good kind of trouble," she adds.

I smile in spite of myself, and Director Hawley leans back more casually in her chair and tilts her head as if appraising me.

"Ms. Martin, I know what it's like to be more powerful than everyone around you and carry the weight of their mistrust and their expectations. But I have no doubt you will find your footing."

"Thank you. I truly hope so."

"You won't know this of course, but your Uncle Mikkel was at Darlings at the same time as my son."

I shake my head. "I don't know much of anything about my father's side of the family."

"Mikkel is several years younger than Lars and was an awful, awful boy. Just horrid. He used to bully my Benjamin terribly. Ben has very powerful magic, but not the kind that excites the young.

"He was frequently targeted for being weak. Mikkel was always the ringleader, as Lars was in his own way before him. Mikkel has the rare ability to nullify magic. There was one incident in particular, where he and a few other boys beat Ben to a bloody mess. Mikkel locked up my son's magic so he couldn't heal himself and then left him out in the elements. If not for a passing stranger, it's likely he would have died."

Even though this happened long ago, the emotion and the fear are still raw in her voice.

"I am so sorry. That's awful."

"I don't tell you this to make you feel worse about your unfortunate relatives. I tell you because I have very good reason to despise your uncle, but I am smart enough to recognize that you are not him. You are not your father either.

"While the options for those of us with extreme power are limited, I trust that you will carve your own path. You will exceed all our expectations, and you will do it without anyone holding your hand."

There's a twinkle in her shrewd eyes.

"Before I call Lundqvist back in, is there anything you would like to ask me or anything I can assist you with?"

I think for a moment. I have so many questions, and I don't want to bother someone so high-ranking with most of them, but there is one thing she could do for me.

"I know it's exceptionally irregular for someone like me to get involved in an investigation into my own family, but I want to help."

She purses her lips thoughtfully.

"I didn't get where I am by avoiding the 'exceptionally irregular,' as you say. I will mention it to Lundqvist."

"Thank you, ma'am."

She puts her hand on mine, and it warms under her touch. I catch the scent of sweet pea flowers and summer berries. She's reading me with her magic.

"Your heart will mend," she says with a motherly smile that I'm certain she doesn't offer many people. "And trust that the pain you've experienced has already made you stronger."

CHAPTER 42

WILLA

THE MORE I pour over my family's case files, the more I want to light something on fire.

With Director Hawley's permission, Stellan has given me access to the current and archived records on my family. There are several boxes now living on a table in Stellan's office.

It seems that Johannes Stromberg, my grandfather, was the biggest villain of them all. He was born with the same strong Winter magic as me and my father. He ran his family and his business with a tyrannical authority that bordered on psychosis. Blackmail and intimidation were his favorite tactics, with too many unsolved murders in the periphery to be coincidence.

Soren's research department is impressively thorough, but they have to be. Mage law mostly mirrors civilian law, but evidence has to be irrefutable and any charges against a Mage must be airtight to move forward with an arrest. Truth is a complicated concept when someone can manipulate people and reality with unseen forces.

The original records on my father were woefully inadequate, but Soren's intelligence team has scoured news reports, local archives, real estate transactions, and anything else they could find. There are several reports of crimes that fit a similar pattern, but never name anyone in my family outright. Even my father's websites for his academic work and his published articles are interfiled.

After Darlings, Lars Stromberg went to Uppsala University, where he earned a PhD in climate science and worked as a professor. He used his career to gain access to lab space that he exploited for his personal use.

Lars traveled regularly back to Stockholm, presumably to "work" for his father. While we don't know what those jobs entail, we can surmise it wasn't anything legal.

I'm sitting at a table in Stellan's office pulling out more files. The older ones are not very well organized, and I've spent the last several days reading over the records and taking notes on anything that strikes me as useful or interesting.

I flip through one of the last boxes, trying to get a sense of its arrangement. It's odd, but the entire period my father spent in Vermont appears to be missing. There's information on Lars's life before he met my mother and a little after, but for the eight years he spent in my hometown, he essentially vanished off the Agency's radar.

My mother told us that she thought Lars was working nearby colleges, but there's nothing in the records to confirm it. He either used a fake identity or was lying. Either scenario seems entirely possible.

I find a transcript of my mother's original interview. After the Agency spoke with her, they created very basic profiles on all of us. Soren's team made a formal dossier on me when it was clear I was becoming involved, but prior to that there isn't much information. Since we never had any contact with Lars and had no discernible enhanced abilities, they left us alone.

But how could an organization so far-reaching have lost someone like Lars for that long?

"What interesting discovery have you made?" Stellan's deep voice startles me. He walks in, loosening his tie. His biceps strain against his suit jacket.

"How do you know I've found something interesting?"

"Your nose scrunches up when you're thinking."

Though I was unaware of it, I realize that I am indeed scrunching my face. I squint my eyes at him. "I'm not sure I like how observant you are."

Stellan stalks closer. As always, I'm acutely aware of his presence. All I have to do is catch the scent of his magic, and my nipples harden and my thighs squeeze together. Not acting on my attraction to him has only grown more difficult as the days pass.

"It's my job to be observant, but I do admit that watching you is no hardship," he says, offering me his most heart-stop-ping smile.

He's done this a lot lately in the days since our meeting with Director Hawley. He's giving me space and letting me lead, but he's also flirtatious and sweet.

I'm still staying at his apartment but sleeping in the guest room. I need the distance, or I'll do something I'm not ready for. Stellan hasn't pressed the issue, and I think he's building back my trust by showing he thinks of me as more than just a bed partner. We eat all our meals together and spend the evenings talking or reading quietly.

As much as I want to trust his open and honest behavior, I'm not quite there yet.

"Thanks, I think."

"Well, what did you find that has you so thoughtful?"

I pick up a file. "How is it possible for the Agency to have lost my father for the years he was in Vermont? Considering his family ties and his Category 5 status, they must have looked for him, right? I guess I don't understand how there's no record of him living in Vermont until after the incident with the lab."

"You're right to question that. Come sit with me," Stellan motions for me to follow him. We sit in the high-backed leather chairs in front of his desk.

He rakes a hand through his hair and leans back with an ankle resting on his knee. The light in this office is a warm amber that turns his complexion the color of honey and contrasts with the sharp blue of his eyes.

"First, you need to understand that when your father left for the States, he was not formally accused of anything. Highly suspected, of course, but there was never enough evidence to do anything about it. As you're discovering, it is incredibly hard to formally charge a powerful Mage. It's why Mikkel still walks free despite everything we know about him.

"We have record that your father's passport was flagged entering Canada about two years before you were born.

"The Agency office closest to your mother's house is in Montreal. Every branch is meant to follow the same guiding principles, but as you can imagine there are political, cultural, and structural differences that determine how all situations are handled.

"It is quite possible that the Montreal Office was aware of your father's presence and decided not to share it with us, or — more likely — they just didn't care one way or the other.

"The North American branches of the IMA are generally less concerned about tracking people with high category magical abilities, especially if they have no prior history of misdeeds."

"Is there an office in Boston? Would they have known?"

"The closest in the US is New York City, and they would have had their hands full already."

"Hmm, I guess I'm feeling annoyed that my mother wasn't protected, but I realize how impossible that would have been."

"I understand your concerns. The IMA doesn't have the best track record of keeping vulnerable people safe." He looks away as if lost in thought. I wait for him to say more, but he doesn't elaborate.

"Thanks for clarifying things for me. Doing such a deep dive into my family history has been a lot," I admit and slump back in the chair and release my hair from its clip, letting it fall down my back. Stellan watches me intently.

"I don't doubt it. You've been at it for days."

Days...

The thought makes my heart sink to my stomach.

"Stellan, what day is it?" I know it's a Thursday because I've been keeping track of the days of the week for my own sanity, but I've otherwise been living in a timeless existence. I've been here almost a month, which means...

"I was wondering if you would notice. It's November 29th. And yes, it is your Thanksgiving."

The words blindside me. I've never missed Thanksgiving at my mother's house. Beatrice makes the most elaborate meal, and I've never spent it without her and Wren. Sam comes over for pie in the evening. I look forward to it every year.

I feel terrible being away from them, but even worse for not remembering. Since I can't tell them anything about my situation, I've struggled with phone conversations and mostly text for updates on their lives.

I can't believe I forgot about Thanksgiving.

Stellan's magic is bombarded with all my inner turmoil. He reaches for me and positions me on his lap, swiveling the chair so we're hidden from the glass walls.

He holds me close, running his hands along my back and into my hair. His touch is warm and welcome.

"I thought you might miss home today, so I took the liberty of arranging something."

Stellan's voice is low and calm, but it rumbles against me. I sit up straighter so I can look into his eyes.

"You did?"

"Yes, I hired a chef to cook for us. I'd like to do it myself, but it seems there aren't enough hours in the day lately. I've invited my sister's family to join us. Soren, Banks, and Greta are coming over as well. We thought it might help take your mind off everything. But if you'd rather not, I can cancel it. It's up to you."

"No, that sounds wonderful. Thank you."

I lean in to kiss his cheek. His beard is growing back, and it's as soft as I remember as I brush my lips against him gently. I draw back, but he turns toward me and my movement slows like I'm trapped in honey.

Stellan dips nearer and takes my hand resting on his chest and holds it tight. We breathe each other in. I'm dizzy from his masculine scent and the taste of his magic on my tongue. I stare into his wild eyes, our breath coming in fast and ragged as we fight the pull of desire.

Just when I think I might actually die from the tension, Stellan slides his other hand up to angle my face exactly how he wants me and presses his lips on mine. My mouth parts, and he deepens the kiss. He groans in satisfaction.

My hands tangle in his hair and grip his back, needing to feel him between my fingers.

It's not gentle or soft. There's no easing into each other,

no holding back. Stellan takes everything I have to give and demands more until I'm breathless and shaking. Deft fingers undo the buttons on my shirt, reaching inside and he palms my breast over my bra. I arch into his touch, seeking more of everything. He nips my lip and kisses across my face and down my neck. My head rolls back and his fingers knit into my hair, gripping to the point of delicious pain.

A gentle knock at his door freezes us to the spot and the sound of high heels clicking against the floor approaches. I sit up and hastily button my shirt while Stellan wipes my lipstick off his mouth with the back of his hand. Greta rounds the corner and though we have both righted ourselves, there is no mistaking what we've just been up to.

She smiles but doesn't otherwise let on. "Sorry to interrupt. I have some news I thought you would want right away."

"Yes, thank you, Greta. What is it?" Stellan says. He deserves some kind of award for pulling himself together so quickly, while I'm still reeling and my lips are tingling and puffy. I can't even look at Greta.

"Albert Wagner has finally consented to meet with us. You were correct that Willa was the dealbreaker. You have a meeting with him on Monday morning at his home outside the city. I will forward the details."

"Excellent, thank you."

Greta walks to the office door with another small smile for me. She'll hound me later, I'm sure. I roll my eyes, and I hear her snicker as she leaves.

I watch Stellan carefully now that we're alone again. I wish I could trust that he meant that kiss. But after everything that happened, I can't help worrying he'll shut down and freeze me out now that it's over.

Stellan leans with his hands against the edge of his desk.

"I wish I didn't deserve the look you're giving me right now."

"What look is that?"

"Like you're waiting for me to disappoint you."

I shrug. There isn't really anything to say.

Stellan smiles sadly. "Would you like to meet your uncle?" he asks, changing the subject.

"I would." I rub my arms until I realize what I'm doing and stop. The moment before Greta walked in is gone.

I turn away so I can return to the files I was looking through. I can't do this. I will not waste energy on someone who desires me against his better judgment.

Stellan stops me with a hand on my arm and guides me back into his orbit. He curls an arm around my waist, pressing me closer.

"You expect me to push you away," he says, rough and serious. The sincerity in his eyes holds me captive. My heart and head are at war. I want this man, but I won't accept anything less than all of him.

Stellan takes my face in his hands and speaks softly. "That is not going to happen. Not anymore. I know I have miles to go until I earn back your trust, but I'm not going anywhere. I'm reaching for you, Willa. Please let me try."

CHAPTER 43

STELLAN

MY SISTER, Clara, lives with her husband, John, and their twin sons not far from me in Södermalm. They arrive in a flurry of activity as always, but today is a little different. The expectations are higher tonight, and everyone can sense it.

Willa's sadness at missing a family holiday was exactly what I wanted to avoid. I had wanted her to stay in Vermont, where her life would carry on as normal. Where she'd be with her family and people who love and care for her.

But I can provide that, too. I'm finding now that I don't want her to leave. I want her with me, with all of us.

Willa fits here seamlessly. It's not just the intelligent way that she questions and observes. It's watching her laugh with Greta, tease Soren, and smile secretly with Banks.

I will do everything in my power to ensure she wants to stay with us, with me.

Introducing her to my family is another layer of myself that I am sharing with her. I have a close relationship with my sister, but we were broken for a while after Lily's death.

We found our way back to each other, but we each had to grieve the loss in our own way. I threw myself into work to an unhealthy degree, and Clara moved to England to escape into her studies. That's where she met John.

My sister looks a lot like me with the same brown hair and blue eyes. She also resembles our sister, except Lily was always more slender and fragile. There's a maternal softness to Clara that existed long before she ever had children.

Clara kisses me on the cheek, and I take their coats. Willa stands a little awkwardly off to the side, not quite sure what to make of the people filing in through the door.

"*Morbor! Morbor Stellan!*" Two little whirlwinds charge past their mother and fling themselves at me. I scoop up my nephews, one in each arm and whisper to them. I tell them that I have a present in the sitting room and that I have a friend I want them to meet.

They are three years old and don't speak English quite as fluently yet, though their father is working on it. They have sandy blonde hair and wide blue eyes and little elfin features. I'm probably partial, but I think they're pretty spectacular. Judging by the wide-eyed expression on Willa's face, I think she's taken with them as well.

"Edwin, Oli, please meet my friend, Willa," I say to them and set them down. They cautiously approach Willa and she bends low to speak to them.

"*Hej! Trevligt att träffas.*" She tells the boys it's nice to meet them in Swedish. I'm impressed and touched that she made the attempt and by the gentle smile on Clara's face, she is as well.

The boys grin back at Willa, already accepting her as a friend. Edwin says something to her that she clearly can't translate, and Oli nods in agreement. Clara and I laugh, and Willa looks to us for help.

"Edwin just said that it's nice to meet you, and that you are very small."

"We're still working on pleasantries." Clara smiles apologetically.

"To be fair," Willa says. "Compared to most people in this country, I am very small." She gives Edwin a bright smile that he returns before burying his face into his mother's leg.

I laugh again and wrap an arm around Willa's shoulders. Clara watches me with a curious expression before smiling at us both. This is the first woman I've ever introduced to her and her family, and I'm certain she will have questions for me later.

I lead them into the flat. We set up a minibar in the open space between the kitchen and living room. Willa hands my sister a glass of wine, and the two of them engage in easy small talk.

Clara lives a much more traditional life than I ever have. Though the comparative weakness of her magic could have been a point of contention, it only made her work harder.

She and John are both well-known and successful physicians in their respective fields. They have a beautiful home and these two gorgeous children. If anything, I'm jealous of her. Especially now that I can picture that life so much more vividly than ever before.

Greta, Banks, and Soren arrive shortly behind Clara and John, and it grows loud and a little raucous. Clara and Greta are already good friends, and they drag Willa to the kitchen, probably to pepper her with questions on what's happening between us. John and Banks argue over football, and Soren and I play with the boys.

Edwin jumps on Soren's back, and he pretends to be defeated in a loud and dramatic fashion. Oli leaps on him while he's down and the two boys crawl all over Soren, shouting and squealing. Then they turn their attack on me, and I let them knock me to the ground. They climb on my chest in victory.

Once they tire of us, they set out to find their mother together. Perhaps it's being a twin myself, but there is something so precious and bittersweet in their obvious bond with one another.

"So, there's been improvement, I take it?" Soren asks while we right ourselves.

I shake my head in resignation. Soren is the biggest gossip I know. It's why he's so good at his job. He has to know everything about everyone.

"I take it Greta already told you what she saw in my office this morning."

Soren smiles wide and slaps me on the back. "Perhaps she did mention something. We're just happy for you."

"Let's not get ahead of ourselves."

"Willa needs time to trust you again, but you'll get there."

I hope he's right.

Willa's face blossoms into a joyful ease as we eat and drink and the conversation flows around her. She still misses her family, but she grows far more content as the evening goes on.

Seated around the table, we toast with John's homemade aquavit, and the candles light everyone in a peaceful glow.

Willa and I make eye contact with our glasses raised.

I let my expression convey everything that hasn't yet been put into words. Sentiments I kept hidden because she needed more time.

Willa's lips part at the intensity in my eyes and she blushes beautifully. I tuck a piece of hair behind her ear. She breaks the tension, looking down at her glass.

I'm aware we have an audience, but I can't help kissing

the top of her head, breathing in the scent of her magic. Clara makes an audible squeal, which causes Greta to laugh, and the spell is broken for the time being.

After dinner, there's dessert and coffee in the living room, and I sit next to Willa on one of the couches. Edwin and Oli inch closer and closer until eventually they're both sitting beside her, too, shoving me out of the way so they can show her their toys and tell her their favorite stories, which I help translate.

Edwin eventually climbs onto her lap, and Oli leans against her with his head on her legs until they're both falling asleep. She rubs their small hands and admires their faces while they settle on her.

Willa glances up at me with a baffled expression, and her alluring blue eyes sparkle against the candlelight. I always assumed I'd be a father, though it felt like a far-off future. But watching Willa with my nephews awakens a deep longing I didn't know I could possess.

"It's your magic," I tell her. "Children and animals are often drawn to us because they can sense our power. And I told you before that you smell like Christmas."

Soren looks over at us from where he is talking to John and laughs. "It's true, Willa. You probably remind them of sweets and presents."

Clara comes over and scoops up a sleeping Edwin. "I hope you don't mind. They've never been this interested in a new person before." Clara gives me a pointed look as she says it. I shake my head but can't deny that she's right.

"Honestly, how could I mind? This is the sweetest thing that's ever happened to me," Willa says and hands a sleeping Oli off to his dad.

Clara hugs me tighter than usual when it's time for them to go home. She then wraps Willa up in a sisterly hug.

"Thank you," she says earnestly and quietly with another glance at me. "I haven't seen this side of Stellan in years, but you bring something out of him. Something I thought we lost."

They leave with Clara's eyes brimming with tears.

CHAPTER 44

WILLA

"Why am I here?" I ask into the void. I'm surrounded by nothing but darkness. I can't see anything, but there's a rustling of clothes and the scent of ice and evergreen.

"We have unfinished business," my father says with a disappointed frown as he comes into focus. Just me and him in a vast expanse of black. "You've been shutting me out."

"Of course, I have. I don't appreciate being manipulated."

I must have had too much to drink tonight, and it's lowered my shields. I've been so good about building them up before bed.

"Oh, my sweet child. It is not me manipulating you. Don't you think it's rather convenient that the one man who's come the closest to finding me suddenly takes an intimate interest in my daughter?"

The implication stings. It rubs against the exposed nerves of my worst insecurities. The fears I can't shake.

I'm so tired of all the uncertainty and the unanswered questions.

"Can you please just tell me why we're doing all this?"

Two leather armchairs appear in the darkness, and my father folds his lean body into one. He motions for me to take the other.

"If I join you, will you talk?"

"Yes, of course. This is a long overdue conversation and one I am grateful to finally have with you."

I sit and place my hands in my lap. I wait for him to speak. He inhales through his nose and exhales slowly as if centering himself.

"Did you know that before the IMA, the Agency was called 'The Order'?"

I shake my head. I want to tell him that of course I don't know this. I don't know anything because he wasn't around to explain it.

"They have updated themselves for the modern age, but their aims haven't changed. They present themselves as this benevolent force, this organization that we can depend on, for safety, for protection. But the cost of our blind faith is our freedom."

"OK, but again, what does this have to do with me?"

"I'm getting there," my father says with a half-smile. "You are a Winter Mage in a long line of powerful Mages. Much of the fear people associate with our kind is because of our family and a handful of others like us.

"There was a time when every category of magic in Europe had its own council, some dating back as early as the 12th century and likely even before. They operated independently, each serving different roles in society. Though they mostly coexisted peacefully, from time to time they fought each other for land or wealth."

The way my father speaks, calm and informed, makes it easy to imagine him in a university classroom.

"None was as ruthless and feared as the *Concilium*

Magorum Hiemalis. The Winter Council served a vital function. If you wanted something done that no one else would do, you asked us. We never questioned ethics or morals, and we never held back our power.

"Eventually, the Industrial Age and too many witch hunts forced us to create cohesion. The Order of Mages was created to unify the four councils and enact more control over our kind in general.

"In the early 20th century, the Order of Mages became the International Monitoring Agency to mirror other governmental organizations and lend it legitimacy in a new world.

"While it pretends to be a modern organization with compassionate goals, it never lost its origins. And more to the point, the original councils never truly disbanded. They still exist, operating mostly in the shadows and are closely restricted by family ties. The *Concilium Magorum Hiemalis* has only a handful of true Winter Mages left in its ranks. Instead, it's made up of powerful Mages of all categories born from the original families."

He pauses, letting all he's said sink in.

"And," I say at last, "you are part of this council?"

"I am. I never had much choice considering our ancestors were founding members. And if we want to maintain our seats at the table, I must have an heir—"

I interrupt. "You mean me," I say.

"Precisely, my girl."

"But why? Why does it matter if we're on this council? Can't we just...not do that?"

My father smiles, but there's no amusement. "If only it were that simple. The councils are strong, but they're also perilously balanced. If we are not there to act as a counterweight, I am terrified of what will happen."

"What other side? What could happen?" He's still

speaking in riddles.

"I'm afraid that is not something I can share with you until I am certain you won't parrot it back to your new *friends*." He says the word as if it disgusts him. "But Willa, I need you. Countless lives are at stake if you do not join me."

I consider his statement. He seems so genuine. His face is tired and the lines are pronounced across his forehead. He's worried. I believe that to be true, but I don't know if I have faith in his reasoning.

"Why should I trust you?"

"Because I am your father, and I'm telling you the truth. I need you, Wilhelmina."

I desperately wish I could trust him, but how can I when I know what he's capable of?

"You stopped being my father the day you tried to kill my mother," I say with a lethal calm.

"What?!" His voice is so sharp and loud that I jump in my seat. "What are you talking about?"

"You heard me," I reply. "You manipulated her. You turned her into a Mage without her consent, and then when you got jealous of her friendship with Tim, you tried to kill her with your magic."

My voice trembles. How can he have done such horrible things? And how can he act like it's a surprise that I'm upset?

My father bends forward in his seat, his expression both confused and desperate.

"Yes, I hurt your mother, and I have regretted it every day since, but try to kill her? Intentionally? Why would you think that?"

"Because it's what she told me."

My father's face slips into a mask of utter devastation. "Is that...is that what she thinks?" His voice is raspy and thick. "That I tried to kill her?"

He can barely speak the words as if they hurt just to say them out loud.

This is definitely not how I expected this conversation to go.

"She told me that she doesn't remember much of that night," I explain. "She said that you accused her of having an affair. After that, it's unclear. Tim filled in the blanks for her. He said you lost your temper and attacked her."

As if being summoned, electricity surges violently around us. The sound of thunder rumbles, heavy and foreboding, as my father's face darkens with rage. But then as quickly as the anger appeared, it's replaced with pure anguish. He falls back against the leather chair, and his magic dissipates.

"She jumped in the way," he says so quietly I almost can't hear and I swear his eyes glisten. "Tim was there. I was under so much pressure at that time. I just lost control. I tried to hurt Tim, Willa. Your mother jumped in front of him."

A tear runs down my father's face, and I realize my own cheeks are wet. "But you left her? Why did you leave? She could have died!"

"I knew she wouldn't die, Willa. She was too strong. But I also knew it was the end of us. The end of anything truly good in my life. I blamed her for running to Tim and I hated him for taking what was mine, but it was my fault for pushing her away. In truth, I have no one to blame but myself."

"What are you talking about? She never ran to Tim."

"She did, Willa. I don't know what she's told you, but the twins are not mine. They're his."

I rub my temples.

"God, what is it with you powerful men? You're all idiots. Beatrice and Wren are absolutely your children. Mom hardly spoke to Tim until recently when I asked him to check on her."

"That's....that's not possible." My revelations are cutting him open, gutting him from the inside. "I thought that she'd be better off. That Tim would help raise you until I could come for you. I always hoped I could come sooner, but I couldn't risk it."

"Tim definitely didn't help raise me. After that night, Mom shut him out, along with everyone else. I raised my fucking self and my sisters," I explain bitterly. "I had to raise us because you broke our mother. She's been completely alone for 20 years. She suffers from extreme anxiety and depression, and she lives almost entirely inside the fantasy world she made up to escape the reality of losing you."

My father's eyes fix on a point in the distance, lost in his thoughts. "All this time...I used your mother's infidelity to excuse my own actions. But instead, she's been...alone? And the girls? They're mine?"

He sounds almost hopeful.

"Yes! That's what I'm trying to tell you. If they aren't yours, then why the hell does Beatrice look just like you?"

My father smiles unexpectedly, and it lights up his face. He's still rough and worn, but the power shines underneath the surface. I can see why my mother was drawn to him all those years ago. But I also notice my mistake too late. His lips curl, calculating and cunning.

"No," I shake my head. "No, Dad. Not Beatrice. She's too sweet and kind. This life isn't for her."

My father rises from his seat and begins to fade as he ends the dream.

"As always, my darling daughter, it's been a pleasure. But I have some business that I must see to."

CHAPTER 45

"No! No!! No!!!"

I run into the guest bedroom like there's a fire at my heels and throw open the door. Willa thrashes under the covers as if fighting an invisible foe.

I switch on the bedside light and gently shake her shoulders.

"Wake up, Willa. Wake up, love."

She opens her eyes and blinks a few times as if registering her surroundings.

"Was it your father?"

She nods and her eyes brim with tears. "I think he's going to go after Beatrice." Her body shakes and rage boils around her.

"Your shields were lowered."

I intentionally kept an ear out knowing she was vulnerable after all that aquavit.

"He wants me to join him on some council," she says, still in a daze. "He said that if he doesn't have an heir there will be an imbalance and lives will be at risk, but he wouldn't tell me anything else because he doesn't trust me. He was worried I'll tell you."

I can't stop my smile. "Considering where you are and what you're telling me, he was correct on that front."

"Yes, I know. But we also had a strange heart-to-heart about my mom. He really thought that Beatrice and Wren were Tim's children. How he missed that Beatrice is basically a carbon copy of him, I can't understand. But I think he's going to go after her. I can't let him get to her, Stellan. He'll destroy her the way he did our mother."

"Willa, take a breath with me." I lift the covers and climb into the bed, urging her closer. I rub her back and she breathes slowly with me, but she's still too riled up.

"I can't let him near her, Stellan. She's too trusting. He'll manipulate her." Willa trembles from all the fear and anger.

"We'll watch over both of them, Willa. I promise I won't let anyone near your sisters."

My arms encircle her waist, and I tuck her against the shelter of my chest. Her cheek rests on my pecs, and her hand curls around my side. Goosebumps appear beneath her fingers and I have to work to keep my breath stable.

Having her so close is wreaking havoc on my control.

My magic is usually enough to ease her, but Willa's anxiety is a wild animal wrestling for supremacy.

"Would it help if I talk to you?" I ask gently. "It might help you relax. There is nothing we can do about your father at this moment in time, and you need to sleep."

"Yes, I think so."

"I know what it's like to feel responsible for your siblings." I speak softly and let the gravity of what I'm about to share with her settle over us. Willa looks up into my face and meets my eyes.

"You don't have to talk about that, Stellan."

"I want to, Willa. I want you to know every part of me. Even the parts I'm not proud of."

"I want that, too." In her weakened state, her emotions are visible to me. They're tender and warm. She snuggles closer, and I lift her so she's closer to my heart.

"Liliana was more than just my sister when we were children. She was my twin and my closest friend. We did everything together. She was beautiful, sweet, kind. She had this inner light that drew people to her. Everyone loved Lily, and she loved us all fiercely."

I catch the faint wisps of Willa's sadness before she tucks them away behind her mental walls.

She knows where this story ends, but not the details. As hard as it is to share this, I find I truly mean what I said. I want her to know.

"We came into our magic around the same time, and it was like a switch flipped inside her. Like me, she was an incredibly powerful Spring Mage. She could do the most intricate and beautiful things with water. She could heal a wound in seconds, but her empathy overwhelmed her.

"An important skill we learn first is not to feel alongside someone else. I can sense someone's fear or sadness and not experience it with them. Liliana struggled with that. It was hard and sometimes impossible for her to differentiate her own feelings from those of the people around her.

"She grew more and more temperamental and she spent long hours alone. It was more than just the natural changes of puberty and adolescence, the time when our magic truly emerges. She was drowning in everyone else's emotions. All of us could see it, but none of us could pull her free.

"Darlings provided a change of scenery, and that helped tremendously. She grew into herself and her abilities. She was happier and steadier than I had seen her in years, but I never got over my fear that she would go back to that dark place. I tried to shield her, and I protected her from too much.

"She started hiding things from me. Small things at first, things I didn't notice, but it got to the point that when she took on a dangerous role for the IMA, she never told me, never even let on. She feared that I'd try to stop her. She was right, of course. I would have done anything in my power to do so, but I only found out after she left. My overprotective tendencies forced her to shut me out.

"When I learned she died in the field, it destroyed me. She was only 23. I have to wonder if I had worked with her instead of against her, could I have changed the outcome? Could my trust in her have helped her survive? I have learned to live with questions that will never be answered, but it's a pain that never truly goes away."

Willa kisses my chest, and she hugs me close. I breathe in the scent of her magic. Just having her with me stitches together all my frayed and broken edges.

We're silent for a time. I run my hands along her back and her arms. "Soren was right that I was repeating history with you. I was trying to control a situation by making decisions that were not mine to make. I'll never get the chance to tell my sister that I'm sorry, but I need you to know that I'll never take your choices from you again." I bend and kiss her forehead.

I can't hide the need for sleep in my voice. The desire to succumb to rest is calling for us both.

Willa presses deeper into my side, and I clutch her to me. Beyond simple attraction, the need for each other exists on an elemental level. I want to embed her scent in my skin and feel her in every cell of my body. I hold her as we fall asleep like I would a precious treasure.

"Stellan?" she asks in a sleep-soaked voice.

"Yes, darling?"

"Why does Soren have 'Liliana' tattooed on his arm?"

I sigh. She's so observant. Of course she had noticed.

"That is not my story to tell. Lily was my sister, but she was the love of his life."

CHAPTER 46

STELLAN

I'M HARD AS A ROCK. I woke up with my cock pressed against the delectable curve of Willa's hip, but I'm afraid she'll wake and feel pressured to do something she'll regret.

I slowly slide away from her and climb out of bed. I sit in the chair opposite and watch her for a moment. I'll find my phone and check messages once I've calmed down.

Willa moans in her sleep and rolls over, the blankets falling down around her waist. Her hard and perfect nipples visible through the satin of her top. I exhale and say a prayer for strength.

Her eyes flutter open, and she looks at me in confusion.

"Why are you over there?" She sits up, and her sleep-tangled hair once again does funny things to my heart.

"I'm trying to exercise some restraint," I say through gritted teeth.

"Why?" she asks, truly confused. She's adorable when she's half-asleep. Adorable is not a word I ever thought I'd associate with a woman I desire, but with Willa, it makes me ache.

She rises to her knees with her eyes locked on me. The satin of her pajama shorts rises up her thighs, and my eyes are ravenous as I trace up the curves of her beautiful body.

"I have already taken so much from you, Willa. I'm not going to take anything else until you tell me it's what you want."

She tilts her head in confusion. "I think we need to set something straight. There has never been a time when you took something from me that I didn't freely give."

My eyes narrow. "That is patently untrue."

"Stellan, I always knew we had insurmountable differences. Just like I knew our time together was temporary. But I was willing to accept whatever you could offer simply because I wanted it. I wanted you for however long I could have you."

I'm desperate to hold her, but I'll wait until she gives me a sign. She needs to tell me this, and I know I need to hear it.

"When I woke up here, I was so hurt. But I was hurt because I thought that beautiful time together and everything that transpired between us was a lie. But now I know the truth, and I'm not mad at you anymore."

"What truth is that?"

"That the man you showed me in Vermont is who you really are."

My legs move before I can stop them. I rise from the chair and stand in front of the bed, leaning over her. My hands thread through her hair. I tip her head back and look into her eyes.

"It was the real me. All of it. It was real."

Her eyes shine. Her chin trembles, and she swallows hard. "I believe you, but I'm scared."

"Please don't be afraid of me." I bend down and kiss her cheeks and taste the tears that spill down her face.

"I'm not scared *of* you. I'm terrified of how badly it will hurt if you leave again."

"That's never going to happen, Willa," I implore her to understand. I run my fingers along her spine. She shivers in my arms. "I will never leave you again. You are my priority and my greatest desire, and I will spend the rest of my days proving it to you."

I kiss her softly. Slowly at first, just the gentle press of my lips against hers. But the moment her lips part to welcome me, I snap.

I kiss her like I'm starved for it, like her kisses are the only thing between me and certain death. The way my heart lurches inside my chest, they might be.

We melt into each other. I crush her to the bed, and she sighs as if my weight on top of her is everything she needed. She wraps her legs around me, her arms pull me closer, and I revel in her soft skin and the peace of holding her, of having her exactly where she belongs.

We lose ourselves to sensation. Gripping each other with hungry hands. I'm everywhere. My hands are in her hair, inside her shirt, trailing up her thighs. I can't get enough. I want to touch all of her all at once.

She's fire and heat and so hungry for me, clutching and clawing at my back like a woman possessed.

I kiss along the delicate column of her throat. Her fingers find my hair, and she tugs just enough to sting. I grunt and roll my hips to press my aching cock against her slick heat. Whimpers escape as she grinds against me.

"Stellan," she begs. "More. I need you."

I remove her top. My mouth waters as her full breasts are bared before me. I raise to my knees and take the tight bud of her nipple into my mouth, swirling it with my tongue. Biting down roughly and soothing the sting with open-mouthed kisses as she writhes and pants beneath me.

I rip away her shorts. I graze my fingers down her stomach and over her needy flesh, teasing and caressing.

Her skin is hot, and when I sink two fingers inside her, she whimpers unintelligibly. Her tight, glistening pussy strangles my fingers, and I ache to replace them with my cock, to sink inside her until I don't know where I end and she begins.

"Please." She shudders and digs her hands into my back and shoulders, pleading with me to give her more.

I move off her to pull down my sweats. My erection stands long and thick.

"I'm clean, Willa. I want to feel you. All of you." I crawl up her body and hold both her hands captive in one of mine above her head.

"Yes, please. I'm on birth control. Please just…"

I don't give her time to finish before I slide into her as deep as I can go. She's so wet, I'm fully inside her in one stroke, groaning in satisfaction. My control hangs by a thread at her little gasps of pleasure and pain as she adjusts to the sudden intrusion.

"That's it. Fuck, you feel so good. So perfect."

I have to breathe so I don't embarrass myself before I even begin moving inside her. Slowly at first, then faster and harder. We unravel together, the sound of our bodies as they join and our cries of pleasure echoing about the room.

"God, yes. Harder," she begs.

I murmur in Swedish against her ear, telling her she's such a good girl, that she's mine, while I work my hips against hers in powerful thrusts.

Willa clenches around me as her orgasm draws close, arching her back. She shatters in a violent explosion that tears through her body, gripping my cock so hard I see stars.

Her body shakes, and her voice grows hoarse as my name and unbridled cries are wrested from her lips.

Before she can catch her breath, I draw out and flip her over with her hips in the air. In one smooth motion, I push myself back into her perfect pussy, gripping her sides as I set a frenzied pace.

"Fuck, look at you. Taking me so deep." My growls turn feral with possessive fury. "You're mine, Willa. I'm never letting you go."

I don't recognize the dark edge to my voice as I thrust into her.

"Yes," she gasps, barely able to speak. "Only yours."

I collar her throat in one hand, squeezing the sides with gentle but firm pressure. My other hand rubs fast circles over her clit and she arches into me. The onslaught of sensation sends her soaring into another orgasm that leaves her contracting around me and her legs shaking.

"*Ah, fuck. Willa*," I moan, unable to stop the pleasure scorching up my spine. My thrusts slow as my own release empties in hot bursts inside her.

As our breathing calms, I roll onto my back, tucking Willa into my chest and caging her against me in my arms.

We're silent for a long moment, my hands roaming her body in gentle exploration. Feeling and touching and reacquainting myself.

"I'm sorry I was too rough with you." My fingers trail over her throat. I've never wanted to do that before, but I've also never craved anyone so ravenously.

"I am not complaining," she says with a sleepy laugh. "I like knowing I'm the one who makes you lose control."

I smile contentedly. "You do, darling. I'm always half out of my mind around you."

I reluctantly leave her and come back from the guest bathroom with a warm cloth and wipe away the evidence of our love making, soothing her overheated skin. I get back in the covers and she snuggles close, sighing in contentment.

"Did you mean it earlier? When you said you were mine?" I ask, needing this moment of vulnerability.

She looks up at me and smiles, shaking her head in disbelief. She's so beautiful when she smiles. I want to capture it. I want to bottle it up and hoard it all for myself.

"Stellan, I was yours the moment you set foot in my library. I've just been waiting for you to catch up."

CHAPTER 47

STELLAN IS at the front of the room in a dark navy suit standing beside a whiteboard covered in images, documents, and maps. It's hard to believe he's the same man who whispered dirty things in my ear just a few hours ago, but this is also who Stellan is. I can learn to trust this version, too.

Soren and Greta sit on one side of the conference room table, and Banks is on the other with a man and a woman I recognize by sight from around the office.

"Willa, thank you for joining us. This is Agent Bergen and Agent Johns. They work closely with Banks. I invited you this morning because I believe that your latest dream changes the trajectory of our investigation."

"Of course," I say, a little uncertain. It was natural telling Stellan about my dream, but it's different explaining it to this room of stone-faced professionals, even ones I consider friends.

I clear my throat. "Well, my father met with me last night in a dream state," I begin. I'm not sure what everyone already knows about my father's magic, but I assume this isn't a revelation.

"He finally shared part of his rationale. As a powerful Winter family, we are part of a Council of Mages, and he needs an heir to act as a counterbalance. But counter to what, he wouldn't say."

"I thought the councils died out in the last century?" Agent Jones asks.

"That is a misunderstanding they use to their advantage," Banks explains. "But business ties, arranged marriages, votes on shared strategies, and everything in between have continued. It serves their purpose to operate in the shadows, but I'm certain high-ranking members in the IMA are aware, perhaps even on a council themselves. We will have to be careful where we dig."

"We already knew the Stromberg family was deeply entrenched in organized crime. How does this change our investigation?" Greta asks.

Stellan spins a pen in through his fingers and considers her question thoughtfully. "In some ways, it doesn't. We will simply cast wider nets and quietly gather intel on anyone in Stromberg's network who might also be a council member. However, we do have a more immediate concern. Willa, can you tell us more about the conversation with your father?"

I'm not thrilled to air my family's dirty laundry, but I know Stellan is right to ask it of me.

I anxiously rub my hands together and think of where to begin.

"It is hard to explain because it's so unbelievable to me, but my father was under the mistaken impression that I am his only child."

I shift uncomfortably in the stiff leather office chair. "He was somehow certain that my mother had an affair resulting in my sisters. I managed to convince him that

Beatrice and Wren are his children. Unfortunately, in my haste to defend my mother, I drew his attention to them. And, now, I believe that he will target Beatrice instead of me."

"Beatrice?" Soren asks with a confused frown. "No, that's not possible. She's too naive. Wren is a much more likely target."

Everyone stops and stares at Soren.

"How could you possibly know that?" I ask, affronted.

"I don't, of course." Soren has the decency to look sheepish. "It's just that with the extensive research I conducted on your family, I created very detailed profiles. I don't know your sisters personally, but I do feel confident that my assessment is correct. Your father would not have much luck with someone as flighty and...well, as vacuous and inattentive as Beatrice."

He trips over the words as if he knows he shouldn't say them, but can't seem to help himself.

"Vacuous?! What the hell, Soren!" I can't keep a lid on my anger, and both Greta and Banks shift in their seats to glower at Soren. "Beatrice might be innocent," I continue. "But she's one of the most intellectually curious people I know and definitely the most emotionally competent. The problem is not that she lacks skill or intelligence, it's that she'd do whatever our father asks because she would want to make him happy. She would be easy to manipulate."

"I hadn't thought about that," he says. "But she wouldn't be a good choice for him long term. Though I suppose that wouldn't prohibit him from targeting her now." The sudden concern on Soren's face is surprising.

"I think what Soren might be trying and failing to adequately explain is that Beatrice is perhaps an unlikely candidate for your father's attention," Stellan attempts to ease the tension in the room. "But in some ways, she might be perfect if he finds her to be malleable. Someone easy to train and control could be exactly what he needs."

"If that's the case, we need to send personnel to their location," Greta says. "It's not safe for her to be unguarded."

"I was hoping you would agree," Stellan says. "Jones, Bergen: the two of you will provide quiet cover until we can confirm the threat and I can commit more resources. I have also asked our counterparts in the New York Office to monitor for unusual movement in the high-ranking families and keep an eye on the area. They have agreed."

"I'll keep track of Beatrice from here," Soren adds, and all eyes turn to him.

"How?" I ask.

"My usual methods." He shrugs as if that explains anything. There's a pink tinge to his cheeks at our scrutiny.

A thought occurs to me that sours my stomach. The threat seems to have passed for me, but has it?

"What about Mikkel?" I ask.

I can't easily forget the man I saw in my dreams. He was meant to be fetching me for my father, but I never got the impression he appreciated the task. The way he looked at me was terrifying. It was as if he didn't just want to find me, he wanted to hurt me, too.

"What about him?" Banks sounds unconcerned. "He'll do whatever your father tells him to like all good second sons in their generation. If Lars is no longer a risk to you, I don't believe Mikkel is either."

How do I explain what I saw and felt when dreaming about my uncle or when confronting his mercenaries? I don't think it's safe to assume anything as far as he's concerned.

"I don't know. I guess I'm just having a hard time accepting the idea that this is over for me."

"It's not," Stellan says emphatically, shaking his head. "It's not over until we can confirm your suspicions and determine that your father really is shifting focus. I won't take the chance that you misinterpreted what he said or that he's manipulating you to let our guard down."

"What are our next steps then?" Banks asks and steeples his fingers. The tattoos that travel all along his arms peek out through his shirt sleeves.

"We need your assistance checking on council activities," Stellan answers. "I know you're careful how much you interact with your family, but in this moment, it's warranted."

Banks frowns, his discomfort obvious, but nods in agreement.

"Greta, I need you to lean on the mercenary angle. There's a link to the UK, and we need to know what it is.

"And, Soren, dig deeper into Stromberg's associates, including those we excluded early on. Check for any regular travel, purchases made in shared locations, anything that might point to a meeting. I doubt very much they're using video conference for major votes, but however they're meeting, I suspect they're careful to cover their tracks."

"On it," Soren says.

"Willa and I are leaving shortly to meet with Albert Wagner. Hopefully that will provide something fruitful."

The others nod in agreement.

"OK, then. Keep me updated on your progress."

Stellan's last statement seems to signal the end of the meeting. The others rise from their seats and begin exiting.

"Soren, may I speak with you for a moment?" I ask.

"Uh, yes, of course," he agrees with some reluctance.

After everyone else is gone, Soren stands in front of me with his hands awkwardly in his pockets.

"I'm sorry for making insinuations about your sister." He's contrite, regretting his outburst.

"I understand how you might have arrived at your

conclusions," I concede. "Beatrice is vibrant and sometimes impulsive. She might not be as organized as I am or as tough and calculating as Wren, but she's the kindest and most loving person I know and I won't let anyone diminish that."

Soren puffs out a breath and pulls me in for a hug before I can stop him. "I'm really sorry, Willa. I promise that I will do everything I can to help keep your sister safe."

"You better, Soren. I'd hate to have to electrocute you," I squeeze him back in a tight, friendly hug. I feel his chest rise and fall in quiet laughter.

"I might be an arrogant know-it-all, Willa, but I do keep my promises."

CHAPTER 48

WILLA

MY UNCLE ALBERT lives in a quaint country home about an hour outside Stockholm.

The exterior of the house is bright yellow with white trim and with what I assume will be beautiful flower gardens in springtime.

Today, it's cold, but bright, and a thick blanket of snow coats the ground.

As we exit the car, we're greeted by a friendly golden retriever and an English bulldog.

"Hans, Björn, leave our guests be," my uncle calls from the doorway.

He is older than I anticipated and walks with a cane. He's dressed in dark blue trousers and a freshly pressed cotton shirt. White hair frames his distinguished face.

Stellan speaks to him with a respectful tone in Swedish, probably thanking him for agreeing to meet with us. My uncle responds with a few cold words, but Stellan doesn't back down.

Albert lets out a resigned sigh and motions for us to follow him. The old house is nicely furnished in dark wood antiques and hand embroidered fabrics. Albert leads us to a living room where a silver tea service has been set out.

"I sent my housekeeper home so we could speak in private, but she left us tea. Please help yourselves."

Stellan and I sit next to each other on one of the floral Victorian settees and he pours us both a cup.

"So," I say, breaking the awkward silence that has settled over us. However uncomfortable this may be, I know that my uncle has information that will help the investigation and will help me better understand my family.

I sip my tea and push ahead. "My mother said you sent a letter. I apologize that she never replied, but she tends to retreat into herself at the mention of my father."

Albert sets his cup on the saucer. There is so much sadness in the smile he gives me.

"You have nothing to be sorry for," he says. His English is slow but confident. "I understand your mother's reticence, but I have become sentimental in my old age and the urge to contact her was too strong. Did you know that I met you once before? When you were very little, I visited my brother in the States."

Some of his sadness ebbs as he recalls the memory.

"My mother mentioned it, but not until very recently."

"Lars is much younger than I am. Our mother remarried when I was already at university, but I was close to Mikkel and Lars when they were boys. I loved them dearly. It is unfortunate that as they grew older, they took after their horrible father."

Albert pauses for a moment. His eyes drag to the floor to where his English bulldog lays by the fire.

"We had lost touch for many years, so I was surprised when I heard from my brother. He said that he was living in the United States and that he needed my help and had no one else to turn to.

"It was rare for him to need anything from anyone, so of course I went. That was when I met you and your mother.

"Anne had such a sweet innocence about her. I am sure you've been told this many times, but you look so much like her."

He smiles warmly at me now, and I return it.

"I have heard that a time or two."

His smile fades. "Lars loved your mother, of that I am certain, but he was ruled by his father and the Stromberg family legacy. It was so deeply ingrained that I don't think he could see beyond it.

"In his mind, there were no options, no alternatives. I know that what I'm about to tell you will be painful," he goes on. "But I am afraid that if I don't share it with you now, there may never be another opportunity."

I fight against the emotion rising up in me. Stellan reaches for my hand, and his magic brushes against me.

"Please tell me whatever it is you need to say. I want to hear it." I sit up straighter and steel myself for whatever revelations he's about to share.

The retriever rests his head on my uncle's lap and Albert pets him absentmindedly. When he speaks next, he's quiet and hesitant.

"Lars invited me to take a walk with him on the second or third day of my visit. On our stroll, he told me that he needed my help because his unborn child's mother was being difficult."

"What?" I interrupt. "That doesn't make sense."

"That was also my reaction, but Lars wasn't talking about your mother."

A chill sweeps over me. My magic swirls painfully inside my chest.

No. There's no way he'd be that cruel.

"Are you...are you telling me what I think you're telling me?"

My hands shake. The tea turns sour in my stomach, and I swallow down my nausea.

Albert bows his head. "Yes. I am sorry to have to tell you this, but since your mother was not born a Mage, he sought out another option to continue the family line. I am certain it was at his father's request."

"Oh, my God." I clasp a hand to my mouth.

"I'm so sorry, Willa," Albert says. "Lars never pretended to love this other woman. They had a business arrangement as far as I can tell.

"Marie Laurent is her name and she wanted more from Lars than he was willing to give her. When he refused to leave your mother, she threatened to tell Anne the truth. So, he asked me to speak with her. In my capacity as Mage legal counsel and, well, as a very wealthy individual, he thought I might be able to reason with her.

"I ended my visit with your parents and traveled to Montreal to find Marie. The person I found was very power-ful, but deeply damaged.

"When she discovered she would never be your father's choice, it hardened her. She didn't want to keep the child, but she didn't want to terminate the pregnancy, or allow Lars to raise it either. She felt trapped and desperate. I was worried what she might do to Anne or to you, if I didn't resolve the situation. In the end, I paid an indecent amount of money for her to vanish, but it was on the condition that we tell Lars she lost the baby naturally.

"She gave birth to a daughter and left her at an orphanage in Quebec."

Stellan shifts closer to me, but my focus is on Albert.

"So, my father doesn't know this other child exists?"

"No, I never told him. I regretted it for a long time, but I lost both my brothers to their father's evil ways long before I agreed to keep this secret."

"What...what happened to the baby?" My voice shakes.

"Her name is Claire Laurent. She's only ever known me as an anonymous benefactor. I paid for her to attend a boarding school for Mages in Quebec. Once she came of age, it became difficult to keep track of her. The last I heard, she was living in Montreal. But what she is doing with herself and how she is fairing, I cannot say.

"I wanted your mother to know, partly out of guilt for keeping this secret, but mostly because I don't believe Claire has ever known a family. I hoped that you could look for her, and perhaps she might find something she's never had."

I release a long breath. I swirl the tea in my cup, thinking through what I've just heard.

There is no way my mother would have been able to handle this information, let alone provide what Albert has imagined. In fact, I'm terrified of what will happen when she finds out. It will devastate her.

But that is not Claire's fault.

Stellan remains quiet, but his steady presence is a comfort.

"Of course, I'd like to find her. She's my half-sister. I can't imagine what it would have been like to...Albert? Albert, are you alright?"

Albert's face turns pale and his mouth opens and closes like he's trying to speak but nothing will come out. Stellan jumps to his feet. Two bright red patches appear on the chest of my uncle's shirt.

He slumps forward. On his back are two large wounds, bleeding heavily. They almost look like bullet holes, but no shots were fired.

Albert falls off the chair, knocking the tea set on the floor.

The dogs scatter from the noise while blood and tea stain his beautiful antique rug. Stellan checks Albert's pulse and shakes his head. The uncle I only just met is already gone.

"Stay here, Willa. I'm going to check in with the guards," Stellan whispers as quietly as possible, in case someone is listening. "Text the others and tell them we need backup immediately. We're about to have a very different kind of family reunion."

CHAPTER 49

WILLA

My HEART POUNDS as I text the team. I do my best to calm my magic, which is running riot in my chest.

As much as we need Greta, Soren, and Banks, it could be an hour before they arrive. Until then, it's just me, Stellan, and the three guards we brought with us—assuming any of them are still alive.

I look down at the body of my uncle. A vital connection to my family and our history is gone. Instead of pain and loss, I feel nothing. I'm numb.

I cannot believe I have another sister. One who doesn't know us. She'd only be a little older than Beatrice and Wren.

It's impossible to stomach what this will mean for my mother. She was so in love with my dad, and he was out fathering a child with another woman.

He may not have intended to physically hurt her all those years ago, but this revelation might be the blow that finally tips her over the edge.

The sound of dogs barking outside stops my morose

thoughts. I may be numb, but I need to focus on my surroundings. I get as close to the window as I can without being seen and peek out. It's midday, but with the winter solstice approaching, the sun is already casting long shadows across Albert's garden. His dogs are nowhere to be seen.

The hair on the back of my neck stands up. I swallow hard and look around the room. There's nothing here. A shiver of fear slithers across my skin. A gun fires outside. The sound of a man groaning. Another shot. Then silence.

My shoes creak along the wood floor to the front entrance. I can't stand waiting in here any longer.

In the hallway, there's a sudden rush in the air, a huge reserve of magic being used at once. I'm blown backwards by this invisible force, as Stellan's massive body comes careening through the closed front door. The wood splinters and sprays in every direction. I shoot my arms up to protect myself from the raining bits of wood and plaster.

A sickening silence follows the aftermath of the crash, and I rush towards Stellan. He's covered in scraps of the blown-apart house. A cold wind blows and snow drifts inside. I wipe the trickle of blood that drips out of the corner of his mouth.

Either by the force of his landing or something that occurred outside, Stellan is completely knocked out. I feel around to the back of his head. There's a shallow wound and my fingers come back bloody. He's breathing, thank God, but his face is deathly pale.

Not knowing what else to do, I bend forward and place a kiss on his forehead. "Our friends will be here soon," I whisper. "I'll take care of us until then."

I don't know if he can hear me. I say it mostly for my own benefit. I'm alone now, and it's time to find my bravery.

"Well, isn't this just the prettiest picture?" A voice I have only heard in dreams speaks from the destroyed doorway.

I rise to my feet and put myself between Stellan and Mikkel Stromberg. I square my shoulders. My insides are in knots, but I tip my chin up in challenge. My magic swirls from my chest down my arms to my hands where it waits for instruction, no longer frantic inside me but poised for battle.

"I have grown tired of your antics, my dear niece," Mikkel says.

With a flick of his wrist, the magic that was active and ready to fight curls back up my arms and shrinks until it's just a tiny spark. I inhale sharply in shock and at the fear from such total vulnerability.

The terror of what he's done sinks in: he's stripped me of my powers with barely any effort. How can I fight him without my magic, when he can turn the air into a weapon?

My heart hammers inside my chest. "What's your endgame here, Mikkel? Are you going to take me to my father?" I try to keep my voice even despite my panic.

Mikkel is pale and blonde and much taller up close. His face is harsh and cruel, and his eyes are such a dark blue that they're almost black. He shifts his weight, favoring one side. As he moves, I catch sight of blood spreading across his t-shirt. Stellan must have attacked before Mikkel sent him flying into the house.

"That was the plan, but not anymore." Mikkel approaches, and I step back on instinct.

"What changed?" I ask. If he's not taking me to my father, does he need me alive?

"You did," he sneers. "Lars was wrong to think he could convince you to join him. I went along with it when I thought you might be amenable to our aims. We were taught to honor the succession of our family line. But your father is trapped in a prison of his own making, where I fully intend for him to stay. And then, of course, without you, I'll be the successor."

Mikkel lifts his hands and sends a surge of energy at me. I duck to the side, but it grazes my hip, slicing deep into me. I fall to the ground and just manage to roll aside as Mikkel sends another wave of his terrifying magic at me. My fear is overpowering, but his frustration is just as real.

"Stop. Making. This. So. Hard." Mikkel fires more magic at me. I dodge it as best I can, but I have grazes all over and a deep cut on my leg.

I'm alive, but how long will I last?

I'm panting and tired while Mikkel has barely broken a sweat. He hurls more magic at me, but this time it isn't physical. He hits me with something far worse.

Terror like I've never thought possible holds me captive. Every horrible thought I've ever had. Every worry. Every nightmare. All of it surfaces at once. Images of my mother ending her life. My sisters lying bloody and broken. Stellan's lifeless eyes.

We are going to die here, and there is nothing I can do about it.

I fracture. I can't move. I collapse onto my knees, breathing hard. Unable to determine reality from my uncle's terrible power.

Mikkel seizes his opportunity. He pulls a knife out of his jacket pocket and standing over me, plunges it deep into my upper thigh. The pain is beyond comprehension and I try to squirm away. Mikkel holds the knife, pushing it deeper.

"We're making this look like an accident. My brother would destroy me if he ever learned about this. But no, it will be nothing more than a tragic little mistake." His cruel voice echoes inside my skull.

Mikkel grits his teeth and twists the knife. I scream. Sharp and hot, the pain is infinite. I can't breathe. I fall onto my back as the sick certainty of death plays over and over inside my mind. My eyesight blurs, and my eyelids flutter closed.

Inside my chest, that tiny spark of my magic pulses just once. A flicker. I can picture it. A little gold sphere, sparkling and powerful, but hidden behind a black veil.

In the darkness, it's all I can see. I reach for it, and I tug at the veil. It shimmers, encouraging me to pull harder.

My uncle is powerful and an expert in his abilities, but I am stronger. My father is a goddamn piece of work, but I'm still his daughter.

My magic pulses again. It glows bright, and I reach for it. It takes all the mental energy I have, but I rip apart my uncle's magic and leave behind nothing except blinding golden light.

Far away, I hear Mikkel shout in anger. I open my eyes. He's staring at me, shock and rage war on his face.

"Impossible!" he cries.

My body lifts off the ground as my magic flows through me. I'm weak and losing blood, but I'm not going to let him hurt me or anyone I love. I can't bear it.

A storm gathers. Thunder rumbles, and electricity crackles. The sky grows ominous and dark. Mikkel scrambles out of the house, and I stumble after him. My magic propels me, seeking connection with the open air.

The second Mikkel crosses the threshold into the snowy garden, I catch him in a violent gale that tears through Albert's yard. Mikkel screams in fear and frustration as I hold him captive in a barrier of snow and wind.

I raise my arms like an offering. Electricity flows through me, and my hair blows around my head like a terrible goddess of the sky. Blood flows out of my wounds. My eyes glow in golden orbs as my power saturates every cell in my body, binding me to the air. A blizzard of my own creation rages around us. My hands fly up, and a lightning bolt strikes the ground right in front of my uncle, singeing his skin.

Thundersnow.

"No! No! Please," Mikkel pleads from the ground.

But I'm beyond forgiveness. My magic is in control, and it requires vengeance. I raise my hands again, and thunder shakes the earth with a violent rumble as lightning strikes Mikkel fully in his chest. He flies backward and lands in a heap in Albert's once-peaceful garden. Smoke rises off his sizzling body. I crumple to the cold ground, breathing hard.

My magic brushes against me in a friendly nudge as it retreats. Light returns to the sky, and the wind and snow disappear.

I stagger back toward the house. Stellan is leaning against the broken door frame. Pale and injured, he uses the wall to support his weight.

"I was going to help, but you had it under control," he says weakly. "Obviously," he adds with a wincing smile.

I'm fading, still bleeding and my head throbs. I shuffle closer, tripping toward him. Stellan catches me as I collapse.

His rainwater magic blankets me in a sense of safety and the profound feeling of home, and I slip into the beautiful darkness.

CHAPTER 50

THE SNOW STARTED FALLING on the second day of mandatory leave. Flurries of white against the steel gray of the Baltic Sea. After Willa and I had recovered enough to travel, I insisted we take the ferry to Sandhamn for rest and recuperation.

There isn't much on the island in December. Summer cottages sealed off against the harsh wind, waiting for the warmer months ahead. But it's exactly what we both need.

The home Clara and I inherited is painted red to match the other traditional houses on the island, but ours is more modern with large windows and an interior of light wood. On the far side of the island, my getaway is perfectly suited for privacy. No one can find us unless we want them to.

I approach Willa as she watches the snow falling outside the window. I hand her a cup of coffee, and for a few moments, watch the snow with her.

I'm in tune with her moods, and Willa's is black. She's mired in negative thoughts and has been since the fight with her uncle. I've been giving her space to work through it, but it's worrying me.

"If you talk about it, I might be able to help," I tell her, wrapping my arms around her waist. She fits into me so perfectly.

She sighs. I think she knows I'm right, but she's afraid to say the words out loud.

"I am worried," she says and pauses to gather herself. "I'm worried I have become someone I no longer recognize."

Our faces are reflected back at us in the window. There's anguish on hers and sadness and concern on mine. But I give her space to continue, hoping she'll elaborate.

"In the last few weeks, I've experienced so much pain. So much agony and death, and all of it is because of this power I have inside me. I understand now why my mother shut down her magic and cut off access to ours. At first, I was thrilled to discover what I could do, but now that I know, I'm not sure I want it."

She rubs her fingers against her sternum as her magic flares inside her. No doubt reminding her that it's there, that it's part of her.

I'll never forget the way her eyes lit up when she asked me if she was a witch. She was delighted then. But now she's finally realizing the cost.

The price of her power is her innocence and freedom.

I turn her to face me and hold her close with my hands on her hips.

"Willa, there's no right or wrong way to adapt to this life. It's hard. It can be brutal at times. But you have already experienced the worst of it.

"You took extreme action to save your own life and the lives of people you care about. That kind of trauma stays with you. But it can swallow you, if you let it.

"You need to remember that there is nothing inherently

bad or cruel about your abilities and the beautiful, caring person you are inside hasn't gone anywhere. Feel what you need to feel, but know that I'm here with you, that I have experienced this myself, and that I want to help you."

She sets her coffee down on the small table by the window. She lifts her hands and frames my face. Her sapphire eyes stare deeply into mine. The connection between us crackles with electricity.

"I love you," she says and rises on her toes to kiss me gently on the lips before pulling back to look at me. A satisfied smile spreads across my face.

"When I thought I might die and never get to tell you that..." her voice breaks.

I stop her with a kiss of my own. I tangle my fingers in her hair, kissing her languidly and deep, pouring myself into it. Her body melts into mine, but I stop us before we get carried away.

"I love you so much, Willa. You are everything I have ever wanted and never thought I deserved. I'm yours for as long as you'll have me."

* * *

WILLA

"Thank you, Director Hawley. I won't let you down."

I hang up the phone and place it on the coffee table next to the sweaters I've been knitting for Edwin and Oli. Stellan eyes me expectantly from across the living room. He's sitting in an armchair with his hands clasped and his eyes trained on me. He looks like he's ready to dive across the room and kiss the life out of me, but he's restraining himself.

"It appears you won't be getting rid of me then," I shrug,

making light of the dark fear that has lodged itself in my mind since the fight with Mikkel.

Stellan's long legs make quick work of the space between us.

"You say that like I would have let you go." He kisses me before pulling back to examine my face. "But your life is on a very different path now, Willa. How do you feel?"

I take stock of everything I'm thinking and the emotions this morning's news has brought up. The relief and the worry. The uncertain future that lays ahead and the unwavering love of the man in front of me.

"It's the right choice," I state firmly. "I will miss Vermont and my mom and friends, but when I think about what it would be like to return, to let go of everything here and try to recreate the life I was living before. Even without the restraints of my magic, it's just not feasible.

"And I have finally come to realize that I wasn't helping my mother by hovering over her. She's forming a community for herself in my absence. She's joined a book club and has taken up cross-country skiing with a new friend. I think we were both stuck in a lot of ways, and this forced us to make necessary changes."

"I believe you're right," Stellan says. He takes my hand in his. "What did Director Hawley say?"

"She offered me a place in the fast-tracked training program. She agrees with you that concerns for my safety are legitimate and that I shouldn't be relocated. She also said that I could join your team on an interim basis and then formally after I complete my training."

The sweet smile that spreads across Stellan's face makes my blood pump faster.

"That's wonderful," he says. "There is no amount of distance that would have kept me from you for long, but having you here is the best outcome."

"I agree." My stomach flips at the urgency in his words and the ardent spark in his eyes.

"But will you miss being a librarian?" Stellan frowns in concern.

"I won't miss my old job. I'm not sure I knew what I wanted to do, but I'm certain it wasn't that. I can take the parts of librarianship that I love and incorporate it into my work with you here. At its core, intelligence gathering is just research. And I'll always be happiest knowing that what I'm doing matters."

His eyes twinkle at my response. "Soren told me you're already making significant headway and finding connections others have missed. You would be an asset to any investigative team, but I'm thrilled you'll be on mine."

"I hate that word," I say and shake my head.

"Asset?"

"Yes, it's what you called me..."

"...when I was being an idiot and a dick. I remember," Stellan cuts me off with a remorseful bow of his head. "I hope you realize you're so much more than that, Willa. Especially to me."

"I know that now."

He stands to grab an envelope off the mantle.

"I have a present for you," he says. He sits back down on the couch and settles me against him in the safety of his arms.

I open the envelope and pull out a flight itinerary for Monday.

First class from Stockholm to New York and then on to Burlington, Vermont.

He bought me a ticket home.

My heart beats out of my chest.

"I can go home?" I ask and my hands shake. I drop the papers on my lap.

"Yes, of course," Stellan takes my chin between his fingers and encourages me to look in his eyes. "I took the liberty of booking a return ticket for you and tickets for myself as well. I hope that's acceptable."

I desperately want to go home and see my family, but not without Stellan with me.

"Your mum and Sam might not be thrilled to see me," he admits. "But there's no other option. Even without the security risks, I'm not comfortable letting you out of my sight for so long."

"They'll be fine. They know that you're important to me and that's all that matters." I kiss his cheek. "Thank you for this. It means so much to me."

"You're welcome." He kisses my forehead.

"Oh, and I thought we could also make arrangements to move your cats here," he says with his cheek resting on the top of my head.

"Really!?" I shriek and spin around to straddle him. I hug him tightly around the neck. Stellan laughs in surprise and hugs me back.

"Yes, really."

"Sam will be so happy. He's been the best Cat Uncle, but I think he's tired of Reg and his antics. Are you sure you're OK sharing a space with him? He's crazy."

"I promise to be the best Cat Dad you've ever seen," he tells me with a twinkle in his eyes. "Even to the complete freak who sleeps on your face."

I smile wide. "Aw, Cat Dad. I love that."

"I love you," he says and his voice turns deep and serious. "I mean it, Willa. You are my family and my future." He places his hand on my lower stomach, where our future children could grow. I have to swallow hard to keep the emotion at bay.

"Do you mean that?" I ask.

"Yes, of course," he says, like it's obvious. "Someday, I want to watch you walk toward me wearing white with pretty flowers in your hair. I want to take pictures of your beautiful belly as it grows round and perfect with my children. I want everything."

"I want that, too."

Stellan's lips blossom into an enormous smile and he bends to kiss me, unhurried and tender.

"We have a lot to do before then though," he says, breaking the kiss with his forehead resting against mine. "Now that we know you're working with us, how would you like to find a long-lost sister?"

Claire has been on my mind a lot. I've wondered what her life has been like and what she might think if she meets us.

"I would love that."

"Excellent. Now let's get undressed so we can celebrate all these decisions properly." He grips my ass with both hands.

"God, you are so bossy." I'm breathless as he slowly kisses up my neck.

"I am," he says with a low groan in his chest as my hands knit through his hair. "But you love that about me."

"You're right," I smile and kiss the man I love more than I ever thought possible. "I do."

EPILOGUE

LARS

The phone shatters against the office wall. How could Mikkel be so reckless? So bloody stupid.

His lust for power finally killed him. Now I have to act.

I turn on my long-unused computer monitor and enter a number I hoped I'd never need again.

A man's face appears almost immediately. Charming and classically handsome with high cheekbones and a square jaw, it's hard to believe the young man is as dangerous as anyone alive. Just like his father before him.

"Stromberg. What a surprise," the man says with little emotion. "I heard about your brother. My condolences."

Of course he would know already.

"Save it," I say. "You know I'm only calling because I'm out of options."

Rhys Anders tents his fingers. "Yes, I admit I am surprised. You never do business with New York. Please enlighten me."

"I need you to find someone for me. And I need new

documents. Passport, bank accounts, the whole package. I'll transfer the money."

"Consider it done. We'll courier the documents to your usual location. And the mark?"

"My daughter," I say, a touch of pride in my voice. I have three daughters. Not just one.

"I thought she was in bed with the Agency?" Anders asks with a curl of his lip.

"Don't remind me," I bark in frustration. "For now, I'm trying another angle. I'll forward you the details through the secure server, but if my information is correct, you'll want to handle this one yourself."

A few strokes on my keyboard and an image pops up. A pretty young woman with blonde hair, fair features, and brilliant blue eyes. She looks so much like me, but there's a whimsical air about her that's all Anne. My daughter is undeniably beautiful, just like her mother.

Anders clears his throat. "Yes. Yes, I will indeed," he says.

"I am trusting you with this Anders. Don't fuck it up. You remember what happened to your predecessor."

"How could I forget?" Anders responds with practiced calm, but his jaw twitches. "I am honored that you considered us. I'll be in touch."

"Do that."

I end the video call and hang my head in my hands. This new plan has to succeed. There is too much at stake to fail now.

ALSO BY STELLA WHITCOMB LANE

Spring: The Storm King's Daughters, Book 2 - Coming Soon

Beatrice and Soren's story

ACKNOWLEDGMENTS

Thank you so much for reading this book!

Willa and Stellan are the first couple in a series of stand-alone romances, and I am so excited for you to meet the other daughters of The Storm King.

This series would not be possible without my husband, Chris. He is my first reader, strictest editor, and favorite person. He makes my writing better, and I am eternally grateful for his expertise, patience, and sense of humor with my chosen genre.

I would also like to thank my earliest readers: Ashley, Alison, Lisa, and Jet. Thank you so much for your support and encouragement even when I gave you truly rough drafts that were probably quite painful to read. Your words of encouragement were invaluable.

Thank you to Katrin Berndt at Slow Swedish (@slowswediish_) for her assistance and knowledge. Any errors in the Swedish found in this book are mine alone.

Thank you to Fran at Merry Book Round (https://www.merrybookround.com/) for her collaborative spirit and fabulous cover art.

Thank you to my parents and sister for their love and their genuine excitement for my stories.

And lastly, thank you to my children for having pride in their mother's work even though they definitely aren't allowed to read my books.

ABOUT THE AUTHOR

Stella Whitcomb Lane writes witty, suspenseful romance with a modern fantasy twist. Set in a contemporary magical world, her characters find their hidden strength and discover that love can sneak up on you when you least expect it.

Stella grew up in the great state of Vermont and lives in Providence, Rhode Island with her husband, two children, and their Bernese Mountain Dog.

Please get in touch! I'd love to hear from you.
https://www.stellawhitcomblane.com
stellawhitcomblane@gmail.com

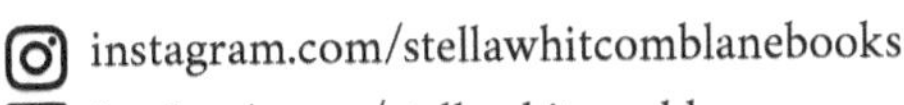

instagram.com/stellawhitcomblanebooks
facebook.com/stellawhitcomblane